MINOR
HAUNTINGS

MINOR HAUNTINGS

Chilling Tales
of Spectral Youth

Edited by
JEN BAKER

This collection first published in 2021 by
The British Library
96 Euston Road
London NW1 2DB

Cataloguing in Publication Data
A catalogue record for this publication is available from the British Library

ISBN 978 0 7123 5319 9
e-ISBN 978 0 7123 6728 8

Frontispiece illustration from the first appearance of 'Walnut-Tree House'
by Charlotte Riddell in *Illustrated London News* 28th December 1878

Cover design by Mauricio Villamayor with illustration by Sandra Gómez
Text design and typesetting by Tetragon, London
Printed in England by CPI Group (UK) Ltd, Croydon, CR0 4YY

Contents

INTRODUCTION

Minor Hauntings: Chilling Tales of Spectral Youth offers a range of Anglo-American and Irish supernatural tales from the nineteenth and early twentieth centuries which feature some form of dead-child spirit or ghostly imprint of the child. The title captures a bitter irony of course; that despite the prevalence of infant mortality in this period and dominant philosophies of the child as not yet fully human or formed, in reality these would not have been "minor" hauntings for those affected by the untimely death of a child. We can see from both the quantity and content of a wider range of narratives and imagery in this period—such as diaries, consolation manuals, prose fiction, elegies, post-mortem portraiture, sculptures, and fine art—that the loss of a child was deeply affecting across different classes, religions, and societies, and a powerful symbol of social attitudes towards the glorification of youth.

Reflecting this exaltation, many poems and elegies which feature spectral or ghostly children are not "Gothic"—the style and tone is twee, the child is a passive and benevolent spirit from heaven, and the motivation for their "return" is comfort; urging parents into a mindset of acceptance and to temper their "excessive" grief. For instance, in Letitia E. Landon's 1832 poem "The Little Shroud", based on a German folk tale (and found in other traditions), a child's ghost appears to his mother and pleads with her not to cry too much over his loss because her tears are soaking his shroud meaning he cannot sleep soundly in his grave. The speaker declares:

7

Oh, love is strong!—the mother's heart
  Was filled with tender fears;
Oh, love is strong!—and for her child
  Her grief restrained its tears.

Once the child spirit could sleep peacefully, the mother "knelt in prayer, / And only asked of Heaven its aid / Her heavy lot to bear".[1]

There are also numerous supernatural short stories—the form and genre being the most prominent textual space for the ghostly child in this period—which follow this pattern, such as Annie Trumball Slosson's "A Speakin' Ghost," (1890) in which a bereaved young woman teaches a "heathen" ghost boy how to be a good Christian so that his soul can transcend; or Katherine Bates' "Whither Thou Goest" (1896), in which a mother and father see and hear the spirits of their lost children who are playing on the land, waiting to guide their parents to heaven; or Rudyard Kipling's "They" (1903), in which a bereaved father comes across the blissful earthly Elysium in which the spirit of his child gets to play eternally. These works mirror the mainstream cultural narrative put forth in the long nineteenth century which, contrary to centuries of doctrine suggesting limbo or even hell awaited unbaptised, sinful, or all children, insisted that heaven and God's grace was the inevitable destination for every child's soul.

However, as guided by the aesthetic of the Tales of the Weird series, this anthology is a selection of short stories where, for the most part, something *is not quite right*. In these examples, the death is caused by abuse, neglect, murder, or even horrific accidents, and customary burial rites are often neglected as in Edwards' and Lawrence's tales. Or, as in the tales by Bell and Everett, disease/biology is the villain, but despite being deemed a "natural" cause, the family are not protected from the strangeness that follows. Most of these tales ask whether children who do not have a good and peaceful death will *definitely* go to heaven; what the *consequences* might be if no glory awaits to compensate the child's suffering; and asks what if the child is angry or even vengeful for their treatment in life and the fate to which they have been consigned? What about children whose parents or society cannot or do not mourn them—perhaps because they are the direct cause of their death? Some of these spectral youths are imprints that do not interact with the present—doomed to replay their scenes of abuse until something is resolved and peace can be achieved (their bodies found and buried, or the perpetrator brought to justice). Others are active and vengeful spirits who engage to some extent with the living and require their assistance but show the potential for (and sometimes cause) harm.

The tales in this collection revive, appropriate, and often merge domestic folkloric and literary traditions where the spirit of a wronged child would passively wander and bewail its fate with the darker traditions of non-Anglophone cultures, in which such spirits would terrorise and sometimes kill those who wronged them or even passers-by. Throughout this collection, haunting the interstices between the literary tales, you will find snippets of customs, ballads, transcribed oral folk tales and some classical "pagan" literature concerning the child or the dead child and its spirit to illustrate the sense of historical and cultural debt. The stories nevertheless also house more contemporaneous concerns that influenced the subversions of, or departure from, these traditions—a greater interest in "the child" figure and its social position, the advent of spiritualism and the alignment of spirits with Christian tenets, as well as changing domestic ideologies and class concerns. Those familiar with ghostly children in contemporary Gothic and Horror film and literature will also recognise the recurring tropes in these ghost stories—pattering feet, twinkling laughter, small and beautiful child bodies—which show signs of being used as subversive elements exploited for the aesthetics of terror, as they are today.

I have endeavoured to include the original versions of these stories where possible, in the form in which they were first consumed by readers in periodicals and magazines, only tidying up incongruences with spacing and any clear typographical errors but leaving idiosyncrasies to best reflect the experience of encountering these stories in their original mode. Those who have previously read the stories "Walnut-Tree House" by Charlotte (J. H.) Riddell, and "The Lost Ghost" by Mary E. Wilkins Freeman from their respective collections *Weird Stories* (1882) and *The Wind in the Rose-Bush* (1903), for instance, will note that the versions included here are far shorter, having first been printed in periodicals where word count was restrictive.

Victorianist scholar Nina Auerbach once stated that "Victorian child-ghosts are not the satanic monsters on which our own Gothic literature feeds. They are something subtler, innocent, admonitory, and terrifying at the same time".[2] But I cannot fully agree; at least not when viewed through our contemporary lens. The innocent/evil binary that underpins the child in Horror is, for anyone aware of such tropes, latent even in the most placid of stories in this period, and certainly I think in the stories in this collection. And so, as they peruse these chilling tales, I invite the reader to revel in the pitiful and the dreadful, the familiar and the unfamiliar of spectral youth.

JEN BAKER

Jen Baker is a Teaching Fellow in Nineteenth and Twentieth Century Literature at the University of Warwick and a Visiting Fellow of the Centre for Death and Society at the University of Bath.

FURTHER READING

Gillian Avery and Kimberley Reynolds (eds.), *Representations of Childhood Death* (London: Palgrave Macmillan UK, 2016).

Baker, Jen, "The Spectral Child" in Clive Bloom (ed.), *The Palgrave Handbook of Steam Age Gothic* (London: Palgrave Macmillan UK, 2021), pp. 711–728.

Hast thou done what some women, filled with the boldness of the devil are wont to do? When any child has died without baptism they take the corpse of the little one and place it in some secret place and transfix it with a stake, saying that if they did not do so the little child would arise and injure many.

Burchard of Worms, *Decretum* (*c.* 1008–1012)[3]

Many persons consider it sinful to give a child the same Christian name as another who is dead: one female remarked to the writer that "id wor gooin ageean God Omeety as hed ta'en t'other away."

Harland and Wilkinson, *Lancashire Legends* (1873)[4]

THE DEAD DAUGHTER: A TALE

Henry Glassford Bell

Born and raised in Scotland, Henry Glassford Bell (1803–1874) was only involved directly with the fashionable literary community for a short period of time and is a comparatively obscure figure today. Nevertheless, before he turned to the law profession, he was well known among contemporaries as an editor, writer, and as a critic.

"The Dead Daughter", first printed in his own publication The Edinburgh Literary Journal *in 1831, was reviewed favourably in* The Literary Gazette *1832 as "a beautiful specimen of the supernatural" and is characteristic of the darker strain of Romanticism found in the writings of English authors such as Byron and Coleridge, German writers Hoffmann and Goethe, and of early nineteenth-century American writers Poe, Hawthorne and Melville. Bell's influence on Edgar Allan Poe, and most particularly the short story "Morella" (1835) was noted in the* Dictionary of National Biography *(1888) and, owing to the literary debt, Bell's story was housed in Peter Haining's* The Edgar Allan Poe Bedside Companion: Morgue and Mystery Tales *(1989). The tale is, I think, one of the first literary sources in English to utilise the ghostly revenant child as the source of terror and grief for the parent and would be used again in "Morella" and later in W. W. Jacobs' "The Monkey's Paw" (1902), to similar effect. It has an unsettling subtext of transgressive sexuality, too, alongside the more obvious depiction of the oppressive domestic scene.*

What may this mean,
So horridly to shake our disposition
With thoughts beyond the reaches of our soul?
SHAKSPEARE

he building was a solitary one, and had a cold and forbidding aspect. Its tenant, Adolphus Walstein, was a man whom few liked: not that they charged him with any crime, but he was of an unsocial temperament; and ever since he came to the neighbourhood, thinly inhabited as it was, he had contracted no friendship, formed no acquaintance. He seemed fond of wandering among the mountains; and his house stood far up in one of the wild valleys formed by the Rhætian Alps, which intersect Bohemia.

He was married, and his wife had once been beautiful. She even yet bore the traces of that beauty, though somewhat faded. She must have been of high birth too, for her features and gait were patrician. She spoke little; but you could not look on her and fancy that her silence was for lack of thought.

They had one only child—a daughter—a pale but beautiful girl. She was very young—not yet in her teens—but the natural mirth of childhood characterised her not. It seemed as if the gloom that had settled round her parents had affected her too; it seemed as if she had felt the full weight of their misfortunes, almost before she could have known what misfortune was. She smiled sometimes, but very faintly; yet it was a lovely smile,—more lovely that it was melancholy. She was not strong; there was in her limbs none of the glowing vigour of health. She cared not for sporting in the fresh breeze on the hill-side.

If ever she gathered wild-flowers, it was only to bring them home, to lay them in her mother's lap, and wreathe them into withered garlands.

Much did they love that gentle child: they had nothing else in the wide world to love, save an old domestic, and a huge Hungarian dog. Yet it was evident Paulina could not live; at least her life was a thing of uncertainty—of breathless hope and fear. She was tall beyond her years; but she was fragile as the stalk of the white-crowned lily. She was very like her mother; though there was at times a shade upon her brow that reminded you strongly of the darker countenance of her father. It was said, that when he took his gun, and went out all day in search of the red-deer, far up among the rocky heights, he would forget his purpose for hours, and seating himself upon some Alpine promontory, would gaze upon his lonely house in the valley below, till the sun went down in the stormy west; and as evening drew on, and a single light faintly glimmered from one of the windows of his mansion, he has brushed a hot tear from his eye, and started into recol-lection. It was dark ere he came home, and the winds howled drearily. In their sitting-room—a room but barely furnished—he found his wife plying her needle beside the lamp, and at a little distance the dying flame of the wood fire threw its ghastly flickerings on the pale face of his daughter. He stood at the door, and leant upon his gun in silence. They knew his mood, and were silent also. His eye was fixed upon his daughter; she would have fascinated yours too. *It was no common countenance.* Not that any individual feature could have been singled out as peculiar, but the general expression was such as, once seen, haunted the memory for ever. Perhaps it was the black eye—blacker than the ebon hair—contrasted with the deadly paleness of her white-rose cheek. It was deep sunk, too, under her brow. But it is needles to form conjectures: none knew in what that expression originated—there was a mystery in it. She had a long thin arm, and tapering fingers, and a hand crossed by many a blue vein. Its touch was in general thrillingly cold, yet at times it was feverishly hot. Her mother had borne many a child, but all died in early infancy. Yet her father's fondest wish was to see a son rising by his side into manhood; nor did he despair of having the wish gratified. It was said his dying commands would have given that son much to do.

Paulina was now thirteen; but the canker was busy within, and even her mother saw at last that she, too, was to be taken from her. It was a stern dispensation; the only child of her heart,—the only one whom her sleepless care had been able to fence in from the grasp of the spoiler,—her meditation and her dream for thirteen years,—the one only sad sunbeam whose watery and uncertain ray lighted up their solitude. But evil had followed them as a doom, nor was that doom yet completed.

She died upon an autumn evening. She had been growing weaker for many a day, and they saw it, but spoke not of it. Nor did she; it seemed almost a pain for her to speak; and when she did, it was in a low soft tone, inaudible almost to all but the ear of affection. Yet was the mind within her busy with all the restless activity of feverish reverie. She had strange day-dreams; and life and the distant world often flashed upon her in far more than the brightness of reality. Often, too, all faded away; and though her eyes were still open, darkness fell around her, and she dwelt among the mysteries and immaterial shapes of some shadowy realm. It would be fearful to know all that passed in the depth of that lonely girl's spirit. It was an autumn evening—sunny, but not beautiful,—silent, but not serene. She had walked to the brook that came down the mountains, and which formed a pool and babbling cascade not a stone-cast from the door. Perhaps she grew suddenly faint; for her mother, who stood at the window, saw her coming more hastily than usual across the field.

She went to meet her; she was within arm's-length, when her daughter gave a faint moan, and, falling forward, twined her cold arms round her mother's neck, and looked up into her face with a look of agony. It was only for a moment; her dark eye became fixed—it grew white with the whiteness of death, and the mother carried her child's body into its desolate home.

If her father wept—it was at night when there was no eye to see. The Hungarian dog howled over the dead body of its young mistress, and the old domestic sat by the unkindled hearth, and wept as for her own first-born; but the father loaded his gun, as was his wont, and went away among the mountains.

The priests came, and the coffin, and a few of the simple peasants. She was carried forth from her chamber, and her father followed. The procession winded down the valley. The tinkling of the holy bell mingled sadly with the funeral chant. At last the little train disappeared; for the churchyard was among the hills, some miles distant. The mother was left alone. She fell upon her knees, and lifted up her eyes and her clasped hands to her God, and prayed—fervently prayed, from the depths of her soul—that he might never curse her with another child. The prayer was almost impious; but she was frantic in her deep despair, and we dare not judge her.

A year has passed away, and that lonely house is still in the Bohemian valley, and its friendless inmates haunt it still. Walstein's wife bears him another child, and hope almost beats again in his bosom, as he asks, with somewhat of a father's pride, if he has now a son. But the child was a daughter, and his hopes were left unfulfilled. They christened the infant Paulina; and many a long day and dreary night did its mother hang over its cradle, and shed tears of bitterness, as she thought of her who lay unconscious in the churchyard away among the hills. The babe grew, but not in the rosiness of health.

Yet it seldom suffered from acute pain; and when it wept, it was with a kind of suppressed grief, that seemed almost unnatural to one so young. It was long ere it could walk; when at last it did, it was without any previous effort.

Time passed on without change and without incident. Paulina was ten years old. Often had Philippa, with maternal fondness, pointed out to her husband the resemblance which she alleged existed between their surviving child and her whom they had laid in the grave. Walstein, as he listened to his wife, fixed his dark penetrating eye upon his daughter, and spoke not. The resemblance was, indeed, a striking one,—it was almost supernatural. She was the same tall pale girl, with black, deep, sunk eyes, and long dark ebon hair. Her arms and hands were precisely of the same mould, and they had the same thrilling coldness in their touch. Her manners, too, her disposition, the sound of her voice, her motions, her habits, and, above all, her expression of countenance—that characteristic and indescribable expression—were the very same. Her mother loved to dwell upon this resemblance; but her father, though he gazed and gazed upon her, yet ever and anon started, and walked with hasty strides across the room, and some times, even at night, rushed out into the darkness, as one oppressed with wild and fearful fancies.

They had few of the comforts, and none of the luxuries of life, in that Bohemian valley. Philippa had carefully laid aside all the clothes that belonged to her dead daughter; and now that the last child of her age was growing up, and was so like her that was gone, she loved to dress her sometimes in her sister's dress; and the pale child wore the clothes, and talked of the lost Paulina, almost as if she had known her.

One night her mother plied her needle beside her lamp, and at a little distance her daughter, in a simple white dress, which had once been another's, sat musing over the red embers of a dying fire.

A thunder storm was gathering, and the rain was already falling heavily. Walstein entered; his eye rested on his daughter, and he almost shrieked; but he recovered himself, and with a quivering lip sat down in a distant corner of the room. His Hungarian dog was with him; it seemed to have caught the direction of his master's eye, and as its own rested keenly on Paulina, the animal uttered a low growl. It was strange that the dog never seemed to love the child. It is probable that she was hardly aware of her father's entrance, for she appeared absorbed in her own thoughts. As the blue and flickering flame fell upon her face, she smiled faintly.

"O God! it is! it is!" cried Walstein, and fell senseless on the floor.

His wife and daughter hurried to his assistance, and he recovered; but he pointed to Paulina, and said falteringly, "Philippa!—send *her* to bed." With a quiet step, his daughter moved across the room; at the door, she was about to kiss her mother, but Walstein thundered out, "Forbear!" and rising, closed the door with trembling violence. Philippa had often seen her husband in his wilder moods, but seldom thus strangely agitated; yet, had she known the conviction that had arisen in his mind, she would have ceased to wonder.

He had watched long and narrowly, and now he was unable to conceal longer from himself the fearful truth. It was not in her wan beauty alone that she resembled her sister—it was not merely in the external development of her form;—he knew, he felt, that the second Paulina, born after her sister's death, was *the same Paulina as she whom he had laid in the grave*. There was horror in the idea, yet could it not be resisted. But even now he breathed it not to his wife, and silently they passed to their chamber. The secret of his soul, however, which he would never have told her by day and awake, the wretched Philippa gathered from him in his unconscious mutterings in the dead watches of the night. When the thought came upon her, it fell upon her heart like a weight of lead. Her maternal affection struggled with it, and with the thousand proofs that came crowding of themselves into her memory, to strengthen and to rivet it, and the struggle almost overturned her reason.

The Paulina, in whom her heart was wrapped up twelve years ago, had frequently dreams of a mysterious meaning, which she used to repeat to her mother when no one else was by. A few days after the occurrences of the evening to which we have alluded, the living child, who had come in the place of the dead, told Philippa she had dreamt a dream. She recited it, and Philippa shuddered to hear an exact repetition of one she well remembered listening to long ago, and which she had ever since locked up in her own bosom. Even in sleep, it seemed that, by some awful mystery, Paulina was living over again.

Time still passed on, and the pale child shot up into a girl. She was thirteen; though a stranger would have thought her some years older. It was manifest that she, too, was dying. (There was a dismal doubt haunted her father's mind whether she had ever lived.) She never spoke of her deceased sister; indeed, she seldom spoke at all; but when they asked if she were well, she shook her head, and stretched an arm towards the churchyard.

To that churchyard her father went one moonlight night. It was a wild fancy, yet he resolved to open his daughter's grave, and look once more upon her mouldering remains. He had a reason for his curiosity, which he scarcely dared own even to himself. He told the sexton of his purpose; and, though the old man guessed not his object, he took his spade and his pickaxe, and speedily commenced his task. It was an uncertain night. The wind came in gusts, and sometimes died away into strange silence. The dim moonlight fell upon the white tomb-stones, and the shadows of the passing clouds glided over them like spirits. The sexton pursued his work, and had already dug deep. Walstein stood by his side.

"I have not come to the coffin yet," said the old man, in a tone bordering upon wonder; "yet I could tell the very spot blindfold in which I put it with these hands thirteen years ago."

"Dig on, for the love of Heaven!" said Walstein, and his heart began to beat audibly. There was a short pause.

"My digging is of no use," said the sexton. "I am past the place where I laid the coffin; and may the Holy Virgin protect me, for there is not a vestige either of it or the body left."

Walstein groaned convulsively and leapt into the grave, but in vain; the sexton had reported truly. He had just stept up again into the moonlight, when a cold hand was laid upon his shoulder. He started, and turning round, saw that his daughter stood beside him.

"Paulina! just Heaven! what can have brought you so far from home?—at night, and weak as you are? it will be your destruction."

She took no notice of the question, but fixing her quiet look upon the grave, she said—"Father, I shall soon lie there."

It was the thirteenth anniversary of Paulina's death, and the swollen brook was brawling hoarsely down the mountains, for a tempestuous autumn had already anticipated winter. The shutters of the upper chamber were closed, and Philippa sat by the sick-bed of her last child. The sufferer raised her pale and languid head, and whilst her dark eye appeared to wander in the delirium of fever, she said, with a struggle,—"Mother, is it not a mysterious imagination,—but I feel as if I had lived before, and my thoughts were happier and better than they are now?" Philippa shuddered, and gazed almost with terror upon her child. "It is a dream, Paulina; one of the waking dreams of over-watchfulness. Be still, sweet girl; an hour's sleep will refresh you." As she spoke Paulina *did* sleep, but there was little to refresh in such slumber. Her whole frame was agitated convulsively;—her bosom heaved with unnatural beating;—her hands alternately grasped the coverlid, as if to tear it into shreds, and were ever and anon lifted up to her head, where her fingers twined themselves among the tresses of her ebon hair; her lips moved incessantly; her teeth chattered; her breath came short and thick, as if it would have made itself palpable to the senses. Terrible gibberings succeeded, and her poor mother knew that the moment of dissolution was at hand. In an instant all was still,—the grasp of the hand was relaxed,—the heaving and the beating ceased,—the lips were open, but the breath of life that had ebbed and flowed between them had finished its task, and was gone: a damp distillation stood upon the brow,—it was the last sign of agony which expiring nature gave.

That night Walstein dreamed a dream. Paulina, wrapt in her winding-sheet, stood opposite his couch. Her face was pale and beautiful as in life, but under the folds of her shroud he discovered the hideous form of a skeleton. The vision became double; a grave opened as if spontaneously, and another Paulina burst the cerements asunder, and looked with her dead eye full upon her father. Walstein trembled, and awoke. A strange light glanced under his chamber door. Who was there stirring at the dead hour of night? He threw the curtains aside. The moon was still up; an indescribable impulse urged him to rush towards the room in which the body of his daughter lay. He passed along the lobby;—the door of the chamber was open; the Hungarian dog lay dead at the threshold; *the corpse was gone*.

Now, as they enter'd, doleful screams they hear;
And tender cries of infants pierce the ear.
Just new to life, by too severe a doom,
Snatch'd from the cradle to the silent tomb![5]

From Virgil, The Aeneid, trans. 1778

It is little more than half a century since the good people of Whittinghame got happily quit of a ghost, which, in the shape of an unchristened wean, had annoyed them for many years. An unnatural mother having murdered her child at a large tree, not far from the village, the ghost of the deceased was afterwards seen, on dark nights, running in a distracted manner between the said tree and the church-yard, and was occasionally heard to greet. It was understood by the villagers, that it was obliged thus to take the air, and bewail itself, on account of wanting a name,—no anonymous person, it seems, being able to get a proper footing in the other world. Nobody durst speak to the unhappy little spirit, out of a superstitious dread of dying immediately after; and, to all appearance, the village of Whittinghame was destined to be haunted till the end of time, for want of an exorcist. At length, however, it providentially happened, that a drunkard, one night, in reeling home, encountered it; "How's a' wi' ye this morning, Short-Hoggers?" cried the courageous villager,—when the ghost immediately ran away, joyfully exclaiming,

OH WEEL'S ME NOO, I'VE GOTTEN A NAME;
THEY CA' ME SHORT-HOGGERS O' WHITTINGHAME!

And, since that time, it has never been either seen or heard of.

Chambers, Popular Rhymes of Scotland (1826)[6]

THE OLD NURSE'S STORY

Elizabeth Gaskell

Elizabeth Gaskell (1810–1865) is probably one of the most well-known writers in this collection, both during her lifetime and now. She was a good friend of Charles Dickens, was the first biographer of Charlotte Brontë, and was a prominent social activist and writer. "The Old Nurse's Story" was first published in the 1851/2 Christmas edition of Dickens' periodical Household Words *and is, I would suggest, the germinal literary story in the subgenre of ghost-child tales. The tale betrays a number of striking resemblances to Emily Brontë's 1847 novel* Wuthering Heights; *firstly, through their narrative modes as both tales are relayed by a lower-class female servant who cares for a young female charge. Secondly, there is clear inspiration from the application and attentiveness to folklore and the oral tradition; particularly the child ghost pleading to be let into the house—a symbol for Heaven or at least rest—from which it is excluded.*

Yet Gaskell's tale signifies the start of a striking departure from customary traditions: nearly all of which centre on the sounds (sighs, wails, shrieks) of the dead-child spirit, but this phantom child is silenced (and a few other examples can only repeat the same whispered words) and so its pleas are evidenced through the body's movements. Nevertheless, the child in Gaskell's tale does not simply "haunt". The unnamed, shunned, and murdered ghost child, although clearly a passive victim in life, actively pursues revenge and will not be appeased until a life is claimed as payment for its suffering.

ou know, my dears, that your mother was an orphan, and an only child; and I dare say you have heard that your grandfather was a clergyman up in Westmoreland, where I come from. I was just a girl in the village school, when, one day, your grandmother came in to ask the mistress if there was any scholar there who would do for a nurse-maid; and mighty proud I was, I can tell ye, when the mistress called me up, and spoke to my being a good girl at my needle, and a steady honest girl, and one whose parents were very respectable, though they might be poor. I thought I should like nothing better than to serve the pretty young lady, who was blushing as deep as I was, as she spoke of the coming baby, and what I should have to do with it. However, I see you don't care so much for this part of my story, as for what you think is to come, so I'll tell you at once I was engaged, and settled at the parsonage before Miss Rosamond (that was the baby, who is now your mother) was born. To be sure, I had little enough to do with her when she came, for she was never out of her mother's arms, and slept by her all night long; and proud enough was I sometimes when missis trusted her to me. There never was such a baby before or since, though you've all of you been fine enough in your turns; but for sweet winning ways, you've none of you come up to your mother. She took after her mother, who was a real lady born; a Miss Furnivall, a granddaughter of Lord Furnivall's in Northumberland. I believe she had neither brother nor sister, and had been brought up in my lord's family till she had married your grandfather, who was just a curate, son to a shopkeeper in Carlisle—but a clever fine gentleman as ever was—and one who was a right-down hard worker in his parish, which was very wide, and scattered all abroad over the Westmoreland Fells. When your mother, little Miss Rosamond, was about four or five years old, both her parents died in a fortnight—one after the other. Ah! that was a sad time. My pretty young mistress and me was looking for another baby, when my master came home from one of his long rides, wet and tired, and took the fever he died of; and then she never held up her head again, but just lived to see her dead baby, and have it laid on her breast before she sighed away her life. My mistress had asked me, on her death-bed, never to leave Miss Rosamond; but if she had never spoken a word, I would have gone with the little child to the end of the world.

The next thing, and before we had well stilled our sobs, the executors and guardians came to settle the affairs. They were my poor young mistress's own cousin, Lord Furnivall, and Mr. Esthwaite, my master's brother, a shopkeeper in Manchester; not so well to do then, as he was afterwards, and with a large family rising about him. Well! I don't know if it were their settling, or because of a letter my mistress wrote on her death-bed to her cousin, my lord; but somehow it was settled that Miss Rosamond and me were to go to Furnivall Manor House, in Northumberland, and my lord spoke as if it had been her mother's wish that she should live with his family, and as if he had no objections, for that one or two more or less could make no difference in so grand a household. So, though that was not the way in which I should have wished the coming of my bright and pretty pet to have been looked at—who was like a sunbeam in any family, be it never so grand—I was well pleased that all the folks in the Dale should stare and admire, when they heard I was going to be young lady's maid at my Lord Furnivall's at Furnivall Manor.

But I made a mistake in thinking we were to go and live where my lord did. It turned out that the family had left Furnivall Manor House fifty years or more. I could not hear that my poor young mistress had ever been there, though she had been brought up in the family; and I was sorry for that, for I should have liked Miss Rosamond's youth to have passed where her mother's had been.

My lord's gentleman, from whom I asked as many questions as I durst, said that the Manor House was at the foot of the Cumberland Fells, and a very grand place; that an old Miss Furnivall, a great-aunt of my lord's, lived there, with only a few servants; but that it was a very healthy place, and my lord had thought that it would suit Miss Rosamond very well for a few years, and that her being there might perhaps amuse his old aunt.

I was bidden by my lord to have Miss Rosamond's things ready by a certain day. He was a stern, proud man, as they say all the Lord Furnivalls were; and he never spoke a word more than was necessary. Folk did say he had loved my young mistress; but that, because she knew that his father would object, she would never listen to him, and married Mr. Esthwaite; but I don't know. He never married at any rate. But he never took much notice of Miss Rosamond; which I thought he might have done if he had cared for her dead mother. He sent his gentleman with us to the Manor House, telling him to join him at Newcastle that same evening; so there was no great length of time for him to make us known to all the strangers before he, too, shook us off; and we were left, two lonely young things (I was not eighteen), in the great old Manor House. It seems like yesterday that we drove there. We had left our own dear parsonage very early, and we had both cried as if our hearts would break, though we were travelling in my lord's carriage, which I had thought so much of once. And now it was long past noon on a September day, and we stopped to change horses for the last time at a little smoky town, all full of colliers and miners. Miss Rosamond had fallen asleep, but Mr. Henry told me to waken her, that she might see the park and the Manor House as we drove up. I thought it rather a pity; but I did what he bade me, for fear he should complain of me to my lord. We had left all signs of a town or even a village, and were then inside the gates of a large wild park—not like the parks here in the south, but with rocks, and the noise of running water, and gnarled thorn-trees, and old oaks, all white and peeled with age.

The road went up about two miles, and then we saw a great and stately house, with many trees close around it, so close that in some places their branches dragged against the walls when the wind blew; and some hung broken down; for no one seemed to take much charge of the place;—to lop the wood, or to keep the moss-covered carriage-way in order. Only in front of the house all was clear. The great oval drive was without a weed; and neither tree nor creeper was allowed to grow over the long, many-windowed front; at both sides of which a wing projected, which were each the ends of other side fronts; for the house, although it was so desolate, was even grander than I expected. Behind it rose the Fells, which seemed unenclosed and bare enough; and on the left hand of the house as you stood facing it, was a little old-fashioned flower-garden, as I found out afterwards. A door opened out upon it from the west front; it had been scooped out of the thick dark wood for some old Lady Furnivall; but the branches of the great forest trees had grown and overshadowed it again, and there were very few flowers that would live there at that time.

When we drove up to the great front entrance, and went into the hall I thought we should be lost—it was so large, and vast, and grand. There was a chandelier all of bronze, hung down from the middle of the ceiling; and I had never seen one before, and looked at it all in amaze. Then, at one end of the hall, was a great fire-place, as large as the sides of the houses in my country, with massy andirons and dogs to hold the wood; and by it were heavy old-fashioned sofas. At the opposite end of the hall, to the left as you went in—on the western side—was an organ built into the wall, and so large that it filled up the best part of that end. Beyond it, on the same side, was a door; and opposite, on each side of the fire-place, were also doors leading to the east front; but those I never went through as long as I stayed in the house, so I can't tell you what lay beyond.

The afternoon was closing in, and the hall, which had no fire lighted in it, looked dark and gloomy; but we did not stay there a moment. The old servant who had opened the door for us bowed to Mr. Henry, and took us in through the door at the further side of the great organ, and led us through several smaller halls and passages into the west drawing-room, where he said that Miss Furnivall was sitting. Poor little Miss Rosamond held very tight to me, as if she were seared and lost in that great place, and, as for myself, I was not much better. The west drawing-room was very cheerful-looking, with a warm fire in it, and plenty of good comfortable furniture about. Miss Furnivall was an old lady not far from eighty, I should think, but I do not know. She was thin and tall, and had a face as full of fine wrinkles as if they had been drawn all over it with a needle's point. Her eyes were very watchful, to make up, I suppose, for her being so deaf as to be obliged to use a trumpet. Sitting with her, working at the same great piece of tapestry, was Mrs. Stark, her maid and companion, and almost as old as she was. She had lived with Miss Furnivall ever since they both were young, and now she seemed more like a friend than a servant; she looked so cold and grey, and stony, as if she had never loved or cared for any one; and I don't suppose she did care for any one, except her mistress; and, owing to the great deafness of the latter, Mrs. Stark treated her very much as if she were a child. Mr. Henry gave some message from my lord, and then he bowed good-bye to us all,—taking no notice of my sweet little Miss Rosamond's out-stretched hand—and left us standing there, being looked at by the two old ladies through their spectacles.

I was right glad when they rung for the old footman who had shown us in at first, and told him to take us to our rooms. So we went out of that great drawing-room, and into another sitting-room, and out of that, and then up a great flight of stairs, and along a broad gallery—which was something like a library, having books all down one side, and windows and writing-tables all down the other—till we came to our rooms, which I was not sorry to hear were just over the kitchens; for I began to think I should be lost in that wilderness of a house. There was an old nursery, that had been used for all the little lords and ladies long ago, with a pleasant fire burning in the grate, and the kettle boiling on the hob and tea things spread out on the table; and out of that room was the night-nursery, with a little crib for Miss Rosamond close to my bed. And old James called up Dorothy, his wife, to bid us welcome; and both he and she were so hospitable and kind, that by-and-by Miss Rosamond and me felt quite at home; and by the time tea was over, she was sitting on Dorothy's knee, and chattering away as fast as her little tongue could go. I soon found out that Dorothy was from Westmoreland and that bound her and me together, as it were; and I would never wish to meet with kinder people than were old James and his wife. James had lived pretty nearly all his life in my lord's family, and thought there was no one so grand as they. He even looked down a little on his wife; because, till he had married her, she had never lived in any but a farmer's household. But he was very fond of her, as well he might be. They had one servant under them, to do all the rough work. Agnes they called her; and she and me, and James and Dorothy, with Miss Furnivall and Mrs. Stark, made up the family; always remembering my sweet little Miss

Rosamond! I used to wonder what they had done before she came, they thought so much of her now. Kitchen and drawing-room, it was all the same. The hard, sad Miss Furnivall, and the cold Mrs. Stark, looked pleased when she came fluttering in like a bird, playing and pranking hither and thither, with a continual murmur, and pretty prattle of gladness. I am sure, they were sorry many a time when she flitted away into the kitchen, though they were too proud to ask her to stay with them, and were a little surprised at her taste; though, to be sure, as Mrs. Stark said, it was not to be wondered at, remembering what stock her father had come of. The great, old rambling house, was a famous place for little Miss Rosamond. She made expeditions all over it, with me at her heels; all, except the east wing, which was never opened, and whither we never thought of going. But in the western and northern part was many a pleasant room; full of things that were curiosities to us, though they might not have been to people who had seen more. The windows were darkened by the sweeping boughs of the trees, and the ivy which had overgrown them: but, in the green gloom, we could manage to see old China jars and carved ivory boxes, and great heavy books, and, above all, the old pictures!

Once, I remember, my darling would have Dorothy go with us to tell us who they all were; for they were all portraits of some of my lord's family, though Dorothy could not tell us the names of every one. We had gone through most of the rooms, when we came to the old state drawing-room over the hall, and there was a picture of Miss Furnivall; or, as she was called in those days, Miss Grace, for she was the younger sister. Such a beauty she must have been! but with such a set, proud look, and such scorn looking out of her handsome eyes, with her eyebrows just a little raised, as if she wondered how any one could have the impertinence to look at her; and her lip curled at us, as we stood there gazing. She had a dress on, the like of which I had never seen before, but it was all the fashion when she was young; a hat of some soft white stuff like beaver, pulled a little over her brows, and a beautiful plume of feathers sweeping round it on one side; and her gown of blue satin was open in front to a quilted white stomacher.

"Well, to be sure!" said I, when I had gazed my fill. "Flesh is grass, they do say; but who would have thought that Miss Furnivall had been such an out-and-out beauty, to see her now?"

"Yes," said Dorothy. "Folks change sadly. But if what my master's father used to say was true, Miss Furnivall, the elder sister, was handsomer than Miss Grace. Her picture is here somewhere; but, if I show it you, you must never let on, even to James, that you have seen it. Can the little lady hold her tongue, think you?" asked she.

I was not so sure, for she was such a little sweet, bold, open-spoken child, so I set her to hide herself; and then I helped Dorothy to turn a great picture, that leaned with its face towards the wall, and was not hung up as the others were. To be sure, it beat Miss Grace for beauty; and, I think, for scornful pride, too, though in that matter it might be hard to choose. I could have looked at it an hour, but Dorothy seemed half frightened of having shown it to me, and hurried it back again, and bade me run and find Miss Rosamond, for that there were some ugly places about the house, where she should like ill for the child to go. I was a brave, high-spirited girl, and thought little of what the old woman said, for I liked hide-and-seek as well as any child in the parish; so off I ran to find my little one.

As winter drew on, and the days grew shorter, I was sometimes almost certain that I heard a noise as if some one was playing on the great organ in the hall. I did not hear it every evening; but, certainly, I did very often; usually when I was sitting with Miss Rosamond, after I had put her to bed, and keeping quite still and silent in the bedroom. Then I used to hear it booming and swelling away in the distance.

The first night, when I went down to my supper, I asked Dorothy who had been playing music, and James said very shortly that I was a gowk to take the wind soughing among the trees for music; but I saw Dorothy look at him very fearfully, and Bessy, the kitchen-maid, said something beneath her breath, and went quite white. I saw they did not like my question, so I held my peace till I was with Dorothy alone, when I knew I could get a good deal out of her. So, the next day, I watched my time, and I coaxed and asked her who it was that played the organ; for I knew that it was the organ and not the wind well enough, for all I had kept silence before James. But Dorothy had had her lesson, I'll warrant, and never a word could I get from her. So then I tried Bessy, though I had always held my head rather above her; as I was evened to James and Dorothy, and she was little better than their servant. So she said I must never, never tell; and, if I ever told, I was never to say *she* had told me; but it was a very strange noise, and she had heard it many a time, but most of all on winter nights, and before storms; and folks did say, it was the old lord playing on the great organ in the hall, just as he used to do when he was alive; but who the old lord was, or why he played, and why he played on stormy winter evenings in particular, she either could not or would not tell me. Well! I told you I had a brave heart; and I thought it was rather pleasant to have that grand music rolling about the house, let who would be the player; for now it rose above the great gusts of wind, and wailed and triumphed just like a living creature, and then it fell to a softness most complete; only it was always music and tunes, so it was nonsense to call it the wind. I thought, at first, it might be Miss Furnivall who played, unknown to Bessy; but, one day when I was in the hall by myself, I opened the organ and peeped all about it, and around it, as I had done to the organ in Crosthwaite Church once before, and I saw it was all broken and destroyed inside, though it looked so brave and fine; and then, though it was noon-day, my flesh began to creep a little, and I shut it up, and ran away pretty quickly to my own bright nursery; and I did not like hearing the music for some time after that, any more than James and Dorothy did. All this time Miss Rosamond was making herself more and more beloved. The old ladies liked her to dine with them at their early dinner; James stood behind Miss Furnivall's chair, and I behind Miss Rosamond's, all in state; and, after dinner, she would play about in a corner of the great drawing-room, as still as any mouse, while Miss Furnivall slept, and I had my dinner in the kitchen. But she was glad enough to come to me in the nursery afterwards; for, as she said, Miss Furnivall was so sad, and Mrs. Stark so dull; but she and I were merry enough; and, by-and-by, I got not to care for that weird rolling music, which did one no harm, if we did not know where it came from.

That winter was very cold. In the middle of October the frosts began, and lasted many, many weeks. I remember, one day at dinner, Miss Furnivall lifted up her sad, heavy eyes, and said to Mrs. Stark, "I am afraid we shall have a terrible winter," in a strange kind of meaning way. But Mrs. Stark pretended not to hear, and talked very loud of something else. My little lady and I did not care for the frost;—not we! As long as it was dry we climbed up the steep brows, behind the house, and went up on the Fells, which were bleak and bare enough, and there we ran races in the fresh, sharp air; and once we came down by a new path that took us past the two old gnarled holly-trees, which grew about half-way down by the east side of the house. But the days grew shorter and shorter; and the old lord, if it was he, played away more and more stormily and sadly on the great organ. One Sunday afternoon,—it must have been towards the end of November—I asked Dorothy to take charge of little Missey when she came out of the drawing-room, after Miss Furnivall had had her nap; for it was too cold to take her with me to church, and yet I wanted to go. And Dorothy was glad enough to promise, and was so fond of the child that all seemed well; and Bessy and I set off very briskly, though the sky hung heavy and black over the white earth, as if the night had never fully gone away; and the air, though still, was very biting and keen.

"We shall have a fall of snow," said Bessy to me. And sure enough, even while we were in church, it came down thick, in great large flakes, so thick it almost darkened the windows. It had stopped snowing before we came out, but it lay soft, thick and deep beneath our feet, as we tramped home. Before we got to the hall the moon rose, and I think it was lighter then,—what with the moon, and what with the white dazzling snow—than it had been when we went to church, between two and three o'clock. I have not told you that Miss Furnivall and Mrs. Stark never went to church: they used to read the prayers together, in their quiet gloomy way; they seemed to feel the Sunday very long without their tapestry-work to be busy at. So when I went to Dorothy in the kitchen, to fetch Miss Rosamond and take her up-stairs with me, I did not much wonder when the old woman told me that the ladies had kept the child with them, and that she had never come to the kitchen, as I had bidden her, when she was tired of behaving pretty in the drawing-room. So I took off my things and went to find her, and bring her to her supper in the nursery. But when I went into the best drawing-room, there sat the two old ladies, very still and quiet, dropping out a word now and then, but looking as if nothing so bright and merry as Miss Rosamond had ever been near them. Still I thought she might be hiding from me; it was one of her pretty ways; and that she had persuaded them to look as if they knew nothing about her; so I went softly peeping under this sofa, and behind that chair, making believe I was sadly frightened at not finding her.

"What's the matter, Hester?" said Mrs. Stark sharply. I don't know if Miss Furnivall had seen me, for, as I told you, she was very deaf, and she sat quite still, idly staring into the fire, with her hopeless face. "I'm only looking for my little Rosy-Posy," replied I, still thinking that the child was there, and near me, though I could not see her.

"Miss Rosamond is not here," said Mrs. Stark. "She went away more than an hour ago to find Dorothy." And she too turned and went on looking into the fire.

My heart sank at this, and I began to wish I had never left my darling. I went back to Dorothy and told her. James was gone out for the day, but she and me and Bessy took lights, and went up into the nursery first and then we roamed over the great large house, calling and entreating Miss Rosamond to come out of her hiding place, and not frighten us to death in that way. But there was no answer; no sound.

"Oh!" said I at last, "Can she have got into the east wing and hidden there?"

But Dorothy said it was not possible, for that she herself had never been in there; that the doors were always locked, and my lord's steward had the keys, she believed; at any rate, neither she nor James had ever seen them: so, I said I would go back and see if, after all, she was not hidden in the drawing-room, unknown to the old ladies; and if I found her there, I said, I would whip her well for the fright she had given me; but I never meant to do it. Well, I went back to the west drawing-room, and I told Mrs. Stark we could not find her anywhere, and asked for leave to look all about the furniture there, for I thought now, that she might have fallen asleep in some warm hidden corner; but no! we looked, Miss Furnivall got up and looked, trembling all over, and she was no where there; then we set off again, every one in the house, and looked in all the places we had searched before, but we could not find her. Miss Furnivall shivered and shook so much, that Mrs. Stark took her back into the warm drawing-room; but not before they had made me promise to bring her to them when she was found. Well-a-day! I began to think she never would be found, when I bethought me to look out into the great front court, all covered with snow. I was up-stairs when I looked out; but, it was such clear moonlight, I could see quite plain two little footprints, which might be traced from the hall door, and round the corner of the east wing. I don't know how I got down, but I tugged open the great, stiff hall door; and, throwing the skirt of my gown over my head for a cloak, I ran out. I turned the east corner, and there a black shadow fell on the snow; but when I came again into the moonlight, there were the little footmarks going up—up to the Fells. It was bitter cold; so cold that the air almost took the skin off my face as I ran, but I ran on, crying to think how my poor little darling must be perished and frightened. I was within sight of the holly-trees, when I saw a shepherd coming down the hill, bearing something in his arms wrapped in his maud. He shouted to me, and asked me if I had lost a bairn; and, when I could not speak for crying, he bore towards me, and I saw my wee bairnie lying still, and white, and stiff, in his arms, as if she had been dead. He told me he had been up the Fells to gather in his sheep, before the deep cold of night came on, and that under the holly-trees (black marks on the hill-side, where no other bush was for miles around) he had found my little lady—my lamb—my queen—my darling—stiff and cold, in the terrible sleep which is frost-begotten. Oh! the joy, and the tears of having her in my arms once again! for I would not let him carry her; but took her, maud and all, into my own arms, and held her near my own warm neck and heart, and felt the life stealing slowly back again into her little gentle limbs. But she was still insensible when we reached the hall, and I had no breath for speech. We went in by the kitchen door.

"Bring the warming-pan," said I; and I carried her up-stairs and began undressing her by the nursery fire, which Bessy had kept up. I called my little lammie all the sweet and playful names I could think of,—even while my eyes were blinded by my tears; and at last, oh! at length she opened her large blue eyes. Then I put her into her warm bed, and sent Dorothy down to tell Miss Furnivall that all was well; and I made up my mind to sit by my darling's bedside the live-long night. She fell away into a soft sleep as soon as her pretty head had touched the pillow, and I watched by her till morning light; when she wakened up bright and clear—or so I thought at first—and, my dears, so I think now.

She said, that she had fancied that she should like to go to Dorothy, for that both the old ladies were asleep, and it was very dull in the drawing-room; and that, as she was going through the west lobby, she saw the snow through the high window falling—falling—soft and steady; but she wanted to see it lying pretty and white on the ground; so she made her way into the great hall; and then, going to the window, she saw it bright and soft upon the drive; but while she stood there, she saw a little girl, not so old as she was, "but so pretty," said my darling, "and this little girl beckoned to me to come out; and oh, she was so pretty and so sweet, I could not choose but go." And then this other little girl had taken her by the hand, and side by side the two had gone round the east corner.

"Now you are a naughty little girl, and telling stories," said I. "What would your good mamma, that is in heaven, and never told a story in her life, say to her little Rosamond, if she heard her—and I dare say she does—telling stories!"

"Indeed, Hester," sobbed out my child; "I'm telling you true. Indeed I am."

"Don't tell me!" said I, very stern. "I tracked you by your foot-marks through the snow; there were only yours to be seen: and if you had had a little girl to go hand-in-hand with you up the hill, don't you think the foot-prints would have gone along with yours?"

"I can't help it, dear, dear Hester," said she, crying, "if they did not; I never looked at her feet, but she held my hand fast and tight in her little one, and it was very, very cold. She took me up the Fell-path, up to the holly-trees; and there I saw a lady weeping and crying; but when she saw me, she hushed her weeping, and smiled very proud and grand, and took me on her knee, and began to lull me to sleep; and that's all, Hester—but that is true; and my dear mamma knows it is," said she, crying. So I thought the child was in a fever, and pretended to believe her, as she went over her story—over and over again, and always the same. At last Dorothy knocked at the door with Miss Rosamond's breakfast; and she told me the old ladies were down in the eating-parlour, and that they wanted to speak to me. They had both been into the night-nursery the evening before, but it was after Miss Rosamond was asleep; so they had only looked at her—not asked me any questions.

"I shall catch it," thought I to myself, as I went along the north gallery. "And yet," I thought, taking courage, "it was in their charge I left her; and it's they that's to blame for letting her steal away unknown and unwatched." So I went in boldly, and told my story. I told it all to Miss Furnivall, shouting it close to her ear; but when I came to the mention of the other little girl out in the snow, coaxing and tempt-ing her out, and wiling her up to the grand and beautiful lady by the Holly-tree, she threw her arms up—her old and withered arms—and cried aloud, "Oh! Heaven, forgive! Have mercy!"

Mrs. Stark took hold of her; roughly enough, I thought; but she was past Mrs. Stark's management, and spoke to me, in a kind of wild warning and authority.

"Hester! keep her from that child! It will lure her to her death! That evil child! Tell her it is a wicked, naughty child." Then, Mrs. Stark hurried me out of the room; where, indeed, I was glad enough to go; but Miss Furnivall kept shrieking out, "Oh! have mercy! Wilt Thou never forgive! It is many a long year ago—"

I was very uneasy in my mind after that, I durst never leave Miss Rosamond, night or day, for fear lest she might slip off again, after some fancy or other; and all the more, because I thought I could make out that. Miss Furnivall was crazy, from their odd ways about her; and I was afraid lest something of the same kind (which might be in the family, you know) hung over my darling. And the great frost never ceased all this time; and, whenever it was a more stormy night than usual, between the gusts, and through the wind, we heard the old lord playing on the great organ. But, old lord, or not, wherever Miss Rosamond went, there I followed; for my love for her, pretty helpless orphan, was stronger than my fear for the grand and terrible sound. Besides, it rested with me to keep her cheerful and merry, as beseemed her age. So we played together, and wandered together, here and there, and everywhere; for I never dared to lose sight of her again in that large and rambling house. And so it happened, that one afternoon, not long before Christmas day, we were playing together on the billiard-table in the great hall (not that we knew the right way of playing, but she liked to roll the smooth ivory balls with her pretty hands, and I liked to do whatever she did); and, by-and-bye, without our noticing it, it grew dusk indoors, though it was still light in the open air, and I was thinking of taking her back into the nursery, when, all of a sudden, she cried out:

"Look, Hester! look! there is my poor little girl out in the snow!"

I turned towards the long narrow windows, and there, sure enough, I saw a little girl, less than my Miss Rosamond—dressed all unfit to be out-of-doors such a bitter night—crying, and beating against the window-panes, as if she wanted to be let in. She seemed to sob and wail, till Miss Rosamond could bear it no longer, and was flying to the door to open it, when, all of a sudden, and close upon us, the great organ pealed out so loud and thundering, it fairly made me tremble; and all the more, when I remembered me that, even in the stillness of that dead-cold weather, I had heard no sound of little battering hands upon the window-glass, although the Phantom Child had seemed to put forth all its force; and, although I had seen it wail and cry, no faintest touch of sound had fallen upon my ears. Whether I remembered all this at the very moment, I do not know; the great organ sound had so stunned me into terror; but this I know, I caught up Miss Rosamond before she got the hall-door opened, and clutched her, and carried her away, kicking and screaming, into the large bright kitchen, where Dorothy and Agnes were busy with their mince-pies.

"What is the matter with my sweet one?" cried Dorothy, as I bore in Miss Rosamond, who was sobbing as if her heart would break.

"She won't let me open the door for my little girl to come in; and she'll die if she is out on the Fells all night. Cruel, naughty Hester," she said, slapping me; but she might have struck harder, for I had seen a look of ghastly terror on Dorothy's face, which made my very blood run cold.

"Shut the back kitchen door fast, and bolt it well," said she to Agnes. She said no more; she gave me raisins and almonds to quiet Miss Rosamond: but she sobbed about the little girl in the snow, and would not touch any of the good things. I was thankful when she cried herself to sleep in bed. Then I stole down to the kitchen, and told Dorothy I had made up my mind. I would carry my darling back to my father's house in Applethwaite; where, if we lived humbly, we lived at peace. I said I had been frightened enough with the old lord's organ-playing; but now, that I had seen for myself this little moaning child, all decked out as no child in the neighbourhood could be, beating and battering to get in, yet always without any sound or noise—with the dark wound on its right shoulder; and that Miss Rosamond had known it again for the phantom that had nearly lured her to her death (which Dorothy knew was true); I would stand it no longer.

I saw Dorothy change colour once or twice. When I had done, she told me she did not think I could take Miss Rosamond with me, for that she was my lord's ward, and I had no right over her; and she asked me, would I leave the child that I was so fond of, just for sounds and sights that could do me no harm; and that they had all had to get used to in their turns? I was all in a hot, trembling passion; and I said it was very well for her to talk, that knew what these sights and noises betokened, and that had, perhaps, had something to do with the Spectre-child while it was alive. And I taunted her so, that she told me all she knew, at last; and then I wished I had never been told, for it only made me more afraid than ever.

She said she had heard the tale from old neighbours, that were alive when she was first married; when folks used to come to the hall sometimes, before it had got such a bad name on the country side: it might not be true, or it might, what she had been told.

The old lord was Miss Furnivall's father—Miss Grace, as Dorothy called her, for Miss Maude was the elder, and Miss Furnivall by rights. The old lord was eaten up with pride. Such a proud man was never seen or heard of; and his daughters were like him. No one was good enough to wed them, although they had choice enough; for they were the great beauties of their day, as I had seen by their portraits, where they hung in the state drawing-room. But, as the old saying is, "Pride will have a fall;" and these two haughty beauties fell in love with the same man, and he no better than a foreign musician, whom their father had down from London to play music with him at the Manor House. For, above all things, next to his pride, the old lord loved music. He could play on nearly every instrument that ever was heard of; and it was a strange thing it did not soften him; but he was a fierce dour old man, and had broken his poor wife's heart with his cruelty, they said. He was mad after music, and would pay any money for it. So he got this foreigner to come; who made such beautiful music, that they said the very birds on the trees stopped their singing to listen. And, by degrees, this foreign gentleman got such a hold over the old lord, that nothing would serve him but that he must come every year; and it was he that had the great organ brought from Holland and built up in the hall, where it stood now. He taught the old lord to play on it; but many and many a time, when Lord Furnivall was thinking of nothing but his fine organ, and his finer music, the dark foreigner was walking abroad in the woods with one of the young ladies; now Miss Maude, and then Miss Grace.

Miss Maude won the day and carried off the prize, such as it was; and he and she were married, all unknown to any one; and before he made his next yearly visit, she had been confined of a little girl at a farm-house on the Moors, while her father and Miss Grace thought she was away at Doncaster Races. But though she was a wife and a mother, she was not a bit softened, but as haughty and as passionate as ever; and perhaps more so, for she was jealous of Miss Grace, to whom her foreign husband paid a deal of court—by way of blinding her—as he told his wife. But Miss Grace triumphed over Miss Maude, and Miss Maude grew fiercer and fiercer, both with her husband and with her sister; and the former—who could easily shake off what was disagreeable, and hide himself in foreign countries—went away a month before his usual time that summer, and half threatened that he would never come back again. Meanwhile, the little girl was left at the farm-house, and her mother used to have her horse saddled and gallop wildly over the hills to see her once every week, at the very least—for where she loved, she loved; and where she hated, she hated. And the old lord went on playing—playing on his organ; and the servants thought the sweet music he made had soothed down his awful temper, of which (Dorothy said) some terrible tales could be told. He grew infirm too, and had to walk with a crutch; and his son—that was the present Lord Furnivall's father—was with the army in America, and the other son at sea; so Miss Maude had it pretty much her own way, and she and Miss Grace grew colder and bitterer to each other every day; till at last they hardly ever spoke, except when the old lord was by. The foreign musician came again the next summer, but it was for the last time; for they led him such a life with their jealousy and their passions, that he grew weary, and went away, and never was heard of again. And Miss Maude, who had always meant to have her marriage acknowledged when her father should be dead, was left now a deserted wife—whom nobody knew to have been married—with a child that she dared not own, although she loved it to distraction; living with a father whom she feared, and a sister whom she hated. When the next summer passed over and the dark foreigner never came, both Miss Maude and Miss Grace grew gloomy and sad; they had a haggard look about them, though they looked handsome as ever. But by and by Miss Maude brightened; for her father grew more and more infirm, and more than ever carried away by his music; and she and Miss Grace lived almost entirely apart, having separate rooms, the one on the west side—Miss Maude on the east—those very rooms which were now shut up. So she thought she might have her little girl with her, and no one need ever know except those who dared not speak about it, and were bound to believe that it was, as she said, a cottager's child she had taken a fancy to. All this, Dorothy said, was pretty well known; but what came afterwards no one knew, except Miss Grace, and Mrs. Stark, who was even then her maid, and much more of a friend to her than ever her sister had been. But the servants supposed, from words that were dropped, that Miss Maude had triumphed over Miss Grace, and told her that all the time the dark foreigner had been mocking her with pretended love—he was her own husband; the colour left Miss Grace's cheek and lips that very day for ever, and she was heard to say many a time that sooner or later she would have her revenge; and Mrs. Stark was for ever spying about the east rooms.

One fearful night, just after the New Year had come in, when the snow was lying thick and deep, and the flakes were still falling—fast enough to blind any one who might be out and abroad—there was a great and violent noise heard, and the old lord's voice above all, cursing and swearing awfully,—and the cries of a little child,—and the proud defiance of a fierce woman,—and the sound of a blow,—and a dead stillness,—and moans and wailings dying away on the hillside! Then the old lord summoned all his servants, and told them, with terrible oaths, and words more terrible, that his daughter had disgraced herself, and that he had turned her out of doors,—her, and her child,—and that if ever they gave her help,—or food—or shelter,—he prayed that they might never enter Heaven. And, all the while, Miss Grace stood by him, white and still as any stone; and when he had ended she heaved a great sigh, as much as to say her work was done, and her end was accomplished. But the old lord never touched his organ again, and died within the year; and no wonder! for, on the morrow of that wild and fearful night, the shepherds, coming down the Fell side, found Miss Maude sitting, all crazy and smiling, under the holly-trees, nursing a dead child,—with a terrible mark on its right shoulder. "But that was not what killed it," said Dorothy; "it was the frost and the cold,—every wild creature was in its hole, and every beast in its fold,—while the child and its mother were turned out to wander on the Fells! And now you know all! and I wonder if you are less frightened now?"

I was more frightened than ever; but I said I was not. I wished Miss Rosamond and myself well out of that dreadful house for ever; but I would not leave her, and I dared not take her away. But oh! how I watched her, and guarded her! We bolted the doors, and shut the window-shutters fast, an hour or more before dark, rather than leave them open five minutes too late. But my little lady still heard the weird child crying and mourning; and not all we could do or say, could keep her from wanting to go to her, and let her in from the cruel wind and the snow. All this time, I kept away from Miss Furnivall and Mrs. Stark, as much as ever I could; for I feared them—I knew no good could be about them, with their grey hard faces, and their dreamy eyes, looking back into the ghastly years that were gone. But, even in my fear, I had a kind of pity—for Miss Furnivall, at least. Those gone down to the pit can hardly have a more hopeless look than that which was ever on her face. At last I even got so sorry for her—who never said a word but what was quite forced from her—that I prayed for her; and I taught Miss Rosamond to pray for one who had done a deadly sin; but often when she came to those words, she would listen, and start up from her knees, and say, "I hear my little girl plaining and crying very sad—Oh! let her in, or she will die!"

One night—just after New Year's Day had come at last, and the long winter had taken a turn as I hoped—I heard the west drawing-room bell ring three times, which was the signal for me. I would not leave Miss Rosamond alone, for all she was asleep—for the old lord had been playing wilder than ever—and I feared lest my darling should waken to hear the spectre child; see her I knew she could not, I had fastened the windows too well for that. So, I took her out of her bed and wrapped her up in such outer clothes as were most handy, and carried her down to the drawing-room, where the old ladies sat at their tapestry work as usual. They looked up when I came in, and Mrs. Stark asked, quite astounded, "Why did I bring Miss Rosamond there, out of her warm bed?" I had begun to whisper, "Because I was afraid of her being tempted out while I was away, by the wild child in the snow," when she stopped me short (with a glance at Miss Furnivall) and said Miss Furnivall wanted me to undo some work she had done wrong, and which neither of them could see to unpick. So, I laid my pretty dear on the sofa, and sat down on a stool by them, and hardened my heart against them as I heard the wind rising and howling.

Miss Rosamond slept on sound, for all the wind blew so; and Miss Furnivall said never a word, nor looked round when the gusts shook the windows. All at once she started up to her full height, and put up one hand as if to bid us listen.

"I hear voices!" said she. "I hear terrible screams—I hear my father's voice!"

Just at that moment, my darling wakened with a sudden start: "My little girl is crying, oh, how she is crying!" and she tried to get up and go to her, but she got her feet entangled in the blanket, and I caught her up; for my flesh had begun to creep at these noises, which they heard while we could catch no sound. In a minute or two the noises came, and gathered fast, and filled our ears; we, too, heard voices and screams, and no longer heard the winter's wind that raged abroad. Mrs. Stark looked at me, and I at her, but we dared not speak. Suddenly Miss Furnivall went towards the door, out into the ante-room, through the west lobby, and opened the door into the great hall. Mrs. Stark followed, and I durst not be left, though my heart almost stopped beating for fear. I wrapped my darling tight in my arms, and went out with them. In the hall the screams were louder than ever; they sounded to come from the east wing—nearer and nearer—close on the other side of the locked-up doors—close behind them. Then I noticed that the great bronze chandelier seemed all alight, though the hall was dim, and that a fire was blazing in the vast hearth-place, though it gave no heat; and I shuddered up with terror, and folded my darling closer to me. But as I did so, the east door shook, and she, suddenly struggling to get free from me, cried, "Hester! I must go! My little girl is there; I hear her; she is coming! Hester, I must go!"

I held her tight with all my strength; with a set will, I held her. If I had died, my hands would have grasped her still; I was so resolved in my mind. Miss Furnivall stood listening, and paid no regard to my darling, who had got down to the ground, and whom I, upon my knees now, was holding with both my arms clasped round her neck; she still striving and crying to get free.

All at once, the east door gave way with a thundering crash, as if torn open in a violent passion, and there came into that broad and mysterious light, the figure of a tall old man, with grey hair and gleaming eyes. He drove before him, with many a relentless gesture of abhorrence, a stern and beautiful woman, with a little child cling-ing to her dress.

"Oh Hester! Hester!" cried Miss Rosamond. "It's the lady! the lady below the holly-trees; and my little girl is with her. Hester! Hester! let me go to her; they are drawing me to them. I feel them—I feel them. I must go!"

Again she was almost convulsed by her efforts to get away; but I held her tighter and tighter, till I feared I should do her a hurt; but rather that than let her go towards those terrible phantoms. They passed along towards the great hall-door, where the winds howled and ravened for their prey; but before they reached that, the lady turned; and I could see that she defied the old man with a fierce and proud defiance; but then she quailed—and then she threw up her arms wildly and piteously to save her child—her little child—from a blow from his uplifted crutch.

And Miss Rosamond was torn as by a power stronger than mine, and writhed in my arms, and sobbed (for by this time the poor darling was growing faint).

"They want me to go with them on to the Fells—they are drawing me to them. Oh, my little girl! I would come, but cruel, wicked Hester holds me very tight." But when she saw the uplifted crutch she swooned away, and I thanked God for it. Just at this moment—when the tall old man, his hair streaming as in the blast of a furnace, was going to strike the little shrinking child—Miss Furnivall, the old woman by my side, cried out, "Oh, father! father! spare the little innocent child!" But just then I saw—we all saw—another phantom shape itself, and grow clear out of the blue and misty light that filled the hall; we had not seen her till now, for it was another lady who stood by the old man, with a look of relentless hate and triumphant scorn. That figure was very beautiful to look upon, with a soft white hat drawn down over the proud brows, and a red and curling lip. It was dressed in an open robe of blue satin. I had seen that figure before. It was the likeness of Miss Furnivall in her youth; and the terrible phantoms moved on, regardless of old Miss Furnivall's wild entreaty,—and the uplifted crutch fell on the right shoulder of the little child, and the younger sister looked on, stony and deadly serene.

But at that moment, the dim lights, and the fire that gave no heat, went out of themselves, and Miss Furnivall lay at our feet stricken down by the palsy—death-stricken.

Yes! she was carried to her bed that night never to rise again. She lay with her face to the wall, muttering low but muttering alway: "Alas! alas! what is done in youth can never be undone in age! What is done in youth can never be undone in age!"

The wife of a Count Tanberg gave birth to a dead child; in the fulness of their faith, the parents mourned that to the soul of their little one Christian baptism had been denied, more than the loss of their offspring. In pursuance of a custom then in vogue in parts of Tirol, if not elsewhere, the Count sent the body of the infant to be laid on the altar of St. Joseph, in the parish church, in the hope that at the intercession of the foster father of the Saviour it might revive for a sufficient interval to receive the sacrament of admission into the Christian family. The servant, however, instead of carrying his burden to the church at Schruns (in Montafonthal), finding himself weary by the time he had climbed up the Christberg, dug a grave, and buried it instead. The next year there was another infant, also born dead; this time the Count determined to carry it himself to the church, and by the time he had toiled to the same spot he too was weary, and sat down to rest. As he sat he heard a little voice crying from under the ground, *"ätti, nüm mi' ô met!"* [Father! Take me also with you] The Count turned up the soil, and found the body of his last year's infant. Full of joy he carried both brothers to the altar of St. Joseph, at Schruns; here, continues the legend, his prayer went up before the divine throne; both infants gave signs of life before devout witnesses; baptism could be validly administered, and they, laid to rest in holy ground.

A legend from the valleys of Tyrol
(Fifteenth century)[7]

THE GHOST OF
LITTLE JACQUES

Ann M. Hoyt

"The Ghost of Little Jacques" was first published, uncredited, in Atlantic
Monthly *in February 1863 and then reprinted (still uncredited) in* Sharpe's
London Magazine *and* The Ladies Companion *in 1864. The* Atlantic's
*1877 index of authors-to-date credits an A. M. Hoyt with the story, while
an Ann M. Hoyt is credited elsewhere with other short stories published
around that period of a similar style, and she is referred to as Anna Hoyt in
various pieces of scholarship (including my own), but without explanation.
No concrete information or detail is yet known on the author, except it is
most likely she is American.*

*The only contemporaneous review I have found so far was not favour-
able—the* New York Times *wrote in 1863 that "'The Ghost of Little
Jacques' is a spirit that we imagine very many readers will attempt to lay,
(and succeed in laying—on the table,) before they reach the end of the
story." And yet the story is rich in detail and its attempts to grapple with the
philosophy and ethics of child death. The narrator, Christine, is particularly
interesting for the misalignment between her apparent disdain of children
and her exalted and lingering imagery over the child form (especially in
death). Through her initial placement as working-class employee and later
her attempts to better herself through marriage and business, she becomes the
unwitting witness of the fatal events and the ghost's attempts to see justice
is served.*

ow quiet the saloon was that morning, as I groped my way through the little white tables, the light chairs, and the dimness of early dawn, to the windows! It was my business to open the windows every morning, finding my way down as I best could, for it was not permitted to light the gas at that hour, and no candles were allowed, lest they should soil the furniture. This morning the glass dome, which brightened the ceiling and helped to lighten the saloon, was of very little effect, so cloudy and dusky was the sky. The high houses which shut in the strip of garden on all sides reflected not a ray of light. A chill struck through me as I passed along the marble pavement: a saloon-dampness, empty, vault-like, hung about the fireless, sunless place; and the plashing of the fountain which dripped into the marble basin beyond—dropping, dropping incessantly—struck upon my ear like water trickling down the side of a cave.

It had never occurred to me to think the place lonely or dreary before, or to demur at this morning operation of opening it for the day. A tawdry, gilded, showy hall, it had seemed to me quite a grand affair compared with those in which I had hitherto found employment. Now I shuddered and shivered, and felt the task, always regarded as a compliment to my honesty, to be indeed hard and heavy enough.

It might have been—yet I was not a coward—that the little coffin in that little room at the end of the saloon had something to do with this uneasiness. On each side of that narrow room (which opened upon a long hall leading to the front of the building) were the small windows looking out upon the garden, which I always unbolted first.

I say I do not know that this presence of death had anything to do with my trepidation. The death of a child was no very solemn or very uncommon thing in my master's family. He had many children, and, when death thinned their ranks, took the loss like a philosopher—as he was—a French philosopher. He philosophised that his utmost exertions could not do much more for the child than bequeath to him just such a life as he led, and a share in just such a saloon as he owned; and therefore, if a priest and a coffin ensured the little innocent admission into heaven without any extra charge, he would not betray such lack of wisdom as to demur at the proposition. Therefore, very quietly, since I had been in his employ (about a twelvemonth), three of his children, one by one, had been brought down to that little room at the end of the saloon, and thence through the long hall, through the crowded street out to some unheard-of burying-ground, where a pot of flowers and a painted cross supplied the place of a head-stone. The shop was not shut up on these occasions—that would have been an unnecessary interference with the comfort of customers, and loss of time and money. The necessity of providing for his little living family had quite disenthralled Monsieur C—— from any weakly sentimentality in regard to his little dead family.

So I do not know why I shuddered, being also myself somewhat of a philosopher—of such cool philosophy as grows out inevitably from the hard and stony strata of an overworked life. The sleeper within was certainly better cared for now than he had ever been in life. Monsieur's purse afforded no holiday-dress but a shroud: three of these in requisition within so short a time quite scanted the wardrobe of the other children. Little Jacques had always been a somewhat restless and unhappy baby, longing for fresh air, and a change which he never got; it seemed likely, so far as the child's promise was concerned, that the "great change" was his only chance of variety, and the very best thing that could have happened to him.

And yet, after all, there was something about his death which individualised it, and hung a certain sadness over its occurrence that does not often belong to the death of children, or at least had not marked the departure of his two stout little brothers. Scarlet-fever and croup and measles are such every-day, red-winged, mottled angels, that no one is appalled at their presence. They take off the little sufferer in such vigorous fashion, clutch him with so hearty a grip, that one is compelled to open the door, let them out, and feel relieved when the exit is made. It is only when some dim-eyed, white-robed shape, scarcely seen, scarcely felt, steps softly in and steals away the little troublesome bundle of life with solemn eye and hushed lip, that we have time to pause, to look, to grieve.

This little Jacques, when I came to his father's house, was a rampant, noisy, cunning child, with the vivacity of French and American blood mingling in his veins, and filling him with strongest tendencies to mischief, and prompting elfish feats of activity. He was not by any means a fascinating child—in fact, no children ever fascinated me—but this little fellow was rather disagreeable, a wonder to his father, a horror to his mother, and a great annoyance generally. We were all rather cross with him, and he was universally put down, thrust aside, and ordered out of the way.

This was the state of affairs when I came. It was little Jacques, with a high forehead, white, tightly curling hair, and mischief-full blue eye, who made himself translator of all imaginable inquisitorial French phrases for my benefit—who questioned, and tormented, and made faces at me—who pulled my apron, disappeared with my carpet-bag, and placed a generous slice of molasses-candy upon the seat of my chair, when I sat down to rest myself.

Little Jacques ardently loved a sly fishing-expedition on the edge of the marble fountain-basin, and had lured one or two unthinking gold-fish to destruction with fly and a crooked pin. He would sit perched up there at an odd chance, when his father was away, and he dared venture into the saloon, his little bare feet twinkling against the water, his plump figure curled up into the minutest size, but ready for a spring and a dart up-stairs at the shortest notice of danger. This piscatory propensity had been severely punished by both Monsieur and Madame C——, who could not afford to encourage such an expensive Izaak Walton; but there was no managing the child. He seemed to possess an impish capability of eluding detection and angry denunciations. To be sure, circumstances were against any very strict guard being kept over the youngster. Madame C—— was a very weak woman, a very weak woman indeed—she declared that such was the case—a nervous, dispirited woman, whom everything troubled, who could not bear the noise and tramp of life, and altogether sank under it. Destiny had had no mercy on her weakness, however, and had left her to get along with an innumerable family of children, a philosophic husband who took all her troubles coolly, and a constant demand for her services either in the shop or at the cradle. She could not, therefore, have patience with the incessant anxiety which little Jacques excited by his pranks.

One day Madame C—— had gone out for a walk, leaving the children locked in a room above—five of them, two younger and two older than Jacques—and these together had been in a state of riotous insurrection the whole morning. Little Jacques was not of a disposition to submit to ignominious imprisonment, when human ingenuity could devise means of escape. While his brothers were running wild together, he soberly hunted up another key, screwed and scraped and got it into the keyhole; it turned, and he was out.

Half-an-hour afterwards, his mother, returning, caught the unfortunate fugitive contemplatively perched on the edge of the fountain-basin. In such a frenzy of anger as only unreasonable people are subject to, she caught the child shivering with terror, and thrust him into the water. The gold-fish splashed and swirled, and the water streamed over the sides of the basin. It was only an instant's work; snatching up the forlorn fisher, she shook him unmercifully, and set him upon the floor, dripping and breathless. I saw nothing of them until night. His mother had then recovered her usual peevishness, weakness, and inefficiency; the ebullition of energy had entirely subsided. I was curious to know whether the summary punishment had had any effect upon Jacques; but he was asleep, as soundly as usual after a day's hard frolic.

My curiosity was likely to be gratified to satiety. A strange change came over the little fellow after this. To one accustomed to his apish activity, and to being annoyed by it, there was something plaintive in the fact of having got rid of that trouble. The child was silent, mopish, "good," as his mother said, congratulating herself on the effect of her summary visitation upon the offender.

When, however, a month passed without any return of the evil propensities, this continued quiescence grew to be something ghastly, and, to people who had only their own hands to depend on for a living, a subject of anxiety and alarm: it was expensive to clothe and feed a child who promised but little service in future.

"The *enfant* will never come to anything," said Monsieur; "we could better have spared him than Jean."

To which his wife shook her head, and solemnly assented.

The "enfant," however, gave no signs of taking the hint. Day after day his little ministerial head and flaxen curls were visible over the top of his old-fashioned arm-chair, and day after day his food was demanded, and his appetite was as good as ever.

Watching the child, whose blue eyes, now the mischief was out of them, grew utterly vacant of expression, I unaccountably to myself came to feel an uncomfortable interest in, and morbid sympathy with him—an uneasy, unhappy sympathy, more physical than mental.

No fault could have been found with the motherly care and attention of Madame C———. It was charmingly polite and French. But the sight of her preparing the child's food, or coaxing him with unaccustomed delicacies and *bonbons*, grew to be utterly distasteful—an infliction so nervously annoying that I could not overcome it. A secret antipathy which I had nourished against Madame seemed to be germinating: every action of hers irritated me, every sound of her sharp, yet well-modulated voice gave me a tremor. The truth was, that plunge into the water, taking place so unexpectedly in my presence, had startled and upset me almost as completely as if it had befallen myself. A hard-working woman had no business with such nerves. I knew that, and tried to annihilate them; but the more I cut them down the more they bled. The thing was a mere trifle: the fountain-basin was shallow, the water healthy—nothing could be more healthy than bathing – and at any rate it was no affair of mine. Yet my mind in some unhealthy mood aggravated the circumstances, and coloured everything with its own dark hue.

I could not give up my place, of course not; I was not likely to get so good a situation anywhere else: I could not risk it; and yet the servitude of horror under which I was held for a few weeks was almost enough to reconcile one to starvation. Only that I was kept busy in the shop most of the time, and had little leisure to observe the course of affairs, or to be in Madame's society, I should have given warning—foolishly enough, for there was not a tangible thing of which I had to complain. But a shapeless suspicion which for some days had been brooding in my mind was taking form, too dim for me to dare to recognise it, but real enough to make me feel a miserable fascination to the house while little Jacques still lived—a magnetic, uncomfortable necessity for my presence, as though it were in some sort a protection against an impending evil.

Such suspicion I did not, of course, presume to name, scarcely presumed to think, it seemed so like an unnatural monstrosity of my own mind. But when, one morning, the child died, holding in his hands the *bonbons* his mother had given him, and Madame C——, all agitation and frenzy and weeping, still contrived to extract them from the tightly closed, tiny fists, and threw them into the grate, I felt a horrid thrill like the effect of the last scene in a tragedy. *I knew that the bonbons were poisoned!*

So that is the reason I shuddered as I passed through the saloon.

Throwing open the window, a dim light flickered through, and a sickly ray fell upon the fountain. It shivered upon the dripping marble column in its centre, and struck with an icy hue the water in the basin below. The fountain was not in my range of vision from the window; but I often turned to look at it as I opened the shutters, thinking it a pretty sight when the drops sparkled in the misty light against the back-ground of the otherwise darkened room. It pleased my imagination to watch the effect produced by a little more or a little less opening of the shutters—a nonsensical morning play-spell which quite enlivened me for the sedate occupations of the day. It was, however, not imagination now which whispered to me that there was something else to look at beside the jet of water and the shadowy play of light. Stooping down upon the fountain-brink, absorbed in contemplating the gold-fish swimming below, and with its naked little feet touching the water's edge, a tiny figure sat. My first thought (the first thoughts of fear are never reasonable) was, that some child from up-stairs had stolen down unawares (as children are quite as fond as grown folks of forbidden pleasures) to amuse itself with the water. But the children were not risen yet, and the saloon was too utterly dark and dismal at that hour to tempt the bravest of them. Second thoughts reminded me of that certainty, and I looked again. The figure raised its head from its drooping posture, and gazed vacantly, out of a pair of dim blue eyes, at me. The eyes were the eyes of little Jacques!

I do not know how I should have been so utterly overcome, but I started up in terror as I felt the dreamy phantom-gaze fixed upon me. Raising my hands wildly above my head, the hammer which I held in my hand to drive back the bolts of the shutters flew from my grasp and struck the great mirror—the new mirror which had just been bought, and was not yet hung up. All the savings of a year were shivered to fragments in an instant. My horror at this catastrophe recalled my presence of mind; for I was a poor woman, dependent for my bread on the family. Poor women cannot afford to have fancies; some prompt reality always startles them out of dream or superstition. My superstition fled in dismay as I stooped over the fragments of the looking-glass. What should I do? Where should I hide myself? I involuntarily took hold of the mirror with the instinctive intention of turning it to the wall. It was very heavy; I could scarcely lift it. Pausing a moment, and looking forward at its shattered face in utter anguish of despair, I saw again, repeated in a hundred jagged splinters, up and down in zigzag confusion, in demoniac omnipresence, the uncanny eye, the spectral shape, which had so appalled me. The little phantom had arisen, its slim finger was outstretched—it beckoned, slowly beckoned, as, growing indistinct, it receded farther and farther out from the saloon towards the shop.

The fascination of a spell was upon me; I turned and followed the retreating figure. The shutters of the show-window were not yet taken down, but thin lines of light filtered through them—light enough to see that the apparition made its way to a forbidden spot slyly haunted by the little boy in his days of mischief—a certain shelf where a box of some peculiar sort of expensive confections was kept. I had seen his mother, with unwonted generosity, give the child a handful of these a day or two before his death. I could go no farther. A mighty fear fell upon me, a dimness of vision and a terrible faintness; for that child-phantom, gliding on before, stopped like a retribution at that very spot, and, raising its little hand, pointed to that very box, glancing upward with its solemn eye, as, rising slowly in the air, it grew indistinct, its outlines fading into darkness, and disappeared.

I did not fall or faint, however; I hastened out to the saloon again. The door of the little room where the coffin stood was open, and Madame C——, stepping out, looked vaguely about her.

"Madame! Madame!" I cried, "oh, I have seen—oh, I have seen a terrible sight!"

Madame's face grew white, very white. She grasped me harshly by the arm.

"What *are* you talking about, you crazy woman? You are getting quite wild, I think. Do you imagine you can bide your guilt in that way?" and she shook me with a savage fierceness that made my very bones ache. "This is carrying it with a high hand, to be sure, to flatter yourself that such wilful carelessness will not be discovered. Do you suppose," she cried, pointing to the fragments of glass, "that *my* nerves could feel a crash like that, and I not come down to see what had happened?"

She spoke so volubly, and kept so firm a grip of my arm, that I could not get breath to utter a word of self-defence—indeed, what defence could I make? Yet I should say, from my mistress's singular manner, that *she* had seen that vision too, so wild were her eyes, so haggard her face.

Little Jacques was buried. His attentive parents enjoyed a carriage-ride, with his miniature coffin between them, quite as well as if the little fellow had accompanied them alive and full of mischief.

Outside matters, as Monsieur said, being now off his mind, he could attend to business again.

The mirror belonged to "business." I had been writhing under that knowledge all the morning of their absence.

Monsieur took the sight of his despoiled glass as calmly as Diogenes might have viewed a similar disaster from his tub. Monsieur's philosophy was grounded upon common sense. He knew that the frame was valuable. He knew also that I had saved enough to pay for the accident. I knew it, too, and was well aware that he would exact payment to the uttermost farthing. Monsieur, therefore, was quite cool. He laughed loudly at Madame's excitement, and the feverish account she gave of my fright, my deceitfulness, and pretending to see what nobody else saw.

"Little Jacques!" I heard him exclaim, as I entered the room, shrugging his shoulders with such a contemptuously good-natured sneer as only a Frenchman can manufacture; and rising both his hands derisively, he went off with vivacity to his business.

In the morning I left. Monsieur endeavoured to persuade me to stay. But my business there was finished. I was quite as cool as Monsieur, in fact a little chilly. I was determined to go. Madame was determined also; we could no longer get along together; each hated and feared the other; and Madame C—— having used over-night what influence she possessed to bring her husband to see the necessity of my departure, his objections were not very difficult to remove.

I could not afford to be out of work, that was true, and it might take me a long time to get it; but I was tired to death, and glad of any excuse for a little rest. What, after all, if I did lie by for a little while? there was not much pleasure or profit either way.

I should not grow rich by my work; I could not grow much poorer by being idle. The past year, which I had spent in the service of Monsieur and Madame C——, had been one of constant annoyance and irritating variety of employment. I had grown fretful in the constant hurry and drive, and the baneful atmosphere of Madame's peevishness. Body and soul cried out for a season of release, which never in all my life of service had I thought of before.

I had my desire now. I had put away my bondage. I had ceased my unprofitable labour. The rest I had so long craved was at hand. I might take a jubilee, a siesta, if I pleased, of half a year and nobody be the wiser. I was responsible to nobody. Nobody had any demands upon my time or exertion. Free! I stood in a vacuum; no rush of air, no tempest or whirlpool stirred its infinite profundity. At length I was at peace—a peace which seemed likely to last as long as my slim purse held out; for employment was not easy to obtain. Did I enjoy it? Did I lap myself in the long-desired repose in thankful quiescence of spirit? Perhaps—I cannot tell; restlessness had become a chronic disease with me. I felt like a ship drifted from its mooring: the winds and the tides were pleasant; the ocean was at lull; but the ship rocked aimless and unsteady upon the waters. The heavy weights of life and activity so suddenly withdrawn left a painful lightness akin to emptiness. The broken chains trailed noisily after me. The time hung heavily which I had so long prayed for. Long years of monotonous servitude had made a very machine of me. I could only rust in inaction. Some other power, to rack and grind and urge me on, was necessary to my very existence.

So it happened that at last, my holiday having spun out to the end of my means, I left the city, and engaged work at very low wages in a country-village. The situation and the remuneration were not in the least calculated to stimulate ambition or avarice; and I remained obscurely housed, incessantly busy, and coarsely clothed and fed, in this place for two years. They were not long years either. I had no hard taskmasters, however hard my task; no uneasy, unexplainable apprehensions, no moody forebodings of evil, no troublesome children to distress me. At the end of that time I heard of a better situation, and returned to the city.

I had been engaged about a twelvemonth in my new place—a very pleasant little shop, though the pay was less, and the work harder than I had had with Monsieur C——, when, one morning, standing at the shop-window, I saw that gentleman pass. Very brisk, very spruce, very plump he looked. Glancing in (I flatter myself that a show-window arranged as I could arrange it would attract any one's eye) he espied me: a speedy recognition and a long conversation were the result. It was early morning, and we had the store to ourselves. Monsieur was very friendly. His business was very good. Poor Madame! he wished she could have lived to see it; but she was gone, poor soul, out of a world of trouble. And Monsieur plaintively fixed his eyes on the black crape upon his hat. The unhappy exit took place a few months after my departure. The children had gone to one or another relative. Monsieur was all alone; he had been away since then himself—had been doing as well as a bereaved man could do, and, having saved a snug little sum, had returned to buy out the old land, and re-establish himself in the old place. No one was with him; he wished he could get a good hand to superintend the concern, now his own hands were so full. It would be a good situation for somebody: in short, Monsieur came again and again, until, as I was poor and lonely, and had almost overworked myself just to keep soul and body together, whose union, after all, was of no importance to anyone save myself, and as I was quite glad to find someone else who was interested in the preservation of the partnership, I consented to be his wife. It was a very sensible and philosophic arrangement for both of us. We could make more money together than apart, and were stout and well able to help each other, if only well taken care of. So we settled the business, and settled ourselves as partners in the saloon.

Three years had passed, and we were in the old place still. We had been very busy that day. Many orders to fill, many customers to wait upon. Monsieur, completely worn out, was sound asleep on the sofa up-stairs. It was late; I was very much fatigued, as I descended, according to my usual custom, to see that everything was safe about the house and shop. The place was all shut and empty; the lights were all out. A cushioned lounge in one corner of the saloon—my saloon now—attracted my weary limbs, and I threw myself upon it, setting the lamp upon a marble table by its side. With a complacent sense of rest settling upon me, I drowsily looked about at the dim magnificence of loneliness which surrounded me. The night-lamp made more shadow than shine; but even by its obscured rays one who had known the old place would have been struck with the wonderful improvement we had made. So I thought. It was almost like a palace, gilded, and mirrored, and hung with silken curtains! Monsieur and I had thriven together, had worked hard and saved much these many years to produce the change. But the change had been, as everything we effected was, well considered, and had proved very profitable in the end. Better reception-rooms brought better customers; higher prices a higher class of patronage. It was very pleasant, lying there, to reflect that we were actually succeeding in the world; and a pleasant and quiet mood fell upon me, as, hopeful of the future, I looked back at the past. I thought of my old days in that saloon; I thought of little Jacques. Little Jacques was still a thought of some horror to me, and I generally avoided any allusion to him. But tonight, in this subdued and contemplative mood, I even let the little phantom glide into my reverie without being startled. I even speculated on the old theme which had so haunted me. I wondered whether my suspicions had been correct, and whether—whether Madame C—— was guilty of sending her little son before her into the other world. So thinking, I might have been almost dreaming, a slight rustle in the shop aroused me. I was not alarmed; my nerves are now much healthier, and I wisely make a point of not getting them unstrung by violent movements, or unaccustomed feats of activity, when anything astonishing happens. I therefore lifted my head calmly and looked about—it might be a mouse. The noise ceased that instant, as if the intruder were aware of being observed. Mice sometimes have this instinct. We had some valuable new confections, which I had no desire should be disposed of by such customers. So, taking up my lamp, and peering cautiously about me, I proceeded to the shop. The light flickered—flickered on something tall and white—something white and shadowy, standing erect, and shrinking aside, behind the counter. My heart stood still; a sepulchral chill came over me. My old self, trembling, angry, foreboding, stepped suddenly within the niche whence the self-confident, full-grown, sensible woman had vanished utterly. For an instant, I felt like a ghost myself. It seemed natural that ghosts, if such there were, should spy me out, and appal my heart with their presence; for there, in that old, haunted spot, where long years ago the spectre of little Jacques had lifted its menacing finger, stood the form of Marie, Madame C——. I knew it well; shuddering and shivering myself, more like an intruder than one intruded upon, I laid my hand upon the chill marble counter for support. It was no creation of imagination; the figure laid its hand also upon the marble, and, stretching over its gaunt neck, stood and peered into my eyes.

"Madame C——! Madame C——!" I cried; "what in the name of God would you have of me?"

"Nothing," she answered; "nothing of you, and nothing in the name of God. Oh, you need not shudder at me, Christine C——! I know *you* well enough. You haven't got over your old tricks yet. I'm no ghost, though. Mayhap you'd rather I'd be, for all your nerves, eh?" And she shook her head in the old vengeful, threatening way.

It was true enough. What evil atmosphere surrounded me? What fell snare environed me? I looked about like a hunted animal brought to bay; like a robber suddenly entrapped in the midst of his ill-gotten gains; for this was no dead woman, but a living vengeance, more terrible than death, brought to my very door. Some unseen power, it seemed, full of evil influence, full of malignant justice, stretched its long arms through my life, and would not let me by any means escape to peace, to rest. A direful vision of horrible struggles yet to come—of want, despair, disgrace in reservation—sickened my soul.

"I will call—I will call," said I, gasping—"I will call Monsieur C——; he"—

"Don't, don't, I beg of you!" she cried, catching me by the sleeve, with a sardonic laugh; low, whispering, full of direful meaning, it stealthily echoed through the saloon. "Don't disturb the good man. He sleeps so soundly after his well-spent days! *He* doesn't have any bad dreams, I fancy—rid of such a troublesome, vicious wife—a wife who harassed her husband to death, and murdered her little boy—he sleeps sound, doesn't he? And yet, I declare, in the name of God, Christine C——" (and she lifted up her bony finger like an avenging fate) "*he did it!*"

I had been endeavouring to calm myself while this woman of spectral face and form stared at me with her maniac eye across the counter: I had succeeded. At any rate, this was a tangible horror, and could be grappled with; it was not beyond human reach, a shadowy retribution from the invisible world. To face the circumstances, however repulsive, is less depressing than to await in suspense the coming of their footsteps, and the descent of that blow we know they will inflict. I had always found that policy best which was bravest. I remembered this now. Dropping my high tone, and soothing my excited features, I beckoned the woman and gave her a chair; I took a chair myself, wrapping a shawl close about me to repress the shivering I could not yet overcome; and I and that woman, returned from the grave, as it seemed to me, sat calmly down in business-fashion, and held a long conversation.

Madame C—— had loved her husband with that sort of respectful, awe-filled affection which lower natures experience towards those which are a grade above them. She had loved her children too, although they were her torment. Her inability to manage or keep them in order fretted and irritated her excessively. Monsieur, as a philosopher, could not understand the anomaly, that a woman who was perpetually unhappy and ill-tempered, while her children— young, buoyant, and mischievous—were about her, should sympathise with and care for them when sick. He could not understand her conscience-stricken misery when little Jacques drooped after her severity towards him. Monsieur was a kind husband, however, and a wise man in many things. He had studied much in his youth, chiefly medical works, of which he had quite a collection. He could not understand the whimsical nervousness of women; but when so slight a thing as a child's illness appeared to be the cause of it, he could unhesitatingly undertake to remove the difficulty. He had prescribed attentively for the two children who died before Jacques, thereby rendering them comfortable and quiet, and saving quite an item in the doctor's bill.

When little Jacques fell ill, and Madame fretted incessantly about his loss of vigour and vivacity, Monsieur, with fatherly kindness, undertook, in the midst of his pressing business to give the child his medicine, which had to be most carefully prepared. Sometimes the powders were disguised in *bonbons*, the more agreeably to dose the patient little fellow; these were prepared with Monsieur's own fatherly hands, and during his absence were once in a while left for Madame to administer. Madame had great faith in these medicines—great faith in her husband's skill; but the child's disease was obstinate, very; no progress could be discovered. It was a comforting thought, at least, that, if his recovery was beyond possibility, something had been done to soothe his pain and quiet the vexed spirit in its bitter struggle with dissolution. Yes, the medicines were certainly very quieting—so quieting, so death-like in their influence—she could not tell how a suspicion (perhaps the strange expression of the child's eye, when they were administered) glided into her imagination (having so great a reverence for her husband, it took no place in her mind for an instant—it was merely a spectral, haunting shadow) that these things were getting the child no better—that they were not medicine for keeping him here, but for helping him away. This suspicion, breathing its baleful breath across her mind, weak, vacillating, incapable of energetic action, had rendered her miserable, morose, irritable, more so than ever before. Yet little Jacques in his last hour hankered for the medicine, and craved feverishly the delicate powder, the sweet confection his father prepared for him.

While inwardly brooding over this unnamed terror, and cowering before this shapeless thought which loomed in the darkness of her mental gloom, an idea entered her mind that I, too, was suspicious that something was going wrong—that I was watching, waiting the evil to come. The child died. Her fear for him was utterly superseded by fear for her husband. What if I should find him out and betray him? The anxiety occasioned by this possibility made her hate me. The agony for her little one's departure, the fear of some dire discovery, the consciousness of guilt near enough of vicinage almost to seem her own, combined to nearly distract her mind, and it seemed like a joyful relief when I departed. The sudden release from that constant pressure of fear (she knew I could do nothing against them without money, credit, or friends) made her ill for a time, quite ill, she said. She knew not what was done for her during this sickness—who nursed her or who gave her medicine. But one morning, on waking from what seemed a long sleep, in which she had dreamed strangely and talked wildly, she beheld Monsieur, smiling kindly, standing beside her bed with a vial and a spoon in his hand.

"It is a cordial, my dear, which will strengthen and bring you round again very soon. You need a sedative—something to allay fever and excitement."

"Is it little Jacques's medicine?"

"Quite similar, my dear—not the powders, the liquid. Equally soothing to the nerves, and promotive of sleep."

She turned her face away. She had slept long enough. She thanked Monsieur, not daring to look up, but capriciously refused to touch little Jacques's medicine.

"And Monsieur," she said—"Monsieur was very angry. He said I was a disobedient wife, who did not wish to get well, but desired to be a constant expense and trouble to her husband.

"And so, Christine C——, I trembled and shook, and let fall words I never meant to have uttered to Monsieur, and I said he had killed the child, and wished to kill me, that he might marry Mademoiselle Christine. I did not say any more that day. In the morning, Monsieur and I discoursed together again. I declared I would get well and go away. Oh! Monsieur knew well I would not betray him. He was willing, very willing to consent to my departure. He cared for me well, and gave me much money; and I went away to my old aunt, who lived in Paris. I have been dead—I have died to Monsieur. I should never have returned, but that my good aunt is gone. When I buried her—shut her kind eyes, and wrapped her so snugly in her shroud—I thought it a horrible thing to be living without a soul to care for me, or comfort me, or even to wrap me up as I did her when the time was come. I felt then a thirsty spirit rising within me to see my old place where I had comfort and shelter long ago, and to see my children. I have been to see them: they are in B——; they did not know me there. I did not tell them who I was. I have been faithful to my promise. I tell no one but you, Christine C——, who have stepped into my place, and stolen away my home. A prettier home you have made of it for a prettier wife; but it's the old place yet, with the old stain upon it."

Wishing to consider a moment what I should do, half paralysed, like one who is stricken with death, I left that other ME (for was she not also my husband's wife?) apparently exhausted, lying upon the sofa, and went wearily upstairs, with heavy steps, like one whose life has suddenly become a weight to her. What indeed, *should* I do? Starvation and misery stared me in the face. If I left the house, casting its guilt and its comfort behind me, where could I go? I could do nothing, earn nothing now. My reputation, now that we were so long established, would be entirely gone. And if I left all for which I had laboured so hard, for another to enjoy, would that better the matter? Great God! would *anything* help me? Before me in terrific vision rose a dim vista of future ruin, of ineffectual years writhing in the inescapable power of the law, of long trial, of horrible suspense, of garish publicity, of my name handed from mouth to mouth, a forlorn, duped, degraded thing, whose blighted life was a theme of newspaper comment and cavil. These thoughts swept over me as a tempest sweeps over the young tree whose roots are not firm in the soil, whose writhing and wrestling are impotent to defend it from certain destruction. There was no one I loved especially, no one I cared for anxiously, to relieve the bitter thoughts which centred in myself alone.

Monsieur awoke as I was sitting thus, in ineffectual effort to compose myself. Seeing me sitting near him, still dressed, the door open, and the light burning, he inquired what was the matter. I had something below requiring his attention, I said, and, taking up the lamp, ushered him down-stairs. My chaotic thoughts were beginning to settle themselves—to form a nucleus about the first circumstance that thrust itself definitely before them. That poor wretch waiting below—that forsaken, abject, dishonoured wife—I would confront him with her, and charge him with his guilt. Opening the saloon-door I stepped in before him. The lamp which I had left upon the stand was out, and the slender thread of light which fell from the one in my hand, sweeping across the gloom, rested upon the deserted sofa. The saloon was empty; no trace, no sign could be discovered of any human being. The hush, the solemnity of night brooded over the place. Monsieur mockingly, but unsteadily, inquired what child's game I was playing—he was too tired to be fooled with. He spoke hotly and quickly, as he never had spoken to me before—like one who has long been ill at ease, and deems a slight circumstance portentous. So I turned upon him, with all the bitterness in my heart rising to my tongue. I told him the story: I charged him with the guilt. He listened in silence: marble-like he stood, with folded arms, and heard the conclusion of the whole matter. When I was silent, be strode up to me, and, stooping, peered into my face steadily. His teeth were clenched; his eyes shot fire; otherwise he was calm, quite composed. He said, quietly, "Would you blame me for making an angel out of an idiot?"

Monsieur's philosophy was too subtile for me. *Guilty* seemed a coarse word to apply to so fine a nature. He denied having attempted to injure his wife in any way. "Women are all fools!" he said: "they are all alike—go just as they are led, and do just as they are taught. They cannot think for themselves: they have no ideas of justice but just what the law furnishes them with. It was silly to complain: it argued a narrow mind to condemn merely because the laws condemn. In that case all should be acquitted whom the laws acquit—did we ever do this? Would his darling Jacques, happy, angelic, condemn his parent for releasing him from the drudgery of life? Was it not better to play on a golden harp than to be a confectioner? Were not all men, in fact, more or less slayers of their brothers? Was I not myself guilty in attributing to Madame a deed in my eyes worthy of death, and of which she was innocent? It was only those whose courage induced them to venture a little farther who received condemnation. In some way or other, every soul is wearing out and overtasking somebody else's soul, and shortening somebody's days. A man who should throw his child into the water, in order to save him from being burnt to death, would not be arraigned for the fierce choice. Little Jacques, if he had lived, would have lingered in misery and imbecility. Was a lingering death of torture to be preferred by a tender-hearted woman to one more rapid and less painful, where the certainty of death left only such preference? Ah, well! it was consolation that his little son was safe from all vicissitude, whatever might befall his devoted father!" And Monsieur wiped his eyes, and drew out a little miniature he always carried in his bosom. It was the portrait of little Jacques.

Well, as I have said, Monsieur was a philosopher, and I was a philosopher; and yet I must have been a woman incapable of reason, incapable of comprehending an argument; for the thought of this thing, and of being in the presence of a man capable of such a deed, made me uneasy, restless, unhappy, as though I were in some sort a partaker of the crime. I could not sleep: I was haunted with horrific dreams; and when, in a few days, among the "accidents," the death of an unknown woman was recorded, whose body had drifted ashore at night, and I recognised by the description poor, unknown, uncared-for Madame C——, a wild fever burned in my veins, a frenzy of anguish akin to remorse, as if *I* had wronged the dead, and sent her drifting, helpless out into the unknown world. A pitiable soul, who preferred misery for her portion rather than betray the man she loved, or become partaker of his crime, had crept back, after years of self-imposed absence, with death in her heart, to see the old place and the new wife—and how had I received her? With horror and shuddering, as though she were some guilty thing, to be held at arm's-length: not as one woman, generous, forgiving, hoping for mercy hereafter, should receive another, however erring. It was a sad boon, perhaps, she had endowed me with; yet it was all she prized and cherished.

With a nobleness of magnanimity, a passionate self-sacrifice, which none but a woman could be capable of, Madame C—— had divested herself of all peculiarities of clothing by which she could be identified. It was only by recognising the features, and a singular scar upon the forehead, that I knew it was herself. She was buried by stranger-hands, however: we dared not come forward to claim her.

The excitement attendant on this miserable death, and the circumstances which preceded it, laid me, for the first time in my life, upon a sick-bed. I was unconscious for many weeks of anything save intolerable pain and intolerable heat. A fiery agony of fever leaped in my veins, and scorched up my life-blood. I believe Monsieur cared for me, and nursed me attentively during this illness.

The fever left me; exhausted, spent, my life shrunken up within me, my energy burned out, a puny, spiritless remnant of the strong woman who lay down upon that couch, I lay despondent, vacant of all interest in the world hitherto so exciting to me. I had not seen Monsieur since this apparent commencement of recovery. A great, good-natured nurse kept watch over me, and fed me with spiritless dainties, tasteless, unsatisfying.

One day, when my senses began to settle a little and things began to take shape again, I asked for Monsieur. He came and stood at my bedside. "Christine," said he, "you have no faith in my power of making angels. I have not made one of you. Being divided in our theories, we will divide our earthly goods. We will part. Should you, as a woman, deem it your duty to inform against me, I shall not think it wrong. I shall bear it as a philosopher. You have no proof: you can substantiate nothing; but it may be a satisfaction. I do not understand women, therefore I cannot tell."

"Monsieur," I answered, "leave it to God to fill his heaven as he thinks best. He has not invited your assistance, neither has he invited me to avenge him. Since He does not punish, dare I invade his prerogative?"

And we did not part. We will live together in peace, we said, and the past shall be utterly forgotten. Shall not a whole lifetime of unwavering rectitude atone for this one crime?

I accepted my fate—weakly, in the dread of poverty, in the horror of disgrace, shrinking within myself with the secret thrust upon me. I said we are all the makers of our own destiny, and there is nothing supernatural in life. If this course is best and wisest in my judgment, nothing evil will come of it. I said this ignorant of the mystery of existence, and inexperienced in that subtle power which penetrates all the windings and turnings of humanity, searching out hidden things—the Purifier and the Avenger, allotting to each one his portion of bitterness, his inexorable punishment. "We will live together in peace": it was the thought of a sudden moment of fervour, which over-leaped the dreary length of life, and assumed to compass the repentance of a whole existence in a single day. But destiny holds always in store its retribution. God suffers no dropped stitches in the web of his universe; and the smallest truth evaded, the least wretch neglected, will surely be picked up again in the unending circle that is winding its certain thread around all beings, connecting by invisible links the most insignificant chances with the most significant events.

When I said we will be one, we will endure together, I thought that so, in my enduring strength, I could bear up whatever burden came. I know not how, by what invisible process, the load which I had lifted to my shoulders grew into leaden heaviness—heavy, heavy, like the weight of some dead soul resting its lifeless shape upon my living spirit, till I staggered under the unbearable presence. I had doomed myself to stand side by side, to work hand in hand with guilt, to feel hourly the dread lest in some moment of frenzy engendered by the dumb anguish within me I might betray the secret whose rust was eating into my soul, and shriek out my misery in the ears of all men.

Monsieur, seeing me grow thin and pale, declared that I must have a change, I must go somewhere, to the sea-shore. To the sea-shore! No, I would not go to the sea-shore, or to any other shore; a stranded vessel, I could not struggle from the place of shipwreck.

Monsieur grew vexed and anxious, when I stubbornly shook my head. And when week after week I still refused, he grew strangely uneasy. I had better go; if I would not go alone, he would go with me, shut up the shop, and take a holiday.

I considered the matter that day. The project was a wild one; at this busiest season of the year, it would be an injury to our business. And what might the neighbours say? It might lead them to unpleasant suspicions. We were not popular among them. No, it would not do.

I explained this to Monsieur very calmly at the supper-table. His face was pale and quiet as usual. He did not interrupt me. When I concluded, he rose as if he would go out, but turning back suddenly and striking the table with his clenched fist—

"God!" he exclaimed. "Woman, would you see me die like a dog? The neighbours, for all I know, they have got me at their finger-ends now—the vile rabble! That old hag, Madame Justine, at the ribbon-shop below—some demon possessed her to look out that night when SHE came crawling home. She noted her well with her greedy eyes; someone *so* like my dear first wife, she told me. There is mischief and death in her eyes. She knows or guesses too much."

"What can she guess?" I asked; "she has only lately come into the neighbourhood."

In answer to this, Monsieur informed me that she professed to have been an old friend of his wife's, who, in times gone by, half bewildered with her troubles, had probably dropped many unguarded words in this woman's presence. Madame C—— had died (to her old home) while this woman was away on her visit. "Ah!" she said, "she had her misgivings many a time. Did the same doctor attend Madame C—— who prescribed for little Jacques? He ought to be hung, then. Ah, well, if all men had their deserts, she knew many things that would hang some folks who looked all fair and square, and held their guilty heads higher than their neighbours."

"Well?" I said.

"Well!—you women are so virtuous, you have no mercy, Madame. Go, hang—go drown the wretch who comes under the malediction of the ladies! Oh, there is nothing too hard for him! And this one owed me a grudge lately about a mistake—a little mistake I made in an account with her, and would not alter because I thought it all right."

The preparations were going on silently and steadily that night. I would go anywhere now, anything would I do, to escape the fate whose stealthy footsteps were tracing us out. Well I knew that, once in the power of the law, its firm grasp would wrest every secret from the deepest depths where it was hidden. Once out of the city, we could readily take flight, if immediate danger threatened.

The doors were all closed; the trunks stood corded in the hall. I was down-stairs getting the silver together. Monsieur was in his room, packing up his medicine-chest. There was no weakness in my nerves now, no trembling in my limbs. I was determined. While thus engaged, pausing a moment amid the light tinkle of the silver spoons, I thought I heard footsteps in the saloon above. Softly ascending the stairs, I met Monsieur at the door. He had come down under the same impression, that someone was walking in the saloon, still holding in his hand the tiny cup with which he measured his medicines. It was full, and Monsieur carried it very carefully, as, opening the door, he looked cautiously about. Nothing stirred; all was silent as death; and walking forward toward the fountain, he straightened himself up, and his white face flushed, as he said in a whisper—

"Christine, everything is ready. We are safe yet; we shall escape. Once away we will never return to this doomed place, let what will come of it. Yes, I am certain that we shall escape!"

Monsieur took a step forward as he said this, and stood transfixed. The light shook which he held in his hand, as if a strong wind had passed over it; his eye quailed; his cheek blanched ghastly whiteness. I thought that undue excitement had brought on a fainting-fit of some kind, and was stooping to dip my hands in the water and bathe his forehead, when I saw, distinctly, like a white mist in the darkness, a visible shape sitting solemn upon the basin-edge; the room was very dim, and the falling spray fell over the shape like a weeping-willow, yet my eyes discerned it clearly. Oh, it was no dream that I had dreamed in my young days long ago! That little figure was no stranger to my vision, no stranger to the changeless waterfall. Did Monsieur see it also? He stood close beside the fountain now, with his face towards the spectre. A portion of the contents of the tiny cup in his hand fell down into the water; a lonely gold-fish, swimming there, turned over on his golden side and floated motionless upon the surface.

I scarcely noticed this, for, at the time, I heard the knob of the shop-door turn quickly, and the door was shaken violently. It was probably the night-watchman going his rounds; but, in my alarm and excitement, I thought we were betrayed. I stepped swiftly to the door, and pushed an extra bolt inside.

"Monsieur!" I cried, under my breath, "hide! hide yourself! Quick! in the name of Heaven!"

But he did not answer, and, hastening to his side, I saw the faint outlines of that shadowy visitant growing indistinct and disappearing. As it vanished, Monsieur turned deliberately towards me; his eyes were clear, the faintness was over: his voice was grave and steady, as he said—

"Christine! I have seen it. It is the warning of death. There is no future and no escape for me. The retribution is at hand"—and he lifted the tiny cup brimming to his lips. "Go you," he said, huskily, "to the sea-shore. I have an errand elsewhere."

In the morning came the officers of justice; my dim eyes saw them, my ears heard unshrinking their stern voices demanding Monsieur C——. I did not answer; I pointed vaguely forward; and forward they marched, with a heavy tramp, to where the one whom they were seeking lay prone upon the marble floor, his head hanging nervelessly down over the water. He had been arrested by a Higher Power. Monsieur C—— was dead.

The wind-demon was said to be attended by the souls of unbaptised children, and English peasants say they hear their wails.

Bassett, *Sea Phantoms* (1892)[8]

Whosoever putteth his child to get his living at sea had better a great deal bind him prentice to a hangman.

Sailor's maxim (sixteenth century)[9]

KENTUCKY'S GHOST

Elizabeth Stuart Phelps

Elizabeth Stuart Phelps Ward (1844–1911) was born in Boston, Massachusetts to an American Congregational minister and his wife. She was another prolific writer and is known as an early feminist intellectual who challenged traditional Christian beliefs of the afterlife and women's traditional roles in marriage and family. Following the end of the Civil War, Phelps published three spiritualist novels which depict the afterlife as a domestic haven and place of reunion for families.

"Kentucky's Ghost" was first published in Atlantic Monthly *in November 1868, and later collected with some of her other supernatural stories in* Men, Women, and Ghosts *(1869). It is a rather unusual example of the subgenre, being the only story I have found set at sea, although William Bottrell's 1873 Cornish story "The Smugglers of Penrose" offers an interesting variant and the subject of the boy stowaway was a prominent concern of real stories and ballads of the period. In the popular ballad and Victorian parlour song "The Little Hero" (also known as "The Stowaway"), the small urchin boy found aboard the ship is threatened with hanging by the savage First Mate, but the boy begins to pray and the innocence he exudes convinces the sailor to save and indeed to love the boy. No such salvation awaits the living Kentucky. His bible is used for gun-wadding and his prayers are scorned by most of the crew, and he is eventually sent to his death. Yet there is a suggestion by the narrator, a fellow kind-hearted sailor, that the boy's godliness saves his soul, for an Old Testament-style divine punishment is wreaked upon the First Mate by the ghost of the boy. Even at sea you are not free from God's judgement, Phelps suggests.*

rue? Every syllable.

That was a very fair yarn of yours, Tom Brown, very fair for a landsman, but I'll bet you a doughnut I can beat it; and all on the square too, as I say,—which is more, if I don't mistake, than you could take oath to. Not to say that I never stretched my yarn a little on the fo'castle in my younger days, like the rest of 'em; but what with living under roofs so long past, and a call from the parson regular in strawberry time, and having to do the flogging consequent on the inakkeracies of statement follering on the growing up of six boys, a man learns to trim his words a little, Tom, and no mistake. It's very much as it is with the talk of the sea growing strange to you from hearing nothing but lubbers who don't know a mizzen-mast from a church-steeple.

It was somewhere about twenty years ago last October, if I recollect fair, that we were laying in for that particular trip to Madagascar. I've done that little voyage to Madagascar when the sea was like so much burning oil, and the sky like so much burning brass, and the fo'castle as nigh a hell as ever fo'castle was in a calm; I've done it when we came sneaking into port with nigh about every spar gone and pumps going night and day; and I've done it with a drunken captain, on starvation rations,—duff that a dog on land wouldn't have touched and two teaspoonfuls of water to the day,—but someways or other, of all the times we headed for the East Shore I don't seem to remember any quite as distinct as this.

We cleared from Long Wharf in the ship Madonna,—which they tell me means, My Lady, and a pretty name it was; it was apt to give me that gentle kind of feeling when I spoke it, which is surprising when you consider what a dull old hull she was, never logging over ten knots, and oncertain at that. It may have been because of Moll's coming down once in a while in the days that we lay at dock, bringing the boy with her, and sitting up on deck in a little white apron, knitting. She was a very good-looking woman, was my wife in those days, and I felt proud of her,—natural, with the lads looking on.

"Molly," I used to say, sometimes,—"Molly Madonna!"

"Nonsense!" says she, giving a clack to her needles,—pleased enough though, I warrant you, and turning a very pretty pink about the cheeks for a four-years' wife. Seeing as how she was always a lady to me, and a true one, and a gentle, though she wasn't much at manners or book-learning, and though I never gave her a silk gown in her life, she was quite content, you see, and so was I.

I used to speak my thought about the name sometimes, when the lads weren't particularly noisy, but they laughed at me mostly. I was rough enough and bad enough in those days; as rough as the rest, and as bad as the rest, I suppose, but yet I seemed to have my notions a little different from the others. "Jake's poetry," they called 'em.

We were loading for the East Shore trade, as I said, didn't I? There isn't much of the genuine, old-fashioned trade left in these days, except the whiskey branch, which will be brisk, I take it, till the Malagasy carry the prohibitory law by a large majority in both houses. We had a little whiskey in the hold, I remember, that trip, with a good stock of knives, red flannel, hand-saws, nails, and cotton. We were hoping to be at home again within the year. We were well provisioned, and Dodd,—he was the cook,—Dodd made about as fair coffee as you're likely to find in the galley of a trader. As for our officers, when I say the less said of them the better, it ain't so much that I mean to be disrespectful as that I mean to put it tenderly. Officers in the merchant service, especially if it happens to be the African service, are brutal men quite as often as they ain't. At least, that's my experience; and when some of your great ship-owners argue the case with me,—as I'm free to say they have done before now, I say, "That's *my* experience, sir," which is all I've got to say; brutal men, and about as fit for their positions as if they'd been imported for the purpose a little indirect from Davy Jones's Locker. Though they do say that the flogging is pretty much done away with in these days, which makes a difference.

Sometimes on a sunshiny afternoon, when the muddy water showed a little muddier than usual, on account of the clouds being the colour of silver, and all the air the colour of gold, when the oily barrels were knocking about on the wharves, and the smells were strong from the fish-houses, and the men shouted and the mates swore, and our baby ran about deck a-play with everybody,—he was a cunning little chap with red stockings and bare knees, and the lads took quite a shine to him,—"Jake," his mother would say, with a little sigh,—low, so that the captain never heard,—"think if it was *him* gone away for a year in company the like of that!"

Then she would drop her shining needles, and call the little fellow back sharp, and catch him up into her arms.

Go into the keeping-room there, Tom, and ask her all about it. Bless you! she remembers those days at dock better than I do. She could tell you to this hour the colour of my shirt, and how long my hair was, and what I ate, and how I looked, and what I said. I didn't generally swear so thick when she was about.

Well; we weighed, along the last of the month, in pretty good spirits. The Madonna was as stanch and seaworthy as any eight-hundred-tonner in the harbour, if she was clumsy; we turned in, some sixteen of us or thereabouts, into the fo'castle,—a jolly set, mostly old messmates, and well content with one another; and the breeze was stiff from the west, with a fair sky.

The night before we were off, Molly and I took a walk upon the wharves after supper. I carried the baby. A boy, sitting on some boxes, pulled my sleeve as we went by, and asked me, pointing to the Madonna, if I would tell him the name of the ship.

"Find out for yourself," said I, not over-pleased to be interrupted.

"Don't be cross to him," says Molly. The baby threw a kiss at the boy, and Molly smiled at him through the dark. I don't suppose I should ever have remembered the lubber from that day to this, except that I liked the looks of Molly smiling at him through the dark.

My wife and I said good by the next morning in a little sheltered place among the lumber on the wharf; she was one of your women who never like to do their crying before folks.

She climbed on the pile of lumber and sat down, a little flushed and quivery, to watch us off. I remember seeing her there with the baby till we were well down the channel. I remember noticing the bay as it grew cleaner, and thinking that I would break off swearing; and I remember cursing Bob Smart like a pirate within an hour.

The breeze held steadier than we'd looked for, and we'd made a good offing and discharged the pilot by nightfall. Mr. Whitmarsh—he was the mate—was aft with the captain. The boys were singing a little; the smell of the coffee was coming up, hot and homelike, from the galley. I was up in the maintop, I forget what for, when all at once there came a cry and a shout; and, when I touched deck, I saw a crowd around the fore-hatch.

"What's all this noise for?" says Mr. Whitmarsh, coming up and scowling.

"A stow-away, sir! A boy stowed away!" said Bob, catching the officer's tone quick enough. Bob always tested the wind well, when a storm was brewing. He jerked the poor fellow out of the hold, and pushed him along to the mate's feet.

I say "poor fellow," and you'd never wonder why if you'd seen as much of stowing away as I have.

I'd as lief see a son of mine in a Carolina slave-gang as to see him lead the life of a stow-away. What with the officers from feeling that they've been taken in, and the men, who catch their cue from their superiors, and the spite of the lawful boy who hired in the proper way, he don't have what you may call a tender time.

This chap was a little fellow, slight for his years, which might have been fifteen, I take it. He was palish, with a jerk of thin hair on his forehead. He was hungry, and homesick, and frightened. He looked about on all our faces, and then he cowered a little, and lay still just as Bob had thrown him.

"We—ell," says Whitmarsh, very slow, "if you don't repent your bargain before you go ashore, my fine fellow, —— me, if I'm mate of the Madonna! and take that for your pains!"

Upon that he kicks the poor little lubber from quarter-deck to bowsprit, or nearly, and goes down to his supper. The men laugh a little, then they whistle a little, then they finish their song quite gay and well acquainted, with the coffee steaming away in the galley. Nobody has a word for the boy,—bless you, no!

I'll venture he wouldn't have had a mouthful that night if it had not been for me; and I can't say as I should have bothered myself about him, if it had not come across me sudden while he sat there rubbing his eyes quite violent, with his face to the west'ard (the sun was setting reddish), that I had seen the lad before; then I remembered walking on the wharves, and him on the box, and Molly saying softly that I was cross to him.

Seeing that my wife had smiled at him, and my baby thrown a kiss at him, it went against me, you see, not to look after the little rascal a bit that night.

"But you've got no business here, you know," said I; "nobody wants you."

"I wish I was ashore!" said he,—"I wish I was ashore!"

With that he begins to rub his eyes so very violent that I stopped. There was good stuff in him too; for he choked and winked at me, and did it all up about the sun on the water and a cold in the head as well as I could myself just about.

I don't know whether it was on account of being taken a little notice of that night, but the lad always kind of hung about me afterwards; chased me round with his eyes in a way he had, and did odd jobs for me without the asking.

One night before the first week was out, he hauled alongside of me on the windlass. I was trying a new pipe (and a very good one, too), so I didn't give him much notice for a while.

"You did this job up shrewd, Kent," said I, by and by; "how did you steer in?"—for it did not often happen that the Madonna got fairly out of port with a boy unbeknown in her hold.

"Watch was drunk; I crawled down ahind the whiskey. It was hot, you bet, and dark. I lay and thought how hungry I was," says he.

"Friends at home?" says I.

Upon that he gives me a nod, very short, and gets up and walks off whistling.

The first Sunday out, that chap didn't know any more what to do with himself than a lobster just put on to boil. Sunday's cleaning day at sea, you know. The lads washed up, and sat round, little knots of them, mending their trousers. Bob got out his cards. Me and a few mates took it comfortable under the to'gallant fo'castle (I being on watch below), reeling off the stiffest yarns we had in tow. Kent looked on at euchre awhile, then listened to us awhile, then walked about oneasy.

By and by says Bob, "Look over there,—spry!" and there was Kent, sitting curled away in a heap under the stern of the long-boat. He had a book. Bob crawls behind and snatches it up, unbeknown, out of his hands; then he falls to laughing as if he would strangle, and gives the book a toss to me. It was a bit of Testament, black and old. There was writing on the yellow leaf, this way:—

"Kentucky Hodge.
"from his Affecshunate mother who prays, For you evry day, Amen."

The boy turned fust red, then white, and straightened up quite sudden, but he never said a word, only sat down again and let us laugh it out. I've lost my reckoning if he ever heard the last of it. He told me one day how he came by the name, but I forget exactly. Something about an old fellow—uncle. I believe—as died in Kentucky, and the name was moniment-like, you see. He used to seem cut up a bit about it at first, for the lads took to it famously; but he got used to it in a week or two, and, seeing as they meant him no unkindness, took it quite cheery.

One other thing I noticed was that he never had the book about after that. He fell into our ways next Sunday more easy.

They don't take the Bible just the way you would, Tom,—as a general thing, sailors don't; though I will say that I never saw the man at sea who didn't give it the credit of being an uncommon good yarn.

But I tell you, Tom Brown, I felt sorry for that boy. It's punishment bad enough for a little scamp like him leaving the honest shore, and folks to home that were a bit tender of him maybe, to rough it on a trader, learning how to slush down a back-stay, or tie reef-points with frozen fingers in a snow-squall.

But that's not the worst of it, by no means. If ever there was a cold-blooded, cruel man, with a wicked eye and a fist like a mallet, it was Job Whitmarsh, taken at his best. And I believe, of all the trips I've taken, him being mate of the Madonna, Kentucky found him at his worst. Bradley—that's the second mate—was none too gentle in his ways, you may be sure; but he never held a candle to Mr. Whitmarsh. He took a spite to the boy from the first, and he kept it on a steady strain to the last, right along, just about so.

I've seen him beat that boy till the blood ran down in little pools on deck; then send him up, all wet and red, to clear the to'sail hal-liards; and when, what with the pain and faintness, he dizzied a little, and clung to the rat-lines, half blind, he would have him down and flog him till the cap'n interfered,—which would happen occasionally on a fair day when he had taken just enough to be good-natured. He used to rack his brains for the words he slung at the boy working quiet enough beside him. It was odd, now, the talk he would get off. Bob Smart couldn't any more come up to it than I could: we used to try sometimes, but we had to give in always. If curses had been a marketable article, Whitmarsh would have taken out his patent and made his fortune by inventing of them, new and ingenious. Then he used to kick the lad down the fo'-castle ladder; he used to work him, sick or well, as he wouldn't have worked a dray-horse; he used to chase him all about deck at the rope's end; he used to mast-head him for hours on the stretch; he used to starve him out in the hold. It didn't come in my line to be over-tender, but I turned sick at heart, Tom, more times than one, looking on helpless, and me a great stout fellow.

I remember now—don't know as I've thought of it for twenty years—a thing McCallum said one night; McCallum was Scotch,—an old fellow with grey hair; told the best yarns on the fo'castle always.

"Mark my words, shipmates," says he, "when Job Whitmarsh's time comes to go as straight to hell as Judas, that boy will bring his summons. Dead or alive, that boy will bring his summons."

One day I recollect especial that the lad was sick with fever on him, and took to his hammock. Whitmarsh drove him on deck, and ordered him aloft. I was standing near by, trimming the spanker. Kentucky staggered for'ard a little and sat down. There was a rope's-end there, knotted three times. The mate struck him.

"I'm very weak, sir," says he.

He struck him again. He struck him twice more. The boy fell over a little, and lay where he fell.

I don't know what ailed me, but all of a sudden I seemed to be lying off Long Wharf, with the clouds the colour of silver, and the air the colour of gold, and Molly in a white apron with her shining needles, and the baby a-play in his red stockings about the deck.

"Think if it was him!" says she, or she seems to say,—"think if it was *him*!"

And the next I knew I'd let slip my tongue in a jiffy, and given it to the mate that furious and onrespectful as I'll wager Whitmarsh never got before. And the next I knew after that they had the irons on me.

"Sorry about that, eh?" said he, the day before they took 'em off.

"*No*, sir," says I. And I never was. Kentucky never forgot that. I had helped him occasional in the beginning,—learned him how to veer and haul a brace, let go or belay a sheet,—but let him alone generally speaking, and went about my own business. That week in irons I really believe the lad never forgot.

One time—it was on a Saturday night, and the mate had been oncommon furious that week—Kentucky turned on him, very pale and slow (I was up in the mizzen-top, and heard him quite distinct).

"Mr. Whitmarsh," says he,—"Mr. Whitmarsh,"—he draws his breath in,—"Mr. Whitmarsh,"—three times,—"you've got the power and you know it, and so do the gentlemen who put you here; and I'm only a stow-away boy, and things are all in a tangle, but *you'll be sorry yet for every time you've laid your hands on me!*"

He hadn't a pleasant look about the eyes either, when he said it.

Fact was, that first month on the Madonna had done the lad no good. He had a surly, sullen way with him, some'at like what I've seen about a chained dog. At the first, his talk had been clean as my baby's, and he would blush like any girl at Bob Smart's stories; but he got used to Bob, and pretty good, in time, at small swearing.

I don't think I should have noticed it so much if it had not been for seeming to see Molly, and the sun, and the knitting-needles, and the child upon the deck, and hearing of it over, "Think if it was *him!*" Sometimes on a Sunday night I used to think it was a pity. Not that I was any better than the rest, except so far as the married men are always steadier. Go through any crew the sea over, and it is the lads who have homes of their own and little children in 'em as keep the straightest.

Sometimes too, I used to take a fancy that I could have listened to a word from a parson, or a good brisk psalm-tune, and taken it in very good part. A year is a long pull for twenty-five men to be becalmed with each other and the devil. I don't set up to be pious myself, but I'm not a fool, and I know that if we'd had so much as one officer aboard who feared God and kept his commandments, we should have been the better men for it. It's very much with religion as it is with cayenne pepper,—if it's there, you know it.

If you had your ships on the sea by the dozen, you'd bethink you of that. Bless you, Tom! if you were in Rome you'd do as the Romans do. You'd have your ledgers, and your children, and your churches and Sunday schools, and freed slaves, and 'lections, and what not, and never stop to think whether the lads that sailed your ships across the world had souls, or not—and be a good sort of man too. That's the way of the world. Take it easy, Tom,—take it easy.

Well, things went along just about so with us till we neared the Cape. It's not a pretty place, the Cape, on a winter's voyage. I can't say as I ever was what you may call scar't after the first time rounding it, but it's not a pretty place.

I don't seem to remember much about Kent along there till there come a Friday at the first of December. It was a still day, with a little haze, like white sand sifted across a sunbeam on a kitchen table. The lad was quiet-like all day, chasing me about with his eyes.

"Sick?" says I.

"No," says he.

"Whitmarsh drunk?" says I.

"No," says he.

A little after dark I was lying on a coil of ropes, napping it. The boys were having the Bay of Biscay quite lively, and I waked up on the jump in the choruses. Kent came up while they were telling

> "How she lay
> On that day
> In the *Bay* of BISCAY O!"

He was not singing. He sat down beside me, and first I thought I wouldn't trouble myself about him, and then I thought I would.

So I opens one eye at him encouraging. He crawls up a little closer to me. It was rather dark where we sat, with a great greenish shadow dropping from the mainsail. The wind was up a little, and the light at helm looked flickery and red.

"Jake," says he all at once, "where's your mother?"

"In—heaven!" says I, all taken aback; and if ever I came nigh what you might call a little disrespect to your mother it was on that occasion, from being taken so aback.

"Oh!" said he. "Got any women-folks to home that miss you?" asks he, by and by.

Said I, "Shouldn't wonder."

After that he sits still a little with his elbows on his knees; then he speers at me sidewise awhile; then said he, "I s'pose I've got a mother to home. I ran away from her."

This, mind you, is the first time he had ever spoke about his folks since he came aboard.

"She was asleep down in the south chamber," says he. "I got out the window. There was one white shirt she'd made for meetin' and such. I've never worn it out here. I hadn't the heart. It has a collar and some cuffs, you know. She had a headache making of it. She's been follering me round all day, a sewing on that shirt. When I come in she would look up bright-like and smiling. Father's dead. There ain't anybody but me. All day long she's been follering of me round."

So then he gets up, and joins the lads, and tries to sing a little; but he comes back very still and sits down. We could see the flickery light upon the boys' faces, and on the rigging, and on the cap'n, who was damning the bo'sen a little aft.

"Jake," says he, quite low, "look here. I've been thinking. Do you reckon there's a chap here—just one, perhaps—who's said his prayers since he came aboard?"

"*No!*"said I, quite short: for I'd have bet my head on it.

I can remember, as if it was this morning, just how the question sounded, and the answer. I can't seem to put it into words how it came all over me. The wind was turning brisk, and we'd just eased her with a few reefs; Bob Smart, out furling the flying jib, got soaked; me and the boy sitting silent, were spattered. I remember watching the curve of the great swells, mahogany colour, with the tip of white, and thinking how like it was to a big creature hissing and foaming at the mouth, and thinking all at once something about Him holding of the sea in a balance, and not a word bespoke to beg his favour respectful since we weighed our anchor, and the cap'n yonder calling on Him just that minute to send the Madonna to the bottom, if the bo'sen hadn't disobeyed his orders about the squaring of the after-yards.

"'From his Affecshunate mother who prays, For you evry day. Amen,'" whispers Kentucky, presently, very soft. "The book's tore up. Mr. Whitmarsh wadded his old gun with it. But I remember."

Then said he: "It's 'most bedtime to home. She's setting in a little rocking-chair,—a green one. There's a fire, and the dog. She sets all by herself."

Then he begins again: "She has to bring in her own wood now. There's a grey ribbon on her cap. When she goes to meetin' she wears a grey bunnet. She's drawed the curtains and the door is locked. But she thinks I'll be coming home sorry some day,—I'm sure she thinks I'll be coming home sorry."

Just then there comes the order: "Port watch ahoy! Tumble up there lively!" so I turns out, and the lad turns in, and the night settles down a little black, and my hands and head are full. Next day it blows a clean, all but a bank of grey, very thin and still,—about the size of that cloud you see through the side window, Tom,—which lay just abeam of us.

The sea, I thought, looked like a great purple pin-cushion, with a mast or two stuck in on the horizon for the pins. "Jake's poetry," the boys said that was.

By noon that little grey bank had grown up thick, like a wall. By sundown the cap'n let his liquor alone, and kept the deck. By night we were in chop-seas, with a very ugly wind.

"Steer small, there!" cries Whitmarsh, growing hot about the face,—for we made a terribly crooked wake, with a broad sheer, and the old hull strained heavily,—"steer small there, I tell you! Mind your eye now, McCallum, with your foresail! Furl the royals! Send down the royals! Cheerily, men! Where's that lubber Kent? Up with you, lively now!"

Kentucky sprang for'ard at the order, then stopped short. Anybody as knows a royal from an anchor wouldn't have blamed the lad. I'll take oath to't it's no play for an old tar, stout and full in size, sending down the royals in a gale like that; let alone a boy of fifteen year on his first voyage.

But the mate takes to swearing (it would have turned a parson faint to hear him), and Kent shoots away up,—the great mast swinging like a pendulum to and fro, and the reef-points snapping, and the blocks creaking, and the sails flapping to that extent as you wouldn't consider possible unless you'd been before the mast yourself. It reminded me of evil birds I've read of, that stun a man with their wings; strike *you* to the bottom, Tom, before you could say Jack Robinson.

Kent stuck bravely as far as the cross trees. There he slipped and struggled and clung in the dark and noise awhile, then comes sliding down the back-stay.

"I'm not afraid, sir," says he; "but I cannot do it."

For answer Whitmarsh takes to the rope's-end. So Kentucky is up again, and slips and struggles and clings again, and then lays down again.

At this the men begin to grumble a little, low.

"Will you kill the lad?" said I. I get a blow for my pains, that sends me off my feet none too easy; and when I rub the stars out of my eyes the boy is up again, and the mate behind him with the rope. Whitmarsh stopped when he'd gone far enough. The lad climbed on. Once he looked back. He never opened his lips; he just looked back. If I've seen him once since, in my thinking, I've seen him twenty times,—up in the shadow of the great grey wings, a looking back.

After that there was only a cry, and a splash, and the Madonna racing along with the gale twelve knots. If it had been the whole crew overboard, she could never have stopped for them that night.

"Well," said the cap'n, "you've done it now."

Whitmarsh turns his back.

By and by, when the wind fell, and the hurry was over, and I had the time to think a steady thought, being in the morning watch, I seemed to see the old lady in the grey bunnet setting by the fire. And the dog. And the green rocking-chair. And the front door, with the boy walking in on a sunny afternoon to take her by surprise.

Then I remember leaning over to look down, and wondering if the lad were thinking of it too, and what had happened to him now, these two hours back, and just about where he was, and how he liked his new quarters, and many other strange and curious things.

And while I sat there thinking, the Sunday-morning stars cut through the clouds, and the solemn Sunday-morning light began to break upon the sea.

We had a quiet run of it, after that, into port, where we lay about a couple of months or so, trading off for a fair stock of palm-oil, ivory, and hides. The days were hot and purple and still. We hadn't what you might call a blow, if I recollect accurate, till we rounded the Cape again, heading for home.

We were rounding that Cape again, heading for home, when that happened which you may believe me or not, as you take the notion. Tom; though why a man who can swallow Daniel and the lion's den, or take down t'other chap who lived three days comfortable into the inside of a whale, should make faces at what I've got to tell I can't see.

It was just about the spot that we lost the boy that we fell upon the worst gale of the trip. It struck us quite sudden. Whitmarsh was a little high. He wasn't apt to be drunk in a gale, if it gave him warning sufficient.

Well, you see, there must be somebody to furl the main-royal again, and he pitched onto McCallum. McCallum hadn't his beat for fighting out the royal in a blow.

So he piled away lively, up to the to'-sail yard. There, all of a sudden, he stopped. Next we knew he was down like heat-lightning.

His face had gone very white.

"What's to pay with *you?*" roared Whitmarsh.

Said McCallum, "*There's somebody up there, sir.*"

Screamed Whitmarsh, "You're gone an idiot!"

Said McCallum, very quiet and distinct: "There's somebody up there, sir. I saw him quite plain. He saw me. I called up. He called down; says he, '*Don't you come up!*' and hang me if I'll stir a step for you or any other man tonight!"

I never saw the face of any man alive go the turn that mate's face went. If he wouldn't have relished knocking the Scotchman dead before his eyes, I've lost my guess. Can't say what he would have done to the old fellow, if there'd been any time to lose.

He'd the sense left to see there wasn't overmuch, so he orders out Bob Smart direct.

Bob goes up steady, with a quid in his cheek and a cool *eye*. Half-way amid to'-sail and to'-gallant he stops, and down he comes, spinning.

"Be drowned if there ain't!" said he. "He's sitting square upon the yard. I never see the boy Kentucky, if he isn't sitting on that yard. '*Don't you come up!*' he cries out,—'*don't you come up!*'"

"Bob's drunk, and McCallum's a fool!" said Jim Welch, standing by. So Welch volunteers up, and takes Jaloffe with him. They were a couple of the coolest hands aboard,—Welch and Jaloffe. So up they goes, and down they comes like the rest, by the back-stays, by the run.

"He beckoned of me back!" says Welch. "He hollered not to come up! not to come up!"

After that there wasn't a man of us would stir aloft, not for love nor money.

Well, Whitmarsh he stamped, and he swore, and he knocked us about furious; but we sat and looked at one another's eyes, and never stirred. Something cold, like a frost-bite, seemed to crawl along from man to man, looking into one another's eyes.

"I'll shame ye all, then, for a set of cowardly lubbers!" cries the mate; and what with the anger and the drink he was as good as his word, and up the ratlines in a twinkle.

In a flash we were after him,—he was our officer, you see, and we felt ashamed,—me at the head, and the lads following after.

I got to the futtock shrouds, and there I stopped, for I saw him myself,—a palish boy, with a jerk of thin hair on his forehead; I'd have known him anywhere in this world or t'other. I saw him just as distinct as I see you, Tom Brown, sitting on that yard quite steady with the royal flapping like to flap him off.

I reckon I've had as much experience fore and aft, in the course of fifteen years aboard, as any man that ever tied a reef-point in a nor'easter; but I never saw a sight like that, not before nor since.

I won't say that I didn't wish myself well on deck; but I will say that I stuck to the shrouds, and looked on steady.

Whitmarsh, swearing that that royal should be furled, went on and went up.

It was after that I heard the voice. It came straight from the figure of the boy upon the upper yard.

But this time it says, "*Come up! Come up!*" And then, a little louder, "*Come up! Come up! Come up!*" So he goes up, and next I knew there was a cry,—and next a splash,—and then I saw the royal flapping from the empty yard, and the mate was gone, and the boy.

Job Whitmarsh was never seen again, alow or aloft, that night or ever after.

I was telling the tale to our parson this summer,—he's a fair-minded chap, the parson, in spite of a little natural leaning to strawberries, which I always take in very good part,—and he turned it about in his mind some time.

"If it was the boy," says he,—"and I can't say as I see any reason especial why it shouldn't have been,—I've been wondering what his spiritooal condition was. A soul in hell,"—the parson believes in hell, I take it, because he can't help himself; but he has that solemn, tender way of preaching it as makes you feel he wouldn't have so much as a chicken get there if he could help it,—"a lost soul," says the parson (I don't know as I get the words exact),—"a soul that has gone and been and got there of its own free will and choosing would be as like as not to haul another soul alongside if he could. Then again, if the mate's time had come, you see, and his chances were over, why, that's the will of the Lord, and it's hell for him whichever side of death he is, and nobody's fault but his; and the boy might be in the good place, and do the errand all the same. That's just about it, Brown," says he. "A man goes his own gait, and, if he won't go to heaven, he *won't*, and the good God himself can't help it. He throws the shining gates all open wide, and he never shut them on any poor fellow as would have entered in, and he never, never will."

Which I thought was sensible of the parson, and very prettily put.

There's Molly frying flapjacks now, and flapjacks won't wait for no man, you know, no more than time and tide, else I should have talked till midnight, very like, to tell the time we made on that trip home, and how green the harbour looked a sailing up, and of Molly and the baby coming down to meet me in a little boat that danced about (for we cast a little down the channel), and how she climbed up a laughing and a crying all to once, about my neck, and how the boy had grown, and how when he ran about the deck (the little shaver had his first pair of boots on that very afternoon) I bethought me of the other time, and of Molly's words, and of the lad we'd left behind us in the purple days.

Just as we were hauling up, I says to my wife: "Who's that old lady setting there upon the lumber, with a grey bunnet, and a grey ribbon on her cap?"

For there was an old lady there, and I saw the sun all about her, and all on the blazing yellow boards, and I grew a little dazed and dazzled.

"I don't know," said Molly, catching onto me a little close. "She comes there every day. They say she sits and watches for her lad as ran away."

So then I seemed to know, as well as ever I knew afterwards, who it was. And I thought of the dog. And the green rocking-chair. And the book that Whitmarsh wadded his old gun with. And the front door, with the boy a walking in.

So we three went up the wharf,—Molly and the baby and me,—and sat down beside her on the yellow boards. I can't remember rightly what I said, but I remember her sitting silent in the sunshine till I had told her all there was to tell.

"*Don't* cry!" says Molly, when I get through,—which it was the more surprising of Molly, considering as she was doing the crying all to herself. The old lady never cried, you see. She sat with her eyes wide open under her grey bunnet, and her lips a moving. After a while I made it out what it was she said: "The only son—of his mother—and she—"

By and by she gets up, and goes her ways, and Molly and I walk home together, with our little boy between us.

A man and his wife and children were once upon a time sitting at their noon-tide meal with a good friend, whom they had invited to share it with them. And while they were so seated, the clock struck twelve, and the stranger saw the door open, and a very little child, dressed all in white, came; it neither looked about nor spake a word; but went right through the chamber. Soon afterwards it came back, as silently as before, and went out of the door again. And it came again in like manner on the second and third days; until at length the stranger asked the good man of the house to whom the beautiful child belonged, who came every day at noon into the chamber? "I have never seen it," said he, "nor do I know to whom it can belong."

On the following day the stranger pointed it out to the father when it came in, but he saw it not, neither did his wife or children see it. Then the stranger arose, went to the door through which it had passed, opened it a little way, and peeped in. Then saw he the child sitting on the ground, groping and raking very busily in the crevices of the floor; as soon, however, as it perceived the stranger it vanished. Then he related what he had seen, and described the child so minutely, that the mother knew it at once, and said, "Alas! that is my own dear child, that died four weeks since." Then he broke up the flooring, and there found two pennies, which the child had once received from the mother, to give to a poor beggar, but it had thought that it could buy sweetmeat with the two pennies, so had kept them and hidden them in the crevices of the floor; and therefore it had found no rest in the grave, but had come every day at noon to search after the pennies. Thereupon the parents gave the money to a poor man, and after that the child was never more seen.

Grimm, "The Stolen Pennies" (1812)[10]

WALNUT-TREE HOUSE: A GHOST STORY

Charlotte Riddell

Charlotte Riddell (1832–1906) was born in County Antrim, Ireland, and moved to London in 1855 to begin her career; publishing predominantly under her married title, Mrs. J. H. Riddell, as well as a few other pseudonyms. Riddell was a prolific writer—publishing over forty novels and a range of short stories, essays, and travel articles and is particularly well known now for her supernatural and sensational works, as well as a theme of commerce and urban life—and became co-proprietor and editor of St. James's Magazine *from 1861. Two of her classic novels can be found in the Tales of the Weird title* Haunted Houses, *edited by Andrew Smith..*

The version of "Walnut-Tree House" printed here is the original version from an 1878 edition of the Illustrated London News; *this is a much shorter version than is usually anthologised, as Riddell expanded the story for her 1882 collection* Weird Stories. *The essence of the story is all there, however; the ability of a lonely bachelor to be a selfless and caring man, not swayed by greed, is tested out through the temporary guardianship and assistance given to the silent and pitiful ghost of a boy who searches his house for a missing will and a missing sister. Despite the boy's apparent benevolence, however, the horror mainly lies (as it does in many such stories) in the cruelty done to him in life. And yet, the boy's very presence has already sent one man "mad", and Edgar is threatened by the same fate if he cannot appease this spirit.*

THE NEW OWNER

any years ago there stood at the corner of a street leading out of Upper Kennington-lane a great red brick mansion, which one very wet evening, in an autumn the leaves of which have been long dead and gone, looked more than ordinarily desolate and deserted.

There was not a sign of life about it. For seven years no one had been found to live in it; for seven years it had remained empty, while its owner wore out existence in fits of moody dejection or of wild frenzy in the mad-house close at hand; and now that owner was dead and buried and forgotten, and the new owner was returning to take possession. This new owner had written to his lawyers, or rather he had written to the lawyers of his late relative, begging them to request the person in charge of the house to have rooms prepared for his arrival; and, when the train drew into the station, he was met by one of Messrs. Timpson and Co.'s clerks, who, picking out Mr. Stainton, delivered to that gentleman a letter from the firm, and said he would wait to hear if there were any message in reply.

Mr. Stainton read the letter—looked at the blank fly-leaf—and then, turning back to the first words, read what his solicitors had to say all through once again.

"Humph," said the new owner, after he had finished. "I'll go and take a look at the place, anyhow. Is it far from here, do you know?" he asked, turning to the young man from Timpson's.

"No, Sir; not very far."

"Can you spare time to go over there with me?" inquired Mr. Stainton.

The young man believed that he could, adding, "If you want to go into the house we had better call for the key. It is at an estate agent's in the Westminster Bridge-road."

"I cannot say I have any great passion for hotels," remarked the new owner, as he took his seat in the cab.

"Indeed, Sir."

"No; either they don't suit me, or I don't suit them. I have led a wild sort of life; not much civilisation in the bush, or at the gold-fields, I can tell you. Then, I have not been well, and I can't stand noise and the trampling of feet. I had enough of that on board ship; and I used to lie awake at nights and think how pleasant it would be to have a big house all to myself, to do as I liked in."

"Yes, Sir," agreed the clerk.

"You see, I have been accustomed to roughing it, and I can get along very well for a night without servants."

"No doubt, Sir."

"I suppose the house is in substantial repair—roof tight, and all that sort of thing?"

"I can't say, I am sure, Sir."

"Well, if there is a dry corner where I can spread a rug, I shall sleep there tonight."

The clerk coughed. He looked out of the window, and then he looked at Messrs. Timpson's client.

"I do not think"—he began apologetically, and then stopped.

"You don't think what?" asked the other.

"You'll excuse me, Sir, but I don't think—I really do not think, if I were you, I'd stay in that house tonight."

"Why not?"

"Well, it has not been slept in for nearly seven years, and it must be blue mouldy with damp; and if you have been ill, that is all the more reason you should not run such a risk. And, besides"—

"Besides"—suggested Mr. Stainton; "Out with it! No doubt, that 'besides' holds the marrow of the argument."

"The house has stood empty for years, Sir, because—there is no use in making any secret of it—the place has a bad name."

"What sort of a bad name—unhealthy?"

"Oh, no!"

"Haunted?"

The clerk inclined his head. "You have hit it, Sir," he said.

"And that is the reason no one has lived there?"

"We have been quite unable to let the house on that account."

"The sooner it gets unhaunted, then, the better," retorted Mr. Stainton. "I shall certainly stop there tonight. You are not disposed to stay and keep me company, I suppose?"

With a little gesture of dismay the clerk drew back. Certainly, this was one of the most unconventional of clients. The young man from Timpson's did not at all know what to make of him.

"A rough sort of fellow," he said afterwards, when describing the new owner; "boorish; never mixed with good society, that sort of thing."

He did not in the least understand this rich man, who treated him as an equal, who objected to hotels, who did not mind taking up his abode in a house where not even a drunken charwoman could be induced to stop, and who calmly asked a stranger on whom he had never set eyes before—a clerk in the respectable office of Timpson and Co., a young fellow anxious to rise in the world, careful as to his associates, particular about the whiteness of his shirts and the set of his collar and the cut of his coats—to "rough" things with him in that dreadful old dungeon, where perhaps he might even be expected to light a fire.

Still, he did not wish to offend the new owner. Messrs. Timpson anticipated he would be a profitable client; and to that impartial firm the money of a boor would, he knew, seem as good as the money of a Count.

"I am very sorry," he stammered; "should only have felt too much honoured; but the fact is—previous engagement."—

Mr. Stainton laughed.

"I understand," he said. "Adventures are quite as much out of your line as ghosts. And now tell me about this apparition. Does the 'old man' walk?"

"Not that I ever heard of," answered the other.

"Is it, then, the miserable beggar who tried to do for himself?"

"It is not the late Mr. Stainton, I believe," said the young man, in a tone which mildly suggested that reference to a client of Timpson's as a "miserable beggar" might be considered bad taste.

"Then who on earth is it?" persisted Mr. Stainton.

"If you must know, Sir, it is a child—a child who has driven every tenant in succession out of the house."

The new owner burst into a hearty laugh—a laugh which gave serious offence to Timpson's clerk.

"That is too good a joke," said Mr. Stainton. "I do not know when I heard anything so delicious."

"It is a fact, whether it be delicious or not," retorted the young man, driven out of all his former propriety of voice and demeanour by the contemptuous ridicule this "digger" thought fit to cast on his story; "and I, for one, would not, after all I have heard about your house, pass a night in it—no, not if anybody offered me fifty pounds down."

"Make your mind easy, my friend," said the new owner, quietly. "I am not going to bid for your company. The child and I can manage, I'll be bound, to get on very comfortably by ourselves."

II

THE CHILD

It was later on in the same evening; Mr. Stainton had an hour previously taken possession of Walnut-Tree House, bidden Timpson's clerk good-evening, and, having ordered in wood and coals from the nearest greengrocer, he now stood by the front gate waiting the coming of the goods purchased.

As he waited, he looked up at the house, which in the uncertain light of the street lamps appeared gloomier and darker than had been the case even in the gathering twilight.

"It has an 'uncanny' look, certainly," he considered; "but once I can get a good fire up I shall be all right. Now, I wonder when those coals are coming!"

As he turned once again towards the road, he beheld on its way the sack of fuel with which the nearest greengrocer said he thought he could—indeed, said he would—"oblige" him. A ton—half a ton—quarter of a ton, the greengrocer affirmed would be impossible until the next day; but a sack—yes—he would promise that. Bill should bring it round; and Bill was told to put his burden on the truck, and twelve bundles of wood, "and we'll make up the rest tomorrow," added Bill's master, with the air of one who has conferred a favour.

In the distance Mr. Stainton described a very grimy Bill, and a very small boy, coming along with the truck leisurely, as though the load had been Herculean.

Through the rain he watched the pair advancing, and greeted Bill with a glad voice of welcome.

"So you've come at last; that's right. Better late than never. Bring them this way, I'll have this small lot shot in the kitchen for the night."

"Begging your pardon, Sir," answered Bill, "I don't think you will—that is to say, not by me. As I told our governor, I'll take 'em to the house as you've sold 'em to the house, but I won't set a foot inside it."

"Do you mean to say you are going to leave them out on the pavement," asked Mr. Stainton.

"Well, Sir, I don't mind taking them to the front door if it'll be a convenience."

"That will do. You are a brave lot of people in these parts I must say."

"As for that," retorted Bill, with sack on back and head bent forward, "I dare say we're as brave about here as where you come from."

"It is not impossible," retorted Mr. Stainton; "there are plenty of cowards over there too."

After he had shot his coals on the margin of the steps, Bill retreated from the door, which stood partly open, and when the boy who brought up the wood was again out with the truck, said, putting his knuckles to his eyebrows—

"Beg pardon, Sir, but I suppose you wouldn't give me a drop of beer. Very wet night, Sir."

"No, I would not," answered Mr. Stainton, very decidedly. "I shall have to shovel these coals into the house myself; and as for the night, it is as wet for me as it is for you."

Nevertheless, as Bill shuffled along the short drive—shuffling wearily—like a man who, having nearly finished one day's hard work, was looking forward to beginning another hard day in the morning, the new owner relented.

"Here," he said, picking out a sixpence to give him, "it isn't your fault, I suppose, that you believe in old women's tales."

"Thank you kindly, Sir," Bill answered; "I am sure I am extremely obliged; but if I was in your shoes I wouldn't stop in that house—you'll excuse me, Sir, meaning no offence—but I wouldn't; indeed I wouldn't."

"It seems to have got a good name, at any rate," thought Mr. Stainton, while retracing his steps to the banned tenement. "Let us see what effect a fire will have in routing the shadows."

He entered the house, and, striking a match, lighted some candles he had brought in with him from a neighbouring oil-shop.

After an inspection of the ground-floor rooms he decided to take up his quarters for the night in one which had evidently served as a library.

In the centre of the apartment there was the table covered with leather. Around the walls were bookcases. In one corner stood a bureau, where the man who for so many years had been dead even while living kept his letters and papers.

He ate his frugal supper, and then, pushing aside the table on which the remains of his repast were spread, began walking slowly up and down the room, thinking over the past and forming plans for the future. Buried in reflection, the fire began to die down without his noticing the fact; but a feeling of chilliness at length causing him instinctively to look towards the hearth, he threw wood into the grate, and, while the flames went blazing up the wide chimney, piled on coals as though he desired to set the house alight.

While he was so engaged there came a knock at the door of the room—a feeble, hesitating knock, which was repeated more than once before it attracted Mr. Stainton's attention.

When it did, being still busy with the fire, and forgetting he was alone in the house, he called out, "Come in."

Along the panels there stole a rustling sort of touch, as if someone were feeling uncertainly for the handle—a curious noise, as of a weak hand fumbling about the door in the dark; then, in similar manner, the person seeking admittance tried to turn the lock.

"Come in, can't you?" repeated Mr. Stainton; but even as he spoke he remembered he was, or ought to be, the sole occupant of the mansion. He was not alarmed, he was too much accustomed to solitude and danger for that; but he rose from his stooping position and instinctively seized his revolver, which he had chanced, while unpacking some of his effects, to place on the top of the bureau.

"Come in, whoever you are," he cried; but seeing the door still remained closed, though the intruder was evidently making futile efforts to open it, he strode half way across the room, and then stopped amazed.

For suddenly the door opened, and there entered shyly and timidly a little child—a child with the saddest face mortal ever beheld; a child with wistful eyes and long, ill-kept hair; a child poorly dressed, wasted and worn, and with the mournfullest expression on its countenance that face of child ever wore.

"What a hungry-looking little beggar," thought Mr. Stainton. "Well, young one, and what do you want here?" he added aloud.

The boy never answered, never took the slightest notice of his questioner, but simply walked slowly round the room, peering into all the corners, as if looking for something. Searching the embrasures of the windows, examining the recesses beside the fire-place, pausing on the hearth to glance under the library table, and finally, when the doorway was reached once more, turning round to survey the contents of the apartment with an eager and yet hopeless scrutiny.

"What *is* it you want, my boy?" asked Mr. Stainton, glancing as he spoke at the child's poor thin legs, and short, shabby frock, and shoes wellnigh worn out, and arms bare and lean and unbeautiful. "Is it anything I can get for you?"

Not a word—not a whisper: only for reply a glance of the wistful brown eyes.

"Where do you come from, and whom do you belong to?" persisted Mr. Stainton.

The child turned slowly away.

"Come, you shall not get off so easily as you seem to imagine," persisted the new owner, advancing towards his visitor. "You have no business to be here at all; and before you go you must tell me how you chance to be in this house, and what you expected to find in this room."

He was close to the doorway by this time, and the child stood on the threshold, with its back towards him. Mr. Stainton could see every detail of the boy's attire—his little plaid frock, the hooks which fastened it; the pinafore, soiled and crumpled, tied behind with strings broken and knotted; in one place the skirt had given from the bodice, and a piece of thin poor flannel showed that the child's under habiliments matched in shabbiness his exterior garments.

"Poor little chap," thought Mr. Stainton. "I wonder if he would like something to eat. Are you hungry, my lad?"

The child turned and looked at him earnestly, but answered never a word.

"I wonder if he is dumb," marvelled Mr. Stainton; and, seeing he was moving away, put out a hand to detain him. But the child eluded his touch, and flitted into the hall and up the wide staircase with swift noiseless feet.

Only waiting to snatch a candle from one of the sconces, Mr. Stainton pursued as fast as he could follow. Up the easy steps he ran at the top of his speed; but, fast as he went, the child went faster. Higher and higher he beheld the tiny creature mounting, then, still keeping the same distance between them, it turned when it reached the top storey and trotted along a narrow corridor with rooms opening off to right and left. At the extreme end of this passage a door stood ajar. Through this the child passed, Mr. Stainton still following.

"I have run you to earth at last," he said, entering and closing the door. "Why, where has the boy gone?" he added, holding the candle above his head and gazing round the dingy garret in which he found himself.

The room was quite empty. He examined it closely, but could find no possible outlet save the door, and a skylight which had evidently not been opened for years. There was no furniture in the apartment, except a truckle bedstead, a rush-bottomed chair, and a rickety washstand. No wardrobe, or box, or press, where even a kitten might have lain concealed.

"It is very strange," muttered Mr. Stainton, as he turned away baffled. "Very strange!" he repeated, while he walked along the corridor. "I don't understand it at all," he decided, proceeding slowly down the topmost flight of stairs; but there all at once he stopped.

"IT IS THE CHILD!" he exclaimed aloud, and the sound of his own voice woke strange echoes through the silence of that desolate house. "IT IS THE CHILD!" and he descended the principal staircase very slowly, with bowed head, and his grave, worn face graver and more thoughtful than ever.

III

SEARCHING FOR INFORMATION

It was enough to make any man look grave; and as time went on the new owner of Walnut-Tree House found himself pondering continually as to what the mystery could be which attached to the child he had found in possession of his property, and who had already driven tenant after tenant out of the premises. Inclined at first to regard the clerk's story as a joke, and his own experience on the night of his arrival a delusion, it was impossible for him to continue incredulous when he found, even in broad daylight, that terrible child stealing down the staircase and entering the rooms, looking, looking—for something it never found.

At bed and at board he had company, or the expectation of it. No apartment in the building was secure from intrusion. It did not matter where he lay, it did not matter where he ate; between sleeping and waking, between breakfast and dinner, whenever the notion seized it, the child came gliding in, looking, looking, looking, and never finding; not lingering longer than was necessary to be certain the object of its search was absent, but wandering hither and thither, from garret to kitchen, from parlour to bed-chamber, in that quest which still seemed fresh as when first begun.

Mr. Stainton went to his solicitors as the most likely persons from whom to obtain information on the subject, and plunged at once into the matter.

"Who is the child supposed to be, Mr. Timpson?" he asked, making no secret that he had seen it.

"Well, that is really very difficult to say," answered Mr. Timpson.

"There *was* a child once, I suppose?—a real child—flesh and blood?"

Mr. Timpson took off his spectacles and wiped them.

"There were two; yes, certainly, in the time of Mr. Felix Stainton—a boy and a girl."

"In that house?"

"In that house. They survived him."

"And what became of them?"

"The girl was adopted by a relation of her father's, and the—boy—died."

"Oh! the boy died, did he? Do you happen to know what he died of?"

"No; I really do not. There was nothing wrong about the affair, however, if that is what you are thinking of. There never was a hint of that sort."

Mr. Stainton sat silent for a minute; then he said,

"Mr. Timpson, I cannot shake off the idea that somehow there has been foul play with regard to those children. Who were they?"

"Felix Stainton's grandchildren. His daughter made a low marriage, and he cast her adrift. After her death the two children were received at Walnut-Tree House on sufferance—fed and clothed, I believe, that was all; and when the old man died the heir-at-law permitted them to remain."

"Alfred Stainton?"

"Yes; the unhappy man who became insane. His uncle died intestate, and he consequently succeeded to everything but the personalty, which was very small, and of which these children had a share."

"There never was any suspicion, you say, of foul play on the part of the late owner?"

"Dear, dear! no; quite the contrary."

"Then you cannot throw the least light on the mystery?"

"Not the least; I wish I could."

For all that, Mr. Stainton carried away an impression Mr. Timpson knew more of the matter than he cared to tell.

"There is a mystery behind it all," he considered. "I must learn more about these children. Perhaps some of the local tradespeople may recollect them."

But the local tradespeople for the most part were new comers—or else had not supplied "the house."

"There is only one person I can think of, Sir," said one "family" butcher, "likely to be able to give you any information about the matter."

"And that is"—

"Mr. Hennings, at the Pedlar's Arms. He had some acquaintance with the old lady as was housekeeper both to Mr. Felix Stainton and the gentleman that went out of his mind." Following which advice, the new owner repaired to the Pedlar's Arms.

"Do I know Walnut-Tree House, Sir?" said Mr. Hennings, repeating his visitor's question. "Well, yes, rather. Why, you might as well ask me, do I know the Pedlar's Arms. As boy and man I can remember the old house for close on five-and-fifty years. I remember Mr. George Stainton; he used to wear a skull-cap and knee-breeches. There was an orchard then where Stainton-street is now, and his whole day was taken up in keeping the boys out of it. Many a time I have run from him."

"Did you ever see anything of the boy and girl who were there, after Mr. Alfred succeeded to the property—Felix Stainton's grandchildren, I mean?" asked the new owner, when a pause in Mr. Hennings' reminiscences enabled him to take his part in the conversation.

"Well, Sir, I may have seen the girl, but I can't bring it to my recollection: the boy I do remember, however. He came over here two or three times with Mrs. Toplis, who kept house for both Mr. Staintons, and I took notice of him, both because he looked so peaky and old-fashioned, and also on account of the talk about him."

"There was talk about him, then."

"Bless you, yes, Sir; as much talk while he was living as since he died. Everybody thought he ought to have been the heir. But if you want to hear all about him, Sir, Mrs. Toplis is the one to tell you. If you have a mind to give a shilling to a poor old lady who always did try to keep herself respectable, and who, I will say, paid her way honourable as long as she had a sixpence to pay it honourable with—you cannot do better than go and see Mrs. Toplis, who will talk to you for hours about the time she lived at Walnut-Tree House."

And, with this delicate hint that his minutes were more valuable than the days of Mrs. Toplis, Mr. Hennings would have closed the interview, but that his visitor asked where he should be able to find the housekeeper.

"A thousand pardons!" answered the publican, with an air; "forgetting the very cream and marrow of it, wasn't I? Mrs. Toplis, Sir, is to be found in Lambeth workhouse—and a pity, too."

Edgar Stainton turned away, heart-sick. Was this all wealth had done for his people and those connected with them?

IV

BROTHER AND SISTER

Mr. Stainton had expected to find Mrs. Toplis a decrepit crone, bowed with age and racked with rheumatism, and it was therefore like a gleam of sunshine streaming across his path to behold a woman, elderly, certainly, but carrying her years with ease, ruddy cheeked, clear eyed, upright as a dart, who welcomed him with respectful enthusiasm.

"And so you are Mr. Edgar, the son of the dear old Captain," she said, after the first greetings and explanations were over, after she had wiped her eyes and uttered many ejaculations of astonishment and expressions of delight. "Eh! I remember him coming to the house just after he was married, and telling me about the dear lady his wife. I never heard a gentleman speak so proud; he never seemed tired of saying the words, 'My wife.'"

"She was a dear lady," answered the new owner.

"And so the house has come to you, Sir? Well, I wish you joy. I hope you may have peace, and health, and happiness, and prosperity in it. And I don't see why you should not—no, indeed, Sir."

Edgar Stainton sat silent for a minute, thinking how he should best approach his subject.

"Mrs. Toplis," at last he began, plunging into the very middle of the difficulty, "I want you to tell me all about it. I have come here on purpose to ask you what it all means."

The old woman covered her face with her hands, and he could see that she trembled violently.

"You need not be afraid to speak openly to me," he went on. "I am quite satisfied there was some great wrong done in the house, and I want to put it right, if it lies in my power to do so. I am a rich man. I was rich when the news of this inheritance reached me, and I would gladly give up the property tomorrow if I could only undo whatever may have been done amiss."

Mrs. Toplis shook her head.

"Ah! Sir; you can't do that," she said. "Money can't bring back the dead to life; and, if it could, I doubt if even you would prove as good a friend to the poor child sleeping in the churchyard yonder as his Maker did when He took him out of this troublesome world. It was just soul-rending to see the boy the last few months of his life. I can't bear to think of it, Sir! Often at night I wake in a fright, fancying I still hear the patter, patter of his poor little feet upon the stair."

"Do you know, it is a curious thing, but he doesn't frighten me," said Mr. Stainton; "that is, when I am in the house; although when I am away from it the recollection seems to dog every step I take."

"What?" cried Mrs. Toplis; "*have you then seen him, too?* There! what am I talking about? I hope, Sir, you will forgive my foolishness."

"I see him constantly," was the calm reply.

"I wonder what it means!—I wonder what it can mean!" exclaimed the housekeeper, wringing her hands in dire perplexity and dismay.

"I do not know," answered the new owner, philosophically; "but I want you to help me to find out. I suppose you remember the children coming there at first?"

"Well, Sir, well—They were poor Miss Mary's son and daughter. She ran away, you know, with a Mr. Fenton—made a very bad match; but I believe he was kind to her. When they were brought to us, a shivering little pair, my master was for sending them here. Ay, and he would have done it, too, if somebody had not said he could be made to pay for their keep. You never saw brother and sister so fond of one another—never. They were twins. But, Lor! he was more like a father to the little girl than aught else. He'd have kept an apple a month, rather than eat it unless she had half; and the same with all else. I think it was seeing that—watching the love they had, he for her and she for him, coming upon them unsuspected, with their little arms round one another's necks, made the old gentleman alter his mind about leaving the place to Mr. Alfred; for he said to me, one day, thoughtful like, pointing to them, 'Wonderful fond, Toplis!' and

I answered, 'Yes, Sir; for all the world like the Babes in the Wood;' not thinking of how lonely that meant—

"Shortly afterwards he took to his bed; and while he was lying there, no doubt, better thoughts came to him, for he used to talk about his wife and Miss Mary, and the Captain, your father, Sir, and ask if the children were gone to bed, and such like—things he never used to mention before.

"So when he made the will Mr. Quinance drew out I was not surprised—no, not a bit. Though before that time he always spoke of Mr. Alfred as his heir, and treated him as such."

"That will never was found," suggested Mr. Stainton, anxious to get at another portion of the narrative.

"Never, Sir. We hunted for it high and low. Perhaps I wronged him, but I always thought Mr. Alfred knew what became of it. After the old gentleman's death the children were treated shameful—shameful. I don't mean beaten, or such like; but half-starved and neglected. He would not buy them proper clothes, and he would not suffer them to wear decent things if anybody else bought them. It was just the same with their food. I durstn't give them even a bit of bread-and-butter unless it was on the sly; and, indeed, there was not much to give in that house. He turned regular miser. Hoarding came into the family with Mrs. Lancelot Stainton, Mr. Alfred's great grandmother, and they went on from bad to worse, each one closer and nearer than the last, begging your pardon for saying so, Sir; but it is the truth."

"I fear so, Mrs. Toplis," agreed the man, who certainly was neither close nor near.

"Well, Sir, at last, when the little girl was about six years old, she fell sick, and we didn't think she would get over the illness. While she was about at her worst Mrs. May, her father's sister, chanced to be stopping up in London, and, as Mr. Alfred refused to let a doctor inside his doors, she made no more ado but wrapped the child up in blankets, sent for a cab, and carried her off to her own lodgings. Mr. Alfred made no objection to that. All he said as she went through the hall was,

"'If you take her now, remember, you must keep her.'

"'Very well,' she replied, 'I will keep her.'"

"And the boy? the boy?" cried Mr. Stainton, in an agony of impatience.

"I am coming to him, Sir, if you please. He just dwined away after his sister and he were parted, and died in December as she was taken in the July."

"What did he die of?"

"A broken heart, Sir. It seems a queer thing to say about a child; but if ever a heart was broken his was. At first he was always going about the house looking for her, but towards the end he used to go up to his room and stay there all by himself. At last I wrote to Mrs. May, but she was ill when the letter got to her, and when she did come up he was dead. My word, she talked to Mr. Alfred! I never heard any one person say so much to another. She declared he had first cheated the boy of his inheritance, and then starved him to death; but that was not true, the child broke his heart fretting after his sister."

"Yes; and when he was dead."

"Sir, I don't like to speak of it, but as true as I am sitting here, the night he was put in his coffin he came pattering down just as usual looking, looking for his sister. I went straight up stairs, and, if I had not seen the little wasted body lying there still and quiet, I must have thought he had come back to life. We were never without him afterwards, never; that, and nothing else, drove Mr. Alfred mad. He used to think he was fighting the child and killing it. When the worst fits were on him he tried to trample it under foot or crush it up in a corner, and then he would sob and cry, and pray for *it* to be taken away. I have heard he recovered a little before he died, and said his uncle told him there was a will leaving all to the boy, but he never saw such a paper. Perhaps it was only talk, though, or that he was still raving."

V

THE NEXT AFTERNOON

Mr. Stainton was trying to work off some portion of his perplexities by pruning the grimy evergreens in front of Walnut-Tree House, and chopping away at the undergrowth of weeds and couch grass which had in the course of years matted together beneath the shrubs, when his attention was attracted to two ladies who stood outside the great iron gate looking up at the house.

"It seems to be occupied now," remarked the elder, turning to her companion. "I suppose the new owner is going to live here. It appears just as dingy as ever; but you do not remember it, Mary."

"I think I do," was the answer. "As I look the place grows familiar to me. I do recollect some of the rooms, I am sure, just like a dream, as I remember Georgie. What I would give to have a peep inside."

At this juncture the new owner emerged from amongst the bushes, and, opening the gate, asked if the ladies would like to look over the place.

The elder hesitated; whilst the younger whispered, "Oh, aunt, pray do!"

"Thank you," said Mrs. May to the stranger, whom she believed to be a gardener; "but perhaps Mr. Stainton might object."

"No. He wouldn't, I know," declared the new owner. "You can go through the house if you wish. There is no one in it. Nobody lives there except myself."

"Taking charge, I suppose?" suggested Mrs. May, blandly.

"Something of that sort," he answered.

"I do not think he is a caretaker," said the girl, as she and her relative passed into the old house together.

"What do you suppose he is, then?" asked her aunt.

"Mr. Stainton himself."

"Nonsense, child!" exclaimed Mrs. May, turning, nevertheless, to one of the windows, and casting a curious glance towards the new owner, who was now, his hands thrust deep in his pockets, walking idly up and down the drive.

After they had been all over the place, from hall to garret, with a peep into this room and a glance into that, Mrs. May found the man who puzzled her leaning against one of the pillars of the porch, waiting, apparently, for their reappearance.

"I am sure we are very much obliged to you," she began, with a certain hesitation in her manner.

"Pray do not mention it," he said.

"This young lady has sad associations connected with the house," Mrs. May proceeded, still doubtfully feeling her way.

He turned his eyes towards the girl for a moment, and, though her veil was down, saw she had been weeping.

"I surmised as much," he replied. "She is Miss Fenton, is she not?"

"Yes, certainly," was the answer; "and you are"—

"Edgar Stainton," said the new owner, holding out his hand.

"I am all alone here," he explained, after the first explanations were over. "But I can manage to give you a cup of tea. Pray do come in, and let me feel I am not entirely alone in England."

Only too well pleased, Mrs. May complied, and ten minutes later the three were sitting round a fire the blaze of which leapt and flickered upon the walls and over the ceiling, casting bright lights on the dingy mirrors and the dark oak shelves.

"It is all coming back to me now," said the girl softly, addressing her aunt. "Many an hour Georgie and I have sat on that hearth seeing pictures in the fire."

But she did not see something which was even then standing close beside her, and which the new owner had witnessed approach with a feeling of terror that precluded speech.

It was the child! The child searching about no longer for something it failed to find, but standing at the girl's side still and motionless, with its eyes fixed upon her face, and its poor, wasted figure nestling amongst the folds of her dress.

"Thank Heaven, she does not see it!" he thought, and drew his breath, relieved.

No; she did not see it—though its wan cheek touched her shoulder, though its thin hand rested on her arm, though through the long conversation which followed, it never moved from her side, nor turned its wistful eyes from her face.

When she went away—when she took her fresh young beauty out of the house her presence seemed to gladden and light up—the child followed her to the threshold; and then in an instant it vanished, and Mr. Stainton watched for its flitting up the staircase all in vain.

But later on in the evening, when he was sitting alone beside the fire, with his eyes bent on the glowing coals, and perhaps seeing pictures there, as Mary said she and her brother had done in their lonely childhood, he felt conscious, even without looking round, that the boy was there once again.

And when he fell to thinking of the long, long years during which the dead child had kept faithful and weary watch for his sister, searching through the empty rooms for one who never came, and then bethought him of the sister to whom her dead brother had become but the vaguest of memories, of the summers and winters during the course of which she had probably forgotten him altogether, he sighed deeply—he heard his sigh echoed behind him in the merest faintest whisper.

More, when he, thinking deeply about his newly found relative and trying to recall each feature in her face, each tone of her voice, found it impossible to dissociate the girl grown to womanhood from the child he had pictured to himself as wandering about the old house in company with her twin-brother, their arms twined together, their thoughts one, their sorrows one, their poor pleasures one—he felt a touch on his hand, and knew the boy was beside him, looking with wistful eyes into the firelight, too.

But when he turned he saw that sadness clouded those eyes no longer. She was found; the lost had come again to meet a living friend on the once desolate hearth, and up and down the wide desolate staircase those weary little feet pattered no more.

The quest was over, the search ended; into the darksome corners of that dreary house the child's glance peered no longer.

She was come! Through years he had kept faithful watch for her, but the waiting was ended now.

VI

THE MISSING WILL

Ere long there were changes in the old house. Once again Mrs. Toplis reigned there, but this time with servants under her—with maids she could scold and lads she could harass.

The larder was well plenished, the cellars sufficiently stocked; windows formerly closely shuttered now stood open to admit the air; and on the drive grass grew no longer—too many footsteps passed that way for weeds to flourish.

It was Christmas-time. The joints in the butchers' shops were gay with ribbons; the grocers' windows were tricked out to delight the eyes of the children, young and old, who passed along. In Mr. May's house up the Clapham-road all was excitement, for the whole of the family—father, mother, grown-up sons and daughters—girls still in short frocks and boys in round jackets—were going to spend Christmas Eve with their newly-found cousin, whom they had adopted as a relation with a unanimity as rare as charming.

Cousin Mary also was going—Cousin Mary had got a new dress for the occasion, and was having her hair done up in a specially effective manner by Crissie May, when the toilette proceedings were interrupted by half a dozen young voices announcing—

"A gentleman in the parlour wants to see you, Mary. Pa says you are to make haste and come down immediately."

Obediently Mary made haste as bidden and descended to the parlour, to find there the clerk from Timpson's, who met Mr. Stainton on his arrival in London.

His business was simple, but important. Once again he was the bearer of a letter from Timpson and Co., this time announcing to Miss Fenton that the will of Mr. Felix Stainton had been found, and that under it she was entitled to the interest of ten thousand pounds, secured upon the houses in Stainton-street.

"Oh! aunt, oh! uncle, how rich we shall be," cried the girl, running off to tell her cousins; but the uncle and aunt looked grave. They were wondering how this will might affect Edgar Stainton.

While they were still talking it over—after Timpson's young man had taken his departure, Mr. Edgar Stainton himself arrived.

"That is all right!" he said, in answer to their questions. "I found the will in the room where Felix Stainton died. Walnut-Tree House and all the freeholds were left to the poor little chap who died, chargeable with Mary's ten thousand pounds, five hundred to Mrs. Toplis, and a few other legacies. Failing George, the property was to come to me. I have been to Quinance's successor, and found out that the old man and Alfred had a grievous quarrel, and that in consequence he determined to cut him off altogether. Where is Mary? I want to wish her joy."

Mary was in the little conservatory, searching for a rose to put in her pretty brown hair.

He went straight to her, and said,

"Mary, dear, you have had one Christmas gift tonight, and I want you to take another with it."

"What is it, Cousin Edgar?" she asked; but when she looked in his face she must have guessed his meaning, for she drooped her head, and began pulling her sweet rose to pieces.

He took the flower, and with it her fingers.

"Will you have me, dear?" he asked. "I am but a rough fellow; but I am true, and I love you dearly."

Somehow, she answered him as he wished, and they all spent a very happy evening in the old house.

Once, when he was standing close beside her in the familiar room, hand clasped in hand, Edgar Stainton saw the child looking at them.

There was no sorrow or yearning in his eyes as he gazed—only a great peace, a calm which seemed to fill and light them up with an exquisite beauty.

A Niðagrísyr is the spirit of an unbaptised child (generally a murdered illegitimate child) that takes the shape of a round-bodied creature that often goes on all-fours and is as a rule malignant, lying in wait for people in the dark and doing them harm [...] Sometimes they haunt a pastor, begging to be given a name, and to be buried in sanctified earth.

Taylor, Faroese Folklore (1902)[11]

WAS IT AN ILLUSION?:
A PARSON'S STORY

Amelia B. Edwards

Amelia B. Edwards (1831–1892) was a journalist, traveller, Egyptologist, and author of various fictional works, including the more well-known supernatural story, "The Phantom Coach" (1864). "Was it an Illusion?" was published as part of the collection Thirteen at Dinner *for Arrowsmith Magazine's first Christmas Annual in 1881. The frame story, "How it Came About", sets the scene of thirteen real friends at a dinner party on a "wild tempestuous night" determining to meet again in a year's time in the same place with original short works that they would then publish as* Arrowsmith's Annual.[12] *Edwards was the only woman in attendance and her contribution of a ghost story commences the collection.*

The story takes a number of key tropes from folklore—in particular the buried body of the murdered illegitimate child and the haunting shadow of a spectre found in wider traditions. Yet, whilst illegitimacy and infanticide were a common theme of folk tales about the dead-child spirit, it is very rare in these literary versions, and here the reason for murder is not hiding the illegitimacy, but social status does create the circumstances for the brutal death of this much older child. So too, it is usually the mother who is blamed as the perpetrator in the ballads and folk tales, but, as in many of the literary stories, the villain here is a male relative.

he facts which I am about to relate happened to myself some sixteen or eighteen years ago, at which time I served Her Majesty as an Inspector of Schools. Now, the Provincial Inspector is perpetually on the move; and I was still young enough to enjoy a life of constant travelling. There are, indeed, many less agreeable ways in which an unbeneficed parson may contrive to scorn delights and live laborious days. In remote places where strangers are scarce, his annual visit is an important event; and though at the close of a long day's work he would some-times prefer the quiet of a country inn, he generally finds himself the destined guest of the rector or the squire. It rests with himself to turn these opportunities to account. If he makes himself pleasant, he forms agreeable friendships and sees English home-life under one of its most attractive aspects; and sometimes, even in these days of universal common-placeness, he may have the luck to meet with an adventure.

My first appointment was to a West of England district largely peopled with my personal friends and connections. It was, there-fore, much to my annoyance that I found myself, after a couple of years of very pleasant work, transferred to what a policeman would call "a new beat," up in the North. Unfortunately for me, my new beat—a rambling, thinly-populated area of something under 1,800 square miles—was three times as large as the old one, and more than proportionately unmanageable. Intersected at right angles by two ranges of barren hills and cut off to a large extent from the main lines of railway, it united about every inconvenience that a district could possess. The villages lay wide apart, often separated by long tracts of moorland; and in place of the well-warmed railway compartment and the frequent manor-house, I now spent half my time in hired vehicles and lonely country inns.

I had been in possession of this district for some three months or so, and winter was near at hand, when I paid my first visit of inspection to Pit End, an outlying hamlet in the most northerly corner of my county, just twenty-two miles from the nearest station. Having slept overnight at a place called Drumley, and inspected Drumley schools in the morning, I started for Pit End, with fourteen miles of railway and twenty-two of hilly cross-roads between myself and my journey's end. I made, of course, all the inquiries I could think of before leaving; but neither the Drumley schoolmaster nor the landlord of the Drumley "Feathers" knew much more of Pit End than its name. My predecessor, it seemed, had been in the habit of taking Pit End "from the other side;" the roads, though longer, being less hilly that way. That the place boasted some kind of inn was certain; but it was an inn unknown to fame, and to mine host of the "Feathers." Be it good or bad, however, I should have to put up at it.

Upon this scant information I started. My fourteen miles of railway journey soon ended at a place called Bramsford Road, whence an omnibus conveyed passengers to a dull little town called Bramsford Market. Here I found a horse and "trap" to carry me on to my destination; the horse being a raw-boned grey with a profile like a camel, and the trap a ricketty high gig which had probably done commercial travelling in the days of its youth. From Bramsford Market the way lay over a succession of long hills, rising to a barren, high-level plateau. It was a dull, raw afternoon of mid-November, growing duller and more raw as the day waned and the east wind blew keener.

"How much farther now, driver?" I asked, as we alighted at the foot of a longer and a stiffer hill than any we had yet passed over.

He turned a straw in his mouth, and grunted something about "fower or foive mile by the rooad."

And then I learned that by turning off at a point which he described as "t'owld tollus," and taking a certain footpath across the fields, this distance might be considerably shortened. I decided, therefore, to walk the rest of the way; and, setting off at a good pace, I soon left driver and trap behind. At the top of the hill I lost sight of them, and coming presently to a little road-side ruin which I at once recognised as the old toll-house, I found the footpath without difficulty. It led me across a barren slope divided by stone fences, with here and there a group of shattered sheds, a tall chimney, and a blackened cinder-mound, marking the site of a deserted mine. A light fog, meanwhile, was creeping up from the east, and the dusk was gathering fast.

Now, to lose one's way in such a place and at such an hour would be disagreeable enough, and the footpath—a trodden track already half obliterated—would be indistinguishable in the course of another ten minutes. Looking anxiously ahead, therefore, in the hope of seeing some sign of habitation, I hastened on, scaling one stone stile after another, till I all at once found myself skirting a line of park-palings. Following these, with bare boughs branching out overhead and dead leaves rustling underfoot, I came presently to a point where the path divided; here continuing to skirt the enclosure, and striking off yonder across a space of open meadow.

Which should I take?

By following the fence, I should be sure to arrive at a lodge where I could inquire my way to Pit End; but then the park might be of any extent, and I might have a long distance to go before I came to the nearest lodge. Again, the meadow-path, instead of leading to Pit End, might take me in a totally opposite direction. But there was no time to be lost in hesitation; so I chose the meadow, the farther end of which was lost to sight in a fleecy bank of fog.

Up to this moment I had not met a living soul of whom to ask my way; it was, therefore, with no little sense of relief that I saw a man emerging from the fog and coming along the path. As we neared each other—I advancing rapidly; he slowly—I observed that he dragged the left foot, limping as he walked. It was, however, so dark and so misty, that not till we were within half a dozen yards of each other could I see that he wore a dark suit and an Anglican felt hat, and looked something like a dissenting minister. As soon as we were within speaking distance, I addressed him.

"Can you tell me," I said, "if I am right for Pit End, and how far I have to go?"

He came on, looking straight before him; taking no notice of my question; apparently not hearing it.

"I beg your pardon," I said, raising my voice; "but will this path take me to Pit End, and if so"—

He had passed on without pausing; without looking at me; I could almost have believed, without seeing me!

I stopped, with the words on my lips; then turned to look after— perhaps, to follow—him.

But instead of following, I stood bewildered.

What had become of him? And what lad was that going up the path by which I had just come—that tall lad, half-running, half-walking, with a fishing-rod over his shoulder? I could have taken my oath that I had neither met nor passed him. Where then had he come from? And where was the man to whom I had spoken not three seconds ago, and who, at his limping pace, could not have made more than a couple of yards in the time?

My stupefaction was such that I stood quite still, looking after the lad with the fishing-rod till he disappeared in the gloom under the park-palings.

Was I dreaming?

Darkness, meanwhile, had closed in space, and, dreaming or not dreaming, I must push on, or find myself benighted. So I hurried forward, turning my back on the last gleam of daylight, and plunging deeper into the fog at every step. I was, however, close upon my journey's end. The path ended at a turnstile; the turnstile opened upon a steep lane; and at the bottom of the lane, down which I stumbled among stones and ruts, I came in sight of the welcome glare of a blacksmith's forge.

Here, then, was Pit End. I found my trap standing at the door of the village inn; the raw-boned grey stabled for the night; the landlord watching for my arrival.

The "Greyhound" was a hostelry of modest pretensions, and I shared its little parlour with a couple of small farmers and a young man who informed me that he "travelled in" Thorley's Food for Cattle. Here I dined, wrote my letters, chatted awhile with the landlord, and picked up such scraps of local news as fell in my way.

There was, it seemed, no resident parson at Pit End; the incumbent being a pluralist with three small livings, the duties of which, by the help of a rotatory curate, he discharged in a somewhat easy fashion. Pit End, as the smallest and farthest off, came in for but one service each Sunday, and was almost wholly relegated to the curate. The squire was a more confirmed absentee than even the vicar. He lived chiefly in Paris, spending abroad the wealth of his Pit End coal-fields. He happened to be at home just now, the landlord said, after five years' absence; but he would be off again next week, and another five years might probably elapse before they should again see him at Blackwater Chase.

Blackwater Chase!—the name was not new to me; yet I could not remember where I had heard it. When, however, mine host went on to say that, despite his absenteeism, Mr. Wolstenholme was "a pleasant gentleman and a good landlord," and that after all, Blackwater Chase was "a lonesome sort of world-end place for a young man to bury himself in," then I at once remembered Phil Wolstenholme of Balliol, who, in his grand way, had once upon a time given me a general invitation to the shooting at Blackwater Chase. That was twelve years ago, when I was reading hard at Wadham, and Wolstenholme—the idol of a clique to which I did not belong—was boating, betting, writing poetry, and giving wine parties at Balliol.

Yes; I remembered all about him—his handsome face, his luxurious rooms, his boyish prodigality, his utter indolence, and the blind faith of his worshippers, who believed that he had only "to pull himself together" in order to carry off every honour which the University had to bestow. He did take the Newdigate; but it was his first and last achievement, and he left college with the reputation of having narrowly escaped a plucking. How vividly it all came back upon my memory—the old college life, the college friendships, the pleasant time that could never come again! It was but twelve years ago; yet it seemed like half a century. And now, after these twelve years, here were Wolstenholme and I as near neighbours as in our Oxford days! I wondered if he was much changed, and whether, if changed, it were for the better or the worse. Had his generous impulses developed into sterling virtues, or had his follies hardened into vices? Should I let him know where I was, and so judge for myself? Nothing would be easier than to pencil a line upon a card tomorrow morning, and send it up to the big house. Yet, merely to satisfy a purposeless curiosity, was it worth while to re-open the acquaintanceship?

Thus musing, I sat late over the fire, and by the time I went to bed, I had well nigh forgotten my adventure with the man who vanished so mysteriously and the boy who seemed to come from nowhere.

Next morning, finding I had abundant time at my disposal, I did pencil that line upon my card—a mere line, saying that I believed we had known each other at Oxford, and that I should be inspecting the National Schools from nine till about eleven. And then, having despatched it by one of my landlord's sons, I went off to my work. The day was brilliantly fine. The wind had shifted round to the north, the sun shone clear and cold, and the smoke-grimed hamlet and the gaunt buildings clustered at the mouths of the coalpits round about, looked as bright as they could look at any time of the year. The village was built up a long hill-side; the church and schools being at the top, and the "Greyhound" at the bottom. Looking vainly for the lane by which I had come the night before, I climbed the one rambling street, followed a path that skirted the churchyard, and found myself at the schools. These, with the teachers' dwellings, formed three sides of a quadrangle; the fourth side consisting of an iron railing and a gate. An inscribed tablet over the main entrance-door recorded how "These school-houses were re-built by Philip Wolstenholme. Esquire: A.D. 18—."

"Mr. Wolstenholme, sir, is the Lord of the Manor," said a soft, obsequious voice.

I turned, and found the speaker at my elbow, a square-built, sallow man, all in black, with a bundle of copy-books under his arm.

"You are the—the schoolmaster?" I said; unable to remember his name, and puzzled by a vague recollection of his face.

"Just so, sir. I conclude I have the honour of addressing Mr. Frazer?"

It was a singular face, very pallid and anxious-looking. The eyes, too, had a watchful, almost a startled, look in them, which struck me as peculiarly unpleasant.

"Yes," I replied, still wondering where and when I had seen him. "My name is Frazer. Yours, I believe, is—is—," and I put my hand into my pocket for my examination papers.

"Skelton—Ebenezer Skelton. Will you please to take the boys first, sir?"

The words were common-place enough, but the man's manner was studiously, disagreeably deferential; his very name being given, as it were, under protest, as if too insignificant to be mentioned.

I said I would begin with the boys; and so moved on. Then, for we had stood still till now, I saw that the schoolmaster was lame. In that moment I remembered him. He was the man I met in the fog.

"I met you yesterday afternoon, Mr. Skelton," I said, as we went into the school-room.

"Yesterday afternoon, sir?" he repeated.

"You did not seem to observe me," I said, carelessly. "I spoke to you, in fact; but you did not reply to me."

"But—indeed, I beg your pardon, sir—it must have been some one else," said the schoolmaster. "I did not go out yesterday afternoon."

How could this be anything but a falsehood? I might have been mistaken as to the man's face; though it was such a singular face, and I had seen it quite plainly. But how could I be mistaken as to his lameness? Besides, that curious trailing of the right foot, as if the ankle was broken, was not an ordinary lameness.

I suppose I looked incredulous, for he added, hastily:—

"Even if I had not been preparing the boys for inspection, sir, I should not have gone out yesterday afternoon. It was too damp and foggy. I am obliged to be careful—I have a very delicate chest."

My dislike to the man increased with every word he uttered. I did not ask myself with what motive he went on heaping lie upon lie; it was enough that, to serve his own ends, whatever those ends might be, he did lie with unparalleled audacity.

"We will proceed to the examination, Mr. Skelton," I said, contemptuously.

He turned, if possible, a shade paler than before, bent his head silently, and called up the scholars in their order.

I soon found that, whatever his shortcomings as to veracity, Mr. Ebenezer Skelton was a capital schoolmaster. His boys were uncommonly well taught, and as regarded attendance, good conduct, and the like, left nothing to be desired. When, therefore, at the end of the examination, he said he hoped I would recommend the Pit End Boys' School for the Government grant, I at once assented. And now I thought I had done with Mr. Skelton for, at all events, the space of one year. Not so, however. When I came out from the Girls' School, I found him waiting at the door.

Profusely apologising, he begged leave to occupy five minutes of my valuable time. He wished, under correction, to suggest a little improvement. The boys, he said, were allowed to play in the quadrangle, which was too small, and in various ways inconvenient; but round at the back there was a piece of waste land, half an acre of which, if enclosed, would admirably answer the purpose. So saying, he led the way to the back of the building, and I followed him.

"To whom does this ground belong?" I asked.

"To Mr. Wolstenholme, sir."

"Then why not apply to Mr. Wolstenholme? He gave the schools, and I dare say he would be equally willing to give the ground."

"I beg your pardon, sir. Mr. Wolstenholme has not been over here since his return, and it is quite possible that he may leave Pit End without honouring us with a visit. I could not take the liberty of writing to him, sir."

"Neither could I in my report suggest that the Government should offer to purchase a portion of Mr. Wolstenholme's land for a play-ground to schools of Mr. Wolstenholme's own building," I replied. "Under other circumstances"...

I stopped and looked round.

The schoolmaster repeated my last words.

"You were saying, sir—under other circumstances?"—

I looked round again.

"It seemed to me that there was some one here," I said; "some third person, not a moment ago."

"I beg your pardon, sir—a third person?"

"I saw his shadow on the ground, between yours and mine."

The schools faced due north, and we were standing immediately behind the buildings, with our backs to the sun. The place was bare, and open, and high; and our shadows, sharply defined, lay stretched before our feet.

"A—a shadow?" he faltered. "Impossible."

There was not a bush or a tree within half a mile. There was not a cloud in the sky. There was nothing, absolutely nothing, that could have cast a shadow.

I admitted that it was impossible, and that I must have fancied it; and so went back to the matter of the play-ground.

"Should you see Mr. Wolstenholme," I said, "you are at liberty to say that I thought it a desirable improvement."

"I am much obliged to you, sir. Thank you—thank you very much," he said, cringing at every word. "But—but I had hoped that you might perhaps use your influence"—

"Look there!" I interrupted. "Is *that* fancy?"

We were now close under the blank wall of the boys' school-room. On this wall, lying to the full sunlight, our shadows—mine and the schoolmaster's—were projected. And there, too—no longer between his and mine, but a little way apart, as if the intruder were standing back—there, as sharply defined as if cast by lime-light on a prepared background, I again distinctly saw, though but for a moment, that third shadow. As I spoke, as I looked round, it was gone!

"Did you not see it?" I asked.

He shook his head.

"I—I saw nothing," he said, faintly. "What was it?"

His lips were white. He seemed scarcely able to stand.

"But you *must* have seen it!" I exclaimed. "It fell just there—where that bit of ivy grows. There must be some boy hiding—it was a boy's shadow, I am confident."

"A boy's shadow!" he echoed, looking round in a wild, frightened way. "There is no place—for a boy—to hide."

"Place or no place," I said, angrily, "if I catch him, he shall feel the weight of my cane!"

I searched backwards and forwards in every direction, the school-master, with his scared face, limping at my heels; but, rough and irregular as the ground was, there was not a hole in it big enough to shelter a rabbit.

"But what was it?" I said, impatiently.

"An—an illusion. Begging your pardon, sir—an illusion."

He looked so like a beaten hound, so frightened, so fawning, that I felt I could with lively satisfaction have transferred the threatened caning to his own shoulders.

"But you saw it?" I said again.

"No, sir. Upon my honour, no, sir. I saw nothing—nothing whatever."

His looks belied his words. I felt positive that he had not only seen the shadow, but that he knew more about it than he chose to tell. I was by this time really angry. To be made the object of a boyish trick, and to be hoodwinked by the connivance of the schoolmaster, was too much. It was an insult to myself and my office.

I scarcely knew what I said; something short and stern at all events. Then, having said it, I turned my back upon Mr. Skelton and the schools, and walked rapidly back to the village.

As I neared the bottom of the hill, a dog-cart drawn by a high-stepping chestnut dashed up to the door of the "Greyhound," and the next moment I was shaking hands with Wolstenholme, of Balliol. Wolstenholme, of Balliol, as handsome as ever, dressed with the same careless dandyism, looking not a day older than when I last saw him at Oxford! He gripped me by both hands, vowed that I was his guest for the next three days, and insisted on carrying me off at once to Blackwater Chase. In vain I urged that I had two schools to inspect tomorrow ten miles the other side of Drumley; that I had a horse and trap waiting; and that my room was ordered at the "Feathers." Wolstenholme laughed away my objections.

"My dear fellow," he said, "you will simply send your horse and trap back with a message to the 'Feathers,' and a couple of telegrams to be despatched to the two schools from Drumley station. Unforeseen circumstances compel you to defer those inspections till next week!"

And with this, in his masterful way, he shouted to the landlord to send my portmanteau up to the manor-house, pushed me up before him into the dog-cart, gave the chestnut his head, and rattled me off to Blackwater Chase.

It was a gloomy old barrack of a place, standing high in the midst of a sombre deer-park some six or seven miles in circumference. An avenue of oaks, now leafless, led up to the house; and a mournful heron-haunted tarn in the loneliest part of the park gave to the estate its name of Blackwater Chase. The place, in fact, was more like a border fastness than an English north-country mansion. Wolstenholme took me through the picture gallery and reception rooms after luncheon, and then for a canter round the park; and in the evening we dined at the upper end of a great oak hall hung with antlers, and armour, and antiquated weapons of warfare and sport.

"Now, tomorrow," said my host, as we sat over our claret in front of a blazing log-fire; "tomorrow, if we have decent weather, you shall have a day's shooting on the moors; and on Friday, if you will but be persuaded to stay a day longer, I will drive you over to Broomhead and give you a run with the Duke's hounds. Not hunt? My dear fellow, what nonsense! All our parsons hunt in this part of the world. By the way, have you ever been down a coal pit? No? Then a new experience awaits you. I'll take you down Carshalton shaft, and show you the home of the gnomes and trolls."

"Is Carshalton one of your own mines?" I asked.

"All these pits are mine," he replied. "I am king of Hades, and rule the under world as well as the upper. There is coal everywhere underlying these moors. The whole place is honey-combed with shafts and galleries. One of our richest seams runs under this house, and there are upwards of forty men at work in it a quarter of a mile below our feet here every day. Another leads right away under the park, heaven only knows how far! My father began working it five-and-twenty years ago, and we have gone on working it ever since; yet it shows no sign of failing."

"You must be as rich as a prince with a fairy godmother!"

He shrugged his shoulders.

"Well," he said, lightly, "I am rich enough to commit what follies I please; and that is saying a good deal. But then, to be always squandering money—always rambling about the world—always gratifying the impulse of the moment—is that happiness? I have been trying the experiment for the last ten years; and with what result? Would you like to see?"

He snatched up a lamp and led the way through a long suite of unfurnished rooms, the floors of which were piled high with packing cases of all sizes and shapes, labelled with the names of various foreign ports and the addresses of foreign agents innumerable. What did they contain? Precious marbles from Italy and Greece and Asia Minor; priceless paintings by old and modern masters; antiquities from the Nile, the Tigris, and the Euphrates; enamels from Persia, porcelain from China, bronzes from Japan, strange sculptures from Peru; arms, mosaics, ivories, wood-carvings, skins, tapestries, old Italian cabinets, painted bride-chests, Etruscan terracottas; treasures of all countries, of all ages, never even unpacked since they crossed that threshold which the master's foot had crossed but twice during the ten years it had taken to buy them! Should he ever open them, ever arrange them, ever enjoy them? Perhaps—if he became weary of wandering—if he married—if he built a gallery to receive them. If not—well, he might found and endow a museum; or leave the things to the nation. What did it matter? Collecting was like fox-hunting; the pleasure was in the pursuit, and ended with it!

We sat up late that first night, I can hardly say conversing, for Wolstenholme did the talking, while I, willing to be amused, led him on to tell me something of his wanderings by land and sea. So the time passed in stories of adventure, of perilous peaks ascended, of deserts traversed, of unknown ruins explored, of "hair-breadth 'scapes" from icebergs and earthquakes and storms; and when at last he flung the end of his cigar into the fire and discovered that it was time to go to bed, the clock on the mantel-shelf pointed far on among the small hours of the morning.

Next day, according to the programme made out for my entertainment, we did some seven hours' partridge-shooting on the moors; and the day next following I was to go down Carshalton shaft before breakfast, and after breakfast ride over to a place some fifteen miles distant called Picts' Camp, there to see a stone circle and the ruins of a pre-historic fort.

Unused to field sports, I slept heavily after those seven hours with the guns, and was slow to wake when Wolstenholme's valet came next morning to my bedside with the waterproof suit in which I was to effect my descent into Hades.

"Mr. Wolstenholme says, sir, that you had better not take your bath till you come back," said this gentlemanly vassal, disposing the ungainly garments across the back of a chair as artistically as if he were laying out my best evening suit. "And you will be pleased to dress warmly underneath the waterproofs, for it is very chilly in the mine."

I surveyed the garments with reluctance. The morning was frosty, and the prospect of being lowered into the bowels of the earth, cold, fasting, and unwashed, was anything but attractive. Should I send word that I would rather not go? I hesitated; but while I was hesitating, the gentlemanly valet vanished, and my opportunity was lost. Grumbling and shivering, I got up, donned the cold and shiny suit, and went downstairs.

A murmur of voices met my ear as I drew near the breakfast-room. Going in, I found some ten or a dozen stalwart colliers grouped near the door, and Wolstenholme, looking somewhat serious, standing with his back to the fire.

"Look here, Frazer," he said, with a short laugh, "here's a pleasant piece of news. A fissure has opened in the bed of Blackwater tarn; the lake has disappeared in the night; and the mine is flooded! No Carshalton shaft for you today!"

"Seven foot o' wayter in Jukes's seam, an' eight in th' owd north and south galleries," growled a huge red-headed fellow, who seemed to be the spokesman.

"An' it's the Lord's own marcy a' happened o' noight-time, or we'd be dead men all," added another.

"That's true, my man," said Wolstenholme, answering the last speaker. "It might have drowned you like rats in a trap; so we may thank our stars it's no worse. And now, to work with the pumps! Lucky for us that we know what to do, and how to do it."

So saying, he dismissed the men with a good-humoured nod, and an order for unlimited ale.

I listened in blank amazement. The tarn vanished! I could not believe it. Wolstenholme assured me, however, that it was by no means a solitary phenomenon. Rivers had been known to disappear before now, in mining districts; and sometimes, instead of merely cracking, the ground would cave in, burying not merely houses, but whole hamlets in one common ruin. The foundations of such houses were, however, generally known to be insecure long enough before the crash came; and these accidents were not therefore often followed by loss of life.

"And now," he said, lightly, "you may doff your fancy costume; for I shall have time this morning for nothing but business. It is not every day that one loses a lake, and has to pump it up again!"

Breakfast over, we went round to the mouth of the pit, and saw the men fixing the pumps. Later on, when the work was fairly in train, we started off across the park to view the scene of the catastrophe. Our way lay far from the house across a wooded upland, beyond which we followed a broad glade leading to the tarn. Just as we entered this glade—Wolstenholme rattling on and turning the whole affair into jest—a tall, slender lad, with a fishing-rod across his shoulder, came out from one of the side paths to the right, crossed the open at a long slant, and disappeared among the tree-trunks on the opposite side. I recognised him instantly. It was the boy whom I saw the other day, just after meeting the schoolmaster in the meadow.

"If that boy thinks he is going to fish in your tarn," I said, "he will find out his mistake."

"What boy?" asked Wolstenholme, looking back.

"That boy who crossed over yonder, a minute ago."

"Yonder!—in front of us?"

"Certainly. You must have seen him?"

"Not I."

"You did not see him?—a tall, thin boy, in a grey suit, with a fishing-rod over his shoulder. He disappeared behind those Scotch firs."

Wolstenholme looked at me with surprise.

"You are dreaming!" he said. "No living thing—not even a rabbit—has crossed our path since we entered the park gates."

"I am not in the habit of dreaming with my eyes open," I replied, quickly.

He laughed, and put his arm through mine.

"Eyes or no eyes," he said, "you are under an illusion this time!"

An illusion—the very word made use of by the schoolmaster! What did it mean? Could I, in truth, no longer rely upon the testimony of my senses? A thousand half-formed apprehensions flashed across me in a moment. I remembered the illusions of Nicolini, the bookseller, and other similar cases of visual hallucination, and I asked myself if I had suddenly become afflicted in like manner.

"By Jove! this *is* a queer sight!" exclaimed Wolstenholme.

And then I found that we had emerged from the glade, and were looking down upon the bed of what yesterday was Blackwater Tarn.

It was indeed a queer sight—an oblong, irregular basin of blackest slime, with here and there a sullen pool, and round the margin an irregular fringe of bulrushes. At some little distance along the bank—less than a quarter of a mile from where we were standing—a gaping crowd had gathered. All Pit End, except the men at the pumps, seemed to have turned out to stare at the bed of the vanished tarn.

Hats were pulled off and curtsies dropped at Wolstenholme's approach. He, meanwhile, came up smiling, with a pleasant word for everyone.

"Well," he said, "are you looking for the lake, my friends? You'll have to go down Carshalton shaft to find it! It's an ugly sight you've come to see, anyhow!"

"Tes an ugly soight, squoire," replied a stalwart blacksmith in a leathern apron; "but thar's summat uglier, mebbe, than the mud, ow'r yonder."

"Something uglier than the mud?" Wolstenholme repeated.

"Wull yo be pleased to stan' this way, squoire, an' look strite across at yon little tump o' bulrashes—doan't yo see nothin'?"

"I see a log of rotten timber sticking half in and half out of the mud," said Wolstenholme; "and something—a long reed, apparently... by Jove! I believe it's a fishing rod!"

"It *is* a fishin' rod, squoire," said the blacksmith with rough earnestness; "an' if yon rotten timber bayn't an unburied corpse, mun I never stroke hammer on anvil agin!"

There was a buzz of acquiescence from the bystanders. 'Twas an unburied corpse, sure enough. Nobody doubted it.

Wolstenholme made a funnel with his hands, and looked through it long and steadfastly.

"It must come out, whatever it is," he said presently. "Five feet of mud, do you say? Then here's a sovereign apiece for the first two fellows who wade through it and bring that object to land!"

The blacksmith and another pulled off their shoes and stockings, turned up their trousers, and went in at once.

They were over their ankles at the first plunge, and, sounding their way with sticks, went deeper at every tread. As they sank, our excitement rose. Presently they were visible from only the waist upwards. We could see their chests heaving, and the muscular efforts by which each step was gained. They were yet full twenty yards from the goal when the mud mounted to their armpits... a few feet more, and only their heads would remain above the surface!

An uneasy movement ran through the crowd.

"Call 'em back, vor God's sake!" cried a woman's voice.

But at this moment—having reached a point where the ground gradually slopes upwards—they began to rise above the mud as rapidly as they had sunk into it. And now, black with clotted slime, they emerge waist-high... now they are within three or four yards of the spot... and now... now they are there!

They part the reeds—they stoop low above the shapeless object on which all eyes are turned—they half-lift it from its bed of mud—they hesitate—lay it down again—decide, apparently, to leave it there; and turn their faces shorewards. Having come a few paces, the blacksmith remembers the fishing-rod; turns back; disengages the tangled line with some difficulty, and brings it over his shoulder.

They had not much to tell—standing, all mud from head to heel, on dry land again—but that little was conclusive. It was, in truth, an unburied corpse; part of the trunk only above the surface. They tried to lift it; but it had been so long under water, and was in so advanced a stage of decomposition, that to bring it to shore without a shutter was impossible. Being cross-questioned, they thought, from the slenderness of the form, that it must be the body of a boy.

"Thar's the poor chap's rod, anyhow," said the blacksmith, laying it gently down upon the turf.

I have thus far related events as I witnessed them. Here, however, my responsibility ceases. I give the rest of my story at second-hand, briefly, as I received it some weeks later, in the following letter from Philip Wolstenholme:—

"Blackwater Chase, Dec. 20th, 18—.

"Dear Frazer,—My promised letter has been a long time on the road, but I did not see the use of writing till I had something definite to tell you. I think, however, we have now found out all that we are ever likely to know about the tragedy in the tarn; and it seems that—but, no; I will begin at the beginning. That is to say, with the day you left the Chase, which was the day following the discovery of the body.

"You were but just gone when a police inspector arrived from Drumley (you will remember that I had immediately sent a man over to the sitting magistrate); but neither the inspector nor anyone else could do anything till the remains were brought to shore, and it took us the best part of a week to accomplish this difficult operation. We had to sink no end of big stones in order to make a rough and ready causeway across the mud. This done, the body was brought over decently upon a shutter. It proved to be the corpse of a boy of perhaps fourteen or fifteen years of age. There was a fracture three inches long at the back of the skull, evidently fatal. This might, of course, have been an accidental injury; but when the body came to be raised from where it lay, it was found to be pinned down by a pitchfork, the handle of which had been afterwards whittled off, so as not to show above the water, a discovery tantamount to evidence of murder. The features of the victim were decomposed beyond recognition; but enough of the hair remained to show that it had been short and sandy. As for the clothing, it was a mere mass of rotten shreds; but on being subjected to some chemical process, proved to have once been a suit of lightish grey cloth.

"A crowd of witnesses came forward at this stage of the inquiry—for I am now giving you the main facts as they came out at the coroner's inquest—to prove that about a year or thirteen months ago, Skelton the schoolmaster had staying with him a lad whom he called his nephew, and to whom it was supposed that he was not particularly kind. This lad was described as tall, thin, and sandy-haired. He habitually wore a suit corresponding in colour and texture to the shreds of clothing discovered on the body in the tarn; and he was much addicted to angling about the pools and streams, wherever he might have the chance of a nibble.

"And now one thing led quickly on to another. Our Pit End shoemaker identified the boy's boots as being a pair of his own making and selling. Other witnesses testified to angry scenes between the uncle and nephew. Finally, Skelton gave himself up to justice, confessed the deed, and was duly committed to Drumley gaol for wilful murder.

"And the motive? Well, the motive is the strangest part of my story. The wretched lad was, after all, not Skelton's nephew, but Skelton's own illegitimate son. The mother was dead, and the boy lived with his maternal grandmother in a remote part of Cumberland. The old woman was poor, and the schoolmaster made her an annual allowance for his son's keep and clothing. He had not seen the boy for some years, when he sent for him to come over on a visit to Pit End. Perhaps he was weary of the tax upon his purse. Perhaps, as he himself puts it in his confession, he was disappointed to find the boy, if not actually half-witted, stupid, wilful, and ill brought-up. He at all events took a dislike to the poor brute, which dislike by and by developed into positive hatred. Some amount of provocation there would seem to have been. The boy was as backward as a child of five years old. That Skelton put him into the Boys' School, and could do nothing with him; that he defied discipline, had a passion for fishing, and was continually wandering about the country with his rod and line, are facts borne out by the independent testimony of various witnesses. Having hidden his fishing-tackle, he was in the habit of slipping away at school-hours, and showed himself the more cunning and obstinate the more he was punished.

"At last there came a day when Skelton tracked him to the place where his rod was concealed, and thence across the meadows into the park, and as far as the tarn. His (Skelton's) account of what followed is wandering and confused. He owns to having beaten the miserable lad about the head and arms with a heavy stick that he had brought with him for the purpose; but denies that he intended to murder him. When his son fell insensible and ceased to breathe, he for the first time realised the force of the blows he had dealt. He admits that his first impulse was one, not of remorse for the deed, but of fear for his own safety. He dragged the body in among the bulrushes by the water's edge, and there concealed it as well as he could. At night, when the neighbours were in bed and asleep, he stole out by starlight, taking with him a pitchfork, a coil of rope, a couple of old iron-bars, and a knife. Thus laden, he struck out across the moor, and entered the park by a stile and footpath on the Stoneleigh side; so making a circuit of between three and four miles. A rotten old punt used at that time to be kept on the tarn. He loosed this punt from its moorings, brought it round, hauled in the body, and paddled his ghastly burden out into the middle of the lake as far as a certain clump of reeds which he had noted as a likely spot for his purpose. Here he weighted and sunk the corpse, and pinned it down by the neck with his pitchfork. He then cut away the handle of the fork; hid the fishing-rod among the reeds; and believed, as murderers always believe, that discovery was impossible. As regarded the Pit End folk, he simply gave out that his nephew had gone back to Cumberland; and no one doubted it. Now, however, he says that accident has only anticipated him; and that he was on the point of voluntarily confessing his crime. His dreadful secret had of late become intolerable. He was haunted by an invisible Presence. That Presence sat with him at table, followed him in his walks, stood behind him in the school-room, and watched by his bedside. He never saw it; but he felt that it was always there. Sometimes he raves of a shadow on the wall of his cell. The gaol authorities are of opinion that he is of unsound mind.

"I have now told you all that there is at present to tell. The trial will not take place till the spring assizes. In the meanwhile I am off tomorrow to Paris, and thence, in about ten days, on to Nice, where letters will find me at the Hotel des Empereurs.

"Always, dear Frazer,

"Yours, &c., &c.,

"P. W.

"P.S.—Since writing the above, I have received a telegram from Drumley to say that Skelton has committed suicide. No particulars given. So ends this strange eventful history.

"By the way, that was a curious illusion of yours the other day when we were crossing the park; and I have thought of it many times. Was it an illusion?—that is the question."

Ay, indeed! that *is* the question; and it is a question which I have never yet been able to answer. Certain things I undoubtedly saw—with my mind's eye, perhaps—and as I saw them, I have described them; withholding nothing, adding nothing, explaining nothing. Let those solve the mystery who can. For myself, I but echo Wolstenholme's question:—Was it an Illusion?

Of the alchemy, magic, black art, sorcery, and "philosophy" of the Dark Ages of Europe, the practice of which lingered in some places well on into the seventeenth century, horrible stories are told, in which children, their bodies, their souls even, appear as fetishes... According to C. F. A. Hoffmann (1817), there lived in Naples "an old doctor who had children by several women, which he inhumanly killed, with peculiar ceremonies and rites, cutting the breast open, tearing out the heart, and from its blood preparing precious drops which were preservative against all sickness."

Chamberlain, *The Child and Childhood in Folk-Thought* (1895)[13]

The story is told of a certain citizen of Cleveland called Richard Rowntree, who, leaving his wife pregnant, went on pilgrimage... He noticed in particular what appeared to be a little child tangled up in swaddling clothes, and he asked who it was and what it might be seeking. It replied, "It is not appropriate for you to address me, for you were my father and I was your stillborn child, buried without being named and baptised..." Hearing this, the pilgrim took off his own shirt and put it on the little child, naming it in the name of the Holy Trinity, and took with him the old swaddling cloth as proof. With its name bestowed, the child went off exultantly, walking upright instead of floundering along as before. When the pilgrim returned from his journey... the midwives then confessed the truth about the premature death and burial of the child, and the husband proceeded to divorce his wife on the grounds that their son had been aborted...

"The Child of Richard Rowntree", *Fragmentary Tales of the Monk of Byland* (Fourteenth century)[14]

LOST HEARTS

M. R. James

Montague Rhodes James (1862–1936) was a Medieval scholar of Oxford and Cambridge colleges and the well-known author of a number of terrifying ghost stories that reflect his antiquarian interests. In 1922, he transcribed into Latin the fragmentary ghost tales of a fourteenth-century Monk from Byland Abbey in Yorkshire, including "The Child of Richard Rowntree" reprinted in part above in which the child spirit appears and reveals the crime committed against it.

"Lost Hearts" was first published in The Pall Mall Magazine *in 1895 and illustrated by Simon Harmon Vedder, and then collected without those illustrations in* Ghost Stories of an Antiquary *(1904). It is the most macabre of the sub-genre in terms of the child deaths and the punishment their ghosts inflict, but also has something unusually mocking, or perhaps just cynical, in terms of its treatment of the subject. The orphaned Stephen is under threat from his guardian; but the motive is not inheritance, or even dislike and sheer brutality, but something far more fantastical than in other stories of this collection: the arrogant quest for immortality. Nevertheless, although it does not seem to follow the similar pattern of social commentary, James' story does reflect on the attitude that the child is both powerful and disposable (particularly the impoverished or orphaned one), and, following the rules of folklore, demonstrates that there are fatal consequences for such attitudes.*

t was, as far as I can ascertain, in September of the year 1811, that a post-chaise drew up before the door of Aswarby Hall, in the heart of Lincolnshire. The little boy, who was the only passenger in it, and who jumped out as soon as the chaise had stopped, looked about him with the keenest curiosity during the short interval that elapsed between the ringing of the bell and the opening of the hall door. He saw a tall, square, red-brick house, built in the reign of Anne; a stone-pillared porch had been added in the purer classical style of 1790; the windows of the house were many, tall, and narrow, with small panes and thick white woodwork. A pediment, pierced with a round window, crowned the front. There were wings to right and left, connected by curious glazed galleries, supported by colonnades, with the central block. These wings plainly contained the stables and offices of the house. Each was surmounted by an ornamental cupola with a gilded vane. An evening light shone on the building, making the window-panes glow like so many fires. Away from the Hall in front stretched a flat park studded with oaks and fringed with firs, which stood out against the sky. The clock in the church tower, buried in trees on the edge of the park—only its golden weathercock catching the light—was striking six, and the sound came gently beating down the wind. It was altogether a pleasant impression, though tinged with the sort of melancholy appropriate to an evening in early autumn, that was conveyed to the mind of the boy who was standing in the porch waiting for the door to open to him.

He had just come from Warwickshire, and was an orphan of some six months' standing: now, owing to the generous and unexpected offer of his elderly cousin Mr. Abney, he had come to live at Aswarby. The offer was unexpected, because all who knew anything of Mr. Abney looked upon him as a somewhat austere recluse, into whose steady-going household the advent of a small boy would import a new and, it seemed, incongruous element. The truth is that very little was known of Mr. Abney's pursuits or temper. The Professor of Greek at Cambridge had been known to say that no one knew more of the religious beliefs of the later pagans than did the owner of Aswarby. Certainly the library at the Hall contained all the available literature of the Mysteries, the Orphic poems, the worship of Mithras, and the Neo-Platonists. In the marble-paved hall stood a fine group of Mithras slaying a Bull, which had been imported from the Levant at great expense by the owner. He had contributed a description of it to the *Gentleman's Magazine*; and he had written a remarkable series of articles in the *Critical Museum* on the superstitions of the Romans of the Lower Empire. He was looked upon, in fine, as a man wrapped up in his books, and it was a matter of great surprise among his neighbours that he should ever have heard of his orphan cousin Stephen Elliott, much more that he should have volunteered to make him an inmate of Aswarby Hall.

Whatever may have been expected by his neighbours, it is certain that Mr. Abney, the tall, the thin, the austere, seemed inclined to give his young cousin a kindly reception. The moment the front door was opened he darted out of his study, rubbing his hands with delight.

"How are you, my boy? how are you? How old are you?" said he—"that is, you are not too much tired, I hope, by your journey to eat your supper?"

"No, thank you, sir," said Master Elliott; "I am pretty well."

"That's a good lad," said Mr. Abney. "And how old are you, my boy?" It seemed a little odd that he should have asked the question twice in the first two minutes of their acquaintance.

"I'm twelve years old next birthday, sir," said Stephen.

"And when is your birthday, my dear boy? Eleventh of September, eh? That's well—that's very well: nearly a year hence, isn't it? I like—ha, ha!—I like to get these things down in my book. Sure it's twelve?—certain?"

"Yes, quite sure, sir."

"Well, well: take him to Mrs. Bunch's room, Parkes, and let him have his tea—supper—whatever it is."

"Yes, sir," answered the staid Mr. Parkes; and conducted Stephen to the lower regions.

Mrs. Bunch was the most comfortable and human person whom Stephen had as yet met in Aswarby. She made him completely at home, and they were great friends after the first quarter of an hour—as indeed they continued. Mrs. Bunch had been born in the neighbourhood some fifty-five years before the date of Stephen's arrival, and her residence at the Hall was of twenty years' standing. Consequently, if any one knew the ins and outs of the house and the district, Mrs. Bunch knew them; and she was by no means disinclined to communicate her information. Certainly there were plenty of things about the Hall and the Hall gardens which Stephen, who was of an adventurous and inquiring turn, was anxious to have explained to him. "Who built the temple at the end of the laurel walk? Who was the old man whose picture hung on the staircase—sitting at a table with a skull under his hand?" These and many similar points were cleared up by the resources of Mrs. Bunch's powerful intellect. There were others, however, of which the explanations furnished were less satisfactory. One November evening Stephen was sitting by the fire in the housekeeper's room reflecting on his surroundings. "Is Mr. Abney a good man, and will he go to heaven?" he suddenly asked, with the peculiar confidence which children possess in the ability of their elders to settle these questions—the decision of which is believed to be reserved for other tribunals.

"Good?—bless the child!" said Mrs. Bunch. "Master's as kind a soul as ever I see! Didn't I never tell you of the little boy as he took in, out of the street, as you may say, this seven years back? and the little girl, two years after I first come here?"

"No: do tell me all about them, Mrs. Bunch—now this minute!"

"Well," said Mrs. Bunch, "the little girl I don't seem to recollect so much about. I know Master brought her back with him from his walk one day, and give orders to Mrs. Ellis, as was housekeeper then, as she should be took every care with. And the pore child hadn't no one belonging to her—she telled me so her own self: and here she lived with us a matter of three weeks it might be; and then, whether she were somethink of a gipsy in her blood or what not, but one morning she out of her bed afore any of us had opened a eye, and neither track nor yet trace of her have I set eyes on since. Master was wonderful put about, and had all the ponds dragged: but it's my belief she was had away by them gipsies, for there was singing round the house for as much as an hour the night she went, and Parkes he declares as he heard them a-calling in the woods all that afternoon. Dear, dear! an odd child she was, so silent in her ways and all; but I was wonderful taken up with her, so domesticated she was—surprising."

"And what about the little boy?" said Stephen.

"Ah, that pore boy!" sighed Mrs. Bunch. "He were a foreigner— Jevanny he called himself—and he came a-tweaking his urdy gurdy round and about the drive one winter day, and Master ad him in that minute, and ast all about where he came from, and how old he was, and how he made his way, and where was his relatives, and all as kind as heart could wish. But it went the same way with him. They're a hunruly lot, them foreign nations, I do suppose, and he was off one fine morning just the same as the girl. Why he went and what he done was our question for as much as a year after: for he never took his urdy gurdy, and there it lays on the shelf."

The remainder of the evening was spent by Stephen in miscellaneous cross-examination of Mrs. Bunch and in efforts to extract a tune from the hurdy gurdy.

That night he had a curious dream. At the end of the passage at the top of the house, in which his bedroom was situated, there was an old disused bathroom. It was kept locked, but the upper half of the door was glazed, and, since the muslin curtains which used to hang there had long been gone, you could look in and see the lead-lined bath affixed to the wall on the right hand, with its head towards the window. On the night of which I am speaking, Stephen Elliott found himself, as he thought, looking through the glazed door. The moon was shining through the window, and he was gazing at a figure which lay in the bath. His description of what he saw reminds me of what I once beheld myself in the famous vaults of St. Michan's Church in Dublin, which possess the horrid property of preserving corpses from decay for centuries. A figure inexpressibly thin and pathetic, of a dusty leaden colour, enveloped in a shroud-like garment, the thin lips crooked into a faint and dreadful smile, the hands pressed tightly over the region of the heart. As he looked upon it, a distant, almost inaudible moan seemed to issue from its lips, and the arms began to stir. The terror of the sight forced Stephen backwards, and he awoke to the fact that he was indeed standing on the cold boarded floor of the passage in the full light of the moon. With a courage which I do not think can be common among boys of his age he went to the door of the bathroom to ascertain if the figure of his dream were really there. It was not, and he went back to bed. Mrs. Bunch was much impressed next morning by his story, and went so far as to replace the muslin curtain over the glazed door of the bathroom. Mr. Abney, moreover, to whom he confided his experiences at breakfast, was greatly interested, and made notes of the matter in what he called "his book."

The spring equinox was approaching, as Mr. Abney frequently reminded his young cousin, adding that this had been always considered by the ancients to be a critical time for the young: that Stephen would do well to take care of himself, and to shut his bedroom window at night; and that Censorinus had some valuable remarks on the subject. Two incidents that occurred about this time made an impression upon Stephen's mind.

The first was after an unusually uneasy and oppressed night that he had passed—though he could not recall any particular dream that he had had.

The following evening Mrs. Bunch was occupying herself in mending his nightgown. "Gracious me, Master Stephen!" she broke forth, rather irritably, "how do you manage to tear your nightdress all to flinders this way? Look here, sir, what trouble you do give to poor servants that have to darn and mend after you!"

There was indeed a most destructive and apparently wanton series of slits or scorings in the garment, which would undoubtedly require a skilful needle to make good. They were confined to the left side of the chest—long, parallel slits, about six inches in length, some of them not quite piercing the texture of the linen. Stephen could only express his entire ignorance of their origin: he was sure they were not there the night before. "But," he said, "Mrs. Bunch, they're just the same as the scratches on the outside of my bedroom door; and I'm sure I never had anything to do with making *them*."

Mrs. Bunch gazed at him open-mouthed, then snatched up a candle, departed hastily from the room, and was heard making her way upstairs. In a few minutes she came down. "Well," she said, "Master Stephen, it's a funny thing to me how them marks and scratches can a come there—too high up for any cat or dog to ave made 'em, much less a rat: for all the world like a Chinaman's finger nails, as my uncle in the tea trade used to tell us of when we was girls together. I wouldn't say nothink to Master, not if I was you, Master Stephen, my dear; and just turn the key of the door when you go to your bed."

"I always do, Mrs. Bunch, as soon as I've said my prayers."

"Ah, that's a good child: always say your prayers, and then no one can't hurt you."

Herewith Mrs. Bunch addressed herself to mending the injured nightgown, with intervals of meditation, until bed-time. This was on a Friday night in March 1812.

On the following evening the usual duet of Stephen and Mrs. Bunch was augmented by the sudden arrival of Mr. Parkes, the butler, who as a rule kept himself rather to himself in his own pantry. He did not see that Stephen was there: he was, moreover, flustered and less slow of speech than was his wont. "Master may get up his own wine, if he likes of an evening," was his first remark. "Either I do it in the daytime or not at all, Mrs. Bunch. I don't know what it may be: very like it's the rats, or the wind got into the cellars; but I'm not so young as I was, and I can't go through with it as I have done."

"Well, Mr. Parkes, you know it is a surprising place for the rats, is the Hall."

"I'm not denying that, Mrs. Bunch; and, to be sure, many a time I've heard the tale from the men in the shipyards about the rat that could speak. I never laid no confidence in that before; but tonight, if I'd demeaned myself to lay my ear to the door of the further bin, I could pretty much have heard what they was saying."

"Oh, there, Mr. Parkes, I've no patience with your fancies! Rats talking in the wine-cellar, indeed!"

"Well, Mrs. Bunch, I've no wish to argue with you: all I say is, if you choose to go to the far bin, and lay your ear to the door, you may prove my words this minute."

"What nonsense you do talk. Mr. Parkes—not fit for children to listen to! Why, you'll be frightening Master Stephen there out of his wits."

"What! Master Stephen?" said Parkes, awaking to the consciousness of his presence. "Master Stephen knows well enough when I'm a playing a joke with you, Mrs. Bunch."

In fact, Master Stephen knew much too well to suppose that Mr. Parkes had in the first instance intended a joke. He was interested, not altogether pleasantly, in the situation; but all his questions were unsuccessful in inducing the butler to give any more detailed account of his experiences in the wine-cellar.

We have now arrived at March 24th, 1812. It was a day of curious experiences for Stephen: a windy, noisy day, which filled the house and the gardens with a restless impression. As Stephen stood by the fence of the grounds and looked out into the park, he felt as if an endless procession of unseen people were sweeping past him on the wind, borne on resistlessly and aimlessly, vainly striving to stop themselves, to catch at something that might arrest their flight and bring them once again into contact with the living world of which they had formed a part. After luncheon that day Mr. Abney said: "Stephen, my boy, do you think you could manage to come to me tonight as late as eleven o'clock in my study? I shall be busy until that time, and I wish to show you something connected with your future life which it is most important that you should know. You are not to mention this matter to Mrs. Bunch nor to any one else in the house; and you had better go to your room at the usual time."

Here was a new excitement added to life: Stephen eagerly grasped at the opportunity of sitting up till eleven o'clock. He looked in at the library door on his way upstairs that evening, and saw a brazier, which he had often noticed in the corner of the room, moved out before the fire; an old silver-gilt cup stood on the table, filled with red wine, and some written sheets of paper lay near it. Mr. Abney was sprinkling some incense on the brazier from a round silver box as Stephen passed, but did not seem to notice his step.

The wind had fallen, and there was a still night and a full moon. At about ten o'clock Stephen was standing at the open window of his bedroom looking out over the country. Still as the night was, the mysterious population of the distant moonlit woods was not yet lulled to rest. From time to time strange cries as of lost and despairing wanderers sounded from across the mere. They might be the notes of owls or water birds, yet they did not quite resemble either sound. Were not they coming nearer? Now they sounded from the nearer side of the water, and in a few moments they seemed to be floating about among the shrubberies. Then they ceased; but just as Stephen was thinking of shutting the window and resuming his reading of Robinson Crusoe, he caught sight of two figures standing on the gravelled terrace that ran along the garden side of the Hall—two figures of a boy and girl, as it seemed: they stood side by side, looking up at the windows. Something in the form of the girl recalled irresistibly his dream of the figure in the bath. The boy inspired him with more acute fear. Whilst the girl stood still, half smiling, with her hands clasped over her heart, the boy, a thin shape, with black hair and ragged clothing, raised his arms in the air with an appearance of menace and of unappeasable hunger and longing. The moon shone upon his almost transparent hands, and Stephen saw that his nails were fearfully long and that the light shone through them. As he stood with his arms thus raised, he disclosed a terrifying spectacle. On the left side of his chest there opened a black and gaping rent; and there fell upon Stephen's brain, rather than upon his ear, the impression of one of those hungry and desolate cries that he had heard resounding over the woods of Aswarby all that evening. In another moment this dreadful pair had moved swiftly and noiselessly over the dry gravel, and he saw them no more. Inexpressibly frightened as he was, he determined to take his candle and go down to Mr. Abney's study; for the hour appointed for their meeting was near at hand. The study or library opened out of the front hall on one side; and Stephen, urged on by his terrors, did not take long in getting there. To effect an entrance was not so easy. It was not locked, he felt sure, for the key was on the outside of the door as usual. His repeated knocks produced no answer. Mr. Abney was engaged: he was speaking. What? why did he try to cry out? and why was the cry choked in his throat? Had he, too, seen the mysterious children who were tracking their prey round that house of terrors? But now everything was quiet, and the door yielded to Stephen's terrified and frantic pushing. He did not come to himself for many hours after he had looked in.

On the table in Mr. Abney's study certain papers were found which explained the situation to Stephen Elliott when he was of an age to understand them. The most important sentences were as follows:—

"It was a belief very strongly and generally held by the ancients— of whose wisdom in these matters I have had such experience as induces me to place confidence in their assertions—that by enacting certain processes, which to us moderns have something of a barbaric complexion, a very remarkable enlightenment of the spiritual faculties in man may be attained: that, for example, by absorbing the personalities of a certain number of his fellow-creatures, an individual may gain a complete ascendency over those orders of spiritual beings which control the elemental forces of our universe. It is recorded of Simon Magus that he was able to fly in the air, to become invisible, or to assume any form he pleased, by the agency of the soul of a boy whom, to use the libellous phrase employed by the author of the *Clementine Recognitions*, he had 'murdered.' I find it set down, moreover, with considerable detail in the writings of Hermes Trismegistus that similar happy results may be produced by the absorption of the hearts of not less than three human beings below the age of twenty-one years. To the testing of the truth of this receipt I have devoted the greater part of the last twenty years, selecting as the *corpora vilia* of my experiment such persons as could conveniently be removed without occasioning a sensible gap in society. The first step I effected by the removal of one Phœbe Stanley, a girl of gipsy extraction, on March 24th, 1792. The second, by the removal of a wandering Italian lad, named Giovanni Paoli, on the night of March 23rd, 1805. The final 'victim'—to employ a word repugnant in the highest degree to my feelings—must be my cousin, Stephen Elliott. His day must be this March 24th, 1812.

"The best means of effecting the required absorption is to remove the heart from the *living* subject, to reduce it to ashes, and to mingle them with about a pint of some red wine, preferably port. The remains of the first two subjects; at least, it will be well to conceal: a disused bathroom or wine-cellar will be found convenient for such a purpose. Some annoyance may be experienced from the psychic portion of the subjects—which popular language dignifies with the name of ghosts. But the man of philosophic temperament—to whom alone the experiment is appropriate—will be little prone to attach importance to the feeble efforts of these beings to wreak their vengeance on him. I contemplate with the liveliest satisfaction the enlarged and emancipated existence which the experiment, if successful, will confer on me; not only placing me beyond the reach of human justice, but eliminating to a great extent the prospect of death itself."

Mr. Abney was found in his chair, his head thrown back, his face stamped with an expression of rage, fright, and mortal pain. In his left side was a terrible lacerated wound, exposing the heart. There was no blood on his hands, and a long knife that lay on the table was perfectly clean. A savage wild cat might have inflicted the injuries. The window of the study was open, and it was the opinion of the coroner that Mr. Abney had met his death by the agency of some wild creature. But Stephen Elliott's study of the papers I have quoted led him to a very different conclusion.

A young girl happened to die of a fever while away on a visit to some friends, and her father thought it safer not to bring her home, but to have her buried in the nearest churchyard. However, a few nights after his return home, he was awakened by a mournful wail at the window, and a voice cried, "I am alone; I am alone; I am alone!" Then the poor father knew well what it meant, and he prayed in the name of God that the spirit of his dead child might rest in peace until the morning. And when the day broke he arose and set off to the strange burial ground, and there he drew the coffin from the earth, and had it carried all the way back from Cork to Mayo; and after he had laid the dead in the old graveyard beside his people and his kindred, the spirit of his child had rest, and the mournful cry was no more heard in the night.

Wilde, "Souls of the Dead" (1887)[15]

THE DOLL'S GHOST

F. Marion Crawford

Francis Marion Crawford (1854–1909) was an American writer who was born in Italy and spent most of his time travelling in Europe, where a number of his fantastical, mysterious, and Weird novels and stories were set. His terrifying tales of a drowned revenant corpse in "The Upper Berth" (1886) and the cursed skull of a murdered spouse in "The Screaming Skull" (1908), are two of his most frequently anthologised horror stories.

"The Doll's Ghost" was first published in the 1896 Christmas supplement of the Illustrated London News *and then in his collection* Wandering Ghosts *(1911). It seems a rather unusual choice in these darker examples of the ghost-child subgenre, as it has a fairly unambiguous "happy" ending in that a living child is saved. However, the doll—that double of a child—is not. It is disfigured and lovingly repaired by the toymaker, only to be "smashed to pieces" by "big boys with bad faces" who attack the man's little daughter: certainly, a metaphor for the most serious dangers for an unaccompanied young girl on the streets. However, I include it here because there is an uncanny eeriness to the emotional investment placed in the doll and in the presence of its "ghost". When coupled with the trope of the ghost in the "machine" or possession of dolls found in fictional cult figures such as Annabelle and Chucky, and in recent works such as Susan Hill's novel* Dolly: A Ghost Story *(2010) and played with in films such as William Brent Bell's* The Boy *(2016), Crawford's tale demonstrates an interesting variation on the intertwining themes of children, death, and Horror.*

It was a terrible accident, and for one moment the splendid machinery of Cranston House got out of gear and stood still. The butler emerged from the retirement in which he spent his elegant leisure, two grooms of the chambers appeared simultaneously from opposite directions, there were actually housemaids on the grand staircase, and those who remember the facts most exactly assert that Mrs. Pringle herself positively stood upon the landing. Mrs. Pringle was the housekeeper. As for the head nurse, the under nurse, and the nursery-maid, their feelings cannot be described. The head nurse laid one hand upon the polished marble balustrade and stared stupidly before her, the under nurse stood rigid and pale, leaning against the polished marble wall, and the nursery-maid collapsed and sat down upon the polished marble step, just beyond the limits of the velvet carpet, and frankly burst into tears.

The Lady Gwendolen Lancaster-Douglas-Scroop, youngest daughter of the ninth Duke of Cranston, and aged six years and three months, picked herself up quite alone, and sat down on the third step from the foot of the grand staircase in Cranston House.

"Oh!" ejaculated the butler, and he disappeared again.

"Ah!" responded the grooms of the chambers, as they also went away.

"It's only that doll," Mrs. Pringle was distinctly heard to say, in a tone of contempt.

The under nurse heard her say it. Then the three nurses gathered round Lady Gwendolen and patted her, and gave her unhealthy things out of their pockets, and hurried her out of Cranston House as fast as they could, lest it should be found out upstairs that they had allowed the Lady Gwendolen Lancaster-Douglas-Scroop to tumble down the grand staircase with her doll in her arms. And as the doll was badly broken, the nursery-maid carried it, with the pieces, wrapped up in Lady Gwendolen's little cloak. It was not far to Hyde Park, and when they had reached a quiet place they took means to find out that Lady Gwendolen had no bruises. For the carpet was very thick and soft, and there was thick stuff under it to make it softer.

Lady Gwendolen Douglas-Scroop sometimes yelled, but she never cried. It was because she had yelled that the nurse had allowed her to go downstairs alone with Nina, the doll, under one arm, while she steadied herself with her other hand on the balustrade, and trod upon the polished marble steps beyond the edge of the carpet. So she had fallen, and Nina had come to grief.

When the nurses were quite sure that she was not hurt, they unwrapped the doll and looked at her in her turn. She had been a very beautiful doll, very large, and fair, and healthy, with real yellow hair, and eyelids that would open and shut over very grown-up dark eyes. Moreover, when you moved her right arm up and down she said "Pa-pa," and when you moved the left she said "Ma-ma," very distinctly.

"I heard her say 'Pa' when she fell," said the under nurse, who heard everything. "But she ought to have said 'Pa-pa.'"

"That's because her arm went up when she hit the step," said the head nurse. "She'll say the other 'Pa' when I put it down again."

"Pa," said Nina, as her right arm was pushed down, and speaking through her broken face. It was cracked right across, from the upper corner of the forehead, with a hideous gash, through the nose and down to the little frilled collar of the pale green silk Mother Hubbard frock, and two little three-cornered pieces of porcelain had fallen out.

"I'm sure it's a wonder she can speak at all, being all smashed," said the under nurse.

"You'll have to take her to Mr. Puckler," said her superior. "It's not far, and you'd better go at once."

Lady Gwendolen was occupied in digging a hole in the ground with a little spade, and paid no attention to the nurses.

"What are you doing?" enquired the nursery-maid, looking on.

"Nina's dead, and I'm diggin' her a grave," replied her ladyship thoughtfully.

"Oh, she'll come to life again all right," said the nursery-maid.

The under nurse wrapped Nina up again and departed. Fortunately a kind soldier, with very long legs and a very small cap, happened to be there; and as he had nothing to do, he offered to see the under nurse safely to Mr. Puckler's and back.

Mr. Bernard Puckler and his little daughter lived in a little house in a little alley, which led out off a quiet little street not very far from Belgrave Square. He was the great doll doctor, and his extensive practice lay in the most aristocratic quarter. He mended dolls of all sizes and ages, boy dolls and girl dolls, baby dolls in long clothes, and grown-up dolls in fashionable gowns, talking dolls and dumb dolls, those that shut their eyes when they lay down, and those whose eyes had to be shut for them by means of a mysterious wire. His daughter Else was only just over twelve years old, but she was already very clever at mending dolls' clothes, and at doing their hair, which is harder than you might think, though the dolls sit quite still while it is being done.

Mr. Puckler had originally been a German, but he had dissolved his nationality in the ocean of London many years ago, like a great many foreigners. He still had one or two German friends, however, who came on Saturday evenings, and smoked with him and played picquet or "skat" with him for farthing points, and called him "Herr Doctor," which seemed to please Mr. Puckler very much.

He looked older than he was, for his beard was rather long and ragged, his hair was grizzled and thin, and he wore horn-rimmed spectacles. As for Else, she was a thin, pale child, very quiet and neat, with dark eyes and brown hair that was plaited down her back and tied with a bit of black ribbon. She mended the dolls' clothes and took the dolls back to their homes when they were quite strong again.

The house was a little one, but too big for the two people who lived in it. There was a small sitting-room on the street, and the workshop was at the back, and there were three rooms upstairs. But the father and daughter lived most of their time in the workshop, because they were generally at work, even in the evenings.

Mr. Puckler laid Nina on the table and looked at her a long time, till the tears began to fill his eyes behind the horn-rimmed spectacles. He was a very susceptible man, and he often fell in love with the dolls he mended, and found it hard to part with them when they had smiled at him for a few days. They were real little people to him, with characters and thoughts and feelings of their own, and he was very tender with them all. But some attracted him especially from the first, and when they were brought to him maimed and injured, their state seemed so pitiful to him that the tears came easily. You must remember that he had lived among dolls during a great part of his life, and understood them.

"How do you know that they feel nothing?" he went on to say to Else. "You must be gentle with them. It costs nothing to be kind to the little beings, and perhaps it makes a difference to them."

And Else understood him, because she was a child, and she knew that she was more to him than all the dolls.

He fell in love with Nina at first sight, perhaps because her beautiful brown glass eyes were something like Else's own, and he loved Else first and best, with all his heart. And, besides, it was a very sorrowful case. Nina had evidently not been long in the world, for her complexion was perfect, her hair was smooth where it should be smooth, and curly where it should be curly, and her silk clothes were perfectly new. But across her face was that frightful gash, like a sabre-cut, deep and shadowy within, but clean and sharp at the edges. When he tenderly pressed her head to close the gaping wound, the edges made a fine grating sound, that was painful to hear, and the lids of the dark eyes quivered and trembled as though Nina were suffering dreadfully.

"Poor Nina!" he exclaimed sorrowfully. "But I shall not hurt you much, though you will take a long time to get strong."

He always asked the names of the broken dolls when they were brought to him, and sometimes the people knew what the children called them, and told him. He liked "Nina" for a name. Altogether and in every way she pleased him more than any doll he had seen for many years, and he felt drawn to her, and made up his mind to make her perfectly strong and sound, no matter how much labour it might cost him.

Mr. Puckler worked patiently a little at a time, and Else watched him. She could do nothing for poor Nina, whose clothes needed no mending. The longer the doll doctor worked, the more fond he became of the yellow hair and the beautiful brown glass eyes. He sometimes forgot all the other dolls that were waiting to be mended, lying side by side on a shelf, and sat for an hour gazing at Nina's face, while he racked his ingenuity for some new invention by which to hide even the smallest trace of the terrible accident.

She was wonderfully mended. Even he was obliged to admit that; but the scar was still visible to his keen eyes, a very fine line right across the face, downwards from right to left. Yet all the conditions had been most favourable for a cure, since the cement had set quite hard at the first attempt and the weather had been fine and dry, which makes a great difference in a dolls' hospital.

At last he knew that he could do no more, and the under nurse had already come twice to see whether the job was finished, as she coarsely expressed it.

"Nina is not quite strong yet," Mr. Puckler had answered each time, for he could not make up his mind to face the parting.

And now he sat before the square deal table at which he worked, and Nina lay before him for the last time with a big brown paper box beside her. It stood there like her coffin, waiting for her, he thought. He must put her into it, and lay tissue paper over her dear face, and then put on the lid, and at the thought of tying the string his sight was dim with tears again. He was never to look into the glassy depths of the beautiful brown eyes any more, nor to hear the little wooden voice say "Pa-pa" and "Ma-ma." It was a very painful moment.

In the vain hope of gaining time before the separation, he took up the little sticky bottles of cement and glue and gum and colour, looking at each one in turn, and then at Nina's face. And all his small tools lay there, neatly arranged in a row, but he knew that he could not use them again for Nina. She was quite strong at last, and in a country where there should be no cruel children to hurt her she might live a hundred years, with only that almost imperceptible line across her face to tell of the fearful thing that had befallen her on the marble steps of Cranston House.

Suddenly Mr. Puckler's heart was quite full, and he rose abruptly from his seat and turned away.

"Else," he said unsteadily, "you must do it for me. I cannot bear to see her go into the box."

So he went and stood at the window with his back turned, while Else did what he had not the heart to do.

"Is it done?" he asked, not turning round. "Then take her away, my dear. Put on your hat, and take her to Cranston House quickly, and when you are gone I will turn round."

Else was used to her father's queer ways with the dolls, and though she had never seen him so much moved by a parting, she was not much surprised.

"Come back quickly," he said, when he heard her hand on the latch. "It is growing late, and I should not send you at this hour. But I cannot bear to look forward to it any more."

When Else was gone, he left the window and sat down in his place before the table again, to wait for the child to come back. He touched the place where Nina had lain, very gently, and he recalled the softly tinted pink face, and the glass eyes, and the ringlets of yellow hair, till he could almost see them.

The evenings were long, for it was late in the spring. But it began to grow dark soon, and Mr. Puckler wondered why Else did not come back. She had been gone an hour and a half, and that was much longer than he had expected, for it was barely half a mile from Belgrave Square to Cranston House. He reflected that the child might have been kept waiting, but as the twilight deepened he grew anxious, and walked up and down in the dim workshop, no longer thinking of Nina, but of Else, his own living child, whom he loved.

An undefinable, disquieting sensation came upon him by fine degrees, a chilliness and a faint stirring of his thin hair, joined with a wish to be in any company rather than to be alone much longer. It was the beginning of fear.

He told himself in strong German-English that he was a foolish old man, and he began to feel about for the matches in the dusk. He knew just where they should be, for he always kept them in the same place, close to the little tin box that held bits of sealing-wax of various colours, for some kinds of mending. But somehow he could not find the matches in the gloom.

Something had happened to Else, he was sure, and as his fear increased, he felt as though it might be allayed if he could get a light and see what time it was. Then he called himself a foolish old man again, and the sound of his own voice startled him in the dark. He could not find the matches.

The window was grey still; he might see what time it was if he went close to it, and he could go and get matches out of the cupboard afterwards. He stood back from the table, to get out of the way of the chair, and began to cross the board floor.

Something was following him in the dark. There was a small pattering, as of tiny feet upon the boards. He stopped and listened, and the roots of his hair tingled. It was nothing, and he was a foolish old man. He made two steps more, and he was sure that he heard the little pattering again. He turned his back to the window, leaning against the sash so that the panes began to crack, and he faced the dark. Everything was quite still, and it smelt of paste and cement and wood-filings as usual.

"Is that you, Else?" he asked, and he was surprised by the fear in his voice.

There was no answer in the room, and he held up his watch and tried to make out what time it was by the grey dusk that was just not darkness. So far as he could see, it was within two or three minutes of ten o'clock. He had been a long time alone. He was shocked, and frightened for Else, out in London, so late, and he almost ran across the room to the door. As he fumbled for the latch, he distinctly heard the running of the little feet after him.

"Mice!" he exclaimed feebly, just as he got the door open.

He shut it quickly behind him, and felt as though some cold thing had settled on his back and were writhing upon him. The passage was quite dark, but he found his hat and was out in the alley in a moment, breathing more freely, and surprised to find how much light there still was in the open air. He could see the pavement clearly under his feet, and far off in the street to which the alley led he could hear the laughter and calls of children, playing some game out of doors. He wondered how he could have been so nervous, and for an instant he thought of going back into the house to wait quietly for Else. But instantly he felt that nervous fright of something stealing over him again. In any case it was better to walk up to Cranston House and ask the servants about the child. One of the women had perhaps taken a fancy to her, and was even now giving her tea and cake.

He walked quickly to Belgrave Square, and then up the broad streets, listening as he went, whenever there was no other sound, for the tiny footsteps. But he heard nothing, and was laughing at himself when he rang the servants' bell at the big house. Of course, the child must be there.

The person who opened the door was quite an inferior person, for it was a back door, but affected the manners of the front, and stared at Mr. Puckler superciliously under the strong light.

No little girl had been seen, and he knew "nothing about no dolls."

"She is my little girl," said Mr. Puckler tremulously, for all his anxiety was returning tenfold, "and I am afraid something has happened."

The inferior person said rudely that "nothing could have happened to her in that house, because she had not been there, which was a jolly good reason why;" and Mr. Puckler was obliged to admit that the man ought to know, as it was his business to keep the door and let people in. He wished to be allowed to speak to the under nurse, who knew him; but the man was ruder than ever, and finally shut the door in his face.

When the doll doctor was alone in the street, he steadied himself by the railing, for he felt as though he were breaking in two, just as some dolls break, in the middle of the backbone.

Presently he knew that he must be doing something to find Else, and that gave him strength. He began to walk as quickly as he could through the streets, following every highway and byway which his little girl might have taken on her errand. He also asked several policemen in vain if they had seen her, and most of them answered him kindly, for they saw that he was a sober man and in his right senses, and some of them had little girls of their own.

It was one o'clock in the morning when he went up to his own door again, worn out and hopeless and broken-hearted. As he turned the key in the lock, his heart stood still, for he knew that he was awake and not dreaming, and that he really heard those tiny footsteps pattering to meet him inside the house along the passage.

But he was too unhappy to be much frightened any more, and his heart went on again with a dull regular pain, that found its way all through him with every pulse. So he went in, and hung up his hat in the dark, and found the matches in the cupboard and the candlestick in its place in the corner.

Mr. Puckler was so much overcome and so completely worn out that he sat down in his chair before the work-table and almost fainted, as his face dropped forward upon his folded hands. Beside him the solitary candle burned steadily with a low flame in the still warm air.

"Else! Else!" he moaned against his yellow knuckles. And that was all he could say, and it was no relief to him. On the contrary, the very sound of the name was a new and sharp pain that pierced his ears and his head and his very soul. For every time he repeated the name it meant that little Else was dead, somewhere out in the streets of London in the dark.

He was so terribly hurt that he did not even feel something pulling gently at the skirt of his old coat, so gently that it was like the nibbling of a tiny mouse. He might have thought that it was really a mouse if he had noticed it.

"Else! Else!" he groaned right against his hands.

Then a cool breath stirred his thin hair, and the low flame of the one candle dropped down almost to a mere spark, not flickering as though a draught were going to blow it out, but just dropping down as if it were tired out. Mr. Puckler felt his hands stiffening with fright under his face; and there was a faint rustling sound, like some small silk thing blown in a gentle breeze. He sat up straight, stark and scared, and a small wooden voice spoke in the stillness.

"Pa-pa," it said, with a break between the syllables.

Mr. Puckler stood up in a single jump, and his chair fell over backwards with a smashing noise upon the wooden floor. The candle had almost gone out.

It was Nina's doll voice that had spoken, and he should have known it among the voices of a hundred other dolls. And yet there was something more in it, a little human ring, with a pitiful cry and a call for help, and the wail of a hurt child. Mr. Puckler stood up, stark and stiff, and tried to look round, but at first he could not, for he seemed to be frozen from head to foot.

Then he made a great effort, and he raised one hand to each of his temples, and pressed his own head round as he would have turned a doll's. The candle was burning so low that it might as well have been out altogether, for any light it gave, and the room seemed quite dark at first. Then he saw something. He would not have believed that he could be more frightened than he had been just before that. But he was, and his knees shook, for he saw the doll standing in the middle of the floor, shining with a faint and ghostly radiance, her beautiful glassy brown eyes fixed on his. And across her face the very thin line of the break he had mended shone as though it were drawn in light with a fine point of white flame.

Yet there was something more in the eyes, too; there was something human, like Else's own, but as if only the doll saw him through them, and not Else. And there was enough of Else to bring back all his pain and to make him forget his fear.

"Else! my little Else!" he cried aloud.

The small ghost moved, and its doll-arm slowly rose and fell with a stiff, mechanical motion.

"Pa-pa," it said.

It seemed this time that there was even more of Else's tone echoing somewhere between the wooden notes that reached his ears so distinctly, and yet so far away. Else was calling him, he was sure.

His face was perfectly white in the gloom, but his knees did not shake any more, and he felt that he was less frightened.

"Yes, child! But where? Where?" he asked. "Where are you, Else?"

"Pa-pa!"

The syllables died away in the quiet room. There was a low rustling of silk, the glassy brown eyes turned slowly away, and Mr. Puckler heard the pitter-patter of the small feet in the bronze kid slippers as the figure ran straight to the door. Then the candle burned high again, the room was full of light, and he was alone.

Mr. Puckler passed his hand over his eyes and looked about him. He could see everything quite clearly, and he felt that he must have been dreaming, though he was standing instead of sitting down, as he should have been if he had just waked up. The candle burned brightly now. There were the dolls to be mended, lying in a row with their toes up. The third one had lost her right shoe, and Else was making one. He knew that, and he was certainly not dreaming now. He had not been dreaming when he had come in from his fruitless search and had heard the doll's footsteps running to the door. He had not fallen asleep in his chair. How could he possibly have fallen asleep when his heart was breaking? He had been awake all the time.

He steadied himself, set the fallen chair upon its legs, and said to himself again very emphatically that he was a foolish old man. He ought to be out in the streets looking for his child, asking questions, and enquiring at the police stations, where all accidents were reported as soon as they were known, or at the hospitals.

"Pa-pa!"

The longing, wailing, pitiful little wooden cry rang from the passage, outside the door, and Mr. Puckler stood for an instant with white face, transfixed and rooted to the spot. A moment later his hand was on the latch. Then he was in the passage, with the light streaming from the open door behind him.

Quite at the other end he saw the little phantom shining clearly in the shadow, and the right hand seemed to beckon to him as the arm rose and fell once more. He knew all at once that it had not come to frighten him but to lead him, and when it disappeared, and he walked boldly towards the door, he knew that it was in the street outside, waiting for him. He forgot that he was tired and had eaten no supper, and had walked many miles, for a sudden hope ran through and through him, like a golden stream of life.

And sure enough, at the corner of the alley, and at the corner of the street, and out in Belgrave Square, he saw the small ghost flitting before him. Sometimes it was only a shadow, where there was other light, but then the glare of the lamps made a pale green sheen on its little Mother Hubbard frock of silk; and sometimes, where the streets were dark and silent, the whole figure shone out brightly, with its yellow curls and rosy neck. It seemed to trot along like a tiny child, and Mr. Puckler could almost hear the pattering of the bronze kid slippers on the pavement as it ran. But it went very fast, and he could only just keep up with it, tearing along with his hat on the back of his head and his thin hair blown by the night breeze, and his horn-rimmed spectacles firmly set upon his broad nose.

On and on he went, and he had no idea where he was. He did not even care, for he knew certainly that he was going the right way.

Then at last, in a wide, quiet street, he was standing before a big, sober-looking door that had two lamps on each side of it, and a polished brass bell-handle, which he pulled.

And just inside, when the door was opened, in the bright light, there was the little shadow, and the pale green sheen of the little silk dress, and once more the small cry came to his ears, less pitiful, more longing.

"Pa-pa!"

The shadow turned suddenly bright, and out of the brightness the beautiful brown glass eyes were turned up happily to his, while the rosy mouth smiled so divinely that the phantom doll looked almost like a little angel just then.

"A little girl was brought in soon after ten o'clock," said the quiet voice of the hospital doorkeeper. "I think they thought she was only stunned. She was holding a big brown-paper box against her, and they could not get it out of her arms. She had a long plait of brown hair that hung down as they carried her."

"She is my little girl," said Mr. Puckler, but he hardly heard his own voice.

He leaned over Else's face in the gentle light of the children's ward, and when he had stood there a minute the beautiful brown eyes opened and looked up to his.

"Pa-pa!" cried Else, softly, "I knew you would come!"

Then Mr. Puckler did not know what he did or said for a moment, and what he felt was worth all the fear and terror and despair that had almost killed him that night. But by and by Else was telling her story, and the nurse let her speak, for there were only two other children in the room, who were getting well and were sound asleep.

"They were big boys with bad faces," said Else, "and they tried to get Nina away from me, but I held on and fought as well as I could till one of them hit me with something, and I don't remember any more, for I tumbled down, and I suppose the boys ran away, and somebody found me there. But I'm afraid Nina is all smashed."

"Here is the box," said the nurse. "We could not take it out of her arms till she came to herself. Should you like to see if the doll is broken?"

And she undid the string cleverly, but Nina was all smashed to pieces. Only the gentle light of the children's ward made a pale green sheen in the folds of the little Mother Hubbard frock.

There lives a lady in London–
　　All alone, and alonie;
She's gone wi' bairn to the clerk's son
　　Doun by the greenwood sae bonnie.

...

She has set her back until a brier–
　　Bonnie were the twa boys she did bear,

But out she's tane a little penknife–
And she's parted them and their sweet life,

...

As she lookit our the castle wa'–
　　All alone, and alonie;
She spied twa bonnie boys playing at the ba'
　　Doun by the greenwood sae bonnie.
"O an thae twa babes were mine–
They should wear the silk and the sabelline,"

"O mother dear, when we were thine–
We neither wore the silks nor the sabelline,"

"But ye took a little penknife, –
An ye parted us and our sweet life,

"But now we're in the heavens hie–
　　And ye have the pains o' hell to dree"–

From "The Cruel Mother"
(Ancient Scottish Ballad)[16]

THE LOST GHOST

Mary E. Wilkins Freeman

Mary Eleanor Wilkins Freeman (1852–1930) was an American novelist and short-story writer whose works are often set in the New England where she was born and raised, and comment on the oppressive and exceptional social and domestic situations of her characters.

The longer version of "The Lost Ghost", published in The Wind in the Rose-Bush *(1903) is no exception, beginning with a rather drawn-out scene between two married women gossiping on a porch. The shorter version, reproduced in this collection and first published in* Everybody's Magazine *that same year, gets to the ghost story much quicker. The tale returns to folkloric tradition by identifying the mother as the perpetrator and for the comparative reader, the difference between the editions offers some very interesting, if seemingly trifling details in this regard. For instance, in the original edition of Freeman's work reprinted here, the child ghost repeatedly calls "I want my mother", but in the extended and anthologised version this is changed to "I can't find my mother". While the latter version of the story still has an eerie feel, the wording in the former implies, I suggest, a more unsettling strength of imperative, a need that is without reason, and more typical of the evil or horrifying ghost child of contemporary Horror. Still, in both versions, that imperative and the sacrifice undertaken by the willing replacement mother is a source for discomfort.*

rs. John Emerson, sitting with her needlework beside the window, looked out and saw Mrs. Rhoda Meserve coming down the street. She rose hurriedly, ran into the cold parlour and brought out one of the best rocking-chairs. She was just in time, after drawing it up beside the opposite window, to greet her friend at the door.

"Good-afternoon," said she. "I declare, I'm real glad to see you. I've been alone all day. John went to the city this morning. I thought of coming over to your house this afternoon, but I couldn't bring my sewing very well. I am putting the ruffles on my new black dress skirt."

Mrs. Meserve settled herself in the parlour rocking-chair, while Mrs. Emerson carried her shawl and hat into the little adjoining bedroom. When she returned Mrs. Meserve was rocking peacefully and was already at work hooking blue wool in and out.

"Well, that's pretty work," said Mrs. Emerson, sitting down at the opposite window and taking up her dress skirt.

"Yes, it is real pretty work. I just *love* to crochet."

The two women rocked and sewed and crocheted in silence for two or three minutes.

"Well, what's the news?" said Mrs. Emerson presently.

"Well, I have got some news," said Mrs. Meserve. "Simon came home with it this noon. The old Sargent place is let."

Mrs. Emerson dropped her sewing and stared.

"Who to?"

"Why, some folks from Boston. The man has got considerable property. He's got a wife and his unmarried sister in the family. The sister's got money, too. He does business in Boston. You know the old Sargent house is a splendid place."

"Yes, it's the handsomest house in town, but—"

"Oh, Simon said they told him about that and he just laughed. Said he wasn't afraid and neither was his wife and sister. Said he'd risk the ghosts rather than little tucked-up sleeping-rooms without any sun, like they've had in the Dayton house."

"Oh, well," said Mrs. Emerson, "it is a beautiful house, and maybe there isn't anything in those stories."

"Nothing in creation would hire me to go into a house that I'd ever heard a word against of that kind," declared Mrs. Meserve with emphasis. "I've seen enough of haunted houses to last me as long as I live."

Mrs. Emerson's face acquired the expression of a hunting hound.

"Have you?" she asked in an intense whisper.

"Yes, before I was married; when I was quite a girl."

Mrs. Meserve hooked up another loop of blue wool. Then she began:

"Of course, I ain't going to say positively that I believe or disbelieve in ghosts, but all I tell you is what I saw. It happened before I was married, when I was a girl and lived in East Wilmington. It was the first year I lived there. You know my family all died five years before that. I told you."

Mrs. Emerson nodded.

"Well, I went there to teach school, and I went to board with a Mrs. Amelia Dennison and her sister, Mrs. Bird. Abby, her name was; Abby Bird. She was a widow; she had never had any children. She had a little money—Mrs. Dennison didn't have any—and she had come to East Wilmington and bought the house they lived in. It was a real pretty house, though it was very old and run down. It had cost Mrs. Bird a good deal to put it in order. I guess that was the reason they took me to board. I thought I was pretty lucky to get in there. I had a nice room, big and sunny and furnished pretty, the paper and paint all new, and everything as neat as wax. I had been there about three weeks before I found it out. I went there in September. I begun my school the first Monday. I remember it was a real cold fall; there was a frost the middle of September, and I had to put on my winter coat. I remember when I came home that night (let me see, I began school on a Monday, and that was two weeks from the next Thursday), I took off my coat downstairs and laid it on the table in the front entry. It was a real nice coat, heavy black broadcloth trimmed with fur; I had had it the winter before.

"Well, though it was hardly the middle of September, it was a real cold night. There was a fire in my little wood-stove. Mrs. Bird made it, I know. She was a real motherly sort of woman; she always seemed to be the happiest when she was doing something to make other folks happy and comfortable.

"Well, that night I sat down beside my nice little fire and ate an apple. There was a plate of nice early apples on my table. Mrs. Bird put them there. I was having a beautiful time, and thinking how lucky I was to have got board in such a place with such nice folks, when I heard a queer little sound at my door. It was such a little hesitating sort of sound that it sounded more like a fumble than a knock, as if some one very timid, with very little hands, was feeling along the door, not quite daring to knock. I said, 'Come in.'

"But nobody came in, and then presently I heard the knock again. Then I got up and opened the door, thinking it was very queer, and I had a frightened feeling without knowing why.

"Well, I opened the door, and the first thing I noticed was a draught of cold air, as if the front door downstairs was open, but there was a strange close smell about the cold draught. It smelled more like a cellar that had been shut up for years, than out-of-doors. Then I saw something. I saw my coat first; the thing that held it was so small that I couldn't see much of anything else. Then I saw a little white face with eyes so scared and wistful that they seemed as if they might eat a hole in anybody's heart. It was a dreadful little face, with something about it which made it different from any other face on earth, but it was so pitiful that somehow it did away a good deal with the dreadfulness. And there were two little hands, spotted purple with the cold, holding up my winter coat, and a strange little far-away voice said, 'I want my mother.'

"'For Heaven's sake,' I said, 'who are you?'

"Then the little voice said again, 'I want my mother.'

"All the time I could smell the cold and I saw that it was about the child; that cold was clinging to her as if she had come out of some deadly cold place. Well, I took my coat, I did not know what else to do, and the cold was clinging to that. It was as cold as if it had come off ice. When I had the coat I could see the child more plainly. She was dressed in one little white garment. I could see dimly through it her little thin body mottled purple with the cold. Her face did not look so cold; that was a clear waxen white. Her hair was dark, but it looked as if it might be dark only because it was so damp, almost wet, and might really be light hair. It clung very close to her forehead, which was round and white. She would have been very beautiful if she had not been so dreadful.

"Then she went away. She did not seem to run or walk like other children. She flitted, like one of those little filmy white butterflies, that don't seem like real ones they are so light, and move as if they had no weight.

"Well, I thought for a moment I should faint away. The room got dark and I heard a singing in my ears. Then I stood in my door, and called first Mrs. Bird and then Mrs. Dennison. It seemed to me I should go mad if I didn't see somebody or something like other folks on the face of the earth. I thought I should never make anybody hear, but I could hear them stepping about downstairs, and I could smell biscuits baking for supper. Somehow the smell of those biscuits seemed the only natural thing left to keep me in my right mind. Finally I heard the entry door open and Mrs. Bird called back:

"'What is it? Did you call, Miss Arms?'

"'Come up here; come up here as quick as you can, both of you,' I screamed out; 'quick, quick, quick!'

"I heard Mrs. Bird tell Mrs. Dennison: 'Come quick, Amelia, something is the matter in Miss Arms's room.' It struck me even then that she expressed herself rather queerly, and it struck me as very queer, indeed, when they both got upstairs and I saw that they knew what had happened.

"'What is it, dear?' asked Mrs. Bird, and her pretty, loving voice had a strained sound.

"'For Heaven's sake,' says I, and I never spoke so before—'for Heaven's sake, what was it brought my coat upstairs?'

"'What was it like?' asked Mrs. Dennison in a sort of failing voice, and she looked at her sister and her sister looked back at her.

"'It was a child I have never seen here before. It looked like a child,' says I, 'but I never saw a child so dreadful, and it had on a night-gown, and said she wanted her mother. Who was it? What was it?'

"I thought for a minute Mrs. Dennison was going to faint, but Mrs. Bird hung onto her and rubbed her hands, and whispered in her ear (she had the cooingest kind of voice), and I ran and got her a glass of cold water. I tell you it took considerable courage to go downstairs alone, but they had set a lamp on the entry table so I could see. I don't believe I could have spunked up enough to have gone downstairs in the dark, thinking every second that child might be close to me. The lamp and the smell of the biscuits baking seemed to sort of keep my courage up, but I tell you I didn't waste much time going down those stairs, and out into the kitchen for a glass of water. I pumped as if the house was afire, and I grabbed the first thing I came across in the shape of a tumbler: it was a painted one that Mrs. Dennison's Sunday-school class gave her, and it was meant for a flower vase.

"Well, I filled it and I ran upstairs. I felt every minute as if something would catch my feet, and I held the glass to Mrs. Dennison's lips, while Mrs. Bird held her head up, and she took a good long swallow; then she looked hard at the tumbler.

"'Yes,' says I, 'I know I got this one, but I took the first I came across, and it isn't hurt a mite.'

"'Don't get the painted flowers wet,' says Mrs. Dennison very feebly, 'they'll wash off.'

"'I'll be real careful,' says I. I knew she set a sight by that painted tumbler.

"The water seemed to do Mrs. Dennison good, for presently she pushed Mrs. Bird away and sat up. She had been laying down on my bed.

"She slid off the bed, and walked sort of tottery to a chair. 'I was silly to give way so,' says she.

"'No, you warn't silly, sister,' says Mrs. Bird. 'I don't know what this means any more than you do, but whatever it is, no one ought to be called silly for being overcome by anything so different from other things which we have known all our lives.'

"Mrs. Dennison looked at her sister, then she looked at me, then back at her sister again, and Mrs. Bird spoke as if she had been asked a question.

"'Yes,' says she, 'I do think Miss Arms ought to be told—that is, I think she ought to be told all we know ourselves.'

"'That isn't much,' said Mrs. Dennison with a dying away sort of sigh.

"'No, there isn't much we do know,' says Mrs. Bird, 'but what little there is she ought to know. I felt as if she ought to when she first came here.'

"'Well, I didn't feel quite right about it,' said Mrs. Dennison, 'but I kept hoping it might stop, and anyway, that it might never trouble her, and you had put so much in the house, and we needed the money.'

"'And aside from the money, we were very anxious to have you come, my dear,' says Mrs. Bird.

"'Yes,' says Mrs. Dennison, 'we wanted the young company in the house; we were lonesome, and we both of us took a great liking to you the minute we set eyes on you.'

"And I guess they meant what they said, both of them. They were beautiful women, and nobody could be any kinder to me than they were, and I never blamed them for not telling me before, and as they said, there wasn't really much to tell.

"They hadn't any sooner fairly bought the house, and moved into it, than they began to see and hear things. Mrs. Bird said they were sitting together in the sitting-room one evening when they heard it the first time. She said her sister was knitting lace and she was reading the *Missionary Herald* (Mrs. Bird was very much interested in mission work), when all of a sudden they heard something. She heard it first and she laid down her *Missionary Herald* and listened, and then Mrs. Dennison she saw her listening and she drops her lace. 'What is it you are listening to, Abby?' says she. Then it came again and they both heard, and the cold shivers went down their backs to hear it, though they didn't know why. 'It's the cat, isn't it?' says Mrs. Bird.

"'It isn't any cat,' says Mrs. Dennison.

"'Oh, I guess it *must* be the cat; maybe she's got a mouse,' says Mrs. Bird, real cheerful, to calm down Mrs. Dennison, for she saw she was 'most scared to death, and she was always afraid of her fainting away. Then she opens the door, and calls, 'Kitty kitty, kitty.' They had brought their cat with them in a basket when they came to East Wilmington to live. It was a real handsome tiger cat, a tommy, and he knew a lot.

"Well, she called 'Kitty, kitty, kitty,' and sure enough the kitty came, and when he came in the door he gave a big yawl that didn't sound unlike what they had heard.

"But Mrs. Dennison, she eyed the cat, and she gave a great screech.

"'What's that? What's that?' says she.

"'What's what?' says Mrs. Bird, pretending to herself that she didn't see what her sister meant.

"'Somethin's got hold of that cat's tail,' says Mrs. Dennison—'somethin's got hold of his tail. It's pulled straight out, an' he can't get away. Just hear him yawl!'

"'It isn't anything,' says Mrs. Bird, but even as she said that she could see a little hand holding fast to that cat's tail, and then the child seemed to sort of clear out of the dimness behind the hand, and the child was sort of laughing then, instead of looking sad. She said that laugh was the most awful and the saddest thing she ever heard.

"Well, she was so dumbfounded that she didn't know what to do, and she couldn't sense at first that it was anything supernatural. She thought it must be one of the neighbour's children who had run away and was making free of their house, and was teasing their cat. So she speaks up sort of sharp.

"'Don't you know that you mustn't pull the kitty's tail?' says she. 'Don't you know you hurt the poor kitty, and she'll scratch you if you don't take care. Poor kitty, you mustn't hurt her.'

"And with that she said the child stopped pulling that cat's tail and went to stroking her just as soft and pitiful, and the cat put his back up and rubbed and purred as if he liked it. The cat never seemed a mite afraid, and that seemed queer, for I had always heard that animals were dreadfully afraid of ghosts; but then, that was a pretty harmless little sort of ghost.

"Well, Mrs. Bird said the child stroked that cat, while she and Mrs. Dennison stood watching it, and holding onto each other; for, no matter how hard they tried to think it was all right, it didn't look right. Finally Mrs. Dennison she spoke.

"'What's your name, little girl?' says she.

"Then the child looks up and stops stroking the cat, and says she wants her mother, just the way she said it to me. Then Mrs. Dennison she gave such a gasp that Mrs. Bird thought she was going to faint away, but she didn't. 'Well, who is your mother?' says she. But the child just says again 'I want my mother—I want my mother.'

"'Where do you live, dear?' says Mrs. Bird.

"'I want my mother,' says the child.

"Everything she would say was, 'I want my mother.'

"Then Mrs. Bird tried to catch hold of the child, for she thought in spite of what she saw that perhaps she was nervous and it was a real child, only perhaps not quite right in its head, that had run away in her little nightgown after she had been put to bed.

"She tried to catch the child; she had an idea of putting a shawl around it and going out—she was such a little thing she could have carried her easy enough—and trying to find out to which of the neighbours she belonged. But the minute she moved toward the child there wasn't any child there; there was only that little voice seeming to come from nothing, saying, 'I want my mother,' and presently that died away.

"Well, that same thing kept happening, or something very much the same. They never knew when they should come across that child, and always she kept saying over and over that she wanted her mother. They never tried talking to her, except once in a while Mrs. Bird would get desperate and ask her something, but the child never seemed to hear it; she always kept right on saying that she wanted her mother.

"After they had told me all they had to tell about their experience with the child, they told me about the house and the people that had lived there before they did. It seemed something dreadful had happened in that house. And the land agent had never let on to them. I don't think they would have bought it if he had, no matter how cheap it was, for even if folks aren't really afraid of anything, they don't want to live in houses where such dreadful things have happened that you keep thinking about them. I know after they told me I should never have stayed there another night if I hadn't thought so much of them, no matter how comfortable I was made, and I never was nervous either. But I stayed. Of course, it didn't happen in my room. If it had I could not have stayed."

"What was it?" asked Mrs. Emerson in an awed voice.

"It was an awful thing. That child had lived in the house with her father and mother two years before. They had come, or the father had, from a real good family. He had a good situation, he was a drummer for a big leather house in the city, and they lived real pretty, with plenty to do with. But the mother was a real wicked woman. She was as handsome as a picture, and they said she came from good sort of people enough in Boston, but she was bad clean through, though she was real pretty spoken, and 'most everybody liked her. She used to dress out and make a great show, and she never seemed to take much interest in the child, and folk began to say she wasn't treated right.

"The woman had a hard time keeping a girl. For some reason one wouldn't stay. They would leave and then talk about her awfully—tell all kinds of things. People didn't believe it at first; then they began to. They said that the woman made that little thing, though she wasn't much over five years old, and small and babyish for her age, do most all of the work. They said they'd seen her carrying in sticks of wood 'most as big as she was many a time, and they'd heard her mother scolding her. The woman was a fine singer, and had a voice like a screech-owl when she scolded.

"The father was away most of the time, and when that happened he had been away out West for some weeks. There had been a married man hanging about the mother for some time, and folks had talked some; but they weren't sure there was anything wrong, and he was a man very high up, with money, so they kept pretty still for fear he would hear of it and make trouble for them; and of course nobody was sure, though folks did say afterward that the father of the child had ought to have been told.

"He set his eyes by his wife, too. They said all he seemed to think of was to earn money to buy things to deck her out in. And he about worshipped the child, too. They said he was a real nice man. The men that are treated so bad mostly are real nice men. I've always noticed that.

"Well, one morning that man that there had been whispers about was missing. He had been gone quite awhile, though, before they really knew that he was missing, because he had gone away and told his wife that he had to go to New York on business and might be gone a week.

"Then folks began to ask where was that woman, and they found out by comparing notes that nobody had seen her since the man went away.

"Well, there was this house shut up, and the man and woman missing, and the child. Then all of a sudden one of the women that lived the nearest remembered something. She remembered that she had waked up three nights running, thinking she heard a child crying somewhere, and once she waked up her husband, but he said it must be the Bisbee's girl, and she thought it must be. The child wasn't well and was always crying. It used to have colic spells, especially at night. So she didn't think any more about it until this came up, then all of a sudden she did think of it. She told what she had heard, and finally folks began to think they had better enter that house and see if there was anything wrong.

"Well, they did enter it, and they found that child dead, locked in one of the rooms. (Mrs. Dennison and Mrs. Bird never used that room; it was a back bedroom on the second floor.)

"Yes, they found that poor child there, starved to death, and frozen, though they weren't sure she had frozen to death, for she was in bed with clothes enough to keep her pretty warm when she was alive. But she had been there a week, and she was nothing but skin and bone.

"Mrs. Dennison said she couldn't really believe that the woman had meant to have her own child starved to death. Probably she thought the little thing would raise somebody, or folks would try to get in the house and find her. Well, whatever she thought, there the child was dead.

"But that wasn't all. The father came home, right in the midst of it, the child was just buried, and he was beside himself. And—he went on the track of his wife, and he found her, and he shot her dead; it was in all the papers at the time; then he disappeared. Nothing had been seen of him since. Mrs. Dennison said that she thought he had either made 'way with himself or got out of the country, nobody knew, but they did know there was something wrong with the house."

"I never heard anything like it in my life," said Mrs. Emerson, staring at the other woman with awestruck eyes.

"But that ain't all," said Mrs. Meserve.

"Did you see it again?" Mrs. Emerson asked.

"Yes, I saw it a number of times before the last time. It was lucky I wasn't nervous or I never could have stayed there, much as I liked the place and much as I thought of those two women; they were beautiful women, and no mistake. I loved those women. I hope Mrs. Dennison will come and see me sometime.

"Well, I stayed, and I never knew when I'd see that child. I can't tell you how I dreaded seeing her, and worse than the seeing her was the hearing her say, 'I want my mother.' It was enough to make your blood run cold. I never heard a living child cry for its mother that was anything so pitiful as that dead one. It was enough to break your heart.

"She used to come and say that to Mrs. Bird oftener than any one else. Once I heard Mrs. Bird say she wondered if it was possible that the poor little thing couldn't really find her mother in the other world, she had been such a wicked woman.

"But Mrs. Dennison told her she didn't think she ought to speak so, nor even think so, and Mrs. Bird said she shouldn't wonder if she was right. Mrs. Bird was always very easy to put in the wrong. She was a good woman, and one that couldn't do things enough for other folks. It seemed as if that was what she lived on. I don't think she was ever so scared by that poor little ghost, as much as she pitied it, and she was 'most heart-broken because she couldn't do anything for it, as she could have done for a live child.

"'It seems to me sometimes as if I should die, if I can't get that awful little white robe off that child and get her in some clothes and feed her and stop her wanting her mother,' I heard her say once, and she was in earnest. She cried when she said it. That wasn't long before she died.

"Now I am coming to the strangest part of it all. Mrs. Bird died very sudden. One morning—it was Saturday and there wasn't any school—I went downstairs to breakfast; there was nobody there but Mrs. Dennison. She was pouring out the coffee when I came in.

"'Why, where's Mrs. Bird?' says I.

"'Abby ain't feeling very well this morning,' says she; 'there isn't much the matter, I guess, but she didn't sleep very well, and her head aches, and she's sort of chilly, and I told her I thought she'd better stay in bed till the house gets warm.'

"'Maybe she's got cold,' says I.

"'Yes, I guess she has,' says Mrs. Dennison. 'I guess she's got cold. She'll be up before long. Abby ain't one to stay in bed a minute longer than she can help.'

"Well, we went on eating our breakfast, and all at once a shadow flickered across one wall of the room and over the ceiling, the way a shadow will sometimes when somebody passes the window outside. Mrs. Dennison and I both looked out of the window; then Mrs. Dennison she gives a scream.

"'Why, Abby's crazy,' says she. 'There she is out this bitter cold morning, and—and—' She didn't finish, but she meant the child. For we were both looking out, and we saw, as plain as we ever saw anything in our lives, Mrs. Abby Bird walking off over the white snow-path with that child holding fast to her hand, nestling close to her as if she had found her own mother.

"'She's dead,' says Mrs. Dennison, clutching hold of me hard. 'She's dead; my sister is dead!' .

"She was. We hurried upstairs as fast as we could go, and she was dead in her bed, and smiling as if she was dreaming, and one arm and hand was stretched out as if something had hold of it; and it couldn't be straightened even at the last—it lay out over her casket at the funeral."

"Was the child ever seen again?" asked Mrs. Emerson in a shaking voice.

"No," replied Mrs. Meserve, "that child was never seen again after she went out of the yard with Mrs. Bird."

Once on a time, a girl, who had exposed her infant, was milking her ewes in the sheepfold. "Alas!" she said to another damsel similarly employed, "What shall I do? I am invited to a party tonight, and I haven't a proper dress to go in."

"Oh! Yes, you have though," muttered a voice from the top of the sheepfold wall. "Be easy on that score. I will lend you my swaddling-clothes to dance in."

It was the voice of the girl's own child, which she had deserted. At the same moment, an arm darted down from the wall, and stabbed the mother dead.

Metcalfe, Icelandic folklore (1861)[17]

THE SHADOWY THIRD

Ellen Glasgow

Ellen Anderson Gholson Glasgow (1873–1945) was a Pulitzer-prize winning American writer, predominantly known for her political, social, and
romance novels dealing with life in Virginia.

"The Shadowy Third" was published in a Christmas supplement of
Scribner's Magazine where it was illustrated by Elenore Plaisted Abbot,
and then reproduced as the title tale in her only short-story collection The
Shadowy Third and Other Stories (1923). Once again, the villain is a
male guardian, and the motive is greed, but what is particularly enjoyable
about this tale is the juxtaposition between the impression of the child ghost
Dorothea (meaning "Gift of God") as innocent and sweet and the look of
knowledge the narrator sees in the child ghost's eyes—a horrible knowledge
only gained through death. Furthermore, the girl's light airiness and tendency to play is exploited rather deliciously in the demise of her (apparent)
murderer.

hen the call came I remember that I turned from the telephone in a romantic flutter. Though I had spoken only once to the great surgeon, Roland Maradick, I felt on that December afternoon that to speak to him only once—to watch him in the operating-room for a single hour—was an adventure which drained the colour and the excitement from the rest of life. After all these years of work on typhoid and pneumonia cases, I can still feel the delicious tremor of my young pulses; I can still see the winter sunshine slanting through the hospital windows over the white uniforms of the nurses.

"He didn't mention me by name. Can there be a mistake?" I stood, incredulous yet ecstatic, before the superintendent of the hospital.

"No, there isn't a mistake. I was talking to him before you came down." Miss Hemphill's strong face softened while she looked at me. She was a big, resolute woman, a distant Canadian relative of my mother's, and the kind of nurse, I had discovered in the month since I had come up from Richmond, that Northern hospital boards, if not Northern patients, appear instinctively to select. From the first, in spite of her hardness, she had taken a liking—I hesitate to use the word "fancy" for a preference so impersonal—to her Virginia cousin. After all, it isn't every Southern nurse, just out of training, who can boast a kinswoman in the superintendent of a New York hospital. If experience was what I needed, Miss Hemphill, I judged, was abundantly prepared to supply it.

"And he made you understand positively that he meant me?" The thing was so wonderful that I simply couldn't believe it.

"He asked particularly for the nurse who was with Miss Hudson last week when he operated. I think he didn't even remember that you had a name—this isn't the South, you know, where people still regard nurses as human, not as automata. When I asked if he meant Miss Randolph, he repeated that he wanted the nurse who had been with Miss Hudson. She was small, he said, and cheerful-looking. This, of course, might apply to one or two others, but none of these was with Miss Hudson. Miss Maupin, the only nurse, except you, who went near her, is large and heavy."

"Then I suppose it is really true?" My pulses were tingling. "And I am to be there at six o'clock?"

"Not a minute later. The day nurse goes off duty at that hour, and Mrs. Maradick is never left by herself for an instant."

"It is her mind, isn't it? And that makes it all the stranger that he should select me, for I have had so few mental cases."

"So few cases of any kind." Miss Hemphill was smiling, and when she smiled I wondered if the other nurses would know her. "By the time you have gone through the treadmill in New York, Margaret, you will have lost a good many things besides your inexperience. I wonder how long you will keep your sympathy and your imagination? After all, wouldn't you have made a better novelist than a nurse?"

"I can't help putting myself into my cases. I suppose one ought not to?"

"It isn't a question of what one ought to do, but of what one must. When you are drained of every bit of sympathy and enthusiasm and have got nothing in return for it, not even thanks, you will understand why I try to keep you from wasting yourself."

"But surely in a case like this—for Doctor Maradick?"

"Oh, well, of course—for Doctor Maradick?" She must have seen that I implored her confidence, for, after a minute, she let fall almost carelessly a gleam of light on the situation. "It is a very sad case when you think what a charming man and a great surgeon Doctor Maradick is."

Above the starched collar of my uniform I felt the blood leap in bounds to my cheeks. "I have spoken to him only once," I murmured, "but he is charming, and, oh so kind and handsome, isn't he?"

"His patients adore him."

"Oh, yes, I've seen that. Every one hangs on his visits." Like the patients and the other nurses, I, also, had come by delightful, if imperceptible, degrees to hang on the daily visits of Doctor Maradick. He was, I suppose, born to be a hero to women. Fate had selected him for the role, and it would have been sheer impertinence for a mortal to cross wills with the invisible Powers. From my first day in his hospital, from the moment when I watched, through closed shutters, while he stepped out of his car, I have never doubted that he was assigned to the great part in the play. If I had been ignorant of his spell—of the charm he exercised over his hospital—I should have felt it in the waiting hush, like a drawn breath, which followed his ring at the door and preceded his imperious footstep on the stairs. My first impression of him, even after the terrible events of the next year, records a memory that is both careless and splendid. At that moment, when, gazing through the chinks in the shutters, I watched him, in his coat of dark fur, cross the pavement over the pale streaks of sunshine, I knew beyond any doubt—I knew with a sort of infallible prescience—that my fate was irretrievably bound with his in the future. I knew this, I repeat, though Miss Hemphill would still insist that my foreknowledge was merely a sentimental gleaning from indiscriminate novels. But it wasn't only first love, impressionable as my kinswoman believed me to be. It wasn't only the way he looked, handsome as he was. Even more than his appearance—more than the shining dark of his eyes, the silvery brown of his hair, the dusky glow in his face—even more than his charm and his magnificence, I think, the beauty and sympathy in his voice won my heart. It was a voice, I heard some one say afterward, that ought always to speak poetry.

So you will see why—if you do not understand at the beginning, I can never hope to make you believe impossible things!—so you will see why I accepted the call when it came as an imperative summons. I couldn't have stayed away after he sent for me. However much I may have tried not to go, I know that in the end I must have gone. In those days, while I was still hoping to write novels, I used to talk a great deal about "destiny" (I have learned since then how silly all such talk is), and I suppose it was my "destiny" to be caught in the web of Roland Maradick's personality. But I am not the first nurse to grow love-sick about a doctor who never gave her a thought.

"I am glad you got the call, Margaret. It may mean a great deal to you. Only try not to be too emotional about it." I remember that Miss Hemphill was holding a bit of rose-geranium in her hand while she spoke—one of the patients had given it to her from a pot she kept in her room, and the scent of the flower is still in my nostrils—or my memory. Since then—oh, long since then—I have wondered if she also had been caught in the web.

"I wish I knew more about the case." I was clearly pressing for light. "Have you ever seen Mrs. Maradick?"

"Oh, dear, yes. They have been married only a little over a year, and in the beginning she used to come sometimes to the hospital and wait outside while the doctor made his visits. She was a very sweet-looking woman then—not exactly pretty, but fair and slight, with the loveliest smile, I think, I have ever seen. In those first months she was so much in love that we used to laugh about it among ourselves. To see her face light up when the doctor came out of the hospital and crossed the pavement to his car, was as good as a play. We never got tired watching her—I wasn't superintendent then, so I had more time to look out of the window while I was on day duty. Once or twice she brought her little girl in to see one of the patients. The child was so much like her that you would have known them anywhere for mother and daughter."

I had heard that Mrs. Maradick was a widow, with one child, when she first met the doctor, and I asked now, still seeking an illumination I had not found: "There was a great deal of money, wasn't there?"

"A great fortune. If she hadn't been so attractive, people would have said, I suppose, that Doctor Maradick married her for her money. Only," she appeared to make an effort of memory, "I believe I've heard somehow that it was all left in trust away from Mrs. Maradick if she married again. I can't, to save my life, remember just how it was; but it was a queer will, I know, and Mrs. Maradick wasn't to come into the money unless the child didn't live to grow up. The pity of it—"

A young nurse came into the office to ask for something—the keys, I think, of the operating-room, and Miss Hemphill broke off inconclusively as she hurried out of the door. I was sorry that she left off just when she did. Poor Mrs. Maradick! Perhaps I was too emotional, but even before I saw her I had begun to feel her pathos and her strangeness.

My preparations took only a few minutes. In those days I always kept a suitcase packed and ready for sudden calls; and it was not yet six o'clock when I turned from 10th Street into Fifth Avenue, and stopped for a minute, before ascending the steps, to look at the house in which Doctor Maradick lived. A fine rain was falling, and I remember thinking, as I turned the corner, how depressing the weather must be for Mrs. Maradick. It was an old house, with damp-looking walls (though that may have been because of the rain) and a spindle-shaped iron railing which ran up the stone steps to the black door, where I noticed a dim flicker through the old-fashioned fan-light. Afterward I discovered that Mrs. Maradick had been born in the house—her maiden name was Calloran—and that she had never wanted to live anywhere else. She was a woman—this I found out when I knew her better—of strong attachments to both persons and places; and though Doctor Maradick had tried to persuade her to move up-town after her marriage, she had clung, against his wishes, to the old house in lower Fifth Avenue. I dare say she was obstinate about it in spite of her gentleness and her passion for the doctor. Those sweet, soft women, especially when they have always been rich, are sometimes amazingly obstinate. I have nursed so many of them since—women with strong ailed ions and weak intellects—that I have come to recognise the type as soon as I set eyes upon it.

My ring at the bell was answered after a little delay, and when I entered the house I saw that the hall was quite dark except for the waning glow from an open fire which burned in the library. When I gave my name, and added that I was the night nurse, the servant appeared to think my humble presence unworthy of illumination. He was an old butler, inherited perhaps from Mrs. Maradick's mother, who, I learned afterward, had been from South Carolina; and while he passed me on his way up the staircase, I heard him vaguely muttering that he "wan't gwinter tu'n on dem lights twel de chile had done playin'."

To the right of the hall, the soft glow drew me into the library, and crossing the threshold timidly I stooped to dry my wet coat by the fire. As I bent there, meaning to start up at the first sound of a footstep, I thought how cosy the room was after the damp walls outside to which some bared creepers were clinging; and I was watching pleasantly the strange shapes and patterns the firelight made on the old Persian rug, when the lamps of a slowly turning motor flashed on me through the white shades at the window. Still dazzled by the glare, I looked round in the dimness and saw a child's ball of red and blue rubber roll toward me out of the gloom of one of the adjoining rooms. A moment later, while I made a vain attempt to capture the toy as it spun past me, a little girl darted airily, with peculiar lightness and grace, through the doorway, and stopped quickly, as if in surprise at the sight of a stranger. She was a small child—so small and slight that her footsteps made no sound on the polished floor of the threshold; and I remember thinking while I looked at her that she had the gravest and sweetest face I had ever seen. She couldn't—I decided this afterward—have been more than six or seven, yet she stood there with a curious prim dignity, like the dignity of a very old person, and gazed up at me with enigmatical eyes. She was dressed in Scotch plaid, with a bit of red ribbon in her hair, which was cut in a fringe over her forehead and hung very straight to her shoulders. Charming as she was, from her uncurled brown hair to the white socks and black slippers on her little feet, I recall most vividly the singular look in her eyes, which appeared in the shifting light to be of an indeterminate colour. For the odd thing about this look was that it was not the look of childhood at all. It was the look of profound experience, of bitter knowledge.

"Have you come for your ball?" I asked; but while the friendly question was still on my lips, I heard the servant returning. Even in my haste I made a second ineffectual grasp at the plaything, which rolled, with increased speed, away from me into the dusk of the drawing-room. Then, as I raised my head, I saw that the child also had slipped from the room; and without looking after her I followed the old butler into the pleasant study above, where the great surgeon awaited me.

Ten years ago, before hard nursing had taken so much out of me, I blushed very easily, and I was aware at the moment when I crossed Doctor Maradick's study that my cheeks were the colour of peonies. Of course, I was a fool—no one knows this better than I do—but I had never been alone, even for an instant, with him before, and the man was more than a hero to me, he was—there isn't any reason now why I should blush over the confession—almost a god. At that age I was mad about the wonders of surgery, and Roland Maradick in the operating-room was magician enough to have turned an older and more sensible head than mine. Added to his great reputation and his marvellous skill, he was, I am sure of this, the most splendid-looking man, even at forty-five, that one could imagine. Had he been ungracious—had he been positively rude to me, I should still have adored him, but when he held out his hand, and greeted me in the charming way he had with women, I felt that I would have died for him. It is no wonder that a saying went about the hospital that every woman he operated on fell in love with him. As for the nurses—well, there wasn't a single one of them who had escaped his spell—not even Miss Hemphill, who could scarcely have been a day under fifty.

"I am glad you could come, Miss Randolph. You were with Miss Hudson last week when I operated?"

I bowed. To save my life I couldn't have spoken without blushing the redder.

"I noticed your bright face at the time. Brightness, I think, is what Mrs. Maradick needs. She finds her day nurse depressing." His eyes rested so kindly upon me that I have suspected since that he was not entirely unaware of my worship. It was a small thing, heaven knows, to flatter his vanity—a nurse just out of a training-school—but to some men no tribute is too insignificant to give pleasure.

"You will do your best, I am sure." He hesitated an instant—just long enough for me to perceive the anxiety beneath the genial smile on his face—and then added gravely: "We wish to avoid, if possible, having to send her away for treatment."

I could only murmur in response, and after a few carefully chosen words about his wife's illness, he rang the bell and directed the maid to take me up-stairs to my room. Not until I was ascending the stairs to the third storey did it occur to me that he had really told me nothing. I was as perplexed about the nature of Mrs. Maradick's malady as I had been when I entered the house.

I found my room pleasant enough. It had been arranged—by Doctor Maradick's request, I think—that I was to sleep in the house, and after my austere little bed at the hospital I was agreeably surprised by the cheerful look of the apartment into which the maid led me. The walls were papered in roses, and there were curtains of flowered chintz at the window, which looked down on a small formal garden at the rear of the house. This the maid told me, for it was too dark for me to distinguish more than a marble fountain and a fir-tree, which looked old, though I afterward learned that it was replanted almost every season.

In ten minutes I had slipped into my uniform and was ready to go to my patient; but for some reason—to this day I have never found out what it was that turned her against me at the start—Mrs. Maradick refused to receive me. While I stood outside her door I heard the day nurse trying to persuade her to let me come in. It wasn't any use, however, and in the end I was obliged to go back to my room and wait until the poor lady got over her whim and consented to see me. That was long after dinner—it must have been nearer eleven than ten o'clock—and Miss Peterson was quite worn out by the time she came to fetch me.

"I'm afraid you'll have a bad night," she said as we went downstairs together. That was her way, I soon saw, to expect the worst of everything and everybody.

"Does she often keep you up like this?"

"Oh, no, she is usually very considerate. I never knew a sweeter character. But she still has this hallucination—"

Here again, as in the scene with Doctor Maradick, I felt that the explanation had only deepened the mystery. Mrs. Maradick's hallucination, whatever form it assumed, was evidently a subject for evasion and subterfuge in the household. It was on the tip of my tongue to ask, "What is her hallucination?"—but before I could get the words past my lips we had reached Mrs. Maradick's door, and Miss Peterson motioned me to be silent. As the door opened a little way to admit me, I saw that Mrs. Maradick was already in bed, and that the lights were out except for a night-lamp burning on a candle-stand beside a book and a carafe of water.

"I won't go in with you," said Miss Peterson in a whisper; and I was on the point of stepping over the threshold when I saw the little girl, in the dress of Scotch plaid, slip by me from the dusk of the room into the electric light of the hall. She held a doll in her arms, and as she went by she dropped a doll's work-basket in the doorway. Miss Peterson must have picked up the toy, for when I turned in a minute to look for it I found that it was gone. I remember thinking that it was late for a child to be up—she looked delicate, too—but, after all, it was no business of mine, and four years in a hospital had taught me never to meddle in affairs that do not concern me. There is nothing a nurse learns quicker than not to try to put the world to rights in a day.

When I crossed the floor to the chair by Mrs. Maradick's bed, she turned over on her side and looked at me with the sweetest and saddest smile.

"You are the new night nurse," she said in a gentle voice; and from the moment she spoke I knew that there was nothing hysterical or violent about her mania—or hallucination, as they called it. "They told me your name, but I have forgotten it."

"Randolph—Margaret Randolph." I liked her from the start, and I think she must have seen it.

"You look very young, Miss Randolph."

"I am twenty-two, but I suppose I don't look quite my age. People usually think I am younger."

For a minute she was silent, and while I settled myself in the chair by the bed I thought how strikingly she resembled the little girl I had seen first in the afternoon, and then leaving her room a few moments ago. They had the same small, heart-shaped faces, coloured ever so faintly; the same straight, soft hair, between brown and flaxen; and the same large, grave eyes, set very far apart under arched eyebrows. What surprised me most, however, was that they both looked at me with that enigmatical and vaguely wondering expression—only in Mrs. Maradick's face the vagueness seemed to change now and then to a definite fear—a flash, I had almost said, of startled horror.

I sat quite still in my chair, and until the time came for Mrs. Maradick to take her medicine not a word passed between us. Then, when I bent over her with the glass in my hand, she raised her head from the pillow and said in a whisper of suppressed intensity:

"You look kind. I wonder if you could have seen my little girl?"

As I slipped my arm under the pillow I tried to smile cheerfully down on her. "Yes, I've seen her twice. I'd know her anywhere by her likeness to you."

A glow shone in her eyes, and I thought how pretty she must have been before illness took the life and animation out of her features. "Then I know you're good." Her voice was so strained and low that I could barely hear it. "If you weren't good you couldn't have seen her."

I thought this queer enough, but all I answered was: "She looked delicate to be sitting up so late."

A quiver passed over her thin features, and for a minute I thought she was going to burst into tears. As she had taken the medicine, I put the glass back on the candle-stand and, bending over the bed, smoothed the straight brown hair, which was as fine and soft as spun silk, back from her forehead. There was something about her—I don't know what it was—that made you love her as soon as she looked at you.

"She always had that light and airy way, though she was never sick a day in her life," she answered calmly after a pause. Then, groping for my hand, she whispered passionately: "You must not tell him—you must not tell anyone that you have seen her!"

"I mustn't tell anyone?" Again I had the impression that had come to me first in Doctor Maradick's study, and afterward with Miss Peterson on the staircase, that I was seeking a gleam of light in the midst of obscurity.

"Are you sure there isn't any one listening—that there isn't any one at the door?" she asked, pushing aside my arm and sitting up among the pillows.

"Quite, quite sure. They have put out the lights in the hall."

"And you will not tell him? Promise me that you will not tell him." The startled horror flashed from the vague wonder of her expression. "He doesn't like her to come back, because he killed her."

"Because he killed her!" Then it was that light burst on me in a blaze. So this was Mrs. Maradick's hallucination! She believed that her child was dead—the little girl I had seen with my own eyes leaving her room; and she believed that her husband—the great surgeon

232

we worshipped in the hospital—had murdered her. No wonder they veiled the dreadful obsession in mystery! No wonder that even Miss Peterson had not dared to drag the horrid thing out into the light! It was the kind of hallucination one simply couldn't stand having to face.

"There is no use telling people things that nobody believes," she resumed slowly, still holding my hand in a grasp that would have hurt me if her fingers had not been so fragile. "Nobody believes that he killed her. Nobody believes that she comes back every day to the house. Nobody believes—and yet you saw her—"

"Yes, I saw her—but why should your husband have killed her?" I spoke soothingly, as one would speak to a person who was quite mad; yet she was not mad, I could have sworn this while I looked at her.

For a moment she moaned inarticulately, as if the horror of her thought were too great to pass into speech. Then she flung out her thin, bare arm with a wild gesture.

"Because he never loved me!" she said. "He never loved me!"

"But he married you," I urged gently after a moment in which I stroked her hair. "If he hadn't loved you, why should he have married you?"

"He wanted the money—my little girl's money. It all goes to him when I die."

"But he is rich himself. He must make a fortune from his profession."

"It isn't enough. He wanted millions." She had grown stern and tragic. "No, he never loved me. He loved someone else from the beginning—before I knew him."

It was quite useless, I saw, to reason with her. If she wasn't mad, she was in a state of terror and despondency so black that it had almost crossed the border-line into madness. I thought once of going up-stairs and bringing the child down from her nursery; but, after a moment's thought, I realised that Miss Peterson and Doctor Maradick must have long ago tried all these measures. Clearly, there was nothing to do except soothe and quiet her as much as I could; and this I did until she dropped into a light sleep which lasted well into the morning.

By seven o'clock I was worn out—not from work, but from the strain on my sympathy—and I was glad, indeed, when one of the maids came in to bring me an early cup of coffee. Mrs. Maradick was still sleeping—it was a mixture of bromide and chloral I had given her—and she did not wake until Miss Peterson came on duty an hour or two later. Then, when I went down-stairs, I found the dining-room deserted except for the old housekeeper, who was looking over the silver. Doctor Maradick, she explained to me presently, had his breakfast served in the morning-room on the other side of the house.

"And the little girl? Does she take her meals in the nursery?"

She threw me a startled glance. Was it, I questioned afterward, one of distrust or apprehension?

"There isn't any little girl. Haven't you heard?"

"Heard? No. Why, I saw her only yesterday."

The look she gave me—I was sure of it now—was full of alarm.

"The little girl—she was the sweetest child I ever saw—died just two months ago of pneumonia."

"But she couldn't have died." I was a fool to let this out, but the shock had completely unnerved me. "I tell you I saw her yesterday."

The alarm in her face deepened. "That is Mrs. Maradick's trouble. She believes that she still sees her."

"But don't you see her?" I drove the question home bluntly.

"No." She set her lips tightly. "I never see anything."

So I had been wrong, after all, and the explanation, when it came, only accentuated the terror. The child was dead—she had died of pneumonia two months ago—and yet I had seen her, with my own eyes, playing ball in the library; I had seen her slipping out of her mother's room, with her doll in her arms.

"Is there another child in the house? Could there be a child belonging to one of the servants?" A gleam had shot through the fog in which I was groping.

"No, there isn't any other. The doctors tried bringing one once, but it threw the poor lady into such a state she almost died of it. Besides, there wouldn't be any other child as quiet and sweet-looking as Dorothea. To see her skipping along in her dress of Scotch plaid used to make me think of a fairy, though they say that fairies wear nothing but white or green."

"Has anyone else seen her—the child, I mean—any of the servants?"

"Only old Gabriel, the butler, who came with Mrs. Maradick's mother from South Carolina. I've heard that those folk often have a kind of second sight—though I don't know that that is just what you would call it. But they seem to believe in the supernatural by instinct, and Gabriel is so old and doty—he does no work except answer the door-bell and clean the silver—that nobody pays much attention to anything that he sees—"

"Is the child's nursery kept as it used to be?"

"Oh, no. The doctor had all the toys sent to the children's hospital. That was a great grief to Mrs. Maradick; but Doctor Brandon thought, and all the nurses agreed with him, that it was best for her not to be allowed to keep the room as it was when Dorothea was living."

"Dorothea? Was that the child's name?"

"Yes, it means the gift of God, doesn't it? She was named after the mother of Mrs. Maradick's first husband, Mr. Ballard. He was the grave, quiet kind—not the least like the doctor."

I wondered if the other dreadful obsession of Mrs. Maradick's had drifted down through the nurses or the servants to the house-keeper; but she said nothing about it, and since she was, I suspected, a garrulous person, I thought it wiser to assume that the gossip had not reached her.

A little later, when breakfast was over and I had not yet gone up-stairs to my room, I had my first interview with Doctor Brandon, the famous alienist who was in charge of the case. I had never seen him before, but from the first moment that I looked at him I took his measure, almost by intuition. He was, I suppose, honest enough—I have always granted him that, bitterly as I have felt toward him. It wasn't his fault that he lacked red blood in his brain, or that he had formed the habit, from long association with abnormal phenomena, of regarding all life as a disease. He was the sort of physician—every nurse will understand what I mean—who deals instinctively with groups instead of with individuals. He was long and solemn and very round in the face; and I hadn't talked to him ten minutes before I knew he had been educated in Germany, and that he had learned over there to treat every emotion as a pathologi-cal manifestation. I used to wonder what he got out of life—what any one got out of life who had analysed away everything except the bare structure.

When I reached my room at last, I was so tired that I could barely remember either the questions Doctor Brandon had asked or the directions he had given me. I fell asleep, I know, almost as soon as my head touched the pillow; and the maid who came to inquire if I wanted luncheon decided to let me finish my nap. In the afternoon, when she returned with a cup of tea, she found me still heavy and drowsy. Though I was used to night nursing, I felt as if I had danced from sunset to daybreak. It was fortunate, I reflected, while I drank my tea, that every case didn't wear on one's sympathies as acutely as Mrs. Maradick's hallucination had worn on mine.

Through the day, of course, I did not see Doctor Maradick, but at seven o'clock, when I came up from my early dinner on my way to take the place of Miss Peterson, who had kept on duty an hour later than usual, he met me in the hall and asked me to come into his study. I thought him handsomer than ever in his evening clothes, with a white flower in his buttonhole. He was going to some public dinner, the housekeeper told me, but, then, he was always going somewhere. I believe he didn't dine at home a single evening that winter.

"Did Mrs. Maradick have a good night?" He had closed the door after us, and, turning now with the question, he smiled kindly, as if he wished to put me at ease in the beginning.

"She slept very well after she took the medicine. I gave her that at eleven o'clock."

For a minute he regarded me silently, and I was aware that his personality—his charm—had been focussed upon me. It was almost as if I stood in the centre of converging rays of light, so vivid was my impression of him.

"Did she allude in any way to her—to her hallucination?" he asked.

How the warning reached me—what invisible waves of sense-perception transmitted the message—I have never known; but while I stood there, facing the splendour of the doctor's presence, every intuition cautioned me that the time had come when I must take sides in the household. While I stayed there I must stand either with Mrs. Maradick or against her.

"She talked quite rationally," I replied after a moment.

"What did she say?"

"She told me how she was feeling, that she missed her child, and that she walked a little every day about her room."

His face changed—how, I could not at first determine.

"Have you seen Doctor Brandon?"

"He came this morning to give me his directions."

"He thought her less well today. He has even advised me to send her to Rosedale."

I have never, even in secret, tried to account for Doctor Maradick. He may have been sincere. I tell only what I know—not what I believe or imagine—and the human is sometimes as inscrutable, as inexplicable, as the supernatural.

While he watched me I was conscious of an inner struggle, as if opposing angels warred somewhere in the depths of my being. When at last I made my decision, I was acting less from reason, I knew, than in obedience to the pressure of some secret current of thought. Heaven knows, even then, the man held me captive while I defied him.

"Doctor Maradick," I lifted my eyes for the first time frankly to his, "I believe that your wife is as sane as I am—or as you are."

He started. "Then she did not talk freely to you?"

"She may be mistaken, unstrung, piteously distressed in mind"—I brought this out with emphasis—"but she is not—I am willing to stake my future on it—a fit subject for an asylum. It would be foolish—it would be cruel to send her to Rosedale."

"Cruel, you say?" A troubled look crossed his face, and his voice grew very gentle. "You do not imagine that I could be cruel to her?"

"No, I do not think that." My voice also had softened.

"We will let things go on as they are. Perhaps Doctor Brandon may have some other suggestion to make." He drew out his watch and compared it with the clock—nervously, I observed, as if his action were a screen for his discomfiture or his perplexity. "I must be going now. We will speak of this again in the morning."

But in the morning we did not speak of it, and during the month that I nursed Mrs. Maradick I was not called again into her husband's study. When I met him in the hall or on the staircase, which was seldom, he was as charming as ever; yet, in spite of his courtesy, I had a persistent feeling that he had taken my measure on that evening, and that he had no further use for me.

As the days went by Mrs. Maradick seemed to grow stronger. Never, after our first night together, had she mentioned the child to me; never had she alluded by so much as a word to her dreadful charge against her husband. She was like any other woman recovering from a great sorrow, except that she was sweeter and gentler. It is no wonder that everyone who came near her loved her; for there was a mysterious loveliness about her like the mystery of light, not of darkness. She was, I have always thought, as much of an angel as it is possible for a woman to be on this earth. And yet, angelic as she was, there were times when it seemed to me that she both hated and feared her husband. Though he never entered her room while I was there, and I never heard his name on her lips until an hour before the end, still I could tell by the look of terror in her face whenever his step passed down the hall that her very soul shivered at his approach.

During the whole month I did not see the child again, though one night, when I came suddenly into Mrs. Maradick's room, I found a little garden, such as children make out of pebbles and bits of box, on the window-sill. I did not mention it to Mrs. Maradick, and a little later, as the maid lowered the shades, I noticed that the garden had vanished. Since then I have often wondered if the child were invisible only to the rest of us, and if her mother still saw her. But there was no way of finding out except by questioning, and Mrs.

Maradick was so well and patient that I hadn't the heart to question. Things couldn't have been better with her than they were, and I was beginning to tell myself that she might soon go out for an airing, when the end came suddenly.

It was a mild January day—the kind of day that brings the foretaste of spring in the middle of winter, and when I came down-stairs in the afternoon, I stopped a minute by the window at the end of the hall to look down on the box maze in the garden. There was an old fountain, bearing two laughing boys in marble, in the centre of the gravelled walk, and the water, which had been turned on that morning for Mrs. Maradick's pleasure, sparkled now like silver as the sunlight splashed over it. I had never before felt the air quite so soft and springlike in January; and I thought, as I gazed down on the garden, that it would be a good idea for Mrs. Maradick to go out and bask for an hour or so in the sunshine. It seemed strange to me that she was never allowed to get any fresh air except the air that came through her windows.

When I went into her room, however, I found that she had no wish to go out. She was sitting, wrapped in shawls, by the open window, which looked down on the fountain; and as I entered she glanced up from a little book she was reading. A pot of daffodils stood on the window-sill—she was very fond of flowers and we tried always to keep some growing in her room.

"Do you know what I was reading, Miss Randolph?" she asked in her soft voice; and then she read aloud a verse while I went over to the candle-stand to measure out a dose of medicine.

"'If thou hast two loaves of bread, sell one and buy daffodils, for bread nourisheth the body, but daffodils delight the soul,' That is very beautiful, don't you think so?"

I said "Yes," that it was beautiful; and then I asked her if she wouldn't go down-stairs and walk about in the garden?

"He wouldn't like it," she answered; and it was the first time she had mentioned her husband to me since the night I came to her. "He doesn't want me to go out."

I tried to laugh her out of the idea; but it was no use, and after a few minutes I gave up and began talking of other things. Even then it did not occur to me that her fear of Doctor Maradick was anything but a fancy. I could see, of course, that she wasn't out of her head; but sane persons, I knew, sometimes have unaccountable prejudices, and I accepted her dislike as a mere whim or aversion. I did not understand then, and—I may as well confess this before the end comes—I do not understand any better today. I am writing down the things I actually saw, and I repeat that I have never had the slightest twist in the direction of the miraculous.

The afternoon slipped away while we talked—she talked brightly when any subject came up that interested her—and it was the last hour of day—that grave, still hour when the movement of life seems to droop and falter for a few precious minutes—that brought us the thing I had dreaded silently since my first night in the house. I remember that I had risen to close the window, and was leaning out for a breath of the mild air, when there was the sound of steps, consciously softened in the hall outside, and Doctor Brandon's usual knock fell on my ears. Then, before I could cross the room, the door opened, and the doctor entered with Miss Peterson. The day nurse, I knew, was a stupid woman; but she had never appeared to me so stupid, so armoured and incased in her professional manner, as she did at that moment.

"I am glad to see that you have been taking the air." As Doctor Brandon came over to the window, I wondered maliciously what devil of contradictions had made him a distinguished specialist in nervous diseases.

"Who was the other doctor you brought this morning?" asked Mrs. Maradick gravely; and that was all I ever heard about the visit of the second alienist.

"Some one who is anxious to cure you." He dropped into a chair beside her and patted her hand with his long, pale fingers. "We are so anxious to cure you that we want to send you away to the country for a fortnight or so. Miss Peterson has come to help you get ready, and I've kept my car waiting for you. There couldn't be a nicer day for a little trip, could there?"

The moment had come at last. I knew at once what he meant, and so did Mrs. Maradick. A wave of colour flowed and ebbed in her thin cheeks, and I felt her body quiver when I moved from the window and put my arms on her shoulders. I was aware again, as I had been aware that evening in Doctor Maradick's study, of a current of thought that beat from the air around into my brain. Though it cost me my career as a nurse and my reputation for sanity, I knew that I must obey that invisible warning.

"You are going to take me to an asylum," said Mrs. Maradick.

He made some foolish denial or evasion; but before he had finished I turned from Mrs. Maradick and faced him impulsively. In a nurse this was flagrant rebellion, and I realised that the act wrecked my professional future. Yet I did not care—I did not hesitate. Something stronger than I was driving me on.

"Doctor Brandon," I said, "I beg you—I implore you to wait until tomorrow. There are things I must tell you."

A queer look came into his face, and I understood, even in my excitement, that he was mentally deciding in which group he should place me—to which class of morbid manifestations I must belong.

"Very well, very well, we will hear everything," he replied

soothingly; but I saw him glance at Miss Peterson, and she went over to the wardrobe for Mrs. Maradick's fur coat and hat.

Suddenly, without warning, Mrs. Maradick threw the shawls away from her, and stood up. "If you send me away," she said, "I shall never come back. I shall never live to come back."

The grey of twilight was just beginning, and while she stood there, in the dusk of the room, her face shone out as pale and flower-like as the daffodils on the window-sill. "I cannot go away!" she cried in a sharper voice. "I cannot go away from my child!"

I saw her face clearly; I heard her voice: and then—the horror of the scene sweeps back over me!—I saw the door slowly open and the little girl run across the room to her mother. I saw her lift her little arms, and I saw the mother stoop and gather her to her bosom. So closely locked were they in that passionate embrace that their forms seemed to mingle in the gloom that enveloped them.

"After this can you doubt?" I threw out the words almost savagely—and then, when I turned from the mother and child to Doctor Brandon and Miss Peterson, I knew breathlessly—oh, there was a shock in the discovery!—that they were blind to the child. Their blank faces revealed the consternation of ignorance, not of conviction. They had seen nothing except the vacant arms of the mother and the swift, erratic gesture with which she stooped to embrace some phantasmal presence. Only my vision—and I have asked myself since if the power of sympathy enabled me to penetrate the web of material fact and see the spiritual form of the child—only my vision was not blinded by the clay through which I looked.

"After this can you doubt?" Doctor Brandon had flung my words back to me. Was it his fault, poor man, if life had granted him only the eyes of flesh? Was it his fault if he could see only half of the thing there before him?

But they couldn't see, and since they couldn't see I realised that it was useless to tell them. Within an hour they took Mrs. Maradick to the asylum; and she went quietly, though when the time came for parting from me she showed some faint trace of feeling. I remember that at the last, while we stood on the pavement, she lifted her black veil, which she wore for the child, and said: "Stay with her, Miss Randolph, as long as you can. I shall never come back."

Then she got into the car and was driven off, while I stood looking after her with a sob in my throat. Dreadful as I felt it to be, I didn't, of course, realise the full horror of it, or I couldn't have stood there quietly on the pavement. I didn't realise it, indeed, until several months afterward when word came that she had died in the asylum. I never knew what her illness was, though I vaguely recall that something was said about "heart failure"—a loose enough term. My own belief is that she died simply of the terror of life.

To my surprise Doctor Maradick asked me to stay on as his office nurse after his wife went to Rosedale; and when the news of her death came there was no suggestion of my leaving. I don't know to this day why he wanted me in the house. Perhaps he thought I should have less opportunity to gossip if I stayed under his roof; perhaps he still wished to test the power of his charm over me. His vanity was incredible in so great a man. I have seen him flush with pleasure when people turned to look at him in the street, and I know that he was not above playing on the sentimental weaknesses of his patients. But he was magnificent, heaven knows! Few men, I imagine, have been the objects of so many foolish infatuations.

The next summer Doctor Maradick went abroad for two months, and while he was away I took my vacation in Virginia. When we came back the work was heavier than ever—his reputation by this time was tremendous—and my days were so crowded with appointments, and hurried flittings to emergency cases, that I had scarcely a minute left in which to remember poor Mrs. Maradick. Since the afternoon when she went to the asylum the child had not been seen in the house; and at last I was beginning to persuade myself that the little figure had been an optical illusion—the effect of shifting lights in the gloom of the old rooms—not the apparition I had once believed it to be. It does not take long for a phantom to fade from the memory—especially when one leads the active and methodical life I was forced into that winter. Perhaps—who knows?—(I remember telling myself), the doctors may have been right, after all, and the poor lady may have actually been out of her mind. With this view of the past, my judgment of Doctor Maradick insensibly altered. It ended, I think, in my acquitting him altogether. And then, just as he stood clear and splendid in my verdict of him, the reversal came so precipitately that I grow breathless now whenever I try to live it over again. The violence of the next turn in affairs left me, I often fancy, with a perpetual dizziness of the imagination.

It was in May that we heard of Mrs. Maradick's death, and exactly a year later, on a mild and fragrant afternoon, when the daffodils were blooming in patches around the old fountain in the garden, the housekeeper came into the office, where I lingered over some accounts, to bring me news of the doctor's approaching marriage.

"It is no more than we might have expected," she concluded rationally. "The house must be lonely for him—he is such a sociable man. But I can't help feeling," she brought out slowly after a pause in which I felt a shiver pass over me, "I can't help feeling that it is hard for that other woman to have all the money poor Mrs. Maradick's first husband left her."

"There is a great deal of money, then?" I asked curiously.

"A great deal." She waved her hand, as if words were futile to express the sum. "Millions and millions!"

"They will give up this house, of course?"

"That's done already, my dear. There won't be a brick left of it by this time next year. It's to be pulled down and an apartment-house built on the ground."

Again the shiver passed over me. I couldn't bear to think of Mrs. Maradick's old home falling to pieces.

"You didn't tell me the name of the bride," I said. "Is she someone he met while he was in Europe?"

"Dear me, no! She is the very lady he was engaged to before he married Mrs. Maradick, only she threw him over, so people said, because he wasn't rich enough. Then she married some lord or prince from over the water; but there was a divorce, and now she has turned again to her old lover. He is rich enough now, I guess, even for her!"

It was all perfectly true, I suppose; it sounded as plausible as a story out of a newspaper; and yet while she told me I was aware of a sinister, an impalpable hush in the atmosphere. I was nervous, no doubt; I was shaken by the suddenness with which the housekeeper had sprung her news on me; but as I sat there I had quite vividly an impression that the old house was listening—that there was a real, if invisible, presence somewhere in the room or the garden. Yet, when an instant afterward I glanced through the long window which opened down to the brick terrace, I saw only the faint sunshine over the deserted garden, with its maze of box, its marble fountain, and its patches of daffodils.

The housekeeper had gone—one of the servants, I think, came for her—and I was sitting at my desk when the words of Mrs. Maradick on that last evening floated into my mind. The daffodils brought her back to me; for I thought, as I watched them growing, so still and golden in the sunshine, how she would have enjoyed them. Almost unconsciously I repeated the verse she had read to me.

"If thou hast two loaves of bread, sell one and buy daffodils"—and it was at that very instant, while the words were on my lips, that I turned my eyes to the box maze and saw the child skipping rope along the gravelled path to the fountain. Quite distinctly, as clear as day, I saw her come, with what children call the dancing step, between the low box borders to the place where the daffodils bloomed by the fountain. From her straight brown hair to her frock of Scotch plaid and her little feet, which twinkled in white socks and black slippers over the turning rope, she was as real to me as the ground on which she trod or the laughing marble boys under the splashing water. Starting up from my chair, I made a single step to the terrace. If I could only reach her—only speak to her—I felt that I might at last solve the mystery. But with my first call, with the first flutter of my dress on the terrace, the airy little form melted into the dusk of the maze. Not a breath stirred the daffodils, not a shadow passed over the sparkling flow of the water; yet, weak and shaken in every nerve, I sat down on the brick step of the terrace and burst into tears. I must have known that something terrible would happen before they pulled down Mrs. Maradick's home.

The doctor dined out that night. He was with the lady he was going to marry, the housekeeper told me; and it must have been almost midnight when I heard him come in and go up-stairs to his room. I was down-stairs because I had been unable to sleep, and the book I wanted to finish I had left that afternoon in the office. The book—I can't remember what it was—had seemed to me very exciting when I began it in the morning; but after the visit of the child I found the romantic novel as dull as a treatise on nursing. It was impossible for me to follow the lines, and I was on the point of giving up and going to bed, when Doctor Maradick opened the front door with his latch-key and went up the staircase. "There can't be a bit of truth in it." I thought over and over again as I listened to his even step ascending the stairs. "There can't be a bit of truth in it." And yet, though I assured myself that "there couldn't be a bit of truth in it," I shrank, with a creepy sensation, from going through the house to my room in the third storey. I was tired out after a hard day, and my nerves must have reacted morbidly to the silence and the darkness. For the first time in my life I knew what it was to be afraid of the unknown, of the invisible; and while I bent over my book, in the glare of the electric light, I became conscious presently that I was straining my senses for some sound in the spacious emptiness of the rooms overhead. The noise of a passing motor-car in the street jerked me back from the intense hush of expectancy; and I can recall the wave of relief that swept over me as I turned to my book again and tried to fix my distracted mind on its pages.

I was still sitting there when the telephone on my desk rang, with what seemed to my overwrought nerves a startling abruptness, and the voice of the superintendent told me hurriedly that Doctor Maradick was needed at the hospital. I had become so accustomed to these emergency calls in the night that I felt reassured when I had rung up the doctor in his room and had heard the hearty sound of his response. He had not yet undressed, he said, and would come down immediately while I ordered back his car, which must just have reached the garage.

"I'll be with you in five minutes!" he called as cheerfully as if I had summoned him to his wedding.

I heard him cross the floor of his room; and before he could reach the head of the staircase, I opened the door and went out into the hall in order that I might turn on the light and have his hat and coat waiting. The electric button was at the end of the hall, and as I moved toward it, guided by the glimmer that fell from the landing above, I instinctively lifted my eyes to the staircase, which climbed dimly, with its slender mahogany balustrade, as far as the third storey. Then it was, at the very moment when the doctor, humming gayly, began his quick descent of the steps, that I distinctly saw—I will swear to this on my death-bed—a child's skipping-rope lying loosely coiled, as if it had dropped from a careless little hand, in the bend of the staircase. With a spring I had reached the electric button, flooding the hall with light; but as I did so, while my arm was still outstretched behind me, I heard the humming voice change to a cry of surprise or terror, and the figure on the staircase tripped heavily and stumbled with groping hands into emptiness. The scream of warning died in my throat while I watched him pitch forward down the long flight of stairs to the floor at my feet. Even before I bent over him, before I wiped the blood from his brow and felt for his silent heart, I knew that he was dead.

Something—it may have been, as the world believes, a misstep in the dimness, or it may have been, as I am ready to bear witness, a phantasmal judgment—something had killed him at the very moment when he most wanted to live.

Many years ago there died, on the estate of Sundshult, in the parish of Nafverstad, a child of illegitimate birth, which, because of this, was not christened and could not be accorded Christian burial, or a place in heaven, and whose spirit, therefore, was left to wander the earth, disturbing the rest and making night uncomfortable for the people of the neighbourhood.

One time, just before Christmas, the parish shoemaker, on his rounds, was detained at the house of a patron, and, having much work before him, he was still sewing late into the night, when he was unexpectedly startled from his employment by a little child appearing before him...

"But who are you that you are here in this manner?"

"I live under the lower stone of the steps to the porch."

"Who put you there?" asked the shoemaker.

"Watch when it dawns, and you will see my mother coming, wearing a red cap. But help me out of this, and I'll never dance again."

This the shoemaker promised to do, and the spectre vanished.

The next day a servant girl from the neighbouring estate came, who wore upon her head a red handkerchief.

Digging was begun under the designated step, and in time the skeleton of a child was found, encased in a wooden tub. The body was that day taken to the churchyard, and the mother, who had destroyed her child, turned over to the authorities. Since then the child spectre has danced no more.

Hofberg, "The Child Phantom" (1882)[18]

TWO LITTLE RED SHOES

Bessie Kyffin-Taylor

Lady Bessie Kyffin-Taylor (1869–1922) was a Welsh philanthropist and the wife of celebrated soldier, solicitor, and MP, Gerald Kyffin-Taylor C.B.E. Very little is known about her now, although one obituary referred to her as "well known in literary circles as a writer of articles and stories" and another obituary claimed her as "one of the first women in the country to drive a motor-car". She published one play called Rosemary, *and one collection of supernatural stories* From Out of the Silence *in 1920, which appears the only place that "Two Little Red Shoes" could be read at the time.*

In this tale, the children themselves do not appear to have any agency—they are visible and audible imprints on the landscape and the ghostly visions of the cruelty they underwent replay for the female narrator without allowing for interaction. Nevertheless, as in some other tales, their very presence, and the sounds they make, drive their perpetrator (once more a male guardian) to distraction and reminders of his crimes are shown to be inescapable.

With thanks to Johnny Mains for assisting me in the search for more about Bessie.

ll my life, or at least as far back as I can remember, empty houses have always had an irresistible attraction for me, though uninhabited gardens are almost as attractive. I cannot call the gardens empty, though people may be absent, for a garden is never really empty—spring, summer or winter—there is always life in a garden! Spring! and the singing of mating birds. Summer! hot, drowsy summer days, with the ceaseless hum of millions of insects; just to lie listening, in what most people call silence, though it is a silence fraught with countless sounds. Winter! the most still, has its sounds and life.

A notice board inevitably draws my footsteps nearer to an empty house, the more weather-worn the "To Let" the greater the attraction.

My infatuation for empty houses has led me into curious situations at times, and has often been the source of very real pleasure and interest. Occasionally I have had unpleasant episodes; but, on the whole, happy hours predominated. Long years ago my prying tendencies had about them the elements of a game of "Let's pretend," for in imagination dwelt in one or other of those silent, houses, always with a tender lover by my side: I used to choose my drawing-rooms, and furnish them—I chose my nurseries, and peopled them with little people; my colour schemes were many and very varied, and in this way I passed many happy hours—so happy indeed, that those hours spent in empty houses were more my real life, than the other.

Years have passed, and part of my game has come true—only part of it—for my colour schemes were somehow never attainable in a work-a-day, practical world, and there were other parts of my day-dreams, and they, too, remained "day-dreams." In spite of passing years, in spite of work, in spite of all, I have never outgrown my fondness for empty houses and uninhabited gardens, and to this day I am known to visit a tenantless house, light a fire, from a hidden store of coal and wood, seat myself in an old broken-down chair, and there, in the silence—a silence unbroken by the ring of telephone or any other bells—I dream my dreams and revel in unbroken solitude—with every nerve at rest, sure in the knowledge that none can disturb my peace, since none know my whereabouts—I have said strange episodes have befallen me at times—one so strange as to be almost unbelievable—yet let those explain who can!

A long hot summer was drawing to an end—a summer of almost tropical heat, which had left the earth parched and brown, green lawns looked like brown felt, and people had at last given up in despair the sprinkling of water in their thirsty gardens—it seemed waste of energy and water, the flowers were too thirsty—so were left to droop and fade away almost before they were fully out; leaves tumbled off trees while yet green, simply because they were sun-baked and dry. Even the birds waited about expecting some thoughtful human creature to give them a dish of water to drink and play in.

Most people had gone either to the sea or hills, certainly all who could afford it had fled, and those unfortunate ones whom work or duties chained to the towns, were deserving of pity, as they toiled through the hours of day, returning, in what they tried to call the cool of the evening, to their dried-up bits of garden, or suffocating rooms. I was one of those unlucky ones—doomed to stay in town until the end of August, after which I was free—Free! with a little sum of money at my disposal to squander as and where I pleased. For some reason it pleased me to save that bit of money and *not* spend it in train travelling other than one short journey, for I had long ago made up my mind that when next the Fates were sufficiently kind as to leave me in undisputed possession of our happy home, and granted me a few days' freedom from the daily round—the common task, I would spend that time in pursuance of my favourite pastime—the hunting out and getting into uninhabited houses and gardens—I already knew of one such house, and had long made up my mind to inspect it—so, on this first day of my freedom, I made a parcel of some food, a book, some paper and pencils, and donning old garments, I set forth. A short train journey and a long walk landed me at a pair of massive old iron gates—they were shut, and, to my intense disappointment, padlocked! I peered through them up a long grassy drive, with high banks of rhododendrons on each side—the drive was not newly grass-grown, it had always been a grass drive—and straight ahead at the far end of it, stood the house—I meant to reach it, I intended to get inside, and I was not going to be daunted by a merely padlocked gate—even though the said gate was too high to climb, and, moreover, had spikes at the top. I wandered on past the gates and spotted a thin part of the close thorn hedge, where the paling behind had rotted and given way. Through this thinned hedge I scrambled, and over the broken paling, but didn't intend to spoil my approach that way, so crept back inside the fence until I reached the gates. "So much for your padlock," I thought, as I started triumphantly to march up the length of that old grassy drive—odd little paths branched off it from time to time, leading I knew not whither, and all of them were grass; gravel or paving of any kind was unknown. As I neared the house, I found myself thinking what a silent place it must have been to dwell in, with all the approaches of soft turf, no sound of feet or wheels would be heard, such silence would have pleased me well.

Probably most people would have gone straight to the house and peered in at the windows. I did not. I sat down on the short turf, under the shadow of a giant copper beech tree, and stared at those many blank windows, looking down on me, as if they were so many eyes. It has always been my way to approach those things which please me in a lingering kind of manner, as if, like the children do, I tried to make them last longer. I felt like this as I sat gazing at the house I had long waited to inspect, but having attained my desire, I lingered, even though longing to get inside.

It was a dull, red brick house, with many windows, but all flat—not a "bay" window or jutting corner anywhere—only the front door broke the monotony, it having a curious porch—two sides glass, with a heavy oak door in the centre. The bell-pull attracted my eye next, it was a heavy copper chain, and green with age in many places—the handle, a horse-shoe—of rusty iron. I wondered if that had been the original, or whether some inmate, with a tendency to superstition, had hung it there.

From my comfortable seat, I let my gaze wander to and fro from window to window, trying to picture the rooms within, yet still putting off my attempt to enter—no thought of being unable to do so entered my mind, for by some means or other I intended to accomplish what to me was a definite purpose. I would eat my lunch first, I decided, then find a way indoors, and later, as it grew cooler, wander in the garden. It was gloriously still there under the beech tree, so still, that I grew drowsy, and all but fell asleep (that would waste time, I thought), so roused myself with an effort, and drew nearer to the house. I believe in my heart I feared being foiled in my desire, and that was one reason why I delayed, but time, relentless always, was passing along, and I must really make a start.

I peered through the windows to the right of the door.

"Oh! Lovely!" I exclaimed, and hurriedly peeped in those on the other side of the door. "What a contrast," I thought, I *must* get in; so almost ran round the back of the house in my eagerness. Window after window I tried in vain, but at last caught sight of one with a broken hasp. This, by using a penknife, and sharp-edged stone, I raised sufficiently to get my fingers in and lift it up, then, jumping on to the sill, I crept through, closing the window softly behind me. I found myself in a big lofty kitchen—minus furniture of any kind, though oddly enough two little dish covers still hung on the walls. From there I wandered along a stone passage, which had many doors—I don't mean doors opening on to them, but heavy doors across them—every few yards—as if the dwellers in the house had intended cutting off all sound from the kitchen premises being heard in other parts of the house—the end door was cedar wood, and as I closed it, I realised that the living rooms seemed quite in another world. I entered the room to the right of the front door, the room which had caused me to exclaim "lovely!" when I peered through its windows. It certainly was a beautiful room—long and low—with walls of white and gold, with a frieze of laughing cupids driving each other with chains of pink roses. This room was likewise devoid of furniture, except for two very small chairs—one upholstered in faded blue, the other in tatters of pink. I smiled, and supposed they were too small to bother to remove, probably the little folks to whom they had once belonged had long since out-grown them. I loved the laughing cupids, and pictured the gay revels they must have looked down upon before the pink of their roses faded. There was another door leading from this room—it was slightly ajar—so I peeped in before continuing my wandering on the other side of the front door. I say at once, emphatically and decidedly, I did not like it. It was a small, round room—with three windows, none of which one could see through without getting on to a chair; the walls were slate coloured, the floor was stone, there wasn't a fire place, but pushed against the wall were two little high wooden stools, and to each stool was attached a long, thin steel chain. I didn't like it. The stools looked as if two small dogs might have been fastened there, and made to sit still. I left it hurriedly and entered the room on the other side of the front door. This had quite a lot of furniture in it, and, to my amazement, many toys—there was a dappled, well-worn rocking-horse—not one of the modern apologies for a rocking-horse, the thing on patent springs which only wobbles to and fro in perfect safety—oh! no, *this* was a real old-fashioned gee, which *really* rocked, until you were rather in danger of slipping over its scanty tail, or sliding forward to grasp its cocked-up ears; there was a broken doll, too, with what had once been a pretty face, not a monstrosity, or fat policeman with a red nose or hideous golliwog; there was a battered engine, some bricks, and on the hearth a little pair of scarlet shoes. I picked these up and fell to wondering what little atom had worn them—someone had once had happy times in this room of toys I thought. I had spent a long time in the few rooms I had prowled through, and already long shadows were dimming the bright glare of the sun. I glanced at my watch, and decided I would move to the garden, the house was beginning to feel chilly—that odd chilliness of a house long tenantless and fireless. I would come again tomorrow, and then explore upstairs, but now would just have one peep at the garden, then trot homewards. The room of toys held me somehow, and I was loth to leave it and the little red shoes! I had a wild desire to put those in my pocket, surely no one would miss them, and I—oh! well—I liked to handle them and imagine the wee soft pink feet that they had covered. It couldn't be stealing, I argued, for by the dust on them they must have been long lying unthought of, besides, I would bring them back tomorrow—but just for tonight I wanted them—so I took them in my hand as I strolled from the room, to commence retracing my steps along the corridor of many doors.

Just as I closed the door behind me I heard a sound—a sound that always had the power to arrest my steps—I heard a long-drawn whimpering cry of a little child!

"Then there *is* a caretaker, and family," I said, aloud. "How stupid of me not to have thought of it, and looked more carefully before I made the house so very much my own."

I went on through another door, and I heard the cry again. I was closer to the sound, or was it nearer to me? I hurried a little, slipping the little red shoes into my pocket for safety. I did not want to be called a thief—beside, I would bring them back tomorrow. I passed through the last door before the kitchen, and again a long, whimpering cry broke the silence, so close to me, so close, I felt as if I had but to stretch out my hand to touch that troubled, little child. I quickened my steps, raised the window, and slipped through, fully intending to explore the back premises to discover the whereabouts of the worthy caretaker and her fractious child. I stood for an instant when safely through the window, and as I stood there, I heard, distinctly, unmistakably, the whimpering cry and the soft tapping of tiny baby fingers on the window pane, tapping as if they could scarcely reach, but tapping insistently and clearly, and always, always, the same little, wailing cry.

I turned away, satisfied that either in rooms above or below, I should next day stumble upon the caretaker, but, though unafraid, I was not by any means sure that I could so easily explain away those persistent, tapping baby fingers.

I travelled home in a thoughtful mood, for though I had enjoyed my day, the memory of those deserted toys lingered in my mind.

Of my home life I need not speak, it was just the usual routine of most women, the everlasting ordering of meals, and the doing of the hundred and one small duties which go to make up the everyday life of the everyday woman, therefore my return home and usual humdrum evening was got through as countless others are—perhaps mine were, at least in the opinion of some folks, duller than the evenings of others, because some of my ideas happened to be different—for instance, I much preferred the silence of my own sanctum with my books and odds and ends to spending an evening in the company of a few other people, with our noses buried in packs of cards, oblivious of all other interests save to win. Cards never attracted me, there is always so much that is more worth while. An evening of music does appeal to me, but people are forgetting how to play and sing, and so I stay at home, dreaming my dreams in my leisure hours of peace.

Tonight, as I sat by my open window, watching the stars peep out, I pondered much on the old empty house. The little scarlet shoes lay on the table at my side, and often I picked them up, trying to picture their wee owner—how old was "she"? for it must have been a girl I was sure—was she fair or dark? where had she gone? and why had her little shoes been left behind? I looked at them carefully; they were not much worn although the tiny soles showed that they had done some running about. She must have been the owner of the broken dome, but who then was the owner of the engine? All my questioning left me no wiser, so I resolved to go early to bed, bent on an early start in the morning, to visit my "House of Mystery," as I called it.

True to my resolve, I was up and away betimes, reaching my house while the dew was still on the grass, part of the house was still in the shadow, the birds were still busy over their morning toilets, otherwise the place looked as silent and deserted as before.

I sat down for a few moments under the copper beech to rest and make up my mind whether to make straight for my window, and go on with my prowl from where I left off, or to try if I could unearth the caretaker. I had a wish to interview the crying baby, who rather spoiled my departure on the previous evening. A sudden thought decided me. I would first hunt up the caretaker, with a view to gaining some sort of permission to prowl as I liked, when and where I liked, it would be worrying if I were turned out, as I might very well be, unless armed with a permit of some kind, and knowing the rules of the game, I ventured to think a promised pound of tea or toy for the baby would in all likelihood grant me a free pass. To this end I would inspect all the back premises first, make my peace with the good lady, and then spend the whole long day in the garden, reserving the house for a wet day or a day too cold for the garden.

Having made up my mind, I proceeded towards the back of the house. There were three or four doors, one labelled "Tradesmen." A useless label I always found, for they inevitably used any other door save the one so marked—our own side door bore a similar inscription, but it never prevented a long line of errand boys tramping past the front of the house, bearing their milk cars, butcher's baskets, or loaves of bread in full view of all and sundry.

I peeped into many out-houses, coal-shed, boot room—I even found the stable yard, but most of the doors there were broken or off the hinges, as if these places had long been known as domiciles for tramps. I was able to see through every window, at the back of the house, every room was empty, dusty and tenantless, not a sound or sign of life was to be heard, so I arrived at the conclusion that the worthy caretaker lived at a distance, only paying occasional visits, and must just have come upon the scene as I was leaving last evening. Then the chances were I should be left in peace today.

The house attracted me, and for a moment I wavered, but the garden called, so I would adhere to my plan, leaving the house for another visit. I would just pop in, replace the little "stolen"—or, as I preferred—"borrowed" red shoes, and then return to the garden.

"Oh, how stupid!" I suddenly exclaimed, aloud, "I have come without the little shoes, I have left them on my dressing table. Well, they are safe, and no one will miss them, and I can bring them tomorrow. I need not enter my window, I can go straight to the garden and explore," but would go to the front door, and start from there. This I did, wandering away to the right, down a winding grassy path, with high bushes on each side interspersed with overhanging laburnums, the golden glory of them had long since departed, but their waving graceful foliage mingling with the darker glossiness of the rhodies, was cool and refreshing.

Quite suddenly the grassy path widened and led me down three rough, stone steps on to a little lawn, closed in with a riotous wilderness of late roses—climbing roses chiefly, but of the old-fashioned kind—I saw a friend of my childhood, a little, squashed-looking white rose, I never knew its name, nor do I now, but it grows in profusion, the buds are just tinged with pale coral, and when open, the little rose is white, with a faint, soft scent—pale pink, monthly roses mingled with them, also crimson peonies and tall, blue larkspurs, while old-fashioned sweet-williams and pansies formed a border, or what once had been a border.

At one side of the lawn was a grassy bank, and opposite to it a huge cedar tree, with a rough, wooden seat below it, or rather the remains of a seat. The shut-in-ness of it, the silence of it, together with the riot of colour and indescribable sweetness of the many flower scents, made me pause enraptured, yet sad to think so much loveliness should be wasting unseen, unknown. I sat down at the foot of the bank, leaning against it, facing the path I had just come down, and closed my eyes with a sense of complete restfulness and peace.

I may have dozed there in the heavily-scented air, or perhaps I was tired, without realising it, but I had probably been lying there an hour, or more, when I suddenly sat up, with the distinct feeling of being no longer alone. I was right, though for the moment I could not see anyone, and yet I heard soft movements. I can't describe them, it was like the passing and repassing of soft footsteps, *little footsteps*, near me. I found myself staring, and then—ah! me—it seems both impossible and useless to describe—yet perchance, some day, someone may read this and believe—I saw two little children, hand in hand, trotting along in the busy little way children have when on affairs entirely their own. Past me they trotted—a tiny boy in a sailor suit, bareheaded, with clustering curls round a pale, resolute little face—and by his side, a dainty wee girl in white, bareheaded, as he was, but with a golden, silky down covering her tiny head. He wore sturdy little brown shoes—she was barefooted—and at times, as I watched them, she pointed with tiny, dimpled fingers to her little bare toes, and seemed half inclined to cry.

No other thought occurred to me in those first few moments except that they had somehow strayed in from somewhere, and—watched them, fascinated, *though I never heard them speak!*

Presently they sat down still intent on each other, and for the first time it struck me how utterly oblivious they were to me.

They were so sweet and lovely, I wanted to run to them, catch them in my arms, and cover them with kisses. Should I try and catch their attention, I wondered—perhaps they would play with me, but I would watch them a little longer first.

Slowly the little lad got up as if listening, and then a change came over the little faces, a dreadful heart-breaking change—and a look of awful fear was in each face—the wee girl stumbled to her feet, and began to cry—I could see, but I could hear no sound—and then, with pale cheeks and trembling little limbs, they started to cross the lawn.

I could not endure it. What had frightened them? I must help them, I sprang to my feet; they reached the tree of white roses by the beginning of the path, just as I came up to them, and as I reached them, putting out my hand to hold them—*they were not there!*

Then, and then only, did I realise that my dream children were dream children indeed. Children from another world, still visiting this one—if, indeed, they had ever really left it!

I sank down, half-faint, and wholly bewildered, and for a long time I lay with my eyes hidden, and feeling unable to stir; I managed to pull myself together after a while, and glanced at my watch. It was four o'clock, the same hour at which I left yesterday when those tapping baby fingers on the window beat themselves into my brain.

I would go, I felt I could not, dare not, venture to the house, but I was determined, though a little shaken, that I would come back. I must, some power compelled me, and I knew I should return.

I reached home again and went at once to my room. There were the wee scarlet shoes just as I had left them, but I handled them in a different spirit, for, vividly before my eyes, I saw those tiny, bare feet, and the odd little pucker of the baby lips as the small girl pointed down to them.

"Very well, baby, you shall have them back, never fear!" For now I felt brave again, and intended to see more of my dream children.

I went to bed wondering what the next day would bring forth.

I suppose I was a bit unnerved, for I passed a restless night, only falling asleep as the dawn came, so sleeping later than my wont, and I woke to find a dull, grey morning, a sobbing wind, and threatening-looking clouds overhead, no trace of sun or blue sky—such is our dear English climate! But, such as it is, I love it in all or most of its moods. Today it suited me. I would journey to my "House of Mystery" and spend the hours indoors. I am not braver than other women, indeed, am a veritable coward over many things, but I am *not* greatly alarmed by the supernatural.

I suppose because of my unchanging belief in a life hereafter, and a very firm faith that those we love, who have passed over, are very, very near us, and not as some would have it, out of our ken for all time, and so, though I have a natural dread of things not understandable, I still was not afraid, certainly not sufficiently afraid to prevent my visiting my dream children at least once more.

I reached the house on this my third visit shortly after one o'clock, and went straight to the window, raised it, and crept through. I had a kind of feeling that if I saw my babies it would not be until four o'clock. Little did I guess what was in store for me, or even I, good as my nerves were, would have gone gladly a hundred miles in another direction.

The house was very still, very silent, as I moved about, my footsteps seemed to make the sounds of a giant at least.

Slowly I wended my way upstairs, through room after room—all had been beautiful, artistic, and varied in colour and design. At last I reached a large, airy room, done in shades of blue, and this room had brass rods before the large window.

"Night nursery," I murmured, and I noticed two small hard-looking beds. Strange, I thought, in all this vast place, just two little things left in various rooms—two little beds, two little dish covers, two little wooden stools, in that horrid room downstairs, what did it mean?

What can have been the story of this house, for story there had been, of that I felt sure. Maybe some little children had died here, or, was it that they had lived, and then gone elsewhere, leaving their little belongings behind them? No! that could not be right, for, almost unwillingly, I was forced to admit that those little beings I had seen and heard were not of this world, nor were they the children of my imagination; so that hidden story was apparently to remain hidden unless—unless—I had the courage and will power to unearth it. Will power I had, I knew that, but courage? Ah! that was a different story, and I felt that a certain amount might be needed in the face of what I had already seen. Resolutely I had made up my mind I would continue to visit the house, trying to take things calmly, trusting nothing would happen to try my powers of endurance too severely.

The garden did not look so attractive today, rain had fallen off and on all morning, beating down the few late flowers, making muddy puddles on the grassy paths, and I did not feel as if I dared to venture as far as the shut-in lawn. I would prowl about indoors, I decided, though to tell the truth, the place was eerie in the chill gloom of this wet day, now and then a moaning wind howled through keyholes and chinks. Sometimes a far-off door slammed to, making me jump, or the sound of a rattling window echoed through the empty rooms, the trees made the house dark, too, lacking the brilliant sunshine of previous days, when I revelled in exploring both house and grounds. However, here I was, and here I intended to remain, at least for another hour or two.

This night nursery, as I called it, was anything but an attractive room, so I decided to leave it and pursue my investigations elsewhere, so merely glanced round it as I wandered towards the door, pausing, as I did so, to look at the two little beds. I felt one of them, and was shocked to feel the hardness of it; for though fully made, even to pillows and blankets, all was of the poorest description, the bedding itself almost like wood, so hard was it.

"Poor babies!" I murmured, "if their sweet, little bodies had been obliged to rest on them." I found it difficult to picture those lovely little people as I saw them in the sunny garden, sleeping uneasily on such hard beds. The room chilled me, and I was glad to leave it, though I paused uncertainly at the door, wondering whether to go further amongst the upstairs-rooms or go down again. It was curious the attraction the toy-room held for me. I liked to look at the toys, picturing the games and frolics of the little ones amongst them; moreover, I had the wee scarlet shoes in my pocket, ready to replace, but first I intended to watch if they were still missed. So, I only gave a passing glance into one or two other rooms on my way to the staircase. All were empty, dusty, cold and faded, though once, as in the rooms below, the decorations must have been beautiful, one large, airy room particularly charmed me, especially the ceiling—hand-painted, apparently—a dull, cream ground with tiny, naked babies flying about, holding up pale blue ribbons, all of them gathered, so to speak, by one baby of a larger size in the centre, who held in his wee hands the ends of the ribbons almost as if driving a team of other babies. What held my attention was the exquisite beauty of the child faces; truly, this house had held one lover of children at any rate. I stayed a little while in that room, sitting on the broad window sill, happy with my fancies amongst those pretty babies. The room, I imagined, was just over the "toy-room," judging from the view from the window, so perhaps this was the room of their mother. Perhaps she rested here where her quick ear could catch the sound of little voices in the room beneath. Happy mother! and happy babies. Was she a mother in the old, real meaning of the word—someone to whom the children could go always sure of sympathy for woes and joy in their joy. Mothers like that are rare today, they have not time. Children weary them, pet dogs are so much less trouble.

This room, with its painted babies, was filling my eyes with useless tears; I felt I was losing time, sitting brooding here of things, which, after all, were probably "Direction that I could not see," so, with a lingering look at the lovely, laughing faces, I quietly stepped away, wending my way back along the long corridor, to the head of the staircase, where there was a quaintly-carved white gate. The babies again, I thought, as I paused beside the gate, noticing that on the top of it was fixed a little silver bell which gave out a sweet deep-toned ring, as the gate was touched, evidently once inside the gate, the bell was a signal if it was opened again; probably for mischief, sometimes a tiny hand would shake the gate, calling instantly some person, maybe nurse, or mother, quickly to gather in the straying baby. I sighed again as I went down the stairs. So far today the house had been singularly quiet. I was glad in a way, yet somehow disappointed. I wanted my babies. Very well, then—the toy-room should be my next room. Softly I opened the door, almost feeling as if I should catch them at their play, but all was silent. I would wait, so went quietly to where an old, much-used rocking-chair stood. No fancy affair this, but a solid yellow, wood chair, with big cane seat and back, and large rockers, the right sort of chair in which to rock tired kiddies. I sat down in it and silently waited. I knew I *was* waiting—it is one thing to merely sit down to rest—it is quite another to sit down to wait—wait—for something—or someone, not knowing what or for whom. I tried to read a little book I had put in my pocket, but my eyes refused to keep on the page, and my ears seemed awaiting sounds. They came at last—the sounds—not the babies, sounds that made me spring from my chair and listen, listen! with thumping heart and cold terror gripping me!

Scream after scream, rang through the silence—piercing shrill, the screams of a little child—no, of little children—not the screams one hears in a nursery, when squabbles occur; not the screams of rage or vexation of thwarted wishes, or bed-time orders, but the awful heart-rending screams of children in dire pain and terror. I could have screamed also, merely hearing them, and yet I felt powerless to move or stir, my limbs refused their office. I could only stand shuddering.

Two more piteous cries reached my ears, and then silence, but only for a brief space, as suddenly the door was flung violently open and two small, naked figures fell rather than walked into the room—fell, as if pushed in, and the door swiftly banged to—the bang brought me more or less to my senses, and I stared horror-stricken, aghast—the two little figures were my sunny smiling children of the garden; but oh! the pity of it, their little faces smiled no longer, tears coursed down each baby face, as they stood clinging together, tremblingly; their lovely, little bodies covered with marks as of a lash or stick, weals and cuts which showed like blood; even across their wee legs were hideous marks.

Even now, as I look back after many years, I find it difficult to believe those little figures were not "real," so real did they appear to me. I wanted to go to them, to kneel beside them, soothing, comforting, but something—was it their absolute unconsciousness of my presence, I wonder—kept me still, and watching, slowly their sobbing ceased, as still trembling they moved together to where an old-fashioned sofa stood. I saw them, with difficulty, drag their little, sore and battered bodies up on to it, and cower down under the old, worn blanket, flung on it; I saw them, arms round each other, fair head and dark, close, close together; I saw the quivering limbs grow still, as I heard little moans die away on their lips, and then I saw a soft, unearthly light hover for one instant over the old couch, and then—I was alone, the sofa empty—the room silent! For a long time I stood staring, and then I knew my first feeling was one of intense relief, that those little, ill-used babies were *not* real—though my heart was aching, sickeningly, at what must once have been; my second feeling was one of stern resolve to know and fathom, to punish, if not too late, the author of such misery. Poor little babies! What had been their fate, and why?

Slowly my wits resumed their balance, and my nerves lost some of the strain. I ventured near the sofa, half-expecting to see the little faces, but only the worn, old blanket lay on the sofa; so, stepping swiftly to the fireside, I knelt down, and taking the little shoes from my pocket, I laid them gently in the spot from whence I had taken them, and, for the first time, glanced at my watch. Five minutes past four! "The usual time," I murmured. "How strange it all is, yet there are those whose fixed and unalterable belief is that *if* there ever are 'ghosts' seen, it can only be at midnight!" How little such people know!

Evidently, then, I had been the witness of varied visions of these little ones—the story of their little lives was rapidly unfolding before me. I had *heard* them on the first afternoon, when I took the little shoes; I had *seen* them happy in the garden on my second visit, and today, my third visit, I had *seen* them tortured, torn. Should I see them again, I wondered, or was this last awful scene the final one! At any rate, I felt I should not see them again today, so prepared to take my leave.

I had just reached the hall, when the sound of a heavy groan fell on my ears—a groan and a sound of a moving chair. Nothing unearthly about that, I thought, though why I was so sure of it I could not tell. The moving chair brought the caretaker to my mind, probably groaning at having to come at all, I thought, but, anyway, I will track her for once. Again something moved. "The other front room," I murmured, as I bravely went towards it, and opened the door. It was empty, but the door leading from it into the little, horrible room, where the two little stools were, was slightly ajar. I hated the thought of entering it, but felt compelled to do so; as I neared it, moving as softly as I could, I heard strange words and mutterings. I had just reached the door when the words—

"My God! is there no peace?" uttered in a man's voice, arrested my steps, and then, in louder tones—

"Help, oh, help!"

Instantly I pushed the door open. "Well," I said.

A gaunt, misshapen figure rose suddenly—a man with long, white beard and hair, eyes sunken and burning, fixed themselves upon me, as with a shriek, he yelled—

"Yes, yes, the well! That is it, the well, it is there they are. Who are you? How did you find out? Oh, God! my sin is found out, my punishment is upon me—I confess—I confess. There, take it, take it, it is all there; too late, too late for reparation, make proper use of it, take it," and he flung a heavily-sealed packet almost in my face, and then—swiftly pulling out a small phial from his coat pocket, he raised it to his mouth, and ere I could stay his hand, had drunk the contents, and, raising his hand upwards, said—

"God forgive me—pardon—I have atoned," and fell forward, face downwards, on the stone floor.

I need not dwell upon the horror I went through, when, in my headlong flight from the house, I stumbled blindly to the nearest police officer, and there, with hurried breath, I told of my visits to the empty house, by way of passing idle hours, and of my suddenly coming upon this man, with my exclamation—"Well?" which apparently startled him into giving up his guilty secret. I did *not* deem it necessary to tell of the little children, at least not to police, because they would, if not openly grin and deride me, most certainly have suggested to the nearest medical man that a young woman who moons about empty houses and sees ghosts was not a fit person to be unattended, so I kept my "dream babies" to myself, and one other.

To my unspeakable annoyance, I was dragged into the affair,

and forced to give evidence as to the finding of the man and of his subsequent act—the taking his own life.

The sealed packet, being addressed to "The person who found him out," was, therefore, proved to belong to me, and to my unfortunate self fell the task of reading and making it known, and later, carrying out the instructions contained therein.

The confession of a man apparently driven to it by awful fear was a terrible thing to read, and for this story need only be put briefly—

"I write this my confession," he wrote, "as the one atonement I can make for a sin which has rendered my life and the life of my son a living torture. I have travelled by land and sea, I have visited many strange lands, I have done all that mind could plan or money achieve, in a vain attempt to deaden the relentless voice of conscience or dull the sound of children weeping, which rings in my ears daylight or dark. Sleep is a friend unknown to me, save only drugged sleep. Joy or happiness I have never known.

"If the sun shines, I remember the Sunny Garden and the children at play, ready to tremble if they heard my voice or that of my son.

"If it rains, I remember the punishment room, where we tortured those innocent little ones. Nowhere can I rest, Oh, God! save in my grave, and only then, if I atone—"

He relates how he was left by his brother, then in India, as Guardian to these children of his, and how he and his son Roger made up their minds from the first to get the vast sum of money, left to the children, into their own hands; and, as later evidence proved, they treated the children with systematic cruelty, though no one suspected it—their torturing of them always taking place during late afternoon or evening hours, but during the day, when people were about, money was lavished upon the children, and a certain amount of care taken of them.

In his confession, he relates how he and his wretched son used to fasten the children to two high stools in the dismal room, and whip them until the blood ran from their little bodies. There was no one to shield them; his son and their nurse, as evil as himself, aided him in his cruelty, having been promised a large sum as soon as the children were safely disposed of.

The father of the children was killed in some Frontier trouble, soon after his return to his regiment, and the shock of his death reduced their mother to a helpless invalid who seldom left her own rooms, believing her little ones were in good hands.

They were always taken to see her at noon—their nurse watching them evilly, having threatened them with punishment if they "told tales."

Systematic cruelty was dealt out to these hapless babes, day by day, until one day, they were beaten so vilely, that both died from shock, and were found on the old couch in the toy-room clasped in each other's arms—dead.

Here his confession reaches frenzy, as he adds—

"Together my son and I took the bodies we had so ill-used and flung them into the old disused well in the sunk garden, where, I am certain, their spirits will haunt us all our days.

"We told their mother that gipsies seen in the neighbourhood must have stolen them, and pretended to try and find them, and use every available means, unavailingly. This added grief killed the poor lady, leaving us to enjoy—if we could—our ill-gotten gains.

"My miserable son was killed in a motor accident, soon after, and I—God knows!—a miserable haunted creature, roam the earth seeking peace and finding none."

*

And finally, the hand of fate drew him back to the scene of his crime, and he endeavoured to make reparation by leaving the vast fortune he now possessed—

"To benefit some children in whatsoever manner the finder of this confession shall decide."

Many years have gone by, and a beautiful "Home for Convalescent Children" has taken the place of my "House of Mystery." Upstairs, in gay, cheery rooms, are long rows of little, white beds. Downstairs, in the "Room of Toys," are still more toys, and little tots in dainty, blue overalls play, and grow strong and well.

In the "Punishment Room," now called "Matron's Room," sits a sunny-faced, gentle lady, ever ready to help her little ones, and adored by her nurses.

In the sunk garden are swings and couches, and many games. One corner of the garden has been opened out, and a high, grass mound made there; on it is an exquisite white marble Angel, holding in her arms two tiny children—that is all. No names or dates are given—simply "In memory of two children."

Only once has the old story been brought vividly to my memory. I was visiting the Home, and the night nurse, a sweet motherly woman, asked me—

"Was there ever a story about this house, ma'am?"

"Why, nurse?" I asked.

"Oh, it may be fancy, ma'am," she replied, "but once or twice I thought I heard a little child crying, but all my little ones were asleep, and at times I've heard tiny pattering feet when none of my babies were out of their beds; and once, ma'am, a woman brought a tiny girl here, and the little thing had on a pair of wee scarlet shoes. That night, I heard soft, baby laughter and little chuckles of glee, and though I, myself, put those little shoes in a safe place, they had been moved by the morning, but this was before the beautiful white angel was put in the garden, ma'am, just about the time the gardeners filled in that unsafe old well. I have not heard anything since then."

I gave no explanation, I could not, I only said—

"If all the babies sleep in peace, nurse, all is well."

In forests and wildernesses the spirits of little children that have been murdered are said to wander about wailing, within an assigned space, as long as their lives would have lasted on earth, if they had been permitted to live. As a terror for unnatural mothers that destroy their offspring, their sad cry is said to be: "Mamma! Mamma!" When travellers by night pass such places, these beings will hang on the vehicle, when the liveliest horses will toil as if they were dragging millstones, will sweat, and at length be unable to proceed a step further. The peasant then knows that a ghost or Pysling has attached itself to his vehicle. If he goes to the horses' heads, lifts the headstall, and looks through it towards the carriage, he will see the little pitiable being, but will get a smart blow on the ear, or fall sick. This is called ghost-pressed (gastkramad).

Thorpe, Swedish folklore (1851)[19]

ANNE'S LITTLE GHOST

H. D. Everett

Henrietta Dorothy Everett (1851–1923) was a British novelist who wrote for many years under the nom de plume Theo Douglas, but even once her identity was revealed she led quite a private life. She wrote three historical novels but most of her other works were in the fantasy and supernatural genre and featured ancient Egyptian mummies, Spiritualism, and psychic vampires.

Her main collection of supernatural tales, The Death-Mask and Other Ghosts (1920), was published under her own name and features two stories that were possible contenders for this collection. "Nevill Nugent's Legacy", the one not included, is an epistolary tale from the perspective of a woman who keeps seeing the ghost of a boy (aged around fourteen) wandering the residence of which she has recently become custodian. No one else is able to see him, although a few others have heard him, and as with a few such stories in this collection, she is more witness than assistant. I encourage readers to seek this one out to note the reliance on themes found elsewhere in this collection. The one chosen for inclusion, "Anne's Little Ghost", may seem tame in comparison, but there are two key factors that swayed me toward it. Firstly, that it is narrated by the father of the ghost itself, which is rare, and secondly, because the father hints that its presence is not quite as harmless as it might seem.

e had planned to take a holiday as soon as I was demobilised, and I claim that we had abundantly earned it, Anne and I. She had been a war worker all the time I was serving abroad—(for there were, alas! no children to tie her to the duties of home)—and she needed relief and change as much as I. It was to be a real holiday and in full measure—no wretched scrap measured by days, but lasting several weeks, and at our own option to extend into months if we so pleased. This gave a peculiar feeling of wealth and spaciousness; for once we were to be millionaires in the holiday linc. But from the £.s.d. point of view, a quite separate matter, the holiday was bound to be cheap. So Anne decreed, and I left it to her to arrange what it should be, and where.

She was in high spirits the last time she came to see me in hospital, about a week before my discharge. She had heard of the very place for us, if I agreed—and of course I was ready to agree. Her friend Adelaide Sherwood recommended Deepdene, but there was no time to be lost; we must write or wire at once if we wanted to secure the rooms. Farmhouse lodgings in Devonshire; would not that be delightful?—with trout-fishing for me thrown in, and the sea not many miles away. It was really half a house, and the farm-mistress would board and cook for us: we could either bring a servant (we did not possess one) or a day-woman would come in from the village to order the rooms. Some friends of Miss Sherwood's had stayed there the previous autumn, and were abundantly satisfied with everything, cleanliness included; the charge was, besides, astonishingly low.

"Just think, Godfrey, of getting the farm produce fresh on the spot—eggs and vegetables, to say nothing of dairy luxuries beyond. And in such pretty country as they say it is. I cannot fancy getting tired of the quiet, but perhaps you may feel differently. A large sitting-room with glass doors on to a verandah, and such a view from it; the farm-buildings quite away on the other side. The bedroom is on the same floor: that will be right for your lame leg, will it not? And then upstairs two more bedrooms, roomy attics. We shall not need to use these, but they are part of the half-house, and are let with it. What do you say?"

A prompt telegram secured us the tenancy of the half-house, and a week later Anne and I were *en route* for our new abode. We took the journey leisurely—a fit prelude to a holiday which was to be all leisure—and stayed a couple of nights at Exeter on our way. So the journey of the last morning was a short one. We arrived at our destination soon after noon, to find all gilded with the cheer of mid-day sunshine, and a white-aproned landlady hospitably welcoming us at the door.

The house was neither picturesque nor old, but it promised comfort, and seemed likely to justify the encomiums of Anne's friend and correspondent. Mrs. Stokes the landlady was openly proud of it, and showed us round expecting appreciation. The kitchen and offices occupied the lower floor, but we had a separate entrance through the garden wicket up steps to the verandah, our private portion of it, which was cut off from the other set of lodgings by a light railing thrown across. This second set was at present vacant, but would be occupied in another fortnight by two ladies, sisters, who came always at this time of year, bringing with them their own maid.

The attic rooms were also shown, though we were not intending to occupy them. My lame leg excused me from a further mounting of stairs, but Anne accompanied Mrs. Stokes aloft. The occupiers of both sets had an equal right to these stairs, and the attic accommodation was impartially divided, two falling to our lot, and two to that of the sisters and their servant.

They were airy rooms, Anne told me, and would make pleasant bedrooms, looking out through smaller windows on the same lovely view that we commanded on the lower floor. This was all that was said at the time, but later, when tea was spread and we were partaking of it, she told me more.

"People must have been here with children," she said presently in an interval of filling my cup. "The attic over our bedroom has evidently been used as a nursery, for there are coloured pictures pasted on the wall, and a child's bed is pushed into one corner. Mrs. Stokes said she would take it out if it was in our way."

There was just the slightest sigh with this communication, and the least possible droop at the corners of Anne's sensitive mouth, but enough to give me a clue to what was in her mind. I can often read Anne's mind as plainly as the page of a book—though I do not tell her so; perhaps because of long association, to say nothing of affection. We two are singularly alone in the world, and so are drawn all the closer, each to each. We have been married rather more than eight years, and in our second year together we possessed, for a brief space of only weeks, a baby daughter. So brief a space that one might suppose both joy and grief would be easily forgotten; but those who so think, know little of a mother's heart—at least, little of Anne's. From the dear memory of that joy and that grief (the sword piercing her soul, as was foretold of another mother) comes the wistful interest she takes in all children. And I could divine her thought: "If only little Clarice had lived and had been with us here, the pictured attic would have been her nursery, and the little bed in the corner would have been ready made for her." But of this I said nothing.

"Perhaps Mrs. Stokes's own children sleep there when they are without lodgers," I suggested, but Anne shook her head.

"No, for I asked the question. They have only three big boys, all in their teens. The eldest works on the farm, and the other two are away at school. None of the Stokes family sleep under this roof; a stable is converted into quarters for them, so that the house may be set apart as lodgings"; and again there came the slight and smothered sigh.

I should be giving a false impression if it were thought from this that there is anything dreary about Anne. No one is more resolutely cheerful, or more keenly and alertly practical, than this wife of mine. These inner feelings of hers, tender regrets and constant thoughts, have their own secret chamber in her mind, the door of which is shut and barred; a sacred threshold, which even I dare not openly approach. No more was said about the empty cot and the pictures, and that first evening of our stay at Deepdene passed delightfully amid country sights and sounds, and the sweet Devonshire air. Miss Sherwood's recommendation was, we thought, justifying itself to the full.

And at night, when the veil of dimness, not quite darkness, was drawn over the garden and the hills, what a healing silence prevailed: bird notes stilled, and at last even the plaintive cry of a lamb which had wandered from its mother, satisfied and at rest. I slept profoundly, but presently what was this? Anne's voice: Anne shaking me awake.

"Godfrey! Godfrey, listen! Do you hear?"

I was for the moment deaf and dazed with sleep.

"No," I said. "What is it? What is the matter?"

"It is a child sobbing. A little child in trouble. A child that has been shut out. I cannot hear it and do nothing. Can you?" Anne was thrusting her feet into slippers, and was already arrayed in her dressing-gown—blue and white, the colours of the Virgin Mother. "I can't make out where the sound comes from—whether it is overhead or out of doors. Listen, and you will hear it too. There are no words, only cries and sobs. I heard it again the instant before you awoke."

I was out of bed by this time and broad awake. I heard no crying, but I did hear footsteps: a child's pattering run across the floor overhead, once from end to end of the room, and then again in return.

"Now I know," said Anne, quite composedly, proceeding to light a candle. "It is upstairs in the attic I told you of; the room like a nursery, which is over ours. I wonder what child it can be. Mrs. Stokes should have let us know. I am going up to see."

That was so entirely Anne-like I was not surprised. She went out carrying the light, and I followed on to the landing in case I should be wanted. As I went, I heard again the pattering feet overhead, and I think Anne heard them too. I waited at the foot of the stairs, not wishing to affright the child by the sight of a grim soldier-man in pyjamas. No child, not even the most nervous, could be frightened at the sight of Anne.

Waiting there, I could be certain that no living soul came down the stairs. I heard Anne pass from room to room, and then she called to me.

"Godfrey, I wish you would come up here."

I went up in the soft twilight that was not wholly dark, even in that enclosed place, entering where I saw her candle shine. She was in the attic with the pictured walls, sitting on the little bed, and her face was white and awe-stricken.

"I can't find anything," she said. "The rooms are all empty, and there is no place in which a child could be shut. I wish you would look too."

Of course I looked with her, and, equally of course, our search was fruitless. Then I persuaded her to go back to our room and listen there, while I hurried on some clothes and made search round the house outside. I talked some nonsense about the way in which sounds reflect and echo, and the difficulty there is about locating their direction, especially at night; but I do not think she believed me: unconvinced myself, I could hardly expect to convince another. And I was privately certain I had heard the footsteps of a child, not echoed over floors from a distance, but distinctly overhead. There must be some way of getting up to those attics, and down from them, that we did not know.

But in the morning Mrs. Stokes could tell us nothing, and had no explanation to offer. No child could have got in without her knowledge. It must have been one out of the village wandering round outside, scared by the darkness, and afraid to go home because it had been threatened with the stick. That was how the good dame dismissed the matter, and we might have been satisfied about the crying, but not as to those footsteps overhead.

It will be well believed that I was eager to sample the fishing, and the next day saw us on the banks of the stream, Anne sitting near me with a book. But somehow in the week following she managed to catch cold, and after that I had for a while to pursue my sport alone, and she spent solitary hours at the Deepdene farm.

I think it was on the second day of her seclusion that she said to me when I came back in the evening: "I have seen the child."

I had better mention here that in the interval we had heard no more of the sobbing voice at night, nor of the footsteps overhead. Anne looked as if something had moved her profoundly, even to the shedding of tears.

"Did you find out whose child it is, and why it is here?"

"No. She did not speak, and it seems so odd that Mrs. Stokes does not know. I was on the landing when I saw her first, and she was running upstairs. There is no carpet on those stairs, and I heard quite plainly the patter of her feet. A little girl. I went up after her, and she ran straight into that room which was a nursery, the room with the pictures."

"And you followed?"

"Yes, I followed, but she was not there. I was puzzled—almost frightened, and I went back again to the sitting-room. I think it must have been half an hour later when I saw her again. If you remember, it began to rain. It was so chilly, I was obliged to shut to the glass doors."

"Yes?" I said. Anne had paused again, with that odd breathlessness which was new.

"She was out there on the verandah, and the rain was slanting in upon her. Such a pretty little girl, and about the age—" (I knew what Anne so nearly said, and why she checked herself and altered the phrase to "about six years old." Clarice would have been six years old had she lived.) "Not a poor woman's child. She had a pretty white frock on, worked cambric and lace, and a silk sash of a sort of geranium red. No cottagers' child would be dressed so. And she had such an appealing little face, as if she was longing to be sheltered and comforted. It was raining, you know, all the time."

"And what did you do?"

"Why of course I opened the window. I said, 'Come in my dear, you will get wet.' I held out my hand and she put hers into it—oh, such a cold little hand, as cold and soft as snow. I can feel the touch of it still. I drew her into the room. 'We should be warm in here,' I said. No, I'm not crying, Godfrey; not really crying; but there was something in her face that touched me: a sort of surprise, as if no one had ever welcomed or been kind to her before. I asked her where she lived, but she only made a sign and put a finger to her lips. She heard me—I am sure she heard me, but I cannot help fancying the poor child is dumb.

"She heard me, for when I said, 'My darling, will you give me a kiss?' she put up both her little arms, and her face was close to mine. I would have had that kiss, only just then that tiresome Mrs. Stokes knocked at the door; the butcher, it seemed, had called, and she wanted to know if we would take a joint. The instant there came the knock, the child slipped away out of my arms. I had left the window open behind us, and she was gone."

"Mrs. Stokes did not see her?"

"No. She saw nothing, and could tell nothing; only I thought she looked a little *odd* when I was putting questions. I couldn't help wondering if there was any secret about it which she was bound to keep."

As the days went on, I began also to wonder this, and after a while that wonder shaped itself into action. But I anticipate.

That night we heard again the footsteps overhead, both of us heard them. It was still completely dark, and the rain, driven against our windows, was mixed with hail. The pattering steps crossed the floor above once, twice, and after an interval a third time. I was still awake, holding my breath to listen should they come again, when I heard another sound beside me. Anne was crying, very quietly, her face buried in the pillow so that all sound should be hushed. I put out my hand to touch her.

"What is the matter?"

"Oh Godfrey—oh Godfrey, that poor child," she sobbed. "It is so sad for her to be up there all alone in the cold and darkness, and only six years old. Six years old! Clarice would have been just that age. Can it be Clarice trying to come back to us? I felt as if she were Clarice when I held her in my arms."

I was not surprised. It was as if I had seen the thought taking shape, somehow as crystals form. But what could I do but dub it foolishness, born out of the sweet fond folly of a mother's love?

We heard no more that night. Next morning, without telling Anne of my intention, I went up to examine the attics for the first time by daylight. The rooms over ours were vacant, and in the one with pictured walls the little bed was gaunt and undraped, with its stripped mattress and uncovered pillow. There was no closet or recess in which it was possible for even the smallest child to hide, and as the walls were of thin modern building, secret entrances and passages were out of the question here.

I was to hear again later of that little bed. Nothing more passed between us touching that strange fancy of Anne's, the confession I had surprised from her in the night, until she said in a sort of shamefaced fashion (but again there were tears in her eyes):

"I made a pretence to Mrs. Stokes today; I hope it was not untrue enough to be wrong. I said we might be expecting a child visitor: we might expect any visitors you know, and some of our friends have children. And I asked her to have the pictured attic put ready, and the bed made up—in case. She did it this morning, and I did not want you to go up there and be surprised. It does not look nearly so miserable now the furniture is in order, and sheets and blankets are on the little bed. Any one who was up there in the night, and who was cold and tired, could lie down."

What was I to say to this, but again that it was folly?—but I could not charge Anne with folly when she looked as she did then. And hardly a night passed without the pattering footsteps overhead.

The parish to which Deepdene belonged was a scattered one; the church was a long half-mile away, and a mere cluster of cottages called itself the village. That cluster, however, contained the post-office, and the inevitable general shop, which included among its wares a few toys of the simpler sort. One day Anne returned from a post-office errand the purchaser of a doll, pretty of head and face, but with its nudity barely covered by a scant chemise of waxed muslin. She said nothing of her intention, but for a day or two that doll lay about in our sitting-room, while her skilful fingers were busied shaping for it more befitting garments—pink and frilly, and with a pinafore of lace. Then it disappeared, but I did not remark, nor for a while did she explain, not until I asked her a week later if she had seen the child again.

"She often comes when I am alone, peeping in at me from the verandah," was the answer. "And she was pleased when I gave her the doll. She took it from me and kissed me, but still she does not speak."

She took the doll! With this the mystery grew. How could an immaterial creature, one we dimly guessed to be spirit and not flesh, accept a material gift, removing it when she withdrew? Yet Anne had given her the toy in exchange for a kiss, and the doll was certainly gone.

Next day when I came in from the stream, Anne was out, and some impulse urged me to go up again to the attic, the attic prepared for our supposed guests, which no one had arrived to occupy. It was vacant as before, but a couple of small vases held fresh flowers, of Anne's filling doubtless, and on the white pillow of the little bed there lay the pink-frocked doll.

I was beginning to be anxious about Anne. There was a change in her I did not like to see; a feverish spot on her cheek, and, slight as she was before, she had fallen away in the few weeks of our sojourn to be very thin. She laughed over it herself, and said her gowns must be taken in; but to me it seemed no laughing matter. Was vitality being drawn from her for the shaping of the child apparition in material form; and, if so, what would be the effect upon her health? I am not instructed in such matters, but I vaguely recalled some of the explanations put forward—material forms built up from the medium, and life-substance drawn away. Ought I to make some excuse, and cut short our stay at Deepdene? That was one question, but another followed it. Now that she fancied the appearance might be that of her dead baby, our little Clarice, would Anne be content to go?

Our little Clarice! Mine as well as hers; the father's tie as valid surely as the mother's, if not so close and fond. If to one of us, why not to both? But in the end I could no longer say this. Though only once, she was visible to me too.

Was it a projection from Anne's mind influencing mine? I have wondered since; but these are questions I can only indicate: they are beyond my power to answer.

We were sitting in the early twilight, the lamp unlit, as Anne had a headache: her head often ached in these days. The glass doors were open, and I dimly saw, first a glimpse of white on the verandah, misty and indefinite, which presently resolved itself into the figure Anne had described to me—the dainty figure of a girl-child in white frock and red silk sash, a cloud of dusky hair hanging about her little head. She was peeping in at me and drawing back; then with more confidence peeping again. Anne took no notice; she was, I think, asleep. I remained motionless, scarcely daring to breathe, lest I should startle this exquisite small creature, as one might fear to affright a bird. Presently she ventured as far into the room as where Anne was sitting, and stood resting her little elbows on her friend's knee, and looking me straight in the face.

I was able now to understand Anne's meaning about the child's pathetic eyes with their wistfulness of appeal, and also to appreciate something more: something that Anne herself had not noticed, was not likely to notice, as people seldom see likenesses to themselves.

It was very marked—the eyes, the brow, the hair: here was Anne as she must have been a quarter of a century ago. Could I doubt that it was our child; and did a longing for the earthly parents' love draw her down to us, away from her safe and happy cradling in the satisfaction of Heaven?

I was still gazing when my wife moved and sighed, waking from her sleep; and the childish figure was gone in a flash, too abrupt for any real withdrawal. In spite of the evidence of those material-sounding footsteps—in spite of the handling of the doll—I never again thought of her as compacted of ordinary mundane flesh and blood.

I had seen her with my own eyes, and I could no longer doubt. But there was a point which I still desired to probe, despite that evidence of the resemblance. I wanted to find out whether the half-house we were renting could be haunted, and whether the child-ghost had been seen or heard by other people than ourselves.

It would be a difficult matter to ascertain, for in defence of their property against depreciation, very good people have before now thought it hardly a sin to pervert the truth. But I reflected that the clergyman of the parish had no interest in letting Deepdene. I would go in the first place to him, and then see what I could make of sounding Mrs. Stokes.

My errand to Mr. Fielding bore only negative fruit. He was a man advanced in years, a gentleman and a scholar, and he received me with suave politeness; if he could serve me in any way he would be glad. But when I put my question, I could see that a faint flicker of amusement underlay his grave attention; he, the minister of the Unseen, was wholly sceptical as to its demonstration. I said very little, merely asking did the house where we were lodging bear the reputation of being haunted? We—I, that is, for I left Anne out of it—had heard sounds that could not be explained, and seen a small figure that appeared to vanish. I should like to know whether it was a matter of common report.

The answer to this was No. There might be some vulgar story of the sort, it was just possible, but it had never reached his ears. Had it done so, he would have discredited it. I would readily see on reflection how easy it was to mistake sounds and their origin; and not only did our ears trick us in such matters, but also our vision. A supposed phantom generally meant that the percipient would do well to resort to an oculist.

I did not argue the point. As I told him, I only wished to ascertain whether there was, or was not, any local tradition. I wished him good morning, and my next resort was to Mrs. Stokes.

Here I was met by indignation, and the good woman was not easy to appease. I was interested, I told her, I was not objecting; rather than otherwise, it increased my interest in Deepdene. I only wished to know if any of the other lodgers—and doubtless in the course of the year she would have many—had mentioned to her any similar sights or sounds.

Her first answer was a flat negative; but there was, I thought, an uneasy consciousness in the eye that did not meet mine as before, and presently modification came. For her own part she knew nothing, as she never slept in the house herself, nor did Stokes *père*, nor the boys—(was this, it occurred to me to wonder, a suspicious circumstance?) She had never seen or heard anything "worse than herself," and I might take that as on her Bible oath; but, now she came to think, some of the lodgers had mentioned a running about on those upper floors, happening when they had the rats in at threshing time. They got some virus when they heard of it, and there were no more complaints after that was put down. If I had been disturbed, no doubt the rats were getting in again. But, certain sure, there were no ghosts.

I wondered, and I wonder still, whether some houses have a psychical atmosphere which can be variously moulded and used; the child employing it to approach us, and the spiritual environment of others putting it to a quite separate use. I think this is not impossible, but as to the truth of the matter, who can say?

As I have shown, I gained nothing by my inquiries, and this is nearly all I have to tell. The end of our sojourn followed quickly. I remember once discussing psychical matters with a friend. He was a believer, and he said to me: "I always know how to distinguish a true ghost-story from a faked one. The true ghost-story never has any point, and the faked one dare not leave it out." This ghost-story of mine, though not faked, has a point, but it is one the ordinary reader would overlook, and I do not insist on it. I am abundantly content to be disbelieved, and Anne is content too.

It was Anne's health which brought our stay at Deepdene to an abrupt close. I think I have said that for some time I had noticed she was looking ill, and wondered vaguely whether her vitality could be drained away to supply material for those manifestations we had witnessed and heard. It was, however, no case of gradually lessened strength, but a threatened crisis which demanded prompt atten-tion—surgeon's investigation and a nursing-home. So, in figurative language, we struck our tents, seeking another encampment, and Deepdene knew us no more.

Woe to the babie that ne'er saw the sun,
All alane and alane, oh!
His bodie shall lie in the kirk 'neath the rain,
All alane and alane, oh!

Late eighteenth-century verse from
the English-Scottish borders[20]

In Annam the spirits of children still-born and of those dying in
infancy are held in great fear. These spirits, called *Con Ranh*, or *Con
Lôn* (from *lôn*, "to enter into life"), are ever seeking "to incorporate
themselves in the bodies of others, though, after so doing, they are
incapable of life.

Chamberlain, *The Child and Childhood in Folk-Thought* (1896)[21]

On a table in the middle of one of these rooms a thing to make you
shudder gleams in a glass box, a fragile thing that failed of life some two
thousand years ago. It is the mummy of a human embryo, and someone,
to appease the malice of this born-dead thing, had covered its face
with a coating of gold–for, according to the belief of the Egyptians,
these little abortions became the evil genii of their families if proper
honour was not paid to them. At the end of its negligible body, the
gilded head, with its great foetus eyes, is unforgettable for its suffering
ugliness, for its frustrated and ferocious expression.

Loti, "The Hall of the Mummies" (1909)[22]

THE CURSE OF THE STILLBORN

Margery Lawrence

Margery Lawrence (1889–1969) was a British author of predominantly romantic, fantasy, horror, and detective fiction, and an illustrator for works by her contemporaries. "The Curse of the Stillborn" was first published in "pulp" magazine Hutchinson's Mystery Magazine *in 1925, prior to its collection with more of her supernatural stories in* Nights of the Round Table *(1926). It is the only story in this anthology featuring British people living and working in the colonies, and indeed while there are a number of Anglophone colonial ghost stories published in the period, I have found few featuring the ghost child. Those who are interested in the theme might turn to Florence Marryat's "Little White Souls" from* A Moment of Madness and Other Stories *(1883) which is set in colonial India. However, in that tale, it is the ghostly mother (and the living mother's own paranoia) that offer the greatest threat. The infant appears, as in some other tales, as a hovering spirit with no character or agency. "The Curse of the Stillborn" turns to the legends found in the colonies and other global traditions as recorded by Anglophone folklorists, in which the child spirit (which is what I read the destructive shadow to be) can shape-shift and exude power much beyond anything it had in life. It is an excellent example of women writers chastising the arrogant Western colonialist, who falters and is, in this case, punished when attempting to enforce their own faith and customs on others, rather than respecting those beliefs and practices of the indigenous inhabitants.*

ammit—why can't you let 'em bury their dead in their own way?"

The words were blurted out. Mrs. Peter Bond raised her sandy eyebrows and stared at the speaker with outraged virtue written large upon her square determined face, burnt brick-red with the Egyptian sun. Little Michael Frith wilted, but stuck to his point.

"I'm sorry—didn't mean to swear, Mrs. Bond—but *don't* you see what I mean, really?" His brown wrinkled brow was lined with distress.

Mrs. Bond pursed her lips disapprovingly. Upright and heavily built, in uncompromisingly stiff white piqué, her thick waist well-belted, her weatherbeaten face surmounted by a pith helmet, she looked impregnably solid and British, reflected Frith exasperatedly—three years among these people and no nearer comprehending them. He tried again.

"You see—Mefren's a child of the desert... and her old mother's a pure-bred nomad... wild as a hawk. Why can't you let 'em bury their dead in peace?"

"I am surprised at your attitude, Mr. Frith! I'm sorry, but I can't undertake to advise my husband any differently. These people are ignorant, childish, superstitious... I and my husband stand here to try and teach them better. And you actually suggest that I allow Mefren to bury her baby as she likes—presumably in the Desert, with I don't know what awful sort of heathen rites—when my husband is here, a minister of the Lord, ready and anxious to give the poor little thing decent Christian burial! I must say I don't think this side of it can have struck you, Mr. Frith!"

Mrs. Bond's voice was genuinely shocked. Restlessly little Michael Frith stirred and kicked a booted foot against the whitewashed wall. He frowned—how *could* he explain? The native point of view... and this good-hearted, narrow, stubborn woman!

Vaguely his mind fled to Mefren, small, slender brown creature, and her mother, Takkari, silent and haggard, with black burning eyes beneath her voluminous haik. Wanderers both, they had appeared at the door of his tent one dawn with a request for food... he was encamped on the lip of the Valley of Blue Stones, a deep cleft between two ridges a few miles away from the tiny town of Ikh Nessan, where Peter Bond's little whitewashed church brooded over the tangle of mud huts like a white hen mothering a scattered handful of brown and alien chicks. Always soft-hearted, Frith had fed them both, and seeing the girl's condition and obvious exhaustion, had sent them into Ikh Nessan with a note to Mrs. Bond—of whose kind heart, despite her irritating ways, none of the tiny colony had the least doubt. Food and shelter were at once forthcoming, and none too soon, for it came to pass, only a few days after the wanderers' arrival at Ikh Nessan, that the girl's time came upon her, but too soon... and a child was born, but dead—stillborn.

Full of well-meaning sympathy and a genuine desire to help, Mrs. Bond had hurried to inform Takkari, grimly silent, crouched in the shadows of the mud hut that sheltered the weeping girl, that despite the fact that the child, poor little soul, had died too early for baptism, her husband was ready at once to conduct the burial service. She was met by blank silence and a vigorous shake of the head. Dashed, and considerably annoyed, the Englishwoman demanded her reasons. Glowering silence again, but repeated attacks elicited the brusque information, in halting English, that "Kistian bury no good. Come night, her bury self—come night, her go aways." Naturally Mrs. Bond was outraged, and withdrew to consult her husband. I fear, had it not been for Nature, whose heavy hand on the young mother forbade anything in the way of flight, Takkari and her daughter would have been away, lost in the heart of the Desert they came from, before that night. But the evening brought little Peter Bond, full of anxious sympathy for this frail member of the flock he genuinely loved, though shocked beyond measure at his wife's report of Takkari's refusal, and the sullen, stubborn silence with which she faced him. It was while awaiting the result of this, Mrs. Bond felt, most momentous interview, standing at the rickety gate of the little walled garden, the evening sun warm on the tamarisks that sprawled, green and lusty, across the whitewashed wall, that Michael Frith, dusty and hot, trudged by and paused with a cheery word. Full of her story, she had poured it forth, and her surprise and indignation were great to meet his gaze at the end—a look in which politeness warred with frank disapproval. His sympathies were entirely with Mefren and her dour, free-striding old nomad mother; why should they who were, at best, mere birds of passage, be obliged to conform to the hidebound ideas of this stupid Englishwoman? Left to himself "Peterkin," as the little chaplain was affectionately known, would have been a sympathetic, understanding father to these wayward children of his—it was the insistent domination of this well-meaning, sincerely religious, but supremely narrow-minded wife of his that drove him into insisting on the "Church's rights." The phrase was on Mrs. Bond's lips as Frith aroused himself from his reverie; she was still talking, her square, hard-featured face stern with strong disapproval as she eyed him.

"Towards a member of his flock—I told my husband he must not admit argument on the subject. As a Father, he must be Firm..."

"But surely, it's not as if Mefren was a Christian," objected Frith drily; "if it was a member of your husband's congregation..."

"Oh, but she *is*!" Mrs. Bond was eagerly assertive. "They are both Christians... I took care to inquire about that when they came first, and Takkari assured me that both she and Mefren had been baptised!"

Michael Frith smiled drily. He could see Takkari's sombre eyes at that first interview, summing up the unconscious Mrs. Bond, and assenting gruffly to any suggestion put forward—anything for a shelter and good food for her ewe-lamb in her trouble. But what was there to say? He shrugged, none too politely.

"Well... I don't agree, I'm afraid, Mrs. Bond. You see, I know these people pretty well. And frankly, I warn you again—I should let them have their own way."

As he spoke there was a quick step from the house, and the Rev. Peter appeared on the threshold. Wiping his moist forehead with a large red handkerchief, he smiled uncertainly on Michael Frith, and turned with a mild air of triumph to his wife. She asked eagerly:

"Well—have you succeeded?"

"With the blessing of the Lord," said Peterkin solemnly. "Poor child—poor child! I feel for her ignorance, and for her mother, though I fear Takkari is still stubborn. But I wrought mightily with Mefren for the soul of her child, and at last I prevailed..."

A shadow seemed to fall upon the group. Old Takkari stood behind them, her lean, muscular feet muffled in the dusty earth. From the dark hooding of her brown haik, pulled close about her head, her uncanny eyes shone out, moving from one face to the other in silence. Mrs. Bond started and drew a sharp breath—the woman was standing at her elbow before she had seen her, and the grim wrinkled face was pregnant with meaning. There was a moment's tense silence, then, turning to Frith, Takkari said something in a low tone, ending with a sardonic laugh... and was gone, flitting through the open gate and down the dusty road towards the little town. The group moved, and Mrs. Bond found her tongue.

"Well, really!" she began, then curiosity fought indignation and conquered. "Whatever did she say to you, Mr. Frith?"

Frith, feeling his patience, like his politeness, nearing its end, moved away in the track of the tireless brown feet that had left delicate tracks, like a greyhound's, in the white dust.

"Nothing in particular," he said over his shoulder, "only a warning. An old Arabic proverb to the effect that your blood must be upon your own head."

As he strode away he saw Mrs. Bond beckon to Said Ullah, idling with a few cronies under the nodding palms, to come and dig the grave.

Like a lean dark wolf returning to its lair at evening, Takkari crept back to her daughter's side that night. Burials are not things, in the tropical heat of Egypt, to be postponed, and already a newly-turned mound beneath a clump of aloes marked the cradle—first and last—of the poor little scrap of humanity that never saw the sun. Alone the chaplain and his wife had committed the tiny body to the warm earth, watched Said Ullah, lean and nonchalant, fill in the grave as they prayed... Mefren was still in a semi-delirious state, and the sound of her distant moaning was disturbing. Mrs. Bond walked down after supper with offers of help, but was confronted by a silent, scowling Takkari in the doorway, whose determined headshake and glowering expression frankly daunted her. She retired, huffed, but somehow not feeling sufficiently sure of herself to adopt the attitude of dignity she felt the situation needed... defeated by the grim silence, the dark hut with its sinister single light spreading a dull red carpet behind the still dark figure of Takkari in her hooded draperies. The stealthy rustle of the bushes that brushed her skirts, the crooning of the faint wind that crept about the garden, combined with the velvet darkness of the night to defeat Mrs. Bond completely, and she beat a retreat to the shelter of the little "parson-house" as graceless Said Ullah called it, in a state of nerves very unusual with her. In fact, she took herself severely to task for her weakmindedness in not reproving Takkari for her lack of manners, but a curious feeling of reluctance to face that silent hut again kept her from a second attempt, and with a frown at herself and a mental note to rectify this leniency by increased severity on the morrow, Mrs. Bond settled herself down to write.

She was a most efficient clerk, in truth, and all the financial affairs, indeed the entire organisation of the secular side of her husband's life, was in her large and capable hands; every evening she set aside an hour at least for checking every item of the day, entering up accounts, engagements made for herself or her husband, requests for help, the thousand and one minor arrangements that make up a parson's life, who, like a doctor, can scarcely dare to call an hour his own. Laboriously on the opposite side of the table little Peter Bond, his high forehead grotesquely wrinkled under the pushed-up glasses, sat writing out his next Sunday's sermon; he was a painstaking preacher, and spent days upon one sermon—conscientious, entirely ineffective orations. It was a pleasant little room, despite the cheap and horrid "Eastern" bazaar stuff with which it was crammed. An oil lamp with a preposterous red shade, not unlike a rakishly poised hat, stood at the chaplain's elbow between him and his wife—the contrast between his slowly scratching pen and frequent pauses and her swiftly decisive scribbling was curiously symbolical of both characters. The room was silent, and outside the lazy, fat-bodied, night moths lunged and bumped against the pane. As a rule the intrusion of the insect tribe after lamp-time was the one thing that maddened Mrs. Bond, but tonight, oddly enough, the room was entirely empty, the churring of the myriad flies that usually found their way in to circle wildly round the lampshade was absent. It may have been the unwonted silence—one misses even a nuisance quite amazingly at first—but once or twice Mrs. Bond stopped her rapid writing, and raising her head, listened intently. The third time she frowned, and spoke.

"Peter—doesn't it strike you how quiet it is? Is there a storm gathering? I feel there must be."

The Rev. Peter raised his large mild blue eyes and regarded her solemnly. In the dead stillness of the room her voice had sounded curiously loud and harsh.

"A storm—I really couldn't say, my dear. There may be one of those desert storms brewing..." He stared over at the window, screwing up his eyes. "You may be correct, my dear. Indeed, I think there is something electrical in the air tonight. For instance, the lamp is burning very badly—very low indeed. Yes."

"Electricity—rubbish!" Mrs. Bond's voice was snappy; now she remembered that the unusually poor light had struck her, subconsciously, and for some obscure reason this worried her faintly. After the manner of many women, the inexplicable always had the effect of sharpening her temper; she hated any deviation from the ordinary as a cat hates getting wet. "Electric conditions can't affect an oil lamp, Peter. Don't be silly—oh!"

The exclamation was, as it were, wrung out of her, for suddenly the lamp, already perceptibly lower, sank to a mere pool of faint light on the table; even as they both exclaimed, though, it flared up again, and irritably Mrs. Bond pulled off the shade to examine it.

"Light the other lamp, Peter. There must be something in the oil, or the wick's a bad one, or something..." Mrs. Bond was an expert at managing a lamp, as she was at most household tasks, and the room sank into silence again as the Rev. Peter resumed his labours beneath a fresh lamp, and his better half wrestled with the internal secrets of the red-shaded one at a little table.

After ten minutes or so spent in patient analysis of the erring lamp, however, she pushed it on one side with an annoyed "Tcha!... There's nothing wrong with it, as far as I can see—it must have been the oil. Well, I can't waste any more time over it."

The Rev. Peter, deep in his sermon, grunted absently, and silence fell again upon the room. Outside the night brooded over the little group of buildings, huts, chapel, the few low-roofed bungalows that, greatly daring, clustered together at the very threshold of the dour, stark Desert. The wind rose among the whispering tamarisks, and the brushing of their green-tufted branches made a dry siffling sound against the low window-sill of the lighted room; the wide sky, a sheet of black-purple velvet, patterned sequin-like with stars, yawned above the Desert, vast, illimitable, a dome of immensity which was at once comforting and menacing. Comforting, at least, it had till now always been to Mrs. Bond, a sincerely pious woman in her stern way. Many a night in her first six months in Egypt she had gazed up at that wide dark peace, and telling herself that that same sky had shone above the Birth at Bethlehem—a star like those immense, unwinking stars had led the Wise Men over hill and dale to their goal at last—the same age-old silence shrouded Joseph and Mary on their flight from Herod's blood-drenched swords. She had gazed up at the stars and felt contentment, peace, a solace in the thought that she, too, lay beneath the Shelter that had made the stars... but for the first time, something faint, tiny, unexplained, seemed to have jarred the usual peaceful spell of the night.

Mrs. Bond felt, bit by bit, her attention wander from her work; irritated, she shrugged the feeling off at first, but it returned, slyly persistent, jogging her shoulder, whispering in her ear—the utter absence of the usual buzz and murmur of the circling insects worried her, at first subconsciously, then consciously. She found herself concentrating on this problem, to the exclusion of anything else; her writing became spasmodic, erratic, and at last ceased altogether. Pushing back her chair with an irritated sigh, she rose from the table.

"Peter—I really think I must have a touch of the sun! Can't concentrate in the least tonight somehow—it must be the heat."

The Rev. Peter looked up solicitously.

"Try an aspirin, my dear," he suggested mildly. His wife shook her head impatiently.

"No—that's no good. I feel oppressed, nervy, somehow—perfectly idiotic, I know, but there it is. It's this—awful stillness, not even a fly in the room. Don't you feel it, too, Peter—or has this life got on my nerves till I'm imagining things?"

"Well—now you come to mention it, I've been feeling a little odd for some time. And now you point it out, it *is* curious, the absence of the—er—usual insect life around the lamp. It must be a storm brewing—or, as you say, we are both a little overdone."

The words were valiant, but there was trepidation in the little man's mild blue eyes—trepidation vague, formless but present. Mrs. Bond struck her hand on the wall in a spasm of irritation, born of the quick inrush of fear that had now seized her, like a stealthy enemy rendered suddenly bolder, at the discovery that the same creeping dread had been working its spell upon her husband's peace of mind as well.

"Peter!" She spoke firmly. "This is either sheer foolishness on our part, of which we ought to be thoroughly ashamed—or else someone is trying to play tricks upon us... for doing our duty as Christians to our flock, despite their ignorant prejudices."

It was odd how, instinctively, it seemed, her mind reverted to the matter of Takkari and Mefren—the former's menacing, sullen eyes.

The little clergyman looked frankly frightened.

"You mean you think Takkari!..." His sentence was unfinished.

"Oh, I don't mean anything *really*—what's-its-name—uncanny!" Mrs. Bond snapped. "I should hope I'm too good a Christian for that—but I wouldn't be surprised if Takkari and some of her precious friends tried to work some of their jugglers' tricks on us, to frighten us... pure nastiness, of course! Nothing else is possible..."

Her tone was a shade too decided; against her will as she talked, partly at random, she could not but realise that the weight and monotony of the silence seemed rising like a sea about them—and... was it so, or was it a trick of her agitated imagination? The fresh lamp now seemed to cast a ring of smaller size, of decreased brilliance; shadows, surely, surely, loomed more deeply in the corners behind the bamboo chairs! There was a curious break in Peter Bond's voice as he answered—a little quake of fear.

"Are you sure, Matilda? I thought so... but tonight, I kept thinking of the witch who tempted Samuel—the Witch of Endor... of Our Lord's strange words of wickedness in high places... And I wondered..."

With a decisive movement, Mrs. Bond strode over to the window and slammed it to, pulling the curtains together to shut out the night—and reeled away with a strangled shriek of terror! Rushing to her assistance, her frightened husband peered out into the darkness, but all was still, save the faint rustling among the tamarisks as the little wind crept through them.

There was no light in the distant hut that housed Takkari and her sullen anger. At the table Mrs. Bond shivered and gasped, gradually regaining her self-control.

"What, my dear... what happened?" The dead silence, the crowding shadows, seemed to listen for her reply. With a huge effort the woman sat up and gulped down her terrors, replying with a steadiness that spoke well for her pluck.

"Peter—something—something awful seized my wrist as I pulled those curtains! Now don't you tell me I'm mad—I was never saner! I grant I was feeling a little nervy—things seem odd tonight somehow—but just at that moment I was perfectly balanced. What—what you said about the... well, you know what you said—suddenly made me realise we were allowing ourselves to become—well, foolishly, unchristianly frightened at nothing at all—it *must* be nothing at all!—and I went to pull the curtains, to shut out the night and the wind and make ourselves cosy and sensible. I was going to suggest we played Patience... and all of a sudden a hand took me by the wrist, strongly, and tried to prevent the curtains being pulled! I told you Takkari was up to something... though how..."

Her eyes, frightened, angry, bewildered, met her husband's—and read there a greater terror than hers.

"Wait!" His voice was a mere whisper. "I can tell you now... but I did not dare to tell you, Matilda, lest it be a mere hallucination on my part. I know"—the humiliated tears were very near—"alas, I am a weak man, Matilda!... I thought perhaps the stillness of the night and—and my own foolish fears, for I must freely admit that I have been far from easy the whole of the evening—were working upon me till I saw, or thought I saw..."

"What?" Mrs. Bond's face was strained; beads of perspiration speckled the little chaplain's lean jaw as he answered, in a voice that shook uncontrollably in the now definitely gathering gloom.

"Something—something swathed and indefinite, but Something that wasn't a shadow—I swear—stand beside you and bend over to watch you write!"

Mrs. Bond shrank back with an involuntary cry of terror. The bald statement was horrible, and the woman shuddered as she listened.

The Rev. Peter's knees were shaking, his voice gathering speed, a hoarse whisper as he rushed on, his frightened eyes seeking from side to side... and still the lamp sank lower and the silence gathered, fold on fold, about the trembling pair.

"I stared and stared... and looked away and forced myself to write. I prayed and sweated and dared not look again, dared not speak for fear it was hallucination and you might think my brain going with the heat and work—till you spoke. Then I dared look—and it was gone! Thank God... I spoke, I believe, rationally enough... and then you rose to draw the curtain, and Matilda, as I am a priest of God and hope for salvation, suddenly It rose at your side again, and Its face pressed close to yours... and the horror of it was Its face was no human face at all, but a gilded mask!"

The hurrying voice rose high and culminated in a half shriek—for on the last word the lamp, now a dying flicker on the table, went out, and with one stride darkness entered the room.

Utterly unnerved, Peter Bond collapsed whimpering on the table, but although shaking in every limb, his wife rose dauntlessly, and biting her lips to still their quivering, faced the darkness that had entered into possession of the room. Silence, dead, heavy, menacing, ruled supreme, broken only by the sobs of the terrified chaplain, the heavy breathing of his wife. Like a cornered creature at bay, she backed sturdily against the table, panting hard, turning her head from side to side, her hands clammy with moisture, clenching and unclenching. There was, indeed, something pathetically valiant about this woman driven thus to fight so hopelessly one-sided a battle, for, in the dire, stealthy strength of the Force that she now dimly realised was arrayed against her, all her shivering, gallant bravery went for no

more than a reed's feeble stand against the gale. Upright in the swirl-
ing shadows that clustered about her, she stood, clutching hard at her
sanity, her self-control, while her little narrow soul shrank within her
and grew shrivelled and puny with terror, like a last year's walnut in its
shell. She knew now—she knew the Thing behind all this—in some
way some streak of lightning clarity had told her—somewhere behind
this awful manifestation moved Something that belonged to Egypt,
that had demanded Its right of Its land, and had through her been
denied it... yet, though sweating with terror, shaking in every limb,
Mrs. Bond, true to her stern type, held grimly to her convictions, and
her shaking lips muttered prayer on prayer, while her soul crawled in
terror, but not regret... But the end was at hand, and mercifully. With
a final huge effort to throw off the spell, with some vague idea that
even to try and light the lamp, anything humdrum, ordinary, might
break the influence that held her so bound, Mrs. Bond stretched
out a fumbling hand along the table for the matches... and touched
another hand! Dry and cold and leathery, with sharply pointed nails,
it lay alongside hers, and as she touched it, withdrew sharply, but it
was too late. Even as Mrs. Bond, her last quivering defences down,
opened her mouth to shriek. It grew beside her swiftly in the darkness,
indefinite, macabre, and of a terror unspeakable; a Thing swathed and
clumsy and vague, shapeless, yet dreadfully, appallingly powerful, a
blind Horror seeking vengeance...

In a frenzy of fear the woman flung herself backwards across the
table where crouched poor little Peter Bond, gibbering, hysterical,
in his panic... but the Shape rose above her against the moving dark,
the crowding shadows, and she saw It clearly, bulbous eyes in a horrible still face of gleaming gold, sinister and pitiless as It bent over her
and... as her senses mercifully left her, laid Its ghastly cheek to hers!

*

Frith knocked out his pipe. As the echoes of his voice died away into the tense silence a little ripple stirred the intent group of listeners, held in the grip of sheer horror. Dennison, the soldier, was the first to find his voice.

"Good Lord—what a beastly yarn! But go on, Frith—that can't be the end? You've got us all on tenterhooks!"

Frith smiled drily.

"That's just where the clever storyteller should leave his audience! I'd rather leave things where they are—on the pitch of the climax, but, of course, there is an aftermath. Fact is, I happened to be strolling near the chapel that night and heard Mrs. Bond scream—rushed in and found her lying in a faint, with poor little Bond perfectly hysterical at her side, burbling wildly, and quite unstrung—for the moment a complete lunatic. Oh, yes, the lamp flared up again just as I got inside the room—no, I saw nothing; but I tell you what I *did* notice—the awful smell in the room!"

"What sort of a smell?" asked Hellier sharply.

"Bitumen," said Frith simply. "Bitumen and natron and dried spices and the intolerably ancient smell of the grave—the smell of the burial rites of old Egypt—stern, undying. The place stank like a newly-opened tomb!"

"But what, actually, was it? The Thing with the gold face, I mean?" My curiosity was greater than my shyness as I put the question.

Frith raised his eyebrows as he poured himself out another liqueur brandy.

"Ah—well, that no one can say for certain. Egypt keeps her secrets now as well as ever she did, but I think I can give a good guess, at least. If I knew the history of Takkari, a strange old daughter of the Nile sands, with the blood, perhaps, of Pharaohs dead ten thousand years ago in her veins... you see, it's true that the system of embalmment died out long ago, yet, like other strange ceremonies, religions, beliefs, no one can swear, even now, that it is utterly dead and forgotten... and who knows what age-old memories, what instincts, what fears, may have haunted those two women from the mysterious Desert as they suffered and agonised over the Stillborn!"

We fell silent, spellbound, as he went on, his voice thrilling, his eyes distant on the blue-gold ancient country he so greatly loved. "You see—in the old days, unless the body of a stillborn child, immediately on its birth, was embalmed with the full ritual, the swathings, the amulets, the golden mask, all the strange symbolic trappings and ceremonies of a full grown being—the Ka, the soul that it had meant to incarnate, would rise in rage and anger at the neglect of the honours due to it, and turn against the house where it was born and all therein, become the evil demon, the Maleficence haunting the unfortunate being who had dared to do it this wrong..."

"Then you think this was the direct result of Mrs. Bond's insisting on Christian burial—that Takkari and her daughter, urged by who knows what instinctive dread and knowledge, meant to secretly steal away with their dead to the Desert, to bury it there with spices and cerements and ceremony to propitiate the Ka thwarted by death of its incarnation?"

Hellier's eyes were alight with interest—Frith nodded.

"Yes. That's what I do think, frankly. In utter ignorance, blundering and narrow, Mrs. Bond forced her weak husband to pit his puny might against a great and ancient Force, and thwarted of its right, the outraged Ka rose against these presumptuous ones... and won... very dreadfully won. In the morning the grave was found empty; the women had dug up the body of their dead in the night and fled with it to the silence of the Desert, which opened and swallowed them. There, perhaps, they laid it to rest in their own way—in Egypt's way. At least the Horror, having worked its will upon those poor well-meaning fools, passed away. I spent many nights after that in the house, and it was perfectly normal. Poor Mrs. Bond—she has paid bitterly enough for her folly, poor soul. She has never been able to tell me what she felt at that supreme moment of horror, when the Thing rose over her and pressed its cheek to hers, except that it was utterly impalpable, no actual touch at all, but a ghastly coldness that scored and burnt like the searing finger of an icicle... then she lost consciousness, thank Heaven. But that terrible moment has left a mark on her that she will never lose. When I picked her up I saw her face was twisted, all wried sideways... where the Gilded Mask had touched."

STORY SOURCES

The following gives the publication details for each story and the sources used. They are listed in chronological order of first publication.

"The Dead Daughter" by Henry Glassford Bell, first published in *The Edinburgh Literary Journal*, Vol. 5, 1831.

"The Old Nurse's Story" by Elizabeth Gaskell was first published in *Household Words*, Vol. 6, no. 144, Christmas special, 1852.

"The Ghost of Little Jacques" by Ann M. Hoyt was first published in *The Atlantic Monthly*, Vol. 11, no. 64, 1863.

"Kentucky's Ghost" by Elizabeth Stuart Phelps was first published in *The Atlantic Monthly*, Vol. 22, no. 133, 1868.

"Walnut-Tree House" by Charlotte Riddell was first published in *Illustrated London News*, 28 December 1878.

"Was It an Illusion?: A Parson's Story" by Amelia B. Edwards was first published in *Thirteen at Dinner and What Came of it* (London: Griffith & Farran, 1881).

"Lost Hearts" by M. R. James was first published in *The Pall Mall Magazine*, Vol. 7, no. 32, 1895.

"The Doll's Ghost" by F. Marion Crawford, first published in *Illustrated London News* Christmas supplement, 1896. Text reproduced in this edition is from *Wandering Ghosts* (New York: Macmillan, 1911).

"The Lost Ghost" by Mary E. Wilkins Freeman was first published in *Everybody's Magazine*, Vol. 8, no. 6, 1903.

"The Shadowy Third" by Ellen Glasgow was first published in *Scribner's Magazine*, Vol. 60, no. 6, 1916.

"Anne's Little Ghost" by H. D. Everett, first published in *The Death-Mask and Other Ghosts* (London: P. Allan 1920).

"Two Little Red Shoes" by Bessie Kyffin-Taylor, first published in *From Out of the Silence* (London: Books Limited, 1920).

"The Curse of the Stillborn" by Margery Lawrence was first published in *Hutchinson's Mystery Magazine*, no. 5, 1925.

NOTES

1 Letitia E. Landon, "The Little Shroud" in *The Literary Gazette* 28th April 1832 (London: Henry Colburn, 1832), p. 266.

2 Nina Auerbach, *Private Theatricals: The Lives of the Victorians* (London: Harvard University Press, 1990), p. 44.

3 Helena M. Gamer & John T. McNeill, *Medieval Handbooks of Penance, a translation of the principal Libri Poenitentiales and Selections from related Documents* (New York: Columbia University Press, 1938), p. 339.

4 John Harland and Thomas Turner Wilkinson, *Lancashire legends, traditions, pageants, sports, &c.* (London: G. Routledge, 1873), p. 220.

5 Rev. Mr. Christopher Pitt (trans.), *The Works of Virgil, in Latin & English. The Aeneid*, v.3. (London: J. Dodsley, 1778), Book 6, Li. 592–5, p. 187.

6 Robert Chambers, *Popular Rhymes of Scotland, with illustrations, chiefly collected from oral sources* (Edinburgh: William Hunter, 1826), pp. 9–11.

7 Rachel Harriette Busk, *The Valleys of Tirol; Their Traditions and Customs, and How to Visit Them* (London: Longman, Green and Co, 1874), p. 27.

8 Fletcher S. Bassett, *Sea Phantoms: or, Legends and Superstitions of the Sea and of Sailors in all Lands and at all Times* (Chicago: Morrill, Higgins & Co., 1892), p. 40.

9 Marcus Rediker, *Between the Devil and the Deep Blue Sea: Merchant Seamen, Pirates and the Anglo-American Maritime World 1700–1750* (Cambridge: Cambridge University Press, 1987), p. 13.

10 Translated by William J. Thoms, *Lays and legends of various nations: illustrative of their traditions, popular literature, manners, customs, and superstitions* (London: George Cowie, 1834), pp. 71–2.

11 A. Lang, William Martin and Elizabeth Taylor, 'Goblins' in *Folklore*, Vol. 13, No. 2 (London: The Folklore Society, 1902), pp. 183–187.

12 Charles Peabody, "How it Came About" in *Thirteen at Dinner and What Came of it: Aka Arrowsmith's Christmas Annual* (London: Griffith & Farran, 1881), pp. 5–8.

13 Alexander Chamberlain, *The Child and Childhood in Folk-Thought: Studies of the Activities and Influences of the Child Among Primitive Peoples, Their Analogues and Survivals in the Civilization of To-Day* (New York: Macmillan and Co., 1896), p. 154.

14 Andrew Joynes (ed.), *Medieval Ghost Stories: An Anthology of Miracles, Marvels and Prodigies* (Boydell and Brewer, 2001), pp. 172–3.

15 Lady Wilde, *Ancient legends, mystic charms, and superstitions of Ireland* (Boston: Ticknor and Co., 1887), p. 153.

16 George Ritchie Kinloch (ed.), *Ancient Scottish ballads, recovered from tradition: with notes* (London: Longman, Rees, Orme, Brown & Green, 1827), pp. 46–8.

17 Frederick Metcalfe, *The Oxonian in Iceland: Or, Notes of Travel in that Island in the Summer of 1860, with Glances at Icelandic Folk-lore and Sagas* (London: Longman, Green, Longman, and Roberts, 1861), pp. 202–3.

18 Herman Hofberg, "The Child Phantom" in *Swedish Fairy Tales*, trans. W. H. Myers (Chicago: Belford-Clarke Co., 1890) [1882] pp. 105–6.

19 Benjamin Thorpe, *Northern Mythology: Comprising the Principal Popular Traditions and Superstitions of Scandinavia, North Germany,*

and the Netherlands, Vol. 2 (London: Edward Lumley, 1851), pp. 94–5.

20 William Henderson, *Notes on the Folk-Lore of the Northern Counties of England and the Borders* (London: W. Satchell, Bryton and Co., 1879), p. 13.

21 Alexander Chamberlain, *The Child and Childhood in Folk-Thought: Studies of the Activities and Influences of the Child Among Primitive Peoples, Their Analogues and Survivals in the Civilization of To-Day* (New York: Macmillan and Co., 1896), p. 353.

22 Pierre Loti, *Egypt (La Mort de Philae)*, trans. by W. P. Baines, (London: T. Werner Laurie Ltd., 1909), p. 49.

'But foliage surrounded him, branches blocked the way; the trees stood close and still; and the sun dipped that moment behind a great black cloud. The entire wood turned dark and silent. It watched him.'

Woods play a crucial and recurring role in horror, fantasy, the gothic and the weird. They are places in which strange things happen, where it is easy to lose your way. Supernatural creatures thrive in the thickets. Trees reach into underworlds of pagan myth and magic. Forests are full of ghosts.

Lining the path through this realm of folklore and fear are twelve stories from across Britain, telling tales of whispering voices and maddening sights from deep in the Yorkshire Dales to the ancient hills of Gwent and the eerie quiet of the forests of Dartmoor. Immerse yourself in this collection of classic tales celebrating the enduring power of our natural spaces to enthral and terrorise our senses.

ALSO AVAILABLE

It is too often accepted that during the nineteenth and early twentieth centuries it was the male writers who developed and pushed the boundaries of the weird tale, with women writers following in their wake – but this is far from the truth.

This new anthology presents the thrilling work of just a handful of writers crucial to the evolution of the genre, and revives lost authors of the early pulp magazines with material from the abyssal depths of the British Library vaults returning to the light for the first time since its original publication.

Delve in to see the darker side of *The Secret Garden* author Frances Hodgson Burnett and the sensitively-drawn nightmares of Marie Corelli and May Sinclair. Hear the captivating voices of *Weird Tales* magazine contributors Sophie Wenzel Ellis and Greye La Spina, and bow down to the sensational and surreal imaginings of Alicia Ramsey and Leonora Carrington.

British Library Tales of the Weird collects a thrilling array of uncanny storytelling, from the realms of gothic, supernatural and horror fiction. With stories ranging from the nineteenth century to the present day, this series revives long-lost material from the Library's vaults to thrill again alongside beloved classics of the weird fiction genre.

From the Depths: And Other Strange Tales of the Sea – ED. MIKE ASHLEY
Haunted Houses: Two Novels by Charlotte Riddell – ED. ANDREW SMITH
Glimpses of the Unknown: Lost Ghost Stories – ED. MIKE ASHLEY
Mortal Echoes: Encounters with the End – ED. GREG BUZWELL
Spirits of the Season: Christmas Hauntings – ED. TANYA KIRK
The Platform Edge: Uncanny Tales of the Railways – ED. MIKE ASHLEY
The Face in the Glass: The Gothic Tales of Mary Elizabeth Braddon – ED. GREG BUZWELL
The Weird Tales of William Hope Hodgson – ED. XAVIER ALDANA REYES
Doorway to Dilemma: Bewildering Tales of Dark Fantasy – ED. MIKE ASHLEY
Evil Roots: Killer Tales of the Botanical Gothic – ED. DAISY BUTCHER
Promethean Horrors: Classic Tales of Mad Science – ED. XAVIER ALDANA REYES
Roarings From Further Out: Four Weird Novellas by Algernon Blackwood – ED. XAVIER ALDANA REYES
Tales of the Tattooed: An Anthology of Ink – ED. JOHN MILLER
The Outcast: And Other Dark Tales by E. F. Benson – ED. MIKE ASHLEY
A Phantom Lover: And Other Dark Tales by Vernon Lee – ED. MIKE ASHLEY
Into the London Fog: Eerie Tales from the Weird City – ED. ELIZABETH DEARNLEY
Weird Woods: Tales from the Haunted Forests of Britain – ED. JOHN MILLER
Queens of the Abyss: Lost Stories from the Women of the Weird – ED. MIKE ASHLEY
Chill Tidings: Dark Tales of the Christmas Season – ED. TANYA KIRK
Dangerous Dimensions: Mind-bending Tales of the Mathematical Weird – ED. HENRY BARTHOLOMEW
Heavy Weather: Tempestuous Tales of Stranger Climes – ED. KEVAN MANWARING
Minor Hauntings: Chilling Tales of Spectral Youth – ED. JEN BAKER
Crawling Horror: Creeping Tales of the Insect Weird – EDS. DAISY BUTCHER AND JANETTE LEAF
Cornish Horrors: Tales from the Land's End – ED. JOAN PASSEY
I Am Stone: The Gothic Weird Tales of R. Murray Gilchrist – ED. DANIEL PIETERSEN

We welcome any suggestions, corrections or feedback you may have, and will aim to respond to all items addressed to the following:

The Editor (Tales of the Weird), British Library Publishing,
The British Library, 96 Euston Road, London NW1 2DB

We also welcome enquiries through our Twitter account, @BL_Publishing.